MURDER
AT
GULLS NEST

ALSO BY JESS KIDD

The Night Ship

Things in Jars

Mr. Flood's Last Resort

Himself

MURDER AT
GULLS NEST

NORA BREEN INVESTIGATES

JESS KIDD

ATRIA BOOKS

New York   Amsterdam/Antwerp   London
Toronto   Sydney/Melbourne   New Delhi

ATRIA
BOOKS

An Imprint of Simon & Schuster, LLC
1230 Avenue of the Americas
New York, NY 10020

First Atria Books hardcover edition April 2025

ATRIA BOOKS and colophon are trademarks of Simon & Schuster, LLC

Interior design by Jill Putorti

Manufactured in the United States of America

1   3   5   7   9   10   8   6   4   2

Library of Congress Cataloging-in-Publication Data has been applied for.

ISBN 978-1-6680-3403-3
ISBN 978-1-6680-3405-7 (ebook)

For Claire Martin

MURDER
AT
GULLS NEST

PROLOGUE

Wait for your eyes to adjust. You are in a tunnel, no, a pit. The walls are patterned, smooth raised bumps, waves and whorls. There's light, cool-toned, so, it must be moonlight. Moonlight through an opening to the sky above. You are alone but for a slumped figure. Need you ask: a woman. If she were alive her hands would be cold. She would hate the chill of this place. The dank walls glisten. She would mind that dripping sound. That scuffle of rats, near and nearer. If she were alive, she would look up to the light. She would shout out. Only her eyes are unseeing, a veil has passed over them. Her mouth is slack. Face bruised, lips blue, one of her hands resting palm upwards. It's dim, not too dim to see that she has gone. Can't you see that she has gone? It's in the angle of her neck, the odd twist of her head. Her hand is held out as if in supplication. Above, a cloud covers the moon, a shadow crosses her face, like a frown. When the dawn comes, it will find no reflection in her dull eyes.

CHAPTER 1

The woman climbs the hill, a favorable wind behind her. Favorable only in that it's going in the same direction, otherwise bitter, with a rough lick of salt, coming in, as it does, off the wide cold gray sea. The woman and the wind make their way along a snake of a promenade, with an incline at the tail. The beachside proceedings have dwindled now. The deck chairs for hire and saucy postcard stands, the donkey rides and Gipsy Roselee Fortune-Teller to Quality, have gone, now that the summer season is over. Along the front, signs have been taken in and hatches boarded shut. Some vendors struggle on, supplying stewed tea and buckets and spades to brave day-trippers out from London for a lungful of bracing October air. At the end of the promenade grand villas hold forth above a grassy bank. The woman takes the steep path and crosses the bank towards them. The villas set their faces to the weather as best they can, some more senile than others, with pitted stone façades, blank windows, dank gardens, and roof tiles like bockety old teeth.

The woman is hatless. Nora Breen is hatless. The hat Nora has been given, a yellow beret affair, is tucked into the suitcase that she has also been given. The hat is not fetching; it gives her an air of a rakish middle-aged schoolgirl. Not that Nora is vain, but she would rather be without the hat, for she's relishing the feel of the wind in her hair, harsh as it is. It chafes her ears and stings her eyes, but she can hear the song in it and tears are not always terrible. Nora has missed the sea all these landlocked years. She is also starting to relish the lightness of her head and the novelty of all-round vision, without the wimple and veil. She reminds herself of the remarkable human ability to adapt. Transplant a person into different soil and although their roots may recoil in shock, gradually they'll stretch out again. She expects this is due to evolution and feels herself very forward-thinking for the notion. But then, as Nora knows, adapting is one thing; flourishing is another matter entirely.

On the first day of leaving the sisters, Nora felt that she might just float away, with her unrestricted vision and her light and airy head. She had thought of St. Joseph of Cupertino levitating in ecstasy around his friary, which was no mean feat for a portly Franciscan. Swooping about the flower beds. Gliding past the bell tower. His brothers below looking up at him with envy and awe. On this second day after leaving the order, Nora has developed a trick. She looks down at the shoes on her feet and tells them to hang on to her as best they can. Heavy and square and of an ugly auld style, the shoes are a grand bit of ballast. They are not her shoes; neither are the clothes on her back. She entered the High Dallow Carmelite monastery thirty years ago, so her own few bits would be long gone. These are the worldly belongings of another woman, discarded in favor of the habit and the veil. Nora can't, for the life of her, imagine which sister in her former order owned the coat she is currently wearing. Puce is a color you could certainly part company with.

Another second-day trick Nora has developed is keeping custody of her eyes. This way she can take in a snippet of this and that, small details, so as not to get drunk on the world. Little everyday things others might not notice: a clubfooted pigeon, a cracked chimney pot, light through a cloud, a child sitting on a doorstep holding a cat too tight and the look on that cat's face. Nora tells herself that the world may seem confusing but it is just the sum of its parts. Take it piece by piece until you can work out the whole.

She keeps custody of her eyes all the way up the hill. Not least because of the alarming nature of the puce horror she is wearing. The flap of the coat's hem or the swing of her arm is enough to draw her eye. For three decades Nora has experienced a muted palette. The colors she has lived with are calming to the eye and to the mind: pastel roses in the gardens, corridors of dark wood and whitewash, brown and black serge and snowy cotton. Apart from dawn and dusk the richest colors were the subtle golden thread of the altar cloth and the gentle gleam of a polished chalice. Adapt, that's what she'll do, to this riot of painted signs, lipstick, and puce coats.

Below, the seaside town falls away. Above, a milkman pushes a handcart downhill, late on his rounds, whistling. He gives her a lazy wink and nod. Nora winks back. A rupture in his whistle, he quickly looks away. Nora smiles to herself and is a girl again, alarming the fellas. It had always amused her.

Nora reaches the house at the tip of the tail of the promenade. Just above the house there is a small squat church with a cozy vicarage and overgrown graveyard. It looks to be peeking over its grander neighbor's shoulder. Farther on still there is scrubland and a jumble of vegetable plots, started during the war no doubt, doing reasonably well despite their proximity to the sea. A narrow path leads on to the uninhabited headlands and dwindles long before it reaches the cliffs.

Nora heads towards the last house. It is quite the aging beauty. Four stories, generous bay windows, a sprinkling of porthole windows, a tower of sorts. There is an undulating quality about the roof tiles that suggest either subsidence or fanciful notions. There are two gates and a half-moon drive that would amply allow for the turning of a carriage. Gloomy huddles of yew trees lend a funereal aspect. It would have been

a grand place in its day. Now it survives as a boardinghouse. Nora notices with surprise the herd of rabbits grazing on a scrappy lawn; they
are too tame to be wild and too muscular to be domesticated. They have
winter-ready fur and a sharp look in their eyes. A few are lop-eared,
some are downright fancy.

Nora climbs mossy stone steps and rings the bell, next to which is
placed a discreet sign:

GULLS NEST
Accommodating Discerning Ladies and Gentlemen
Breakfast, Half or Full Board
Hot Baths and Housekeeping Available
Welcomes long-term residents
VACANCIES

A stout, wide woman opens the door. The rabbits immediately scatter. Nora sees that the woman is sturdy with the chapped and water-
logged hands of a lifelong charlady. There's sweat on her brow and the
pepper-salt hair that escapes from her headscarf is wet too. Her apron
is none too clean and on her feet are clogs of the kind worn by slatterns
back in the day. A doughy red face is garnished with currant-y eyes. The
narrowing of these eyes serves as a greeting.

Nora Breen states her name, only it feels strange in her mouth. It's
a name she hasn't used for thirty years, the name she gladly dropped to
become Sister Agnes of Christ. When she last used this name, her hair
was bright auburn and her skin smooth. The coat on her back was her
own and the shoes on her feet weren't lined with newspaper.

Nora is shown into the parlor, where she waits. Divested of the puce
coat, she feels calmer, more at ease. The secondhand dress she wears is
high-necked, a nice charcoal color, although loose on the bust, for she
hasn't one. Nora in middle age is boyish in shape, of a type considered

sporty. She entered the order before curves and left without them. In the interim years, who knows? As Sister Agnes her body was negligible, swathed in serge. Her body rose at dawn and daily observed the Hours. It knelt or mopped with equal devotion. It conveyed her to chapel or about her work in the infirmary. It was washed in cold water, fed on bland foods, kept largely in silence, and laid down on a narrow bed nightly. Consequently, Nora is of robust health, suffering from none of the vices her contemporaries at large in the world have enjoyed. Slim-limbed, smooth-skinned, tallish, with the long quiet hands of a saint. A glance in the mirror above the mantel there would tell her what she already knows. She has a face that looks severe unless it's smiling, with a strong jaw, wide mouth, straight nose, clear gray eyes. There's a gap in her front teeth that was adorable in youth and will be endearing in old age. Her brown hair, salted with white strands around the temple, was cropped for the veil. Now it is growing back, pelt-like, a short fringe framing her face, like a middle-aged Joan of Arc.

Nora sits straight-backed on an easy chair. She is not given to loll-ing. Neither is she given to fidgeting. She rests her hands on her lap, divested of tunic, scapular, and the rest now that she is no longer a bride of Christ. She wonders what relation she is to Him at all. A woman unattached, unbound, out in the world. She looks down at her shoes and bids them: *hang on to me.* A rising panic sets her doubting her decisions of the past few months. That insidious thought needles her again: what kind of fool throws up thirty years of dedication to solve a puzzle, albeit a troubling one?

Nora tries to smooth this snagging thought. Leaving the order was both simple and complicated, impulsive and the product of decades of deliberation. At some point she might well unravel this knotty decision, but right now she'll roll it to a dusty corner of her mind and concentrate on the job at hand.

She steadies herself in her waiting while the housekeeper fetches the landlady. The parlor is dusty and the fire unlit. The furnishings are solid, in the dark wood of a different era. The wallpaper is ancient too: flock with a sinister pattern, moths perhaps, or urns. Somewhere in the house there is the sound of receding footsteps and then the slamming of doors. A clock ticks solemnly on the mantelpiece, two china dogs slight one another from opposite ends. Outside, the sky is brightening, which is of no concern to the room, daylight being dissuaded by heavy velvet drapes and the somber yews that crowd about the window. The drapes move. Nora notices. The movement increases to a gentle sway.

The curtain twists open to reveal a child cocooned in its folds. The girl—Nora estimates her to be around eight years old—is clad in a cast-off cocktail dress and tatty elbow-length opera gloves. She hangs upside down, a few feet above the ground, her limbs tangled in the frayed curtain lining. She shifts her position to upright with the practiced ease of an aerial acrobat. A face pale enough to be luminous, a small, pointed chin, and large blue eyes, all in a nest of unruly red hair. There is a fox-like quality to the child, a watchful, untamed intelligence. She fixes her eyes on Nora and nods with grave formality.

Nora returns the greeting.

Two generals appraising one another across the battlefield of a dingy hearth rug.

At the sound of the door opening, the curtain twists again and the girl is concealed, the material left swaying only very slightly.

A woman enters, fair-haired and in her thirties, what dressmakers might term petite but proportioned. Despite her best efforts at plain dressing—a simple black dress and court shoes—she has a polish to her, a gleam. Like an actress playing a funeral scene.

She walks over to Nora. "Please, don't get up. I'm Helena Wells. You made the early train? Wonderful." Turning to the housekeeper, who has followed her into room, she cautiously asks, "Irene, could we possibly find some tea for Miss Breen?"

Irene exhales sharply and turns on her heel.

Mrs. Wells perches on a nearby chair and gestures towards the curtain with a questioning air.

Nora nods.

Mrs. Wells lowers her voice. "It's best to let Dinah come to you. My daughter doesn't talk, please don't expect her to. She rather inhabits a world of her own." She smiles as if to indicate that this is no bad thing.

Nora smiles too. "Thank you for accommodating me, Mrs. Wells, at such short notice."

"Helena, please. Not at all; as I said, a room has unexpectedly become available. Its previous occupant was due to stay until spring but left with no notice at the end of August. Fortunate for you, less so for me."

"Such a sudden departure?" Nora attempts to sound indifferent.

From Helena, a measured response: "It was no fault of the room, I can assure you. It's lovely, quite the best view in the house."

The curtain begins to sway again. Helena seems at pains to ignore it.

"The previous occupant was a lady?" asks Nora smoothly.

"Yes. Is that important?"

Some impulse prevented Nora from disclosing her true reason for visiting Gulls Nest when she wrote to Helena Wells, and she feels that same impulse now.

Nora smiles, ignoring the question. "And she left unexpectedly? How curious."

"Guests come and go. I can't help that." Helena looks carefully at Nora, her eyes pale, clear. "Where do you hail from, Miss Breen?"

The curtain flaps wildly.

"Nora, please."

Helena smiles and nods.

"The north of England," Nora says kindly but with finality. "You're not originally from Kent, are you?"

"No, London. I came here in the last year of the war, just after Dinah was born. Eight years ago." She frowns, as if the impact of her decision has just caught up. "How time goes."

"What brought you here, Helena?"

A shadow seems to cross Helena's face. "The fresh air, I suppose."

The curtain settles and stills, as if listening.

"Gulls Nest was a guesthouse when I got here," Helena continues. "Already carved up into rooms; flatlets, they call them now. One old boarder even came with the fixtures and fittings. Irene thought it best to continue." She flushes.

With embarrassment, Nora wonders, for her change of position, socialite to seaside landlady? Helena is clearly too grand for such shabby surroundings, with her high-class accent and glossy poise. Or perhaps something else is troubling Helena? Nora detects something fearful in her demeanor, a shrinking, a nervousness—she even looks afraid of her own charwoman.

"The war changed everything," Nora offers. "We are none of us where we expected to be. Did Irene come with the fixtures and fittings too? What's that saying . . . an old broom knows the corners?"

Helena laughs; the tension in the room dissolves. "I knew Irene in London; she was of help to me there. You will find us rather a curious assortment, Nora." She smiles, as if to indicate that this is no good thing.

The clock ticks. The door opens abruptly and Irene, with a mutinous glint in her eyes, sets down the tea tray with a clatter, slamming the door as she exits.

Helena breathes out. She pours tea and dispenses milk and sugar graciously and rather with the air of someone who has just remembered their stage directions.

"Forgive me for not joining you, Nora. It's not very English, I know, but I never drink tea."

Nora takes up her cup.

"Irene will come and help you with your luggage." The merest glance at Nora's suitcase, secondhand, tied about with parcel string. "I do hope the room will be to your liking."

"Thank you."

"Irene will fill you in about the rules. She is a stickler for the rules; I suppose they contribute to the efficient running of the place. Supper is served at six p.m. sharp. Today is Thursday, so braised liver is on the menu."

A groan comes from the direction of the curtains.

The women look at one another and smile.

Helena arranges her hands on her lap. She appears lost in thought, save for occasional glances at her new guest. The landlady has something to say, Nora thinks. She finishes her tea and reaches to put her empty cup back on the tray. Helena leans forward and touches her arm. Nora catches the sudden scent of peppermint and something underneath that she can't quite place.

"Please don't mind the stories," Helena whispers urgently.

"Stories?"

"The people round here like to tell stories. The last guest simply left. There is no mystery, whatever they say."

Nora keeps her voice level. "What do they say?"

Helena shakes her head and stands up. "One ought never to repeat gossip." Her smile is forced, her eyes are blank. "You must be tired after your journey. I'll leave you to settle in, Nora."

Nora, carrying her own suitcase, is conducted up the main staircase by Irene, who has changed her apron for a housecoat. The thick gravy-brown paint and threadbare carpet, the smell of stale kippers rising and the dust motes falling, cannot detract from the elegant sweep of the staircase. The wallpaper is faded red with brighter scarlet patches marking the positions of paintings long gone. In these squares the pattern is clearer, garlands of chrysanthemums. Handwritten signs decorate most of the walls. Tacked to the back of the front door:

NO ADMITTANCE AFTER 9 P.M.

Passing through the hallway Nora reads:

LAUNDRY

For BAGWASH leave laundry at kitchen door MONDAYS

Unless you request IRONING your linens will be returned DAMP

NO DAMP LAUNDRY TO BE AIRED IN ROOMS

Pasted on a door on the first-floor landing:

BATHROOM

For the use of GENTLEMEN Monday, Wednesday, and Friday

For the use of LADIES Tuesday, Thursday, and Saturday

Sunday by arrangement

Along the corridor a small white dog wearing a red and blue striped ruff sits, still as a statue, on its hind legs. Nora discerns a low growl as Irene approaches, but the dog holds its position, guarding the door behind it.

"First-floor back," Irene huffs in the dog's direction. "Professor Poppy."

"Professor? A learned man, then?"

Irene is all scorn. "A *show*man. Punch and Judy." She nods towards the dog. "Before you ask: pets ain't allowed. The old man has dispensation to keep that thing for his work. Although there's precious little of that as I see."

The dog fixes Irene with a cool glare. Irene looks away.

She opens a door across the corridor. "First-floor front."

Nora follows the char into a room that's all sea. Faded green on the walls, worn blue on the floor, and the ocean filling all the windowpanes. Nora sets her suitcase down inside the door and walks to the window. She sees a break in the clouds and a mackerel streak of light on the water.

"How beautiful," she murmurs.

"No visitors," says Irene. "No burning of coal what isn't supplied by myself, at three shillings a bucket. There are no electrical fires for your convenience at Gulls Nest, so don't ask. No livestock of any kind is permitted in the house either on foot or upon your person. No cooking in the room except to boil the kettle what's provided. You may draw the water from the bathroom but only on your designated days. All meals are served in the dining room and you are expected to be prompt. The times are noted on the dining room door. No refreshments are offered outside these times. Luncheon is not available, so don't ask. Boarders are not served meals in their rooms on a tray, not even if they are infirm. Housekeeping is weekly, on a day of my choosing. Boarders must vacate your room weekdays between nine a.m. and two p.m. The parlor is for guest use between three p.m. and ten p.m. and all day Sunday. You'll find the privy in the garden, behind the rhododendrons. House shoes are recommended to preserve the floors. Rent is a week in advance, unless you have prior arrangements with Mrs. Wells." She stops, sniffs. "Miss Breen, do you have a prior arrangement with Mrs. Wells?"

Nora turns away from the window, smiling. "I've no prior arrangement with Mrs. Wells."

Irene waits, unsmiling.

Nora nods, finds her purse, counts out coins.

Irene pockets the money. "Coal?"

Nora shakes her head. "I prefer a cold room."

Irene casts her a look that approaches approbation. "Your latchkey is on the table. Don't encourage the child. Miss Wells is not to mix with the boarders."

Nora turns back to the window, opens it. Almost immediately a gull descends and walks along the windowsill.

Nora laughs. "How tame he is!"

Irene pushes past her and slams the window closed. The bird flutters away. "We do not encourage the gulls either. Feeding of birds is prohibited. Should Miss Wells come into your room—"

"I must shoo her out as I would a gull."

Irene snorts and bustles from the room.

"Thank you, Irene."

"Mrs. Rawlings, *if you please*."

Nora pulls a face at the closing door. Then, by force of habit, offers up a prayer for patience and humility. She stops, reconsiders. Controlling her temper was her greatest trial at High Dallow. But this wasn't the worst of her shortcomings. Her inquisitive nature was judged to be disrespectful. Her cleverness the sin of pride. These were traits that found her scrubbing a far greater share of bathtubs than any other postulant. Now, out in the world, she can exercise these unfavorable traits. This thought fills Nora with a strange mix of relief and alarm.

She looks around the room. Large windows, high ceiling, with dusty cornices picked out in gold paint. An airy room, worn but still lovely. Not a nun's cell. Nor, she was thankful to see, like the room she slept in last night, which was in a hotel in Paddington and quite the den.

The clock on the mantelpiece tells the wrong time, twelve o'clock, when the day is clearly between None and Vespers. Without the structure of prayer, yesterday, her first day back in the world, had been flabby and endless until midmorning, then it galloped past. A worldly day must be marked in other ways, she remembered: the morning paper, luncheon, a glass of sherry, and a walk. Nora reminds herself about the whole adapting thing as she considers her surroundings. Instead of her cell's hard cot there's an overstuffed single divan. In place of viciously laundered sheets, a pile of old silk counterpanes. A lacquered modesty screen is set around the bed. Four panels depict a flock of herons over a river. Looking closer Nora realizes the herons are far from companionable; they are fighting over one fish, a great fat salmon arching upwards out of the water. Looking past the elegant arcs of wing and feather, she notices spatters of blood and beak-ripped gashes, blinded eyes and drifts of plucked plumage. Nora shudders and pushes the screen closed. She crosses over a frayed rug in the palest of blues to a vast mahogany wardrobe you could set sail in. Upon opening the door, Nora discovers a powerful smell of mothballs and one lonely hanger. A sturdy chair stands next to a spindly table. On the table lies a key attached to a fob the size of a bed knob. On the washstand there is a large pitcher and a very small bowl. There is something unsettling about the objects in this room, washed-up and unmatched. Like living in a doll's house furnished by a child who cares little for scale. Nora lifts her case onto the divan and opens it. She takes out a tissue-paper-wrapped parcel. Handling it as gently as a relic, she places it in the drawer of the nightstand.

Deciding against the mothballs, she hangs her other dress behind the door; the puce coat she hooks over it. She throws a tangle of modern undergarments in the dresser drawer and arranges a brush and comb on top. Then she pulls the chair to the window and because the table looks stranded without the chair, she moves that too. She opens the window wide in case the gull decides to return.

The darkening sky makes the sea look cold and the great swath of sand uninviting. Nora sees figures farther down the beach. They draw closer, a man and a woman, a young couple. Him tall, her slender, their coats fluttering in the breeze off the sea. A young couple in love perhaps, only that they are walking at incompatible speeds. At this distance Nora cannot read their faces, so she reads their bodies. The man, holding his hat on his head, strides. The woman, holding the man's arm, lags. The man, impatient, is pulling away. The woman, pleading, is holding him back. He wrenches his arm free and storms forward alone. His trilby is taken by the wind, but he keeps walking. The hat, blown on, skips over the hard sand. The woman hesitates, watching the hat waltz away, then sets off after the man. The hat dances on with newfound freedom. Nora watches and ponders, for a moment, the mystery of human relationships. A lovers' squall, a misunderstanding, which will hopefully be as quickly forgotten as that hat.

The couple, the man ahead, the woman behind, cross the beach and turn up through the grassy bank and head towards Gulls Nest. Nearer now, Nora can see the expressions on their faces—the man's bitter, the woman's weary—before she loses sight of them as they pass behind the front wall heading towards the front gate.

Now Nora's eye is drawn to a third figure, who has stepped out from a hut farther along the promenade. A small man clad, almost comically, in a too-big army greatcoat with a camera slung over his shoulder. He stalks onto the beach and moves into the path of the freewheeling hat, to catch it, surely.

Instead, he stamps on it. The hat momentarily flutters and is dead. He lifts his foot to inspect, yes, the hat is crushed into the sand.

Malignant little shite, thinks Nora.

Tying the belt tighter on his coat, he follows in the direction of the young couple, tailing off before he reaches the uphill path. Nora loses sight of him to some cut-through unknown to her yet.

And now the beach is empty.

Somewhere in the north a religious community prepares for Vespers. Here on the southeast coast, Nora prepares for braised liver and a dining room full of strangers. Although the light is failing, she leaves the curtains open in her room, for she would not block this view for anything. The one bulb high in the airy ceiling and the lamp by the bedside do little to light this space; there are telling nubs of half-spent candles in the drawer. The water in the pitcher is cold but, sure, isn't that only what she's used to? Faintly, she hears a noise at the door. Drying her hands, she crosses the room to listen. She hears it again, at the gap beneath the door; a faint snuffling.

Nora opens the door. The landing is empty. The door opposite is closed and presently unguarded by the white terrier. She steps out onto the landing and peers down the stairs to the ground floor. The stairs and the hallway below are empty too. The rising odor of burnt onions confirms that supper is imminent. Nora climbs the flight of stairs to the next floor. The doors here, to rooms at the front and back of the house, are closed. There's a further flight of stairs, steep and narrow between wallpapered walls. Nora takes these. The wallpaper is that of a nursery, ducklings, gouged and scratched, perhaps by the hauled suitcases of guests over the years. At the top of the stairs a door stands open into a curious room.

An attic, all slopes and beams and sky. Into the roof a constellation of windows has been installed. Nora can only imagine how lovely a clear night sky would be through these windows, or a bright dawn, for that matter. Even on a gray day it is impressive. The room is immaculately tidy. A shelf holds a modest library of cheap paperbacks and larger reference books along with a few box cameras. The bed is no more than a mattress on the floor, but it is carefully made up. At the end of the bed lies a battered trunk. A pile of clothes is arranged on a nearby chair with military neatness, a pair of old but polished boots placed below. Nora's eye is drawn to the far wall, where orderly rows of photographs are pinned. She draws forward; the images are black and white and oddly engrossing. Blurry scenes, sometimes low-lit, with subjects barely framed within the picture: a faceless passerby, a bird in flight, an endless line of deck chairs. Among the monochrome photographs several images in startling blue stand out. Nora wonders at the shapes of flowers and leaves, abstract compositions, delicate silhouettes against a deep blue background. That the resident of this room is strangely talented she has no doubt. Taking up much of the corner of the large space is a sizable wooden framework draped at the entrance with black cloth: a darkroom.

Hearing footsteps on the stairs, Nora turns. "Dinah!"

The child has added a bedraggled fox stole and a cloche hat to her outfit. She takes a deliberate step right up to the threshold of the doorway and then halts. She lifts the fox's head so that it regards Nora with two glass eyes. Her own eyes she makes round and startled.

"What is it, Dinah?"

She glances behind her, then stretches her other hand out to Nora. There is a theatricality about her actions, each movement exaggerated. She's scared of me being in this room, thinks Nora. Dinah, harkening to something with a cupped ear, hugs the fox stole and takes flight back down the stairs. Nora follows. Leaving the room, she catches sight of an army greatcoat hung behind the door.

CHAPTER 2

In the center of the dining room is a round table. In the center of the table is a lidded tureen. There are six chairs, three of them taken; two by the couple from the beach, the third by an older man. All seem absorbed in their own musings. As Nora enters the room, the young woman looks up first.

"The new guest!" She gestures to the seat next to her. "Please, join us, we are waiting on the others."

The men half stand from their chairs. Nora waves them to be seated.

The young woman smiles; it goes some way to offset the dark circles around her eyes. She holds out her hand. "I'm Stella Atkins and this is my husband, Teddy."

Teddy's nod is cool, barely polite.

The couple are handsome. Stella is in her midtwenties, brown-haired and freckled, her face rounded with youth, her eyes hazel and kind. Teddy looks a little older, fair-haired and unshaven. His suit has seen better days; it is crumpled and wearing thin. Nora notices that the fingers that play with the cigarette package on the table are stained yellow. Teddy suffers with his nerves, she thinks.

The older man holds out his hand. "Mr. Bill Carter."

"Miss Nora Breen." She returns his firm handshake.

Bill is balding and impeccably smart, with a gold tiepin and matching cuff links. His nails are filed and his mustache beautifully trimmed. In contrast to the slouched figure of Teddy he looks upright, if a little rigid. But when Bill speaks his voice, with its rounded Kent accent, is casual and warm.

"Irene has deposited the main event." He gestures at the tureen. "She's gone to fetch the *peripherals.*"

"Heaven help us!" Stella turns, laughing, to Nora. "You've come to Gulls Nest on just about the worst day, I'm afraid, Miss Breen. Braised liver. Teddy will eat just about anything but this— What do you call it, Teddy?"

Teddy attempts a smile. "Penance."

Irene returns with a tray of steaming dishes. She clatters them down on the vast dark-wood sideboard that hunkers along the length of the back wall.

"Ten minutes past six and two guests not arrived," remarks Teddy. "Isn't that tardy, Irene?"

Stella intervenes, pacifying. "I'm sure they will be along directly, Mrs. Rawlings."

Irene, tucking the tray under her arm, ignores the young couple and addresses Bill. "For the peripherals this evening we have—"

"Cabbage," Teddy snorts. "One day surprise us! Would it be so impossible to have carrots?"

Irene shoots him a withering look as she leaves the room.

"You shouldn't, Teddy," says Stella softly.

"She's an old baggage."

Bill Carter rises and, with the air of a maître d', drapes a napkin over his arm and picks up a pile of plates from the sideboard. He nods and smiles at the old man doddering into the room. "Good evening, Poppy."

The old man grunts back and takes a chair with an authority that would put him at the head of the table, even a round one, waving away Stella's attempts to assist him. He is cadaverous and frail in the extreme, but his eyes are bright and his white hair has been carefully brushed, as has his maroon velvet suit. He wears a brightly colored paisley cravat and greets each of the guests by name in a voice as rich as old sherry. Arriving at Nora, he pauses.

"A new lady-guest. So, the last one—"

"Professor Poppy," interrupts Stella. "This is Miss Breen."

The old man offers Nora a gallant salute. "Poppy, please. Madam Breen, you are most welcome."

Bill, napkin on arm, regards the tureen.

"With trepidation he approaches," observes Professor Poppy. "Mr. Carter, I've said this before: you are equal to Irene's braised liver. Double portion for young Teddy."

Teddy's smile is unguarded and it momentarily lights his face. Stella, watching her husband, smiles too.

"And tonight's peripherals—need I ask, young Teddy?"

"Cabbage, I believe, Poppy."

"Exactly to be expected," replies the professor sagely. "Distract us from this repast, Madam Breen; tell us something about yourself and please don't say there's nothing to tell."

Bill takes the lid off the tureen; the unpleasant savory smell in the room gets stronger. Stella holds a napkin up to her nose and laughs. Bill takes a plate and serves a glutinous brown portion with a flourish. He presents the first plate to the old man.

"I'm not entirely sure I should be thanking you for this, Mr. Carter."

Nora is next to be served. She nods her thanks to Bill and turns to the old man. "Now, Professor," she says. "Would you really expect your newest addition to share her life story without prior knowledge of her fellow housemates? Aren't I rather outnumbered?"

"My manners! Forgive me. By the seniority bestowed by my years, I shall start. Although, how can any individual even begin to tell their story? Their likes and longings and their histories varied and often hidden."

Teddy's and Stella's eyes meet. Teddy frowns and returns his gaze to his package of cigarettes.

Bill elegantly serves the young couple their meals and then takes a small portion for himself.

"Might I suggest," the professor continues, "that we inmates limit our divulgences to the basics—occupation and where we reside in this house. As to the length of our sentences, Bill and I are the longest internees—why, I'm almost a lifer. This young couple have served just shy of a year, is that right, dear?"

Stella nods.

Poppy smiles. "So now, the bare minimum please, folks. Miss Breen will become acquainted with the finer points of our characters in her own time. How does that sound?"

"A solid plan," agrees Nora.

"Marvelous," says Poppy. "I am your nearest neighbor, residing in the first-floor back with my faithful dog, Toby, who accompanies me everywhere. Apart from this dining room, for he would no doubt feature in tomorrow's tureen should I dare to bring him down to dinner."

"Poppy!" laughs Stella.

"I am a showman of modest talents—"

"He's a genius, Miss Breen! He has the children roaring with laughter at his Punch and Judy show. Adults too."

"Dear Stella, you are quite my biggest fan." The old man smiles. "Serving our swill tonight is Mr. Bill Carter, second-floor back, mixer of sublime cocktails and collector of curiosities."

"Retired navy chef," explains Bill. "Barman at the Marine Hotel. But I do like acquiring antiques and so forth."

Stella whispers, "He has arrows, Miss Breen, tipped in poison. He has an elephant's foot."

The old man intervenes. "Stella Atkins, second-floor front, is a fantasist. She's also a clerk at the town hall and my guardian angel. She looks out for me; no trouble is too great."

Stella grimaces but is pleased.

"Her husband, Theodore, *not* Edward, also second-floor front, is a man who can turn his hand to anything."

"I'm a caretaker at the amusement park, that is all," replies Teddy plainly.

Nora gestures to the empty chair. "And your absent housemate, the last guest, what should I know about them?"

The temperature in the room seems to cool. Stella glances at Teddy, who resolutely studies his plate. Bill smooths his immaculate mustache.

"You'll meet him soon enough," says the professor, quietly. "Now, Miss Breen. A few easy facts about yourself, so that you will no longer be a stranger in our midst."

Nora glances about the table. "But we haven't touched our food. Will I say grace?"

The professor bows his head in dutiful assent. The others follow his example, even Teddy.

And after grace comes the taking up of napkins. Stella picks up a fork and gingerly pokes the mess on her plate. Poppy clatters about with a soup spoon. Bill attempts to carve up his portion. Teddy lights another cigarette. Footsteps along the corridor; Irene, red-faced, carrying a vast serving bowl.

The professor puts down his spoon, in apparent relief at the distraction. "I must say you are on the ball this evening, Mrs. Rawlings. Here you are with afters and I've hardly masticated your liver."

Irene grunts at the old man, dumps the bowl on the sideboard, and blusters out again.

The old man turns to Nora. "Continue, please, madam."

Nora hesitates. She is long used to taking her meals without talking, with only the soothing lull of a sister reading out loud and the careful handling of cutlery. But then, she would not be eating at this time if she were back at High Dallow.

"I have mostly worked in an infirmary."

The professor takes interest. "In your native Ireland, Mayo, if I guess your accent correctly?"

"Indeed, you do."

"I had a bottler from Mayo." He glances around the table at mystified faces. "A Punchman's assistant, grand fellow, gift of the gab, do go on."

"I have been nursing in the north of England."

"You are a nurse, Miss Breen!" exclaims Stella. "I thought you had that look about you, sort of calm, nurturing."

Teddy turns to his wife. "Don't make judgments. Why must you always make judgments, Stella?"

A long and awkward silence ensues, filled with the sound of scraping cutlery. A different sort of hush than Nora is used to at mealtimes, grim rather than reflective.

The professor puts down his spoon. "Well, that was a trial. Anyone ready for afters? I predict stewed fruit. Teddy, what say you?"

Teddy makes an effort to smile at the old man.

"The room I have been given, the first-floor front," says Nora, "I believe it unexpectedly came available, my predecessor—"

The old man raises his hand as if stopping a horse. Nora follows his gaze. The last guest enters the dining room.

"Mr. Ježek," says the professor. "Join us."

The small man from the beach, the hat killer, takes the last chair. A ravenous look to him, intense and gaunt. Nora senses a fierce intelligence, the alertness of one often on their own. He throws a glance around the room, his dark eyes resting on Teddy a fraction longer than on the other guests. So, he's known to the young couple, thinks Nora. A fellow boarder, of a similar age, in a friendly house would surely be familiar to them? With this in mind his actions on the beach suddenly seem far more malign to Nora. His stalking perverse. Was the destruction of Teddy's hat a gesture of soured friendship? A small act of revenge. She watches with curiosity the diners' responses to this latecomer.

Stella glances at her husband, a fleeting expression of contempt crossing her face. Teddy smokes his cigarette, his color rising, and between inhalations his hand twitches. Bill finishes his last mouthful of supper, carefully washing it down with polite sips of water. He sits back with the air of a man ready for the evening's entertainment.

The professor alone addresses the man. "We didn't wait for you, Karel. Apologies."

"Why should you?" Taking up the last plate Karel Ježek helps himself from the tureen.

He has dressed very carefully, Nora can see that; unlike the greatcoat he wore on the beach these clothes fit him well. Although they are plain, devoid of personality somehow. He is clean-shaven and slim, his dark curly hair is unruly, despite his efforts to neaten it. The latecomer calmly gathers his cutlery, begins to eat.

He turns to Nora, speaks softly, with just a trace of an accent. "You have taken Miss Brogan's old room?"

At the mention of the name, Teddy pushes up violently from the table, sending dishes crashing, toppling a water glass. Stella's eyes close, as if by reflex, as her husband storms out of the room.

Karel looks up at the departing Teddy. Nora sees no victory in his dark eyes. Only a sort of bitter longing. Karel returns his focus to his plate.

Stella rises, throws down her napkin, and runs after her husband.

Nora steels herself. "The previous occupant—"

The professor leans over and takes her hand. His own hands are gnarled with age, as dry as paper. "Please, let us converse no more on this matter, dear. Quite simply, she left us."

Nora sits alone in the dining room among cruets and mustard pots and discarded napkins. Teddy and Stella Atkins did not return, but then she didn't expect that they would. Karel Ježek had finished his meal in silence and left immediately. Bill Carter had collected the plates and Professor Poppy had waived any offers of assistance as he doddered back out of the room.

Nora pours herself a glass of water and drinks it, sitting in the pool of light thrown down on the table by the lamp above. The shadows seem to draw in. A growing sense of being watched prickles the nape of Nora's neck. Behind her comes a faint scrabbling sound. Nora startles and turns. She watches as the door of the sideboard opens and two small pale feet emerge, followed by a ghostly little face.

Dinah Wells straightens up and extends her arms in an elaborate stretch. Ignoring Nora, she softly closes the sideboard door behind her and tiptoes away.

On returning to her room Nora finds she has need of the candle stubs to look around herself. She means to detect the difference in the dim, for something has shifted—of that she is certain. There is no change in the big details; the divan, the heron screen, the wardrobe, the dresser, are exactly as she left them. The change is in the small details. First off, the brush and comb on the dresser have swapped sides. She had left the chair tucked under the table; now they are inches apart. The tilt on the cheval mirror on the dresser is different. Nora looks closely. The dust on the mirror has been disturbed, wiped clean at the top and the bottom.

Nora crosses the room and opens the drawer to the nightstand.

With relief she sees that the parcel is still there. She sits down on the divan and unwraps it. Inside, a neat pile of letters tied with ribbon. She touches the inked address on the topmost envelope.

Dr. Agnes of Christ
Carmelite Monastery
High Dallow

She turns over the pile to see the sender's address on the bottommost envelope.

Miss Frieda Brogan
Gulls Nest
The Promenade
Gore-on-Sea

Nora puts the letters down and surveys the room. Frieda slept here. She gazed at this view through this window. In this place her friend ate braised liver on a Thursday with the motley people below: amiable old Professor Poppy, kindly Stella Atkins, irritable Teddy, dapper Bill Carter, and the mysterious Karel Ježek.

Would Frieda have warmed to any of them?

Most likely. Frieda loved people. She especially gravitated to the lost and the difficult. Nora had seen it during the first days of Frieda's postulancy, crabbed old nuns opening up to her, like flowers feeling the warmth of spring after a long winter. Nora, with her usual clarity of self-sight, knew herself to be one of them. The girl couldn't help but spread joy. With Frieda around, cut roses in egg cups decorated the refectory, potatoes were peeled ready, needles were threaded, knitting tangles unraveled. Unpopular chores were found to be mysteriously completed. With Frieda around, sudden outbursts of laughter were heard in quiet corridors. Frieda would sing in the garden and talk to the cabbages. With Frieda around, sweet peas were sown among the tomatoes and an injured jackdaw was saved and tamed to hop along the path after his young mistress. Mother Superior had words with the charming novice. The roses in the refectory stopped, but the singing and laughing could sometimes still be heard. Then Frieda became dreadfully sick.

The doctors diagnosed a limiting condition of the heart and lungs. This struck Nora as ironic, for a person with a bigger heart she had yet to meet, and to hear Frieda sing, you would not guess that she struggled for breath. And so, Frieda became a regular patient in the infirmary. She was not always easy to nurse. For one, Frieda liked to break the rules. Nora would find her out of bed, barefoot at an open window looking at the stars when she ought to be warm and resting. Or she would discover that Frieda had read all night to the auld nun taking a decade to die in the next bed. Frieda would give away her last bite and the blanket from her shoulders. But like all those people born to care for others, accepting help made her cantankerous. Then Frieda would scowl or fidget or bluster or complain, until Nora made her laugh again.

Frieda's illness showed how dear she had become to everyone. No one was untouched by her joy and kindness. When Frieda was sick the sisters were hushed and drawn and worried. When Frieda was well, life seemed kind and bright and full of possibilities for everyone. None of this escaped Mother Superior's notice but she appeared to bide her time.

Nora had also known from the start, although it would increasingly pain her to admit it, that Frieda the irrepressible was not cut out for the hidden life. But Frieda herself was determined.

Late at night in the infirmary, Frieda and Nora would talk. If Frieda was breathless Nora would fill in the gaps. It was a distraction from Frieda's worst symptoms and the deep fear that comes to every seriously ill person late at night, whether they are full of faith or have none at all. Nora would sit by Frieda's side during those long hours. Frieda seemed strong of faith, yet the look of relief when she saw the first light of dawn was telling.

During these nights Nora heard Frieda's story. She had come to the order by way of an orphanage in County Sligo and had grown up bright and pleasant and popular. A religious vocation had been her chosen path ever since she could remember. As she had no family to claim her, she was determined that the sisters would be her family. After Nora learnt Frieda's story, something inside her shifted. So that she would steal back to Frieda's bedside to watch her sleep. Her face had been familiar from the start, although Nora told herself she couldn't have known this young woman.

And Nora began to think very often about baby Frieda. How she was swaddled in the basket and left on the steps of the orphanage. In her mind's eye Nora saw it all: the ashy, mizzling dawn and the mewling newborn. The shape of her little nose, her delicate fingers, the bleary slate-gray eyes. Nora knew too the pain of a mother who gave up her child.

Then Nora reminded herself that this knowledge was strictly that of another lifetime. She chided herself and went about her duties; nevertheless she returned, time and again, to sit at Frieda's bedside and watch over a lost child returned to her. With her medical training Nora understood Frieda's prognosis well enough. She prayed the girl would have a full life if not a long life, should that please God.

When Frieda's symptoms worsened, a visiting doctor advised relocating the patient to the coast. This granted Mother Superior the impetus she needed. Frieda agreed to leave and was sent to a sanitorium, and on improving, was discharged. So it was that she found herself at liberty for the first time in her young life.

Nora frowns. This tired room in a down-at-heel house wasn't what she'd imagined for Frieda. She had dreamt up an elegant seaside resort with comfort and calm, not these uncared for, shabby surroundings.

Nora sits down at the table. Frieda likely sat at this ridiculous spindly thing to write to her. Since she had left the order eight months ago, Frieda had written weekly, without fail, just as she had promised to. Only without warning, on the last week of August, her letters stopped. All September Nora had waited, her instincts warning her that something was very wrong. Mother Superior had dismissed her concerns and warned against the distraction of human attachments. With almost three decades of spiritual service behind her, Sister Agnes ought to know better. Perhaps she didn't. Now Sister Agnes acted quickly and perhaps even rashly, driven more by intuition than logic. And by one plain fact: for the entire year Nora had known her, Frieda had never once gone back on her word, or broken a promise, whether big or small.

It had taken Sister Agnes three weeks to receive the dispensation that released her from her vows. She became Nora Breen again and duly followed Frieda's footsteps out of the monastery gate.

She considers again a line in Frieda's final letter. The line that has churned over in her mind all these weeks:

I believe every one of us at Gulls Nest is concealing some kind of secret—I shall make it my business to find out and so I shall finally have something riveting to write to you, dear friend!

It was exactly this line—and Nora's deep sense of unease reading it—which had made her hesitate to disclose her relationship to Frieda and the true reason for her stay at Gulls Nest. After the meal taken with the other boarders, she is somehow glad of this decision. There was camaraderie, certainly, but was it just surface? What of that undercurrent of tension? Had they known the puzzle Nora was intent on solving would they have shut down, clammed up?

Nora carefully folds Frieda's letters and puts them away. They unsettle her, they have from the start. She hadn't expected letters full of adventure; she was content with a litany of her friend's quietest days. But Frieda somehow believed she was living for both of them, that she must be diverting, entertaining. Not for the first time, Nora wishes Frieda was less generous. Frieda had been at Gulls Nest for less than a month when she wrote those lines. She had intended to stay until spring at least, doctor's orders.

So why did Frieda leave—and more to the point—where did she go?

CHAPTER 3

Dawn comes, witnessed by Nora Breen, who is up and dressed. She has the chair set next to the open window and the sea air blowing all kinds of cobwebs out of her mind. If she prays, she's unaware of it. But there's a communication, she knows, between her and the fierce colors of the sky. Between her and the miles of wet sand that reflect the colors of the sky. Between her and the wind that brings with it the kiss of sea salt and streams the curtains like banners. Nora is in the world and the world is beautiful, and for now that gives her some peace.

By the time the dawn colors have leached from the sky and the heavens are a clear brash blue, Nora has the visiting gull eating out of her hand. A great, fat, proud-looking fella, dapper in white and gray, with a long, curved beak and a steely expression in his eye. She names him for Father Patrick Conway, the priest who saw her through her novitiate.

With the feeding of Father Conway, she finds herself late for breakfast but still two guests remain in the dining room: Bill Carter, lost in a newspaper, and Stella, picking at an egg.

Stella greets her brightly. Inquiries are made as to the comfort of

Miss Breen's bed and whether she could sleep a wink with the keening of the gulls for don't they drive all newcomers to distraction at first?

"Eventually you won't even hear them cry," says Stella. "If you learn to turn a blind eye you really can get used to anything."

Bill puts down his paper with a smile. "Perhaps you mean a blind ear, Mrs. Atkins?"

Nora considers the selection on the sideboard. The tureen now contains porridge of a gruel-like consistency. Otherwise, there is an arrangement of hard-boiled eggs, slices of thinly buttered bread with the edges curling, and a collation of grayish meats.

"It is Mrs. Rawlings's day off," explains Stella. "She has a girl come in and set this up. At least we are spared the kippers."

Nora helps herself to tea from the pot and takes a seat.

Stella abandons her egg and rises. "I must fix a tray for the professor; I do it most days although Irene strictly forbids it. Mr. Carter, can I help you to anything?"

Bill holds up his hand. "Thank you, no, Mrs. Atkins, you are endlessly kind."

Stella is all bustle, forking meat on a plate, adding a slice of bread. "Poppy sleeps badly and doesn't always wake well, poor old thing."

"Do you still read to him?" asks Bill.

Stella nods. "Most mornings, to distract him from the worst of his aches. He likes detective novels, the grislier the better! What are your plans this morning, Miss Breen?"

"After this cup of tea, a walk into town."

"Well, enjoy. I must go and heat up some milk for Poppy. I really can't be late for work again today!" Stella is off with the plate.

Bill folds his napkin and slips from his pocket a cigarette case. "Would you care to join me?"

Nora has never smoked in her life. "I would. Thank you."

He leans forward to light her cigarette. Nora is knocked out by the

cologne on the man. She will try not to inhale, either him or the cigarette.

"What brings you to Gore-on-Sea, Miss Breen?"

"Nora, please. Doctor's orders, for the healthy air." She puffs a cloud
of smoke out into the room. "And you, Mr. Carter?"

"Bill, please. I've put in at this town for several years now. To be
honest with you, standards are slipping. There's not the flow of gentry
anymore, the Quality are holidaying elsewhere. Don't get me wrong,
Nora, I have nothing against working people—I like them, I'm one of
them—all I'm saying is that standards are slipping. Otherwise, it's a
good enough place to dock."

"You were a naval chef?"

"On the high seas."

"Many years?"

"Too many."

"And you work at the Marine Hotel?"

"I do, but I am finding it needful to reconsider my position there on
account of their clientele."

"Slipping standards?"

"You could say that."

"And exactly how long have you lived at Gulls Nest?"

Bill gives a tense smile. "I'm sorry, is this an interrogation?"

Nora feels herself color slightly. "Is that what it seems like?"

"Somewhat."

"My mother used to say that my nose would never get rusty."

"Evidently." Bill is watching her, waiting for some kind of explanation.

Nora thinks on the hop. "I haven't been around many people lately."

"You were nursing?"

"Sick people don't have a lot of banter."

Bill laughs, the tension gone from his face. Nora makes a mental note to be more cautious. To make questioning more of a conversation. Hadn't Frieda written that every resident was concealing a secret? Well, now Nora is one of them and she ought to guard her secret as closely as any of the other boarders might be guarding theirs.

Bill is still watching her, stroking one side of his mustache and then the other.

She senses he is making some sort of reckoning. He smiles; the outcome appears to be positive.

"I have favored a different line of business for some time, Nora. Commerce really. There is no greater joy than in helping people find what they are seeking. Whatever that might be."

He inhales deeply, savoring his cigarette. Nora takes a shallow puff of hers and tries to suppress the resulting cough.

Bill's voice is soft, with the air of the confessional. "Whether it's a leg of lamb, or a new set of pans, French perfume, *anything* you seek . . ."

Nora makes a bigger puff, blinking against the smoke. "Many goods are still hard to acquire I should imagine?"

"Not if you know the right people, Nora." He stoops to the case at his feet and places a peach in front of her. "On the house."

"A perfect peach in October! So, you are a magician too?"

"I'll leave that to Poppy." He beams. "*Anything* you require."

Nora takes a final puff of her cigarette and stubs it out in the ashtray.

"And it doesn't have to be a cigarette, Nora."

Nora laughs. She glances out of the door to see Stella pass with a laden tray heading for the staircase. Nora can see she has laid things out nicely for the professor: a cup with a saucer set on top, a little posy of garden flowers; it will be cheering to an old man who has seen a painful dawn.

Bill stands and gathers his newspaper, his case. "Your inquiries last night fell on blind ears, didn't they? About your predecessor?"

Nora looks up at him. "They did."

Bill taps his nose, lowers his voice, as if he's about to give a racing tip. "She went out very late, that last evening. Not Miss Brogan's usual thing."

"You saw her?"

"I was enjoying a cigar by the front door. I don't have a view from my room, you see."

"Did she tell you that she was leaving Gulls Nest?"

"She told me she would see me at breakfast, so I supposed she was coming back."

Nora feels light-headed. She wills her shoes to hang on to her. "Was she alone?"

"Yes. On her way past she dropped a letter in the post tray to go out the next morning. I'm no snoop but I was right next to it."

"You saw the address on the letter?"

"A religious order." Bill regards Nora closely. "In the north of England."

"Do you remember the date?"

Bill nods. "It was the last Friday in August."

Nora had received Frieda's final letter the week before. This meant there was one more letter written before Frieda disappeared.

A letter that never arrived. Was it posted? Or did someone take it from the post tray? Was it incriminating to the residents in some way?

Finding herself unable to speak, Nora picks up the peach, holds it carefully.

"Miss Brogan seemed a nice young woman, agreeable, forthright," says Bill. "Not at all the kind to do a moonlight flit."

Nora turns the peach in her hands, finds a bruise; it's not perfect after all. "So, she must have made friends locally. Anyone in particular?"

Bill hesitates. "I wouldn't know, I'm afraid."

"Thank you, Bill."

"You are most welcome, Nora. As I said: if I can help people find what they are seeking."

After a long cliff walk Nora stands at the shore with her bare feet in the cold, wet sand and the hair plastered to her head by the wind. It is reviving. She concentrates on trying to feel her toes before they drop off. On calming her mind. She was unprepared for the way that the world has set her thoughts swirling. She thinks back to the time before she took the veil; did her thoughts swirl then? As a passionate young woman, how could they not? At High Dallow she learned to make her thoughts deep and slow, gentle ripples on the still pond of her mind. Now her mind is a bucketful of tadpoles; thoughts slip by, squirm away, grow legs—

A hand on her arm and she jumps, but it is only Stella, who makes gestures of apology for startling her. Stella heads a little way down the beach while Nora looks for her shoes and makes an effort to return to herself. When she looks up, the young woman is fetching flat stones out of her coat pocket. She holds them in her hands a moment, palms them, before skimming them over the water. Stone after stone, her aim is accurate, practiced, and they bounce across the incoming waves. When Stella's eyes meet Nora's, her smile is radiant.

They walk into town together. Halfway along the promenade they are on first-name terms. Stella slips her arm through Nora's with the easy air of a confidante and Nora is reminded of when she was a young one herself. The sun is on their faces and the wind dies down a little. The gulls dip and wheel. The vendors, such as there are out of season, are opening their stalls.

"Do you like living at Gulls Nest, Stella?"

"We arrived at the start of this year. Seems like an age ago now. The summer season was dreadfully hectic. But I like my work. I'm only a lowly clerk but I'm grateful for the employment."

Nora, feeling sympathy for the young woman, lets her question go unanswered. "Work can bring great satisfaction, unless perhaps you are Mrs. Rawlings."

Stella laughs. "She can be a bit formidable but . . ."

"But you try and see the good in everyone?"

Stella smiles, shrugs.

"You are good to the old professor."

"I like him," says Stella simply. "Teddy does too."

"Forgive me if I speak out of turn but I sensed some tension between your husband and the young man who came later to dinner last night." Nora glances at her companion.

Stella's smile has faltered, her sunny face clouds.

Nora feels a pang of pity. "There now, I *have* spoken out of turn."

"No, really—"

"We'll say no more about it."

They continue along the promenade, Stella deep in thought, Nora enjoying the freshness to the air.

"Teddy has an irrational idea about Mr. Ježek."

"And what is that?"

Stella looks awkward.

"Ah, I'm sorry—I'll mind my own business."

"It's fine, Nora. Really it is." Stella squeezes her arm. "Teddy thinks that Mr. Ježek is in love with me. That he has *designs*. Isn't that scandalous?"

"Do you think the same?"

"No. I don't know. Teddy can be a little jealous. I try very hard not to give him cause to be, but he only has me in the world."

"And has your husband taken this idea up with Mr. Ježek?"

"I found them arguing a few days ago. Teddy said he'd had it out with him. The whole thing is mortifying."

"I could imagine."

"I just didn't want us to be part of the local gossip. It's bad enough living at Gulls Nest. It attracts all kinds of shabby characters—" Stella hesitates, color rising in her face. "I'm sorry, I didn't mean—"

Nora squeezes her arm back. "Not at all. So, tell me all the gossip about this boardinghouse for strays."

Stella lowers her voice. "During the war Mr. Carter sold goods on the black market."

"That's true. He still does."

"Nora! And he poisoned his entire family when he came back from sea. The doctors couldn't trace it because it was an exotic preparation he'd found on his travels."

"We'll need to watch him with that tureen."

Stella laughs. "Aren't we awful?"

"What else?"

"Professor Poppy is really landed gentry. An earl. His family disowned him when he became a showman. He once lived in a castle."

"Now that could be true. He speaks just like the old king did."

Stella nods, her eyes shining. "Mrs. Rawlings killed a man in her youth and spent years in prison."

"Irene an ex-con? That I could imagine. And Mrs. Wells?"

Stella shakes her head. "It's too scandalous."

"Ah, go on."

Stella gestures for Nora's ear and whispers, "She smokes opium." She shoots her a look of pure mirth. "That's why she's in bed all day with 'her head.'"

"Wouldn't you do the same if you always had to deal with Mrs. Rawlings?"

"And Dinah was brought up by foxes."

"Bless her."

"And Miss Brogan ran away because she was found to be carrying on with a married man."

Nora's breath catches in her. She turns it into a cough.

Stella looks at her, concerned. "I'm so sorry—I have shocked you."

"Not at all."

Stella appears chastened. "I shouldn't have said that; you see, it might have a grain of truth about it."

Nora is incredulous. "You saw her with this man?"

"Never. But I knew she was walking out with someone less than suitable."

"Miss Brogan divulged this?"

"She didn't have to. I read between the lines. As women do. I could tell that it was complicated and that she was in too deep."

"Could you? How?"

Stella reddens. "Oh, the usual: distracted, one moment high in the sky, the other practically underground. Sometimes she went out after dark, for a walk, she said. If Frieda was courting someone suitable, wouldn't he have seen her back to her boardinghouse? She always returned alone." Her voice is almost inaudible. "Sometimes our hearts win out over our heads. You know how love is."

"Actually, I don't. I've never been in love, so to speak."

Nora catches Stella's glance, questioning, sympathetic. Nora looks away.

They walk apace. Nora, built to range over distances, easily keeps up with the younger woman, who moves at a neat clip.

Nora keeps her voice light. "It sounds as if you and Miss Brogan were close. Confidantes?"

"Not so much. I liked Frieda. If I hadn't been so busy with Teddy and my work, I'm sure we would have been the best of friends."

Nora could see that, the two of them with the same kind of openness about them. But Frieda and a married man? Nora couldn't see that.

"I found her very agitated one day, not long before she left. She said that she had a decision to make about something that would change many lives." Stella catches Nora's expression. "She didn't say what it was."

"Did you tell anyone about this?"

"Only Teddy. After Frieda left, I heard the rumors going about and put two and two together."

"About the married man?"

"Yes."

"And did the rumors suggest the man's identity?"

Stella hesitates, then shakes her head. "Not that I heard."

They stop outside the Town Hall, a neoclassical building with a stuffy symmetry about it. Workers are filing inside; a few of them nod briskly to Stella.

She smooths down her hair. "I must go in, I'm already late." She frowns. "I hope you don't think badly of me, or of Gulls Nest, now."

"Only about the braised liver."

Stella gives Nora a warm smile. "It's fried fish tonight, one of the better ones."

Nora returns her smile. "Isn't there always something to be grateful for?"

The housekeeper brings the tea and the priest pours, which means he's progressive. The housekeeper looks on with indulgent disdain. He tells her thank you and he'll bring the tea things into the scullery afterwards. The woman walks from the room in bewilderment at the new ecumenical generation. This is a youngish priest, new to the parish, with a freshness to him. It is with enthusiasm he takes the photograph Nora holds out to him. Taken on the day Frieda began her postulancy, it pictures a bright-eyed young woman with a smile that would break your heart from the pure joy in it. Yes, *of course* he knew Frieda. She spoke to him, and several members of the congregation he believed, about her journey—leaving the order, her health struggles, her hopes for the future.

Nora scrutinizes the priest's face as he talks, for a hint of a shadow passing, the trace of a frown, the merest suggestion of tension in the jaw. There is nothing. His relaxed countenance suggests nothing of a dark or difficult nature passed between him and Miss Brogan in the confessional.

The priest regards the photograph and nods, untroubled. "She seemed an eminently sensible young woman. I really shouldn't worry unduly, Nora."

"Frieda wrote that she was taking Mass here."

"She was, very regularly at first."

"But not latterly, Father?"

"Latterly I saw her somewhat less. Frieda had other distractions, which is perfectly natural. But she never missed Mass on a Sunday."

"What sort of distractions?"

The priest smiles. "Oh, forging friendships and making herself useful in some way, finding occupation and so forth."

"Did she speak of any future plans she might have had to leave Gore-on-Sea?"

"No, indeed, she seemed to be quite settled."

Nora deduces that if the priest's benign, unlined face is anything to go by, Frieda's future plans didn't involve a moonlight flit after an affair with a married man.

The local infirmary has no record of a twenty-year-old woman, cheerful and kind, with a joyful smile and a limiting heart and lung condition (or some other difficulty, mishap, or accident, unforeseen) being admitted during the last seven weeks.

None of the three local doctors has had the pleasure of treating Miss Brogan, nor any young person matching her description, for an emergency or otherwise.

Nora reminds herself that she held little hope on this score. Gulls Nest, as Frieda's place of residence, would surely have been notified of any sickness or mishap. With a sense of unease growing in the pit of her stomach, Nora asks directions to the police station.

Thus, Nora finds herself waiting before a small desk and a large officer. The problems with scale in this town just continue. The desk officer is seemingly engrossed in the cataloging of a complicated misdemeanor, red-faced in the effort of it. He has yet to look up. Nora doesn't mind standing, not that she's been offered a seat. After some minutes she coughs politely. The officer writes more slowly. Somewhere a clock ticks, a metallic sound to offset the laborious scratchings on the page.

Tick, scratch, tick, scratch—

Nora notices something strange about herself. A movement to her person. It starts with a shifting of weight from side to side, it increases to the tapping of toes, then a stepping of each foot, toe to heel. She should check herself, but then, is there really a need for stillness? She's not waiting for the sanctified voice of the Holy Lord, only for the desk officer. Nora slips off her shoes. The cool of the linoleum is nice for one used to the airiness of a sandal. She regards the sand still between her toes. Now her bare soles make a pleasant patter.

Tick, patter, scratch, tick, patter, scratch, tick—

She examines the shoes; the ghosts of her own sweaty toes are in there. The shoes are hers now. Isn't that a novelty after thirty years of owning nothing?

"Put your shoes back on, madam," says the desk officer, not looking up.

It talks, thinks Nora.

"How do you know I'm wearing no shoes, Officer?" she asks. "You haven't looked at me once."

The officer's pen on the page slows to a halt.

"I've come to report a missing person."

"You'll have to put your shoes on for that."

"Is that the law?"

The officer says nothing; after a few moments he returns to his writing.

Tick, patter, scratch, tick—

"Officer," says Nora smoothly and with effort. "My friend has disappeared under mysterious circumstances, I'd like to report her missing."

"Shoes."

"That's an *urgent* report—"

The officer puts down his pen, crosses his arms, and looks at Nora. It's a look that unites irritation and a particular distaste that Nora knows to be reserved for mouthy middle-aged women.

Nora's rage, which has been on a low simmer, ignites. "All manner of harm may have befallen her—"

The officer narrows his eyes and points to Nora's shoes.

"This is not about my bloody shoes! It's about a lovely young woman who is lost and possibly in danger and there's you wasting time pretending to be writing something important with a big red face on you."

"Shoes."

"My friend—"

"*I said—*"

Detective Inspector Rideout surveys Nora Breen across a tacky, cup-ringed table. The weapon of assault, a pair of ugly auld shoes, lies between them.

Rideout looks amused, Breen looks unrepentant.

The inspector leans forward, chin on his hand. Nora both likes and dislikes the way he's looking at her. As if she's the entertainment, or a puzzle he could solve. Either way she'll be sure to disappoint.

"I misunderstood what your officer was requesting of me."

"You threw a shoe and hit him in the eye. Did you think that's what he was asking for?"

Nora can hardly answer that. "Actually, I threw both shoes but only one hit its target."

Rideout raises his eyebrow.

Nora has to admit it is rakish, the eyebrow. She has always liked the rakish ones. If she winked back at him, he wouldn't look away. Not that she'd try it, with the gravity of her current situation. And why would a man of his trusted position be winking at her in the first place? There's a swagger to him, although he looks as though he sleeps on a bench. The crumpled jacket, the opened shirt with a ring of grime about the neck.

He catches her looking. "I was at a stake-out last night. I was about to leave for home when you assaulted my constable."

"A stake-out? And was that very exciting?"

His face shows no excitement.

Nora wonders at the man. Wouldn't being a detective be entirely invigorating? Solving puzzles, indulging your curiosity, studying people and their motivations. People are endlessly fascinating to Nora. Even the nuns in her community moved in far more mysterious ways than the Good Lord Himself did. She thinks of the case of Sister Brendan and her secret pet mouse and Sister Gobnait and the broken chalice. Little enigmas she herself solved, much to Mother Superior's chagrin. Nora smiles to herself; perhaps she would have made a better detective than a nun. If she had had the choice.

Magnanimously she includes Rideout in her smile. "Tell me: would your stake-out have been at a criminal's lair or a bank full of bullion?"

"Don't change the subject." He searches in his pocket and withdraws a cigarette case. "It was at a woodyard, Miss Breen. Someone has been knocking off timber."

"Did you catch 'em?"

"Yes. I did."

"Fair play to you."

Rideout takes out a cigarette and taps it on the table in a way that looks both natural and swish to Nora. He sees her looking and offers her the case.

"Don't mind if I do," says Nora.

He strikes a match and lights his cigarette.

Nora tries the tapping, naturally swish. Looking up, she sees he's there holding out the lit match to her, waiting.

The two of them sit puffing. Nora is more proficient now. She's a quick learner.

She examines him through the cloud of smoke. Light brown eyes, light brown hair with flecks of gray. A mustache just the right side of finicky. Several scars to his neck and jaw that are not quite hidden by the stubble of days. Shrapnel, thinks Nora, although as a nurse to a confined religious order her experience of war injuries is negligible. The only traumatic wound she treated in the last thirty years was Sister Julien's when she impaled herself arse-wards on the point of a railing while pruning an unruly shrub rose.

Nora admits to herself that Rideout's face is handsome, although not as handsome as his voice. He has the crisp, clear vowels of a radio broadcaster that would make even Lord Professor Poppy sound like a guttersnipe.

"You have to ask, Inspector, what is the best use of your time? Is it arresting me for accidentally aiming those shoes at your officer's head, or finding my missing friend, a lovely young woman, who could be in great trouble?"

Rideout regards Nora, inhales, breathes out again. "So now we come to it, you're here to report a missing person?"

Nora extracts the photograph from her coat pocket and holds it out to him. "Mind now, don't put it down. The filth of that table."

Rideout takes the photograph and looks at it.

"You could get that desk officer up off his backside, give this room the once-over," Nora murmurs.

"You left your order to find this girl?"

Nora meets his eyes. "I left my order. Finding Frieda is another matter."

Rideout, perhaps seeing the steel there, swallows his next question and just nods. "Can I keep hold of this photograph?"

"You can."

"People come and go all the time at Gore-on-Sea."

"She wasn't the coming-and-going kind."

"I'm not promising anything."

"Good man yourself."

He looks at her narrowly. "You say your housemates at Gulls Nest have no knowledge of your prior friendship with Miss Brogan?"

"I thought it best to come undercover. I usually trust my instincts."

Rideout nods. "Instincts count but so too do facts, Miss Breen."

"Breen, please. Call me by my surname like the detectives do in the books."

Rideout slips the photograph into the inside pocket of his jacket. As he does so, Nora catches a glimpse of some marvelous variety of silk lining. The colors bright, the design birds of paradise if she's not mistaken.

The inspector stands and conducts her to the door. "I suggest you might put your shoes back on rather than keeping them to hand." His wry expression returns. "Resist temptation and all that, Miss Breen."

Nora takes the path across the grassy verge up towards Gulls Nest. The wide stretch of the beach is behind her and the toes in her shoes are sandy again. It's a feeling she's missed all these long years. Having grown up by the sea, she sometimes felt it was a cruelty to be landlocked at High Dallow. Gulls bicker and swear overhead. She looks up to see if Father Conway is among them; she has bought a few wee herrings for him. She marvels at herself, out shopping, bag in hand, coat on her back. She is of the world experiencing things of the world. She gives thanks for the sea and the sky and the gulls and her cold, sandy feet. She doesn't name God as the recipient of her thanks. If he's still around he stays quiet; perhaps he doesn't want to push his luck.

A small boy runs down the path towards her, his face grave with some errand. "Are you the nurse, missus?" he asks, breathless. "Are you Missus Breen?"

Professor Poppy sits at the kitchen table, his terrier close by his feet. The old man wears a coat over his pajamas and holds a teacup. He is unable to drink from the cup with the shaking of his hands. His white hair is untamed. When he looks up, he doesn't see Nora. She recognizes the wild-eyed look of one in shock. She knows his mind is resting on some other sight.

Next to his chair waits a girl not above sixteen, aproned and wearing socks inside beach shoes. She is pale but excited. She stands awkwardly by, not quite knowing what's expected.

"Has he taken sick?" Nora asks of her, laying a hand on Poppy's arm, automatically feeling for his pulse.

"He says he found something terrible," says the girl. "Out there, in his workshop."

CHAPTER 4

Nora kneels before Professor Poppy. In the daylight he looks old and spare and ratty in his weatherworn mackintosh. His pajamaed legs are tucked into wellington boots and his chin is stubbled. His eyes are fixed on the back door with a fear that's almost pantomime.

The girl's name is Rose and her employment at Gulls Nest consists of the daily washing of pots and crockery and the weekly turning down of beds. On Mrs. Rawlings's day off Rose has free rein of the kitchen and the additional responsibility of serving the breakfast as well as clearing up after.

"With all due respect," says Rose, not unkindly, "my duties don't include *terrible findings.*"

At the mention of terrible findings, Poppy lets out a moan. His eyes swivel to Nora, rheumy and imploring.

Nora pats his hand. "Fetch him some water, Rose. I'll go out to the workshop and take a look."

Nora finds she is glad of the fresh air as she steps out of the house. This is the time of seedpods and dankness, wet earth and bare twigs. Nora sees the bones of a beautiful, albeit neglected, garden. She passes the privy lodged behind a bank of rhododendrons, a gazebo stuffed with old furniture, a toolshed, a sundial on a mossy, sloping lawn, a Victorian greenhouse with delicate ironwork and moldering panes. A pond with fallen yellow leaves bright against dark water. The overgrown path takes her closer to the old high boundary wall, adorned with the skeletons of espaliered fruit trees. She notes a tree house, no more than a platform with a rope ladder, way up high in a lovely sprawling oak. Too high perhaps for a young child, certainly not for someone without a head for heights. But doubtlessly with a good view over the wall, towards the rectory and the church and the cliff path beyond. Now and again Nora catches sight of a rabbit. These are no wild creatures but of a fancy do-mesticated kind like those she saw at the front of the house—lop-eared and masked, white and ginger, slate blue and doe-eyed sable. As she nears, they cast her baleful glances and hop away. Nora hopes they are not destined for Irene's tureen.

She reaches an old stable building with a few bockety deck chairs set outside. It would be a pleasant place to sit; the trees that are prolific in this garden have been cut back to allow for some light here. One of the stable doors has been propped open, and the others have been glazed or boarded over. Above the open door a grotesque carved head is hung, Mr. Punch himself. This is Professor Poppy's workshop. The old man's walking stick is still looped over the handle of the door. Presumably he hadn't needed it when he galloped back up the garden path after the terrible finding.

Nora steps inside.

A body lies supine on the floor not far from the door. Nora instantly knows this person is beyond medical help. Even in the dim she can see a terrible lividity to the face. She needn't bend to take a pulse, but she does.

The corpse surveys her slyly through the corner of one eye, but really Teddy Atkins is in a better place now. He is dressed in work clothes and heavy boots. One leg twisted under him and his arms thrown out. Teddy's mouth is open and, taking a delicate sniff, Nora discerns the faint scent of bitter almonds.

She straightens and steps back from the corpse. She must move carefully now and touch nothing. She glances around, taking in the details of the room. Teddy is alone. An oil lamp has been lit on the workbench. In its pool of light lies a saucer, a cup, and a spoon, all in a line, methodically laid out. Nora glances into the cup; the dregs of something dark can be seen at the bottom. She swishes the cup and sniffs. The aroma of coffee and beneath that, bitter almonds.

A piece of wood is clamped in the vise, otherwise the bench is clear and swept clean. The stables have been converted to give one long, narrow room with the workbench along the wall opposite the door. Above the workbench, shelves hold paint pots and brushes, wood in various stages of being worked, and baskets of fabric remnants and fringing. Tools hang on the wall and all look to be accounted for: files and chisels hung in size order, mallets and hammers all in their designated places. Finished puppets hang on the wall at the far end of the workshop. The cast of a Punch & Judy show, their costumes bright even in the dim. Propped in the corner there are furled backdrops and dismantled puppet booths. Otherwise, there's a comfortable chair and a wood-burning stove. A small table holds a selection of aperitifs and the pipe rack above is stocked with gnarled old-timers. This is a year-round workshop and, if not for the body on the floor, would prove a cozy retreat.

Nora retraces her steps down the garden. She prays by habit for the repose of Teddy's soul, in thanks for a wet garden, for the safety of rabbits. She notices that her prayers have a stiff formality now. Like the first inroads after a bad argument with someone. She doesn't expect an answer. Back in the kitchen, Rose is collecting pots and dishes to bring into the scullery. Professor Poppy has regained some composure. He sips a glass of brandy and trains a watery eye on Nora's approach. He gives her a rakish salute and she wonders how many drinks he's downed. Rose turns to her with a coffeepot in her hand.

"Put down the coffeepot, Rose. Don't touch another thing in this kitchen."

Rose looks startled and does what she's told.

"Now, run and fetch a policeman and a doctor, in that order."

"A doctor?" pipes up Poppy. "But surely the poor dear boy is beyond—"

"Professor, come with me to the parlor."

"Before three o'clock? But the rules—"

"I think we can bend them a little."

He stands and takes Nora's arm in a way that appears chivalrous but actually hides his need for support.

"I saw your stick down at your workshop," says Nora. "I ought to have brought it back."

"I don't really need it."

"Is that true?"

The old man pulls a face.

Nora smiles. "We'll say no more about it."

They shuffle out of the kitchen as Rose puts on a hat and coat and is out the back door in a jiffy.

Poppy stops to take a breath when they are halfway across the hallway. He cries briefly, almost angrily, his frail frame racked by sobs, then collects himself. He sniffs and nods and they continue into the parlor.

Over the threshold a pained expression crosses his face. "Stella, the poor child, someone must find her."

Nora conducts him to a chair by the fire. "All in good time."

She deftly lights the fire and draws a blanket around his shoulders.

"You are so calm, Nora. Even with what you've just seen: a young man, in his prime, struck down."

Nora pats his hand. "I am a nurse."

"Well used to the vicissitudes of life and death." He shakes his head. "My poor dear Teddy. He did not die from natural causes, did he?"

"Poppy, we can't make assumptions—"

"Madam, I saw his face too. He took something, didn't he?" He frowns, considering. "He had been sick lately. Not in body, in mind." Poppy delicately taps the side of his head, the expression in his eyes one of profound sadness.

He doesn't judge, thinks Nora, he's a man with his own demons.

"By all accounts he had a difficult war and found it hard to reconnect."

Nora nods. "By whose account?"

"Stella's. She confided in me, only a few weeks ago now." Poppy gathers the blanket around him. "Teddy was hardly sleeping, she said. He would be out walking at all hours. But the bad dreams found him day or night. It was our plan, mine and Stella's, to make the workshop available to him at all times. Save him wandering the cliff path or down to the sea."

A beat passes between them and a look. Nora understands what Poppy is saying.

"Consequently, Teddy was often in my workshop early mornings or late at night. Helping me with my carvings, doing a few little jobs. Stella said it took his mind off things."

A question forms in Nora's mind. She looks at Poppy; his eyes are wet.

The old man, as if reading the inquiry in her face, answers. "Poor, poor, impulsive Teddy. He looked in on me this morning. We sometimes have a coffee together first thing but this morning he wouldn't stop. But dash it to hell—he seemed brighter."

Nora speaks carefully. "Are you saying you think Teddy took his own life?"

"What else?" Poppy frowns. "You can't seriously suggest that this was malicious? If you knew him, you wouldn't— Teddy was a dear boy."

Dear boys and girls are killed every day, thinks Nora, only she keeps it to herself.

She pats Poppy's hand and tries to speak brightly. "The finished puppets displayed in your workshop look very old."

The professor's face relaxes. "My first set. Not the best, but then I didn't make them."

"But you have affection for them, displaying them as you do?"

"I should have, I carted them all over the country, man and boy!"

"That would do it. You have a full cast on that wall?"

"Of course! All the traditional characters. Even Toby Dog." He glances down at the old terrier who has followed them in from the kitchen and installed himself on the hearth rug. "The kiddies like a living dog better. He would sit up with his ruff on the board there, smart as anything, proud as Punch. Now we are both old and shabby."

Nora smiles. "But with a wealth of memories?"

Poppy nods. "Let's just say it was a winding road which brought us here. With lots of odd turnings." He throws her a shrewd look. "But Gulls Nest is that sort of a place, isn't it? Where the dreamers and schemers wash up."

The sound of a motorcar pulling up on the driveway. Nora opens the front door to Inspector Rideout and a young officer she hasn't seen before. Rose has ridden back to Gulls Nest with them, her face pink with all the excitement.

Rideout addresses Nora, offering no preliminary. "You found him?"

"No, Professor Poppy did, another resident."

"This is Miss Breen, sir, she's a nurse," Rose volunteers.

"Miss Breen, take me to the body, if you will?"

Rose visibly shudders.

Nora turns to her. "Wait with the professor in the parlor, make sure he's kept warm."

Rose is aghast. "The parlor, before three o'clock?"

"Yes, before three o'clock. And keep out of the kitchen."

Rideout kneels down beside the corpse. He has a neat torch and he uses it to note Teddy's expression. Nora draws nearer.

"You can wait outside, Miss Breen. Leave this to me."

"It's no bother."

Rideout glances up at her. "I meant: wait outside."

Nora ignores him. "Presumably cyanide," she volunteers. "You can tell by his complexion, all that excess oxygen in his bloodstream. And a faint bitter almond smell if you get close enough."

"Presume nothing," says Rideout. He returns his attention to the corpse. "And I suppose you regularly came across cyanide poisoning in your order?"

"No, in detective novels."

"I don't for a moment believe that nuns read detective novels."

Nora grins. "Not all nuns."

Rideout glances over at the cup, saucer, and spoon laid out on the workbench. "Well, he was methodical about it."

"*He* was? That sounds like a presumption to me."

Rideout grunts. He bends down and takes a tentative sniff at Teddy's open mouth. "I can't smell it but then not everyone can. I'll have to take your word."

Rideout glances around.

Nora points to the bench. "It was in the coffee cup."

"And you say Teddy Atkins was in the habit of taking coffee with Professor Poppy?"

"Yes, only not this morning, it seems; Teddy wouldn't stop but his wife found the time to read to the auld fella."

"That's a regular occurrence too?"

"Yes, according to Stella."

"So, the young couple look out for Professor Poppy. How touching." Rideout is musing. "And it was Poppy who found the body? When?"

"Shortly before my return. Around eleven twenty. I'd say Teddy has been dead for a couple of hours."

"What makes you think that?"

"His rigidity, temperature. I took his pulse."

"A dead man's pulse. I would say that would be hard to find."

"I mean to say that I touched him. So, I can make an educated guess."

"In my profession we generally steer clear of guesses, Miss Breen, educated or otherwise. Anyone else in the house?"

"At the time of Teddy's death or the discovery of his body?"

"Death, preferably."

"You'll have to ask Rose. I was out all morning."

Rideout shines his torch on the puppets along the far wall. "Not out assaulting police officers, I hope?" he murmurs. "Ah, there's Mr. Punch, another great one for battering the constabulary."

Nora ignores the dig. "Something isn't quite right here."

"No, Punch and his gang are pretty grotesque-looking."

"That's it!"

Rideout considers the puppets, frowns. "What's it?"

"That isn't the whole gang," observes Nora. "One character is missing."

"Is that right?"

Nora nods. "Jack Ketch. The executioner."

"Coincidental?"

She casts a look at Teddy's body. "Or a message from the killer?"

"Let's not get ahead of ourselves."

Nora catches sight of something and bends down to study the corpse. She frowns, her voice suddenly urgent. "Look at this, stuffed in his right pocket."

Rideout peers. "A handkerchief?"

"It's not his."

"How could you possibly know that, Miss Breen?"

"See those forget-me-nots?"

Rideout shines the torch, squints. "I see little blue dots."

"I can assure you they are flowers," replies Nora. "And when you unfold that handkerchief, you will also discern the letters F.B., in blue thread."

"What makes you so sure?"

"I embroidered it, for Frieda Brogan."

Rideout notes the coffeepot Rose had deposited on the kitchen table and gives a cursory check in the scullery and pantry.

"We'll go through and take samples."

"It's likely the cyanide was added to Teddy's coffee cup directly," observes Nora. "The murderer may not have wanted to run the risk that others would die accidentally."

Rideout gives her a stern look. "I am not yet investigating a murder, Miss Breen."

"Are we not?"

"No, *I* am not."

"And then there's the link to Frieda's disappearance. We need to establish why he had her handkerchief in his possession."

From the direction of the parlor comes a commotion. A polite voice raised, Mrs. Wells's certainly. Nora recognizes the sound of rising panic, if not the exact words being said. A second voice, rougher, can be heard: Irene Rawlings.

The young police constable peers around the kitchen door. "Sir, two ladies have arrived since, one of them has lost her little girl. And the doctor is here."

Rideout looks momentarily weary. "Take the doctor down to the workshop and tell the ladies I'll be there directly, Griggs."

Nora regards Helena Wells. The woman is a wonder: despite her tears she does not suffer the indignity of a red nose or puffy eyes. She is handsomely distraught. Irene Rawlings, still in her hat and coat, looks on sourly, with barely concealed disgust, at the invasion of the parlor outside designated hours and the lavish use of coal. Professor Poppy sleeps openmouthed in an armchair. A bright-eyed Rose watches the proceedings from a chair by the fire. Nora has no doubt the girl is enjoying herself.

"She must have taken fright, or worse," says Helena to the inspector. "Dinah would never, ever stray past the boundaries of Gulls Nest. We have a terrible job getting her to visit a dentist or so forth."

"And your daughter always comes when you call her?" Rideout asks.

"No, Constable."

Rideout lets his demotion pass.

"She almost never comes," continues Helena. "Especially when she thinks she's in trouble."

Irene, frowning at her employer, quickly interjects. "What Mrs. Wells means is that the child can sometimes make mischief, that's all."

Rideout looks exasperated. "Well, there you go. She's not lost at all, then, but simply ignoring—"

"You don't understand." Helena's voice is raised. "Dinah and I have a special call, *life or death*. It's one of the few things I absolutely insist upon." She takes from her pocket a little silver whistle.

Rideout's expression is incredulous. "You blow a dog whistle?"

"Well, yes, I do, Constable."

"And Dinah returns?"

"Always. Without fail."

Rideout glances at Irene, whose grim nod substantiates this.

At the recounting of this little pact with her daughter, Helena's expression crumples in a way that is not at all becoming. She hides her face in her hands and sobs. Nora feels a pang of pity for her. Even Irene's scowl softens.

Rideout turns to Nora. "You search upstairs, Miss Breen. I'll search the ground floor and the gardens. The rest of you remain in the parlor please."

Religious life has made Nora proficient in turning a gorgon's eye on errant feelings, should they arise. Now she notices a slight swelling of pride, a wee preening about herself. It comes from being singled out by Rideout to help with the detection. She reminds herself that his choosing her is not flattery; it is expedience. She is a person known to him already—that is all. Besides, if she wants to play detective it won't depend on Detective Inspector Rideout's say-so. Nora hesitates; identifying pride again, she silently berates herself.

Irene looks disgruntled. "I can't stay cooped up in here! There's the supper to be getting on with."

"Supper can wait." Rideout addresses Helena. "Are any of the doors in this house locked? Do you keep master keys?"

"We supply keys to our residents," Irene answers for her employer. "Whether they use them or not is down to them. There is no need for locked doors in Gulls Nest. There is no wrongdoing here."

With impeccable timing, Professor Poppy lets out a loud snort of a snore.

Nora starts with her own room, searching all the spaces a child as tricksy as Dinah might hide. Under the sprung metal bed, inside the wardrobe, hanging by her monkey feet from the back of the curtains. There is no sign of the girl. She crosses to Professor Poppy's room, braving the smell of stale alcohol and the fug of pipe tobacco. There is no Dinah to be found amidst the clutter of books and blankets. Nora climbs the stairs to the landing above. Bill Carter's bedroom door is locked. Nora is a touch surprised given how amiable the man is. She applies Irene's master key and is unsurprised by the condition of the room, as neat as a nun's cell but with a wall of glass cabinets such as you would see in any museum. And inside? Curiosities, from Bill's travels no doubt, displayed carefully. Some a little macabre: blowpipes and spears, odd carved dolls. Nora wishes she had the time to look.

Dinah is not in Stella and Teddy's room, sadly touching with its domestic clutter. Two brushes in a glass on the dressing table, the slippers lined up by the door, his one suit and her few dresses limp in the wardrobe. Their wedding photograph takes pride of place on the mantelpiece. The couple look impossibly young, Stella lovely in white, Teddy scowling up at the sun. They are barely adults, thinks Nora, as she notices a battered toy car on the shelf and a nightie case on the bed, shaped like a scruffy dog.

Nora departs the room and shuts the door, moving with the customary quietness brought about by life in a contemplative order. She takes a moment to say a prayer on behalf of the young wife whose life is about to be shattered. Not to Himself but to St. Monica. In her mind Nora sees the face of the saint, wan, grave-eyed, wearing a simple nun's habit. The patron saint of married women. Nora frowns at a niggly little thought: *What else is St. Monica patron of?* She pushes this thought from her mind. She thinks instead about Stella. The young constable Rideout sent in the car to collect her will perhaps be imparting the terrible news right now. She will be driven back to Gulls Nest a widow. At least this way Stella would not hear carried news and speculation, broadcast over fences, in the shops and on street corners, of the terrible finding here.

Nora climbs the narrow stairs to the attic room, between the scraped nursery-papered walls. She emerges into a space that is empty of Dinah but full of sky.

She instantly sees that much has changed in the room.

Photographs still adorn the wall, only they are no longer in regimented lines. Some have been pulled down; there are gaps now. The army coat is missing from behind the door, which is only to be expected if Karel Ježek is not at home. But gone too is the battered trunk at the end of the bed, the pile of clothes from the chair and the boots that had lodged beneath. Has no one mentioned Karel's movements today? Nora did not see him at breakfast—had he breakfasted early and gone straight out? His bed is carefully made, which perhaps isn't a sign of a hasty departure. Much has been left behind. Could this signal that he means to return?

Nora parts heavy black curtains and steps into the wood-framed cubicle of the makeshift darkroom. She startles as something brushes past her head. She puts up her hand, discovers a cord, pulls it, and the space is flooded with red light.

The darkroom seems to tell a different story from Karel's room. The shelves of bottles and packets have been ransacked. A chemical smell emanates from trays of solution on the bench, which Nora thinks is perhaps as it should be. A spool of film lies disemboweled on the floor. Streamers of film negatives hang from the ceiling. With the ammonia smell and the red light and the stark black shadows Nora could fancy herself to be in some sort of confined hell. She bites down the urge to flee and squints at the images on the negatives but can make nothing out. It is with relief she switches off the lamp and emerges into the brightness and clean air of the attic room.

It is also with relief that she hears Rideout calling up to her that the child has been found.

Dinah is no worse for her experience, it seems. Other than her face is even more grubby and her hair even more matted than usual. She grabs the glass of water that the police constable hands her and drinks greedily, ignoring her mother, who is smiling at Rideout very prettily, as if he's a conquering hero. Irene looks on, arms folded, mouth down-turned.

Dinah, it appears, became trapped in the sideboard during breakfast time when the lock failed. When no one had heard her pounding on the doors she had simply curled up and fallen asleep.

"That will teach you," says Helena Wells indulgently to her daughter. "Not to hide in confined spaces to earwig conversations."

Dinah turns her large blue eyes to her mother and regards her blankly.

Rideout crouches down, leans in, addressing the girl. "Is that what happened, Dinah? You got yourself stuck in the sideboard?"

Nora watches as Dinah turns her gaze on the detective. Her expression doesn't change.

Rideout waits, frowns.

Nora catches the merest blink in answer before Dinah throws her glass—which smashes—on the floor and runs from the room.

"Dinah!" calls Helena.

Irene sullenly sets about picking up the shards of broken glass.

Nora takes the opportunity to catch Rideout's attention. He follows her into the hallway. They talk in low voices.

"What is it, Miss Breen?"

"It appears as if Karel Ježek has gone. He's taken a trunk from his attic room."

Rideout frowns. "A planned departure or a coincidence?"

"There was some tension between the two men: Teddy was allegedly under the impression that Karel was after his wife."

"You heard this from?"

"Stella herself."

"Any truth in that, were they lovers?" Rideout stops, looks awkward. "Sorry, what a question to ask you."

"Nonsense. There appeared to be animosity between the two men at supper. I also saw Karel stamping on Teddy's hat."

"From hat stamping to murder by cyanide?"

"So, you agree that it was murder?"

Another commotion in the parlor. Rose is calling.

Nora regains the room to find Rose up at the window, peering out at the next installment of the day's drama.

"It's Mrs. Atkins," she says. "They are bringing her up the drive."

A hush has descended on the room. Irene Rawlings scowls at the dying embers in the grate, Professor Poppy dozes, frowning in his sleep. Rose stands by the door straining to hear what is going on. Helena Wells elegantly reclines on the sofa with a cold flannel over her eyes; the shock of Teddy's untimely death and the uproar over Dinah have given her one of her heads. Dinah has scurried up behind the curtains and apart from sending the dusty velvet swaying from time to time, causes no further commotion. Nora sits quietly watching the others.

Professor Poppy wakes, he glances at Irene. "No sign of a pot of tea, then? I'm absolutely parched."

Irene scowls on, unhearing it seems.

The old man coughs, as if to make a point.

Nora gets up from the chair and goes to sit near him. "Soon, Professor, we'll find you some tea."

"And I suppose there won't be any kind of supper." He grimaces at Nora and whispers, "Perhaps that's no tragedy."

From the dining room next door: a woman's loud sobs. Helena Wells peers sadly out from under her flannel. Irene stops scowling momentarily and looks forlorn. Only Rose seems unaffected by this outpouring of grief. Hearing the crunch of gravel on the drive she's already back at the window.

"Some men have arrived in a van. They have a stretcher," she observes. "The doctor is leaving. Here is Mr. Carter walking up the drive.

He's looking all around, his head moving this way and that; he can't believe what he sees!"

"Come away from that window, girl," Irene barks.

Rose looks mutinous but does what she's told.

A firm knock is heard, even Helena sits up to attention. Constable Griggs puts his head around the door.

"Miss Breen, would you be so kind as to come into the dining room?"

Nora rises. She can feel the eyes of the others upon her.

Professor Poppy huffs. "Is this going to take much longer, Constable?"

"It's hard to say, sir. I'm sure the inspector will let you know soon enough."

Rideout opens the door to Nora, he keeps his voice low. "She asked for you."

Nora looks at Stella Atkins and her heart lurches. The young widow sits at the dining room table, her face pale and her eyes sore and red. Her crying has abated to an exhausted misery. She stares down at the dirty breakfast things yet to be cleared. A world of difference from the bright-faced woman Nora met this morning.

She looks up. "It's not true what they are saying. It's not really him, is it, Miss Breen?"

Nora pulls a chair next to Stella's and sits down. She holds her desperate gaze.

Softly, she says, "Stella, I'm so sorry but Teddy is dead."

Stella takes a gulp of breath and nods with conviction. Like a child who finally understands a problem they have been set.

Rideout takes a seat opposite. "Mrs. Atkins, there are a few questions I need to ask."

"Now?"

"I'm afraid so; we need to build a picture of what happened." He glances at Nora. "Miss Breen can stay, if that will be of comfort?"

Stella nods, resigned. She takes Nora's hand.

"Was your husband in trouble of any kind?"

"Of course not."

"Mr. Atkins had a position at the amusement park?"

"Yes."

"In the employ of the Ladd family? Is that right?"

"Yes."

"Any issues there?"

"Not at all. He loves his work—" Stella's eyes fill with tears again, she takes a deep breath—"*loved*."

"Do you need a moment, Mrs. Atkins?" asks Rideout.

Stella shakes her head. Nora squeezes her hand.

Rideout continues. "Did Mr. Atkins drink?"

"No more than anyone else."

"Did he owe money?"

Stella smiles up at him bitterly. "No more than anyone else."

"Gamble, perhaps?"

"Never."

"His behavior, his interests, had they changed lately?"

"No."

"Was there anything troubling him? Any arguments or fights?"

Stella hesitates. "No."

"You can think of no ill feeling, towards, or from, another resident here?"

Stella purses her lips and shakes her head.

"I'm sorry, Mrs. Atkins, but I have to ask: how were relations between the two of you? Any quarrels?"

"We never quarreled."

Nora remembers the first time she saw the young couple. Teddy with his face like thunder, storming away, Stella seeming to plead with him, holding him back.

Nora speaks kindly. "You can tell the inspector anything, Stella, he will not judge."

The younger woman lets go of Nora's hand, a flash of anger in her eyes. "What do you want me to say? That I drove Teddy to it?"

Rideout, fleetingly, looks pained. Nora notices his expression. He feels too deeply to do this job, she thinks. It costs him.

Stella starts to cry again.

"Is there anyone we can send for, dear?" asks Nora softly and waits.

After a time, Stella recovers her composure, accepts Nora's handkerchief, wipes her eyes.

"Teddy was my only family. I've no one else." She looks down at Nora's handkerchief balled in her fist. "It was poison, wasn't it? He killed himself with poison."

Rideout's face is grave. "Mrs. Atkins, why would you think that?"

Stella hesitates. "Your officer told me. Do you know, I had a horrible feeling as soon as my manager came to get me? I somehow knew something had gone very wrong."

Nora wonders if Rideout is angry with his young officer for letting slip this information. If so, he doesn't give it away, only perhaps with those spots of high color on his cheeks.

"It is too soon to make such judgments." He hesitates and proceeds in a tone that's carefully neutral. "Mrs. Atkins, your husband's routine, was there anything exceptional this morning?"

Stella takes a ragged breath. "I woke early, Teddy was already dressed and gone."

"Just a moment, Stella. Can you recall, did Teddy have the benefit of a clean handkerchief this morning?"

Stella and Rideout both look at Nora. Stella with an expression of confusion. Rideout with a glare.

"Miss Breen," he snaps. "You are party to this interview solely because Mrs. Atkins requested your presence. I would ask you to refrain from interrupting."

"Right you are."

"Sorry, Mrs. Atkins, please continue, your husband was gone when you woke?"

Stella turns to Nora. "Why do you ask about Teddy's hankie?"

Rideout groans.

"Is it possible that Teddy had someone else's hankie in his possession?" whispers Nora.

"Did he?" Stella frowns. "Whose?"

Rideout is half out of his chair. "Miss Breen! This is your final warning. One more peep out of you and you'll leave the room!"

Nora looks mutinous.

Stella turns to Rideout. "My husband always had a fresh handkerchief. I leave a pile of them in his drawer. I generally see to our laundry unless I'm very busy at work."

"Thank you, Mrs. Atkins."

"You see Irene has Rose organize the bagwash and everything comes back in a dreadful muddle. Everyone's things mixed up. Teddy hated that."

Nora opens her mouth. Rideout shoots her a warning glare. She closes it again.

Rideout addresses Stella. "Is it possible that Mr. Atkins might inadvertently have had another resident's handkerchief in his possession?"

Stella looks back at them, from one to the other, like a child confused by a trick question. "No—yes—I don't see that he would."

Rideout glances at Nora with an *are you satisfied* expression. "Let's return to my previous question, Mrs. Atkins—your husband was gone when you woke?"

She takes a slow, deep breath. Nora senses Stella's effort to compose herself.

"Yes, he often does a few jobs for Poppy before he goes to work."

"In the workshop?"

"Yes. I readied myself and went down to breakfast; I saw Miss Breen there."

"At what time?"

"Oh, I don't know." Stella looks to Nora. "Around eight o'clock."

Nora nods encouragingly.

"Did you see your husband at this point?"

"No, I went into the kitchen to prepare a tray for Poppy and took it up to his room. I read to him in the mornings, you see, when he has had a bad night." She sniffs, finds out a handkerchief. "Lately he has had many bad nights."

"You took the tray directly up to him? Can you describe what you prepared for him?"

"Warm milk."

"Which you heated using—"

"The milk pan—I don't see why this is relevant."

"Please just answer as best you can," says Rideout, not unkindly. "So, you took Poppy his milk?"

"Yes, but there was hardly a drop left for him. Rose said the birds had got into the milk bottles. I set the tray and carried it upstairs to Poppy. Moments later Rose popped up and offered to go and fetch another bottle. Honestly, that girl will find any excuse to duck out, especially when Mrs. Rawlings is away. I heard her go out. When she returned and called up to me, I went downstairs."

"How long was Rose gone for?"

"I couldn't say, not very long."

"And then?"

"And then it was time for work. I said goodbye to Poppy, went downstairs, took my hat and coat from the hall stand, and left. I spotted Miss Breen down on the beach and we walked to town together."

"Did you at any point go out to the workshop and see your husband there?"

"No, Inspector, if only I had . . ."

Rideout gives her a moment to regain her composure. "And you waited until Rose returned before you left the house? Why was that?"

"I suppose I was engrossed in the story I was reading. The sound of the back door brought me back to the world." She pauses, frowns.

"What is it?" asks Nora.

"I remember now: I heard the back door go. I thought perhaps Rose had forgotten something; she is rather scatty."

"Professor Poppy's room is directly over the kitchen and the pantry at the back of the house," Nora observes. "Did you look out, Stella?"

"No, because there isn't a clear view."

"Who has access to the garden?"

"We all do, Inspector."

"The residents use the narrow hallway that runs between the kitchen and the pantry to reach the garden and back gate," Nora adds.

Rideout nods. "I know it."

"Only Poppy really uses the garden," Stella volunteers. "Everyone else is discouraged. Mrs. Rawlings doesn't like the boarders passing her kitchen unless . . ." She hesitates and glances at Nora.

"It's to use the privy," says Nora plainly.

Rideout smooths his mustache. The gesture seems to settle him. He turns to Stella. "So, you presumed it was Rose you heard going out of the back door and then returning?"

"Yes. The back door sticks, you see, it's impossible to open or close it quietly. We all apply the same knack to it. A deft kick to the bottom and a hard push."

Nora turns to Stella. "Would you say it was someone familiar with the door then?"

"Miss Breen!"

She puts up her hand in a gesture of apology. "I'll leave the questions to you, Detective Inspector."

Rideout turns to Stella. "So, you believe the door was opened by a resident?"

"Or rather, someone *familiar* with the door," Nora corrects.

"Yes, almost certainly," Stella answers.

Rideout, a little red in the face, seems to be making some effort to control himself. "How many times did you hear the door being opened and closed, Mrs. Atkins?"

Stella shakes her head. "A few times, I can't be sure."

"More than once?"

"I think so. Can I go now?" says Stella wearily. "I want to be alone, to lie down."

"Of course. Could you take Mrs. Atkins to her room, Miss Breen? Then I would ask that you return directly to the parlor."

Stella rises, wobbles, accepts Nora's steadying arm.

At the door Stella turns and looks the inspector in the eye. "It was an accident, I'm sure. Teddy would never have left me by choice."

Nora taps on the dining room door. Rideout bids her enter. The inspector stands by the fireplace, smoking. He gestures with his cigarette for her to take a seat.

"The doctor has given Stella something to help her sleep. The residents you've questioned have taken to their rooms, apart from Poppy, who is dozing in the parlor. What now?" Nora asks.

"I'll interview you."

"I suppose we are all of us suspects here—"

"Miss Breen, I've already told you this isn't a murder investigation—"

"I'll take one of those cigarettes."

Rideout offers her his case. Nora makes a big point of selecting one. He offers her a light. She nods her thanks, puffs, considers herself an old hand.

She glances up at Rideout. "Come on, you must have gleaned something from the residents. What's your hunch? Did Teddy die by his own hand, or was there foul play?"

Rideout takes a seat opposite. "Miss Breen, I don't have hunches."

"And the handkerchief—"

"Will you stop going on about that bloody handkerchief!" Rideout rubs his head. "Apologies, it's been a long day."

"Accepted. Perhaps the killer planted it. A clue." Nora frowns. "That makes me very uneasy about Frieda."

Rideout holds up his hands. "Look. Try to avoid jumping to any more conclusions. Or divulging details that could compromise the integrity of the interview."

"Oh." Now it is Nora's turn to redden. "The hankie again, is it?"

"I understand that you are concerned regarding the whereabouts of your friend. If you could just let me do my job—"

"Of course."

Rideout narrows his eyes. "No more interfering."

"None at all." Nora attempts a smoke ring, fails.

Rideout gathers his cigarettes, his notebook—

"Just one question, Rideout."

His expression is pained.

Nora continues. "The person Stella heard ducking into the kitchen. It could have been Teddy, or his killer, or even just Rose returning because she'd forgotten something, like Stella said. Call Rose in. We'll ask her now, rule her out."

"Unless Rose is a distraught widow requesting your support you can't be present at her interview."

"Was Stella distraught? I thought she handled it with remarkable composure. Her husband dead only hours and from unnatural causes. But perhaps she's no stranger to tragedy, she has no family after all."

"This is gossip."

"I never gossip." Nora considers. "Any leads on Karel Ježek yet? I could pop down to the train station, a distinctive young man like that—"

"Miss Breen." Rideout looks exasperated. "Really, must I say this until I'm blue in the face: leave this investigation to me!"

"So," says Nora. "It is an investigation."

CHAPTER 5

Supper is a very late and somber affair for the surviving residents of Gulls Nest. Bill Carter presides at the tureen, his hair immaculately slicked and his black jet cuff links and tiepin befitting the occasion. Professor Poppy is dressed now in his shabby velvet suit and, despite attempts to be chipper, looks frail and haggard. Toby Dog sticks close to his master, his eyes watchful. He has been given special dispensation to stay with his master for this evening's meal, although truth be told, says Poppy, the dog will not leave his side. Stella has also been given special dispensation to take her meal on a tray in her room. When Nora looked in, the food remained untouched and Stella was a small sad huddle in the bed.

Nora says grace. The others bow their heads. The words of the prayer, spoken softly, seem to calm everyone.

Bill removes the lid from the tureen. Irene, it seems, was able to knock up a stew after all. Nora peers over. Beneath a surface slick of grease is a mess of clotted gravy. The smell is at once savory and awful. Bill lifts the ladle.

"There was no time for fish frying apparently. It's scrag-end stew again. Shall we?"

Professor Poppy pushes forward his bowl, Nora does the same. Bill fills his own.

The old man raises his glass, his jowls shaking with emotion, his hand trembling. "To Teddy."

The others join him in a solemn toast.

Then, in a show of trust, they raise their spoons together. The stew is heavily peppered and burnt-tasting, unpleasant but, they hope, not fatal. They reach for water. While they eat in silence Nora considers what might drive a person to poison someone. Such an intimate and vengeful act, serving up death in a domestic setting.

"We all of us have had a traumatic day," says Poppy. "But I found Inspector Rideout thorough and not without tact."

Bill ponders. "It was a trying day whatever way you cut it. For poor Stella and for Mrs. Wells."

Poppy rolls his eyes. "Every day is trying for Mrs. Wells."

Bill frowns.

"The child is no worse for wear, at least," adds Poppy. "I saw her hanging out of her nest in the old oak in the garden earlier."

Nora, who was distracted by supporting Stella, has spared no thought for Dinah. She glances over at the sideboard.

Bill catches her glance. "I shouldn't imagine she'd stow herself in there again. She's likely learnt her lesson. From what I heard she was accidentally trapped in there all morning."

Poppy leans forward. "Now, that's where you could be wrong, Bill. Perhaps Dinah wasn't stuck. Perhaps she *chose* to stay inside."

Bill lays down his napkin. "She was found fast asleep behind locked doors, wasn't she? The latch stuck, how was that a choice?"

Poppy laughs. "Dinah is a miniature Houdini! Give her any lock and she'll pick it. She's likely picked yours a few times. We all know you lock your door, Bill."

Bill frowns down at his plate. "It's habit, nothing more."

"We don't take it as a slight here." Poppy is gentle.

"Well, then she likely sabotaged the lock herself, if she's the escape artist you say she is." Bill speaks with surprising venom. "Wouldn't that be just like the child to draw attention, provoke a scene, cause her mother trouble?"

"Come now, Bill, you get Dinah wrong!"

Bill snorts. His usually calm feathers ruffled. "That child wants a firm hand, she wants civilizing."

Poppy turns to Nora. "Our friend here has certain ideas on the bringing up of children."

"I have ideas about manners." Bill's voice is surly. "That child has no upbringing; she's feral."

"Well don't go telling Mama, you know how she dotes on her cub."

"What is the world coming to, Poppy, if letting a kiddie run wild is considered *doting*?" Bill grumbles.

Poppy sips at his water, his attention turned back to the sideboard. "There are several possibilities; Dinah was trapped inside by accident, or by her own inclination, or she was the victim of a deliberate act and a jammed lock that even a little monkey couldn't pick."

Poppy eyes Bill closely. "I would hazard a guess at the latter."

"Are you saying someone shut her in?"

Poppy looks at his glass. "The lock has never been faulty before."

Bill's face reddens. "Who among us would lock the child in?"

Who among us would poison a man's coffee? Nora thinks.

Bill scrapes back his chair, gets to his feet. "All I'm saying is this is no way to go about things. That child running wild, spying on everyone, the rabbits, the dreary rooms, the dreadful food—I really don't know why I stay." He gives a slight bow, speaking stiffly now. "Good evening to you both."

Bill leaves the room.

"He knows exactly why he stays." Poppy winks at Nora. "Our friend Bill has a liking for the finer things of the world."

"Finer things?"

"A certain widow."

She startles. "Stella?"

Poppy startles too. "Good God, no—Helena Wells. You have to hand it to him, setting his sights so high. Mr. Carter is entirely smitten."

Nora cautions herself against gossip.

There's a glint in the old man's eye. "Go on, ask the question, Miss Breen. You know you want to."

She gives in. "Does Helena Wells return his interest?"

"Somehow, I don't think she is even aware of his interest. Let's just say she lives on a higher plane."

"He doesn't stand a chance?"

"Not if he lets slip his opinions about Dinah! Poor little misunderstood soul."

Nora collects up their dishes and serves them both pudding, stewed fruit of some kind.

They raise their spoons together, wincing against the sharpness.

Poppy laughs. "No one would stay for this food."

"Why do you stay, Poppy?"

Poppy smiles at Nora, a world of sadness in it. "I used to stay because my work was here, now because I have nowhere else to go. It's a terrible thing to be old and alone in the world."

A sigh from the dog under the table.

"Apart from my Toby."

They eat their fruit silently, reflectively. Afterwards Poppy leans back in his chair, wipes his mouth.

"Time will tell, but if we're poisoned, I suspect it will be by Mrs. Rawlings's questionable cooking rather than cyanide."

Nora looks at the old man. "What makes you think it was cyanide?"

"Wasn't it?" Poppy's expression is sober. "I saw Teddy's body too, Miss Breen."

Nora nods. "I know."

The professor nudges her elbow. "They could have been meaning to kill me, you know?"

Nora is taken aback. "What do you mean?"

"It was my coffee in that cup."

"Stella says you take warm milk in the mornings?"

"I do. But sometimes I enjoy an early coffee with young Teddy. Not every morning, the stuff is costly." He leans forward, taps his nose. "But Bill procures a decent roast at a fair price."

"So, your coffee comes from Bill?"

"Always. But what I'm saying is the coffee and the coffeepot are mine, everyone in this house knows that." He frowns. "If Teddy's death was deliberate, perhaps that drink was meant for me."

"Who usually makes the coffee you two share?"

The old man thinks. "Rose, sometimes. Or Teddy did. The thing is, Teddy didn't make it today, else he would have brought me a cup. You see, he never drinks the stuff alone."

"Why not?"

Poppy smiles sadly. "He never really liked it. I could tell. Teddy was far more of a tea drinker. He drank it along with me to be sociable. So, he'd hardly brew it just for himself, would he?" The old man considers. "Would coffee mask the taste of poison? The bitterness?"

"I don't think it would," says Nora. "In all its forms cyanide would be acrid and, I should imagine, taste deeply unpleasant. But if he drank it quickly, or distractedly, perhaps the damage could have been done before he realized?"

"Someone brought him a cup and held his attention while he drank it?"

"Plausibly."

"But who would do such a thing?" He shakes his head. "Though the alternative is just as bleak: that the poor boy felt bad enough to dose himself. Suicide or murder? That is the question, Miss Breen."

"Or an accident?"

"I'm not in the habit of keeping cyanide in my coffee jar."

Nora nods. "That's what I thought."

Poppy's eyes rest on Teddy's empty seat across the table. His expression is pained. A light snore from the terrier asleep under the table brings him back into the room. He busies himself with the folding and rearranging of his napkin.

Nora decides to chance it. "Do you have a handkerchief and is it your own?"

Poppy looks up at her in surprise. "I'm not sure I follow."

"I've heard the laundry provision in the house is a bit hit and miss."

Poppy rummages in his pocket and extracts a blousy spotted affair. "What? Laundry? I have on several occasions inadvertently worn Bill's underpants. Forgive me for the personal nature of that disclosure. It was uncomfortable for both of us."

"Rose gets in a muddle?"

"The dear girl—who wouldn't under the auspices of the dragon Irene."

Nora, heartened by the old man's openness, frames another question. "You told me earlier that the full cast of Punch puppets are displayed on the wall of your workshop?"

"I did."

"Jack Ketch is missing," Nora replies, watching Poppy closely.

He doesn't hide his surprise. "If that is the case, I have no explanation for it. Everyone in this house knows not to touch my puppets."

"Even Dinah?"

"Especially Dinah." The old man turns his gaze upon her. "That has put rather a sinister cast on my question now, Miss Breen."

"How so?"

"Is it conceivable that poor Teddy's death could be an execution made to look like a suicide?"

Nora frowns and finishes his sentence in her own mind: *or a suicide dressed up as an execution?*

Nora sits alone at the dining table. The others have retired but she does not feel inclined to do so yet. The light pools on the tablecloth and the dark corners of the room are as murky as Irene Rawlings's gravy. The house is quiet but not silent. A wind is picking up outside and the branches at the window tap and scrabble a wild message. Nora listens to the weather and to the nighttime sounds of the old house settling. The knocks and burbles of the plumbing. The creaks of floorboards and joists settling. She is relishing time without speech, free of human voices. It is what she is used to, it is what she has always craved. Her life at High Dallow was mostly spent in silence, although she was comforted daily by the presence of the members of her community. Other women going about their business, the patter of sandaled feet and the rustle of skirts. During the recreation time, when talking was permitted, each sister would regain her likes and dislikes, her personality, accent, and individuality. The rest of the time, while they prayed or worked, they would simply merge, one and the same. Life was ordered, prescribed, and predictable.

She pours herself another glass of water and feels still the strangeness of sitting up alone late at night like this. Of deciding what to eat and drink and when to sleep. She thinks of the sisters, each slumbering in a neat and identical cell. Remembering the late-night calm that would blanket the building, moonlight stretching out along the empty corridors. The peace to be found at the end of a day of work and prayer. The security of waking into a familiar routine.

Gulls Nest may be quiet but Nora does not feel at peace here. Who knows what dark thoughts are brewing, what chaos is being hatched? In her old life Nora was a ship anchored firmly to the bedrock. Tumultuous waves might come and go but she knew she had a lifeline. At Gulls Nest she feels like a frantically bobbing cork in an unfriendly ocean.

The grandmother clock in the hallway chimes midnight. It's a sweet sound, a little discordant. Nora stirs herself. She tucks the chairs under the table and piles up the supper things on the sideboard for Irene or Rose to deal with come the morning.

On second thought Nora bends down and peers into the sideboard. It is empty, a cavernous affair; the stale air inside speaks faintly of polish and loudly of kippers. Nora can only hope Dinah has found a more suitable place to lurk now. There are signs of the child's recent occupation along the bottom shelf: a nub of chalk and a furry jam tart, a circle of beach stones and a sticky handprint. Nora inspects the lock; it doesn't appear to be faulty in any way. The key is present in the lock. A simple enough mechanism. The lock looks to have been recently oiled. She turns the key; the action is silent, smooth. If someone wanted to lock Dinah inside, they could easily do so without making her aware.

Nora closes the sideboard and leaves the room, switching off the lights. The landing light is on, a single bulb with a dingy shade. In this gloom Nora takes the stairs to her room. Toby Dog sleeps in a tight furry ball outside the professor's door. He opens one eye at her passing and, sensing no foe, closes it again and snuffles his snout farther under his paw.

Nora casts a quick glance up the unlit staircase to Karel Ježek's attic room. Perhaps the morning will bring his return? Although she suspects that tomorrow may just offer more questions than answers.

CHAPTER 6

Nora roams Gulls Nest looking for something. The house in her dreams is not unlike the real house, only the angles are all wrong and the rugs are treacherous so that her feet sink with every step. She tries door handles. Some spin so wildly that she can't grab them, some are burning hot to the touch and sear her palm. When she can open the doors, different rooms and areas present themselves: the first-floor back and the second-floor front, attic and kitchen, workshop and cellar, gazebo and toolshed and privy. All in the wrong order. Peering inside each room she glimpses scuttling figures—the residents are hiding from her! They slide under beds and scrabble about in the curtains. A yawning wardrobe snaps closed around a little muffled laugh; the furniture is in on their game too! Nora tries another handle. It turns but the door sticks; she tugs and tugs, sweating with effort. Then, with a sudden sickening sucking noise, the door opens. Nora stands on the threshold of the dining room. The table is set for dinner; at the center there is a tureen the size of a small bathtub. Irene Rawlings presides, ladle in hand, held out in front of her like a weapon of war. Helena Wells lies stretched out along the sideboard in her widow's costume. The guests seated around the table turn to look at Nora, unsmiling: Poppy in his velvet suit with Toby Dog at his feet, Stella in her dressing gown with her eyes pink from crying, Bill dapper in cuff links, Karel in his army greatcoat. Dinah hops around the room in a white fur coat. Now and again, she stops and twitches her nose, just like rabbits do. Nora notices the empty seat at the table but knows, with the strange wisdom of a dreaming mind, it is not hers. Irene lifts her ladle and, with the deftness of a magician, whips the lid from the tureen. Nora is propelled forward to look down into a vast lake of gravy. It bubbles and boils, thick and gloopy, muddy and evil. There is movement in the liquid, something surfaces. The severed head of Teddy Atkins bobs into view. Handsome, frowning, flushed bright cherry red. A collective gasp from the assembled guests and Nora looks up. The empty chair has been filled. Frieda Brogan, her head lowered, is saying grace. She raises her face and Nora cries out in horror. In place of shining blue eyes, Frieda has flat beach pebbles. In place of clear skin, her flesh is sickly and green, sloughing from her temples. Frieda smiles, revealing teeth in a state of terrible decay. She opens her folded hands, in her palms a perfect shell. And now the *tick, tick, tick* of the grandmother clock marking time that's always running out, whether in dreams or—

Nora wakes to the *tick, tick, tick* of Father Conway's beak on the glass. She can tell by the sky framed in her windows that she has slept late. The rhythm of her days and nights all out of kilter. She is drenched in sweat but that isn't an unusual occurrence these days; even without the nightmare she would likely have woken in this way. In the weeks leading up to her departure from the order it was as if her body's thermostat had broken. One moment she would be wringing wet with a big red face on her. The next she would be frozen to the bone. There were other issues too: the dry eyes, the aches and pains where there previously were none, the prickly rages that came and went, the lapses in memory. And then her monthly visitor became quarterly and then not at all. As

High Dallow's senior nurse she diagnosed herself, prayed for fortitude, and left off her vest and long drawers.

Nora opens the window and Father Conway skews her with one bright eye.

"Morning, Father," she says. "Will you take some fish?"

He will.

She spoons tinned mackerel onto the windowsill. The gull looks at her with a half tilt of the head.

"It's Bill Carter's finest."

The gull flaps his wings and deigns to eat. Nora watches him and considers her dream. A certain nun pops into her mind, Sister Angela, long gone now. Sister Angela opined the importance of "nightly wisdoms" and would voice her theories at length during recreational hour. Several of the sisters were captivated and dreams were duly reported to Sister Angela, who took pains to interpret them. Nora, then Sister Agnes, was suddenly the focus of attention. Her dreams were found to be complete little detective stories, involving mislaid sandals and stolen statues. The sisters laughed and suggested that Sister Agnes had spent every night of her vocation padding about the corridors in her sleep after some miscreant or other. Sister Agnes's nighttime investigations soon began to inspire the nocturnal adventures of the others. The Pope featured highly, once as a pink-eyed guinea pig, mislaid among wood shavings in a drawer in the Vatican. St. Teresa of Ávila appeared nightly to one nun, searching for lost crockery in the compost heap. Sister Angela prescribed the liberal consumption of mustard and cheese at supper to heighten the intensity of nighttime visions. This went on until Mother Superior got wind of it and strongly advised more suitable discussions during recreation. Sister Agnes and Sister Angela, the apparent ringleaders, were called before her. Sister Angela was admonished for her fanciful nature and Sister Agnes was reprimanded for her interrogatory tendency, which was not the best trait for a cloistered nun.

* * *

Nora is mildly relieved that she has the dining room to herself this morning. It appears no one has taken breakfast, for the porridge pot is untouched and the platter of thinly buttered bread is undisturbed.

She pours stewed tea and helps herself to a bowl of sinister-looking prunes. The milk in the jug smells questionable so she will take her tea black. It's a cheerless repast, as cheerless as the room, unlit and without a fire on a dreary October morning. But the wind has died down and the sky is a lighter shade of gray now.

Nora studies the dark, peaty liquid in her cup and is reminded of Teddy's own fatal drink. A thought suddenly occurs to her: Teddy's coffee was taken black. Nora thanks her mind for this flotsam and feels perhaps it is somehow important. Isn't the solving of crimes all about misplaced objects and timetables? Tiny coincidences or deviations from everyday habits are usually the key to solving big misdemeanors. She braves the last of her tea and resolves to walk down to the station to hear Rideout's findings.

The desk officer is no more mannerly than before, but Nora keeps her shoes on her feet and hasn't long to wait before Inspector Rideout stalks into the office. He manages to look both pristine and exhausted all at once. His face is rumpled but his suit is immaculate. Nora suspects that Rideout's dreams—if he even sleeps—would be quite haunting enough without the liberal consumption of mustard and cheese. Nora reads that in the hollows of his face, the shadows under his eyes and the shadows behind them. He greets Nora with a sharp nod and motions her into the back office.

"You kept your shoes on this time?" His voice is polite, although his smile is wayward.

Nora can't help but feel a tingle. "I'll be brief: what window have you been given for Teddy Atkins's death?"

"Miss Breen, you know I can't divulge that."

"Between eight a.m. and eleven a.m.?"

Rideout doesn't have to answer, his face agrees.

"Narrow it," says Nora. "Let's say Teddy's death occurred when Rose went out to buy the milk. What time did the girl put on that when you interviewed her?"

Rideout looks at her with exasperation.

"Save asking Rose myself," adds Nora.

Rideout relents. "Approximately eight forty-five."

"Teddy took his coffee black, didn't he? I remember from his cup."

"What are you getting at?"

"Would that have been his preference? Teddy hated the stuff; Poppy said he only drank it to keep him company. Taking it without milk would hardly make it more palatable, would it?"

"Possibly not," Rideout concedes. "So, the poison was served when the milk ran out. Presumably during the time Stella heard someone enter and leave the kitchen in Rose's absence."

"There may have been an advantage to the killer serving black coffee," Nora muses. "They could have blamed the bitter taste on the fact that there was no milk."

"I've told you already we are not investigating—"

"Whoever handed Teddy that cup must have had some influence over him. Why else would he have taken a drink he didn't like?" Nora reflects a moment. "He didn't strike me as an overly polite variety of man."

"So, they forced it on him?"

Nora's eyes twinkle. "The murderer, you mean?"

Rideout groans.

"I don't believe he was forced," she says. "Not a drop was spilt from that cup, there was no sign of a scuffle. Teddy willingly drank a cupful of something he didn't even like. Perhaps for someone he did like?"

"Well, he would hardly drink it for an enemy."

"No." Nora muses. "What of Mr. Ježek, have you located him?"

"We haven't been looking for him, as well you know, Miss Breen."

"Don't you think it a little suspicious that he cleared out? Teddy's dead and your man is nowhere to be found. Another mystery needing to be solved, just like the disappearance of my friend Frieda. In case you were forgetting."

Rideout sits back in his seat with a sigh, rifles in his pocket, and brings out his cigarette case. Nora sits back too. Perhaps her opening gambits have worked? A free and frank conversation will ensue. Rideout glances at her, takes out a cigarette, finds matches, lights it, slides case and matches both across the table.

"Help yourself, why don't you? To my smokes and my investigation."

Nora selects a cigarette, applies a match, gives a good puff to get it going, then waves it at the policeman. "Inspector Rideout, I wouldn't have put you down as the selfish sort."

Rideout raises an eyebrow. "Not that I need to divulge this: it is a habit of Mr. Ježek to go away at short notice; his work sometimes necessitates it."

"Who told you that?"

"His employers."

"So, you *have* made inquiries about him?"

"In passing." Rideout takes a drag on his cigarette, exhales, his eye on Nora. "Don't get any ideas. We are treating the unfortunate demise of Mr. Atkins as a suicide."

"That is an error. What about the missing puppet? Jack Ketch—the executioner—surely that's a clear sign?"

"That a poisoner is on the loose at Gulls Nest?"

"Exactly."

"Did you all survive supper? Anyone else croak overnight?"

Nora frowns. "I consider that in bad taste, Rideout."

Rideout taps his cigarette on the ashtray with the finesse of a movie star. "Apologies," he says. "It was."

Nora nods. Tries the same deft tapping technique with her cigarette.

"Miss Breen, I know you are rattled by your young friend going missing and now a sudden alarming death has occurred in your place of residence. Really, it would shake the sturdiest of minds."

"I was a nurse for thirty years. I have met with death, alarming and otherwise."

"Alarming, really?" Rideout raises his eyebrows. "At a convent?"

"At a Carmelite *monastery*, as we call it," Nora clarifies. "The case of Sister Elizabeth of the Holy Trinity for one at first sight seemed quite disturbing."

"Pray, do tell."

The sarcasm in his voice is not lost on Nora but she continues all the same. "Sister Elizabeth, who had always enjoyed very good health, was discovered bolt upright in the bed. Dead entirely. Her face contorted by an expression of such profound horror that the community feared some unholy evil had stalked our peaceful corridors and slithered into her cell to terrify the life out of her."

"But not you, presumably?"

"Many people pull quite remarkable facial expressions as they pass on. That is natural. Of course, a grimace would also be commensurate with seeing the Bad Man Below. If there was something Sister Elizabeth wasn't confessing to us . . ."

"As I said: the sturdiest of minds . . ."

"Detective." Nora is steely. "I will have you know that my mind is unshakable."

Rideout hesitates, then nods. "Which is why I will be open with you. I knew of Mr. Atkins prior to his death, I had seen him around. I served with men just like him. The experiences he had in the war . . ." He falters. "The experiences many of us had are not always surmountable. Some struggle to rehabilitate; returning to civilian life is not always easy."

"I can relate to that."

Rideout looks at her. "Yes, I daresay you can. But some people, some *men*, young or otherwise, find it necessary to take a way out that offers the least pain. It is hard for someone like you, with your background, to condone—"

Nora speaks calmly. "Please don't presume what I would or would not condone."

They sit smoking in silence. When Rideout speaks again his voice is weary. "Sometimes in life there is no mystery, Miss Breen. Your young friend merely forgot to write. Teddy Atkins merely wanted peace."

"That's as may be. But you must ask: Were their actions *in character*? Frieda always kept a promise. Teddy's wife believes her husband would never leave her."

"With all due respect, we are not always the best judges of our loved ones." Rideout stubs out his cigarette with a rapid twist. "As far as Teddy Atkins goes, I will keep an ear to the ground but unless further information is unearthed the case is closed. Suicide, plain and simple. The coroner will agree."

He gets up to leave. Nora remains seated.

"There's another aspect of Teddy Atkins's so-called suicide that bothers me," she continues calmly. "The method. Young men are far more likely to shoot themselves, hang themselves, or jump off a cliff. Cyanide doesn't seem like an obvious choice."

Rideout wavers, sighs, regains his seat. "Perhaps it was expedient? What he had on hand at that moment?"

"But aren't most suicides planned? Teddy would have had to go to the effort to seek out the cyanide in some form or other."

Rideout nods. "He would. We are checking local suppliers, registers, as a matter of course. Anything else?"

"What about a suicide note? Wouldn't he have left one?"

"Perhaps Teddy wasn't in a corresponding frame of mind."

"Don't be facetious, Inspector. Teddy had promised his wife never to leave her; you'd think he would offer something more by way of explanation, at least say goodbye?"

Rideout frowns. "That's where you might be wrong, Miss Breen. Men, especially young men, often find that kind of communication hard, you know. It is damnably difficult to talk about one's emotions."

Nora concedes. "Yes, I've noticed. And not just for men."

"Well, then." Rideout rises. "I have work to do, Miss Breen—if you've any further spanners to throw into the works?"

"At this moment, no."

Nora steps into a cheap café and orders a pot of tea. When it arrives it is what she hoped for: decent and strong with a skin a mouse could skate on. The windows are running with condensation, but the tables are clean and the décor nicely austere. The place is packed, even at this time of day, too late for breakfast, too early for lunch. The clientele seems to be a mix of workingmen and off-duty charladies, judging by the paint-spattered overalls and the blousy hats. Nora is the only one sitting alone but finds this preferable when she has a plan to make and thoughts to think. Without the wimple and veil, she still feels a little naked and not entirely immune to the glances she knows herself to be receiving. She puts these down to the puce coat and her habit of going hatless. Picking up a discarded newspaper on the table, she makes a big act of unfolding it. She lights on the racing news and reads it avidly. Soon enough, interest wanes in the puce-coated newcomer and Nora feels herself settling. Her mind unwinds with every sip she takes. She thanks God (in a manner of speaking) for the restorative powers of tea. Feeling peckish, she considers ordering a sandwich or a bun but a quick check in her purse tells her what she already knows: frugality would be a good idea. She has been given a small stipend by the order, to tide her over while she finds a way to support herself. Her advance rent has taken a fair proportion of her available funds. She must budget sensibly, just the necessaries: a few bites of food and the odd morsel for Father Conway. She distracts herself from her rumbling stomach by considering the people around her. Gassing, gossiping, gesticulating, their facial expressions exaggerated to Nora's eyes after the restrained communication at High Dallow. A young girl muffled in a scarf comes in. She goes up to the counter and makes some request of the waitress there. The waitress listens and replies, pointing up to the clock on the wall above the counter. The girl nods and turns to leave. Nora, recognizing the socks inside the beach shoes, stands up and gestures for the girl to join her.

Rose cradles her teacup in her hands, her fingers pink with cold and hard work. "And you won't tell Mrs. Rawlings?"

"Why would I? It's up to you where you choose to work, isn't it? This café has a bit of life to it." Nora wonders about whether there was truth in what Stella said about the girl. If so, Rose would struggle to slack off here. "Bit busier than Gulls Nest though?"

Rose nods. "But the pay is better."

"Well good luck to you. I've to start looking myself for gainful employment."

Rose's eyes widen so that Nora feels amused; surely the girl hadn't taken her for a fine lady with independent money?

"It's harder to find a place out of season," the girl remarks.

"I expect it is."

"Depending on your line."

"Fortune-teller."

Rose smiles. "Give over, Miss Breen."

Nora smiles too.

They sip their tea.

"Why do you want to leave your job at Gulls Nest?"

Rose throws her an incredulous look.

"The death of Mr. Atkins aside, Rose."

Rose sniffs, unfurls her scarf, becomes a little formal. "The position isn't without its annoyances."

"Mrs. Rawlings?"

"Oh, she's all right really, if you do things her way. Bark is worse than her bite."

"Her bark sounds bad enough."

Rose shrugs. "Mrs. Rawlings isn't the worst thing about Gulls Nest."

"What is?"

"That weird bloody kid. She gives me the jitters."

Nora feels a pang of sympathy for Dinah.

"Always up to mischief," Rose says. "Spying and skulking. Stealing anything that isn't nailed down, especially the guests' trinkets. If I nip out of the room for half a minute, I'll return to handprints in the butter and bite marks in the loaf. She even pelted me with rotten apples once."

"Dinah did?"

Rose nods. "Mrs. Wells will do nothing to check her. And despite her threats, Mrs. Rawlings won't either. I think they're scared of her. Imagine, a little kid!"

"You organize the laundry at Gulls Nest too?"

"Sometimes. Only, if you've something missing best take it up with Mrs. Rawlings—"

"No, Rose. What I meant is, it must be quite a job, tricky to keep it all separate?"

"That's just it, you can't with a bagwash. It all gets lumped in together. Then, when it comes back, I have a hard time sorting out their socks and shirts and bleeding petticoats!"

"Course you do, Rose. So, it's not impossible a guest might find themselves with someone else's handkerchief."

"There's another reason for that." Rose gives a cheeky grin. "Maybe, if they are sweet on them? Are we talking about Bill and Mrs. Wells here?"

Nora frowns. No. She wasn't. Not at all. Now she considers what Rose has implied. Was Frieda's handkerchief a keepsake for Teddy? As soon as she thinks it Nora dismisses it.

Why? Wasn't Teddy a married man?

Nora gives another moment's thought to this, wondering if her gut has anything to add. Finding it doesn't, she glances up to see Rose watching her, amused.

"Would you say the Atkinses were close at all to Frieda Brogan?"

Rose looks surprised. "No more than anyone else. Miss Brogan was cheerful to everyone but I wouldn't say they were close friends. I mean, I saw her walk out with Mrs. Atkins once or twice."

"Not Mr. Atkins?"

Rose regards her strangely. "No, of course not. Miss Breen, are you saying there was something *untoward*—"

"I wasn't."

Rose seems disappointed. "Well, if there had been, I for one would have known."

"Would you?"

"I have eyes, Miss Breen."

"And you read a lot of romance novels?"

The girl blushes a little.

It is as Nora thought: Frieda was friendly to the other residents but for all that kept herself to herself.

"Did any of the guests ever give you any trouble?"

"Oh, they're all right. The professor is a dear. Mr. Carter is always good for a tip. Mrs. Atkins is a total doll." She frowns.

"What is it, Rose?"

"I didn't like Mr. Atkins at all. Is it wrong to say that, with him being dead?"

"No, I don't think so, you don't have to like the dead."

"He was a sulky sod." Rose bites her lip. "I'm sorry, Miss Breen, my mouth—"

"Not at all. In what way was Mr. Atkins sulky?"

"He was always moping about the workshop, snapping at his wife if she went down the garden to him."

Nora thinks a moment. "You would make his morning coffee?"

Rose shakes her head. "Never, at least, not for *him*. I made it on the professor's asking only."

"Did Mr. Atkins ever make their coffee?"

"Not that I know of." Rose is watching her closely. "He was poisoned, wasn't he?"

Nora hesitates.

"To be honest, I'm not surprised." Rose looks at Nora out of the side of her eye. "With that temper he'd hardly win friends."

"There's one guest you haven't mentioned, Rose."

"You?"

Nora smiles. "Not me. Mr. Ježek."

"The photographer? I wouldn't know what he's like. He keeps himself to himself. I see him up and down the promenade, that big coat on him, even in the summer, like he is trying to hide in plain sight."

Nora pours them both another cup. Rose nods her thanks.

Nora speaks in an easy tone. "Did you notice anything unusual yesterday morning?"

Rose stops sipping and looks at Nora with a shrewd eye. "I've been through all that with the inspector. What, are you the police now?"

"Not at all." Nora smiles reassuringly. "Would you like a bun?"

Rose would. Nora gestures to the waitress, then continues. "There are just a few things that puzzle me, Rose. About yesterday morning."

Rose shivers, a pinkness to her cheeks, the morbid excitement of recent events returning. "You think someone did him in, don't you, Miss Breen?"

"Don't be macabre, Rose."

Rose hides a grin.

They sip their tea as the waitress brings the bun.

When the waitress walks away, Rose resumes. "Thing is, I do too, Miss Breen."

"What makes you say that?"

"There are easier ways to top yourself, aren't there?"

Nora waits while Rose finishes her bun. She dabs her mouth in a ladylike way, then guzzles the last of her tea.

"Smashing. So, yesterday morning: Mrs. Rawlings had already left the house when I arrived, she always goes out early on her day off. I just got on with it; I know the setup backwards."

"What is the setup?"

"Butter the bread, put out the meat, start the porridge, and set the kettle on the stove. Then I've to keep an ear out for the guests finishing and clear up after them. Then I might have a bit of dusting or a few items of hand washing." She thinks. "It started off a better morning than most."

"Why is that?"

"Dinah was nowhere to be seen. But then the trouble started when the milk ran out."

"When did you realize the milk had run out?"

"Mrs. Atkins was fretting over milk for the professor. There was hardly any in the kitchen jug, but when I went out to the windowsill there was carnage."

"I don't understand, Rose."

"In the cooler months Mrs. Rawlings keeps the bottles outside rather than in the pantry cold store. The milkman sets stones over the tops and we bring it in as we need it."

"Understood. Why carnage?"

"The birds like to get at the cream, you see; they'll peck through the bottle tops given half a chance." Rose lowers her voice. "That morning the birds looked to have had a right squabble over it, bottles pecked and upset."

"And you reckon that was the birds?"

"Well, some kind of pest. Mrs. Atkins took what she had to the professor. But figuring the old man might want more, I bobbed upstairs and offered to go and fetch another bottle."

"So, you went out for milk, at what time, Rose?"

"Quarter to nine, or thereabouts. I was hoping to catch Jimmy Durling to save a walk to the dairy."

"Jimmy Durling?"

"The milkman."

"Did you catch him?"

"I did. He was late on his rounds, as I'd hoped. He's one for chatting up the ladies. He's known to haunt a few doorsteps." Rose gives Nora a mischievous glance. "He's my alibi, if you want to interrogate him too?"

"You're not my prime suspect, Rose."

Rose grins.

"Did you forget anything and have to pop back into the house for any reason?"

Rose shakes her head. "No, I went straight out. As soon as I came back, I called up to Mrs. Atkins and she came down but by then she had to leave for work."

"Did you see anything out of place on your return?"

"I did. The coffeepot was left out and the kettle had been left off the stove."

"So, someone had entered the kitchen and used the coffeepot while you were out getting the milk?"

"Exactly."

"Any idea who?"

"If you are asking me who the poisoner is, Miss Breen, I've no idea." The girl pauses. "But I won't eat as much as a crumb in that house from now on."

"What about the rest of the morning? Did you notice anything strange or different? Think carefully, Rose."

"Nothing. Until the professor went out to the workshop and then came stumbling straight back again like he'd seen a ghost. Then I sent the boy down for you."

"Why did you send for me?"

"The professor said that you were a nurse and to call you if you were in the house. But I spotted you walking back up when I was calling the gardener's boy to run the message."

Nora considers this a moment. It makes sense. That Poppy would have seen Teddy was dead is certain from their earlier conversation. But then the old man had just had a terrible shock; sometimes people don't think rationally in such situations. Perhaps he initially thought Teddy could be revived?

Rose, having long finished her tea and bun, begins to look around herself. She wants to get going now. Nora considers carefully her last questions.

"Apart from the coffeepot and the kettle, did you see anything else that had been moved or left out of place on your return? Think hard: footprints, handprints, a smell?"

Rose shakes her head. "Not a thing."

"But if you remember?"

"You'll be the first to know, Miss Breen."

"Good girl yourself."

Rose swaddles herself in her scarf. "Thank you for the bun."

"Anytime."

She buttons her coat. "You are better at asking questions than the inspector. I suspect you are just a lot more interested in other people's business." She blushes. "I didn't mean—"

"No offense taken, Rose. I think you may be right."

With time to kill before returning to Gulls Nest, Nora explores the town. By force of habit, she looks out for Frieda wherever she goes. Sometimes she is sure she catches a glimpse of her—there in a stranger's smile, or the tilt of a head, a young woman's walk, or the sunlight on soft brown hair. Nora wanders up and down the lanes wondering which shops her friend would have visited. Then she remembers how Frieda always said she preferred window shopping. All the fun, none of the expense. Nora tries it out, reminding herself that given her limited means it would be better to be frugal.

Then she realizes that the purchases she needs to make all have a purpose. They are not just the whims of a wastrel. Having charge of money again is strange, as is seeing the prices on display, some of which seem eye-wateringly high. Nora reminds herself that it is three decades since she last went shopping. She stops at a dry grocers and marvels at the goods, despite the country being in the tail end of rationing. Throughout the war years food was relatively plentiful at High Dallow. The sisters grew much of their own produce and ate plainly. Although the staples were frequently missing, they never starved. Now Nora delights at shelves of tinned goods and baskets of fancy chocolates, bottles of Camp Coffee and jars of cough candies. The products are ranged nicely on polished wooden shelves or displayed in glass cabinets. As each customer reels off the choices from their list, the goods are deftly brought together and wrapped up by a grocer in a white coat. Nora soon spots exactly what she wants. She waits with the other customers, who form orderly lines, baskets looped over their wrists, some with coats bobbed on over their aprons, some in smarter attire. When it is Nora's turn, she points to a little box on the counter. The grocer selects a handful of sugar mice, pink and white, pear-shaped with tiny cotton tails, and twists them into a bag.

"Granny is spoiling someone today," he says.

Nora is startled. Yes, she would likely be a grandmother now. She is of that age. She imagines the years that have fallen away from her. She feels dizzy at the thought of all that life gone. She sees glimpses of it as it hurtles away—like a rug pulled out from under her, sending her crashing. Wool socks in leather sandals, early rising, mopping miles of corridors, the smell of starched linen, endless hours on her knees, plain food, silence, and a great big void where love ought to have been—

"Are you all right, dear?" The grocer peers at her doubtfully.

"They are for a little girl," says Nora. "But not my own."

The plump housewife with the shopper standing next to her throws Nora a sympathetic look. Nora sees herself through the other woman's eyes: hatless, borrowed clothes, a shabby old spinster, never married.

"Righto," says the grocer. "Will there be anything else?"

Nora notices that her hands are shaking as she counts the money.

Outside the shop she takes a few deep breaths and feels better. She is back on track. With this pocketful of sugar mice, she can cajole Dinah into communicating, when the opportunity presents itself.

Nora decides that her next two purchases will be something of an investment. First, she calls at the tobacconists and emerges an hour later with smoking apparel suited to the amateur sleuth: a dashing cigarette holder and smart case. Afterwards a visit to the stationers sees Nora spending an inordinate amount on a nicely bound notebook and fountain pen. The ink she selects is raven-black, as befitting her line of interest: the solving of dark mysteries. One final stop at the fishmongers for scraps for Father Conway and her errands are complete. She walks back to Gulls Nest, the wind tucking in behind her, for all the world as if they are of the same mind: that there's work to be done and deductions to be made.

CHAPTER 7

Nora considers the first two words written in raven-black ink on the first page of her new notebook: *Murder Weapon*. She glances over at Father Conway, who is wiping his beak against the window frame, having just downed a pound of fish heads.

"I'm setting out my stall here, Conway."

The gull doesn't comment.

Nora underlines the words and adds three more. *Cyanide, possible sources?* She frowns and looks out of the window. It is not yet three o'clock and shadows are already drawing in down in the garden below. The wind is cold but not squally. A few clumps of bunnies continue to graze the lawn; despite their soft appearance they must be hardy.

Nora Breen has an idea.

She negotiates the passage between the kitchen and the pantry as quietly as she can. There is nothing that can be done about the sticking door. She gives a well-aimed kick to the base of it and a sharp push to the handle and she's out. She takes her time to poke about the corners of the garden. The privy she knows well enough: a place of dampness and spiders, squares of newspaper cut neatly and sewn onto loops within grabbing distance. A high flush and a comfortable, if chilly, seat. A rusting lock and a high-set window provide some security and light. There is nothing stored here so Nora moves on to the moldering gazebo. Perhaps it was a lovely place to take a tea once, but now it is packed with a jumble of the same washed-up ilk that furnishes the rooms of the lodgers: spindly occasional tables, old iron bedframes, fraying armchairs, and tatty screens. These are joined by a profusion of copper coal scuttles. Peering inside, Nora notices that a nest has been made; judging by the dog-eared paperbacks and cigarette ends that litter the floor, this is Rose's bolt-hole. Nora moves on. The toolshed offers a muddle of seed packets and some earthy roots. A few saws with broken teeth are hung on the wall and a clatter of garden rakes and hoes are propped in the corner. Nora closes the door and keeps on up the path. Tucked away behind a bank of dank bushes is a wooden hut. Unlike the other outbuildings, efforts have been made to secure this one's door and a path has been trampled recently through the weeds.

"Bingo," says Nora.

She inspects the door; it is well secured with two padlocks. Around the side of the hut is a window that has been boarded up, willowy saplings providing a further barrier. Nora fancies she spies a crack between the boards. She rounds the hut, thorns snagging, nettles stinging. It is the work of moments to slide the boards open, for the screws at the bottom are missing. Nora, a monkey in her youth and sprightly yet, swings herself up and into the open window.

In the dim of the hut, she looks around. Tins and bottles are ranged on makeshift shelves. There are old jars of paintbrushes and bottles of turpentine. On the top shelf she finds what she is looking for: a row of small red and white tins with the name Cymag printed on them. Next to the tins, a pump.

Nora takes up a tin noting that the preparation is suitable for the extermination of rabbits, rats, and other rodents. Alongside a neat little skull and crossbones, there's a list of ingredients, amongst them: sodium cyanide.

So engrossed is Nora in her thoughts that she doesn't hear the stealthy opening of the door behind her.

"I should put that down if I were you, Miss Breen."

The shadow of a stout, wide woman fills the doorway.

Nora, her heart beating, places the tin back on the shelf.

"You might just have asked," Irene says. "Rather than shimmying through the bleeding window."

Nora realizes all at once how inappropriate her behavior is. She feels a familiar prickly heat rising, followed by a sudden drench of perspiration.

"I have a tea for that," says Irene.

They sit together in the kitchen. Irene Rawlings's expression has turned from sourly begrudging to amused as she watches her errant guest closely.

Nora warily eyes the steaming pot. Her flush has passed, leaving her cold and shivery, and she has no desire to drink the concoction the housekeeper has brewed, which smells as enticing as ditch water.

Irene sets out cups and saucers and with the aid of a strainer pours two drinks. Wordlessly she pushes one to Nora and takes up her own.

Nora sips and finds that the taste is no better than the smell. She is careful to breathe through her nose, and in this way manages to drink more than half.

"I use it for the rabbits," says Irene. "The poison. In case you haven't noticed we are overrun."

"I thought they were pets."

Irene snorts. "No pets of mine." She leans forward; lifting the pot she tops up Nora's cup with a wry smile. "The vicar next door breeds them."

"The vicar?"

"Reverend Audley, he's inventing a new hardy variety. I've tried putting them in the pot but there's no real eating on them. It's better just to gas the bleeders."

Nora puts down her cup, feeling slightly queasy. "Are you the only person with access to the store?"

Irene smooths an imaginary wrinkle in the tablecloth. "I told all this to the inspector. I thought you of all people would know that?"

"Why should I know?"

"Aren't you in league with him?"

"What makes you think that?" Nora's reply is sharper than she intends.

Irene's face shows momentary satisfaction. "Poring over that poor lad's body, up and down to the police station, having confabs."

She's been following me, thinks Nora. In future she'll bear in mind that Irene is not the stodgy pudding she looks.

Irene takes a sip of her tea and seems to relish it. "No one goes into that store but me. I keep it locked."

"And the key?"

"About my person. Couldn't be more secure, before you broke in."

"For that I apologize. But I wasn't the first; several screws on the boards are missing, were you aware of that?"

Irene hesitates. "I was not."

"Are all the tins of pesticide accounted for?"

"Of course."

"Would anyone else have had access to the store over the past few days?"

"No one is allowed there but me." Irene lowers her voice. "No one else knows what's in there."

"Not even Mrs. Wells?"

Irene looks momentarily puzzled.

"So, your employer hasn't asked you to exterminate the vicar's rabbits?"

Irene's eyes narrow at the question. "I have taken that duty upon myself."

"Interesting. Would she approve, do you think? It isn't very neighborly, is it?"

Irene's meaty face reddens. "She doesn't like to be bothered by details; I oversee the running of the house."

"Of *her* house?"

Irene, provoked, glowers.

Nora nods. "There's a question I would like to ask you, if I may?"

Irene gives the merest of nods.

"Where did you go to on your day off yesterday, Mrs. Rawlings?"

Nora can tell from Irene's face that this is precisely the wrong question. When the housekeeper finally speaks the words are no more than a hiss. "That, Miss Breen, is none of your bleeding business."

In the safety of her room, before windows full of sky and sea, Nora records the finer points of today's investigation in raven-black ink in her nicely bound notebook. *Upset milk, flighty milkman, bunnies, poison, missing screws, evasive housekeeper.* She is unsettled, and not just by the ditchwater tea. That Teddy Atkins was poisoned—either by his own or by another's hand, during the time it took Rose to procure more milk—is clear. The sodium cyanide in the form of pesticide could be obtained at any time; a small amount would have sufficed, an entire tin would not have been needed. Teddy himself or Teddy's killer could easily have unscrewed the panel and gained access to the contents of the hut. Irene Rawlings's sinister store is the most obvious source of Teddy's poisoning.

Nora looks out at the priceless view. There's a break in the cloud and enough blue to clothe any number of sailors. But the sand furrowed by the waves looks hard and cold. The few figures on the beach do not linger long; soon enough they retreat from view down the promenade or between the boarded-up kiosks. Today there are no lurking photographers or blown-away hats to be stamped on.

Nora returns her thought to the matter in hand. A question floats up through the flotsam. Where else would potentially dangerous chemicals be stored in a house like this? She has an answer hooked and landed before the beach is empty.

Climbing the stairs to the attic, Nora disregards Irene's reproof. The movements of the residents are entirely her business, as is Frieda's disappearance—and by extension, Teddy's murder. Especially as the dead man had Frieda's handkerchief bunched in his pocket.

Nora scoffs. Irene would no doubt have her leave it all to Detective Inspector Rideout—something she is not about to do while she has eyes and a fecking brain in her head.

Even so, she hesitates outside the door.

She reminds herself that Stella wouldn't suspect the man without some cause and this suspicion alone should necessitate further investigation. Although snooping about in a man's private room perhaps oversteps the line of reasonable inquiry, that can't be helped. Nora will tread lightly and disturb nothing, and no one—apart from herself—will be any the wiser.

Karel Ježek's attic room is exactly as he left it. The remaining photographs pinned on the wall are no less intriguing than before. Nora's eye is caught again by the vivid blue images. A quick search of the shelves and Nora finds exactly what she needs: a well-thumbed darkroom manual. She takes it over to the chair that latterly housed Karel's folded clothes. She turns the pages and grapples with chemical measurements and mixtures, detailed processes and desirable outcomes. In the margins are meticulous notes made in pencil, not in Karel's original tongue, as Nora half expected, but in English. She flips back to find the initials *J. M.* written on the cover page in the same hand. It's possible that the book and the notes are secondhand.

Nora reads with interest the section on cyanotypes. The reader's attention is directed to the color plates, where she recognizes a faded version of the beautiful blue examples on the wall before her. Her eye is drawn to a paragraph where two words are underlined: *potassium ferricyanide*. It is highlighted lightly and with precision and not with the rabid underscoring of a madman. What is of even greater interest is a slip of notepaper sandwiched between the next two pages. Written in the way of a shopping list in the penciled hand that features throughout, it refers to the process of making potassium cyanide from ferricyanide. A complicated process, Nora judges, hardly involving the conditions found in an average cup of coffee.

Nora carries the book to the makeshift darkroom cubicle and switches on the red light. She squints at packages and bottles in the dim. The ransacked shelves in an otherwise immaculate space must be taken to be suspicious. Teddy, or his killer, must have been in a hurry. In the darkroom, Nora finds none of the equipment, or chemicals, listed in the book. This proves nothing. They still could have been stored here prior to being taken and then disposed of by the killer after the poisoning.

Exiting from the darkroom, Nora's eye alights on something. A wrinkle at the corner of the rug to the side of the bed. Nothing of note, except, perhaps, in a meticulously tidy room like this one. Nora rolls the rug back to see that one of the floorboards is slightly proud. A light press is rewarded by the squeak of a loose floorboard.

Nora hesitates. But then she tells herself that now is perhaps not the time to question the propriety of nosing about, trespassing in fact, in another guest's room. Casting round, she finds a paper knife and carefully levers up the board. With disappointment she finds nothing but an empty cavity and a dusty floor joist. She returns the floorboard to its previous position and puts the rug back where she found it, complete with wrinkle. The manual too she returns to the shelf.

If Mr. Ježek does return, he will be none the wiser.

Nora, congratulating herself for her stealth, looks up to see Dinah watching her.

Dinah holds up a finger and slowly shakes her head.

Dinah follows Nora down the attic stairs. She is dressed in her usual incongruous style, a tattered dressing-up gown, only today she has added a pair of ears made from ratty fur and wire. It takes Nora a few moments to realize Dinah is dressed as a bunny with ears and a corresponding bedraggled powder-puff tail.

Nora leaves the door open on entering her room. Dinah hesitates to cross the threshold but then she clears it with a hop. She makes a big show of touching the objects, as if she's never seen them before. She wows at the wardrobe, tentatively turns the cheval mirror, appears alarmed at the heron screen.

Nora takes from a drawer the paper bag of sugar mice she selected at the grocer's shop. Dinah's attention is caught. Nora holds the bag out, Dinah's eyes light up. She bounds forward, snatches the bag, and takes it off into the corner of the room, where she sits down cross-legged on the floor. Nora watches as Dinah takes out the sugar mice and arranges them in a neat line on the floor, nose to tail. Then the little girl smooths and folds the paper bag very nicely and tucks it away in her grubby beaded purse. Turning back to the sugar mice, Dinah eats them quickly, jealously, one after the other. As if Nora might at any moment ask for them back.

The mice gone, Dinah casts her eyes around the room.

Noticing Nora's notebook and pen on the table, she clambers up on the chair and grabs them.

"Dinah!"

But Dinah has the notebook open and is making a mime of reading Nora's words, turning her head from side to side then glancing up with a sly smile.

Nora tries to settle her indignation; the child is only playing—she is harmless enough.

Dinah pulls the lid off the pen with her teeth and turns over to a blank page. She sets about writing slowly, swinging her legs as she scrawls. Nora sees that like Dinah's face, her feet are very grubby.

Nora hesitates to admonish her now that the damage is already done. Besides, she feels a pang of pity for this silent little girl. Regretting the ruin of her beautiful book, Nora bites back her words and sits down on the edge of the bed. She looks out at the sky, darkening now. Soon enough it will be time for the ordeal of another meal; she wonders if she will ever look at a tureen again without a sense of dread.

Dinah hops down from the chair and pushes the book under Nora's nose.

Nora is astonished to read a question in near-perfect copperplate.

WHAT YOU LOOKING FOR?

She looks up at Dinah in surprise.

"None of your beeswax," says Nora. "Who taught you to write so beautifully?"

Dinah looks shyly pleased. She hops off with the book and pens another line. She returns to Nora.

PROFESOR POPPY.

Nora nods, somehow reassured that her spelling is not as excellent as her handwriting.

"He's your great friend?"

Dinah nods. This time she brings over the pen and sits next to Nora on the bed to write her communication.

YOUR NOT ALOWED IN BORDERS ROOM.

"Neither are you."

The girl grins, shrugs.

"Would you like to feed Father Conway? It's almost his suppertime."

Dinah looks puzzled until Nora goes to the window and opens it wide. In a flurry of breeze and feathers the fat gull lands. Dinah laughs soundlessly in delight.

She bravely holds out sprats to the gull, who edges along the windowsill to snatch them. Nora looks on smiling. Dinah insists on feeding the bird two days' rations. When all the fish are gone and Father Conway is more interested in preening, Dinah wipes her hands on the curtains and hops back across the room. She takes up the pen again.

TEDDY IS DEAD.

"He is." Nora looks at Dinah closely. "It was a shock, wasn't it?"

Dinah shrugs, her face strangely blank. She writes again.

THE OFICERS WAS HERE.

"They were. Did the inspector talk to you about what happened to Teddy?"

NO. HE TALKED ABOUT RABBITS.

"Did he? That's a surprise."

HE DOES NOT LIKE CHILDREN.

"You think?"

TEDDY WAS SAME.

Nora looks at her. "So, Teddy wasn't a friend?"

HE DID NOT LIKE CHILDREN. STELLA DOES BECOSE SHE
GIVES PRESANTS.

"Does she?"

Dinah nods, unknots her little bag from her waist, the sort olden-
days ladies would carry to the opera, only the satin is filthy and the
beading unraveling. She spills the contents onto the counterpane. There
are ribbons and tiny pearl buttons, tarnished coins and a fluffy boiled
sweet. The usual treasures of a young child. Dinah pulls an earring from
the muddle—paste stones arranged like petals. She holds it out in the
palm of her hand.

"From Stella?"

Dinah fishes out a clothes-peg lady, complete with a painted face
and a dress.

"She gave you this too?"

Dinah nods.

"You have many lovely things in your collection."

She beams.

Nora's eye is caught by a glint of silver; looking more closely she
sees a small plain crucifix tangled in the muddle. Her heart lurches, she
points to it. "Where did you get this?"

Dinah begins to gather her things together, pushing them quickly
back into her bag.

"Did you take it?"

She shakes her head.

Nora's voice is sharp. "Dinah?"

She takes up the pen and scrawls across a whole page: *FOUND*. She throws down the pen and without a backwards look, stalks from the room.

Nora turns over the page of her notebook. Dinah's scrawl bleeds through. There are no words to add right now. She rises and pulls down her suitcase from the wardrobe. Wrapped in tissue paper in the pocket inside the lid is her own crucifix and chain, the one gifted to her when she was a novice. Not unlike the one Frieda was wearing, the day she left the order—now jumbled among Dinah's treasures. Dinah might have found it, but would Frieda have been careless enough to lose it? Is it so impossible that Frieda gave it away? She had given away the life she had vowed to live, hadn't she? But then, Nora knows she cannot judge the complexities of her friend's relationship with the Big Man Above. Oddly, they rarely discussed their faith all the nights that Nora had sat up with Frieda in the infirmary. Nora remembers them now: Frieda's eyes wet with tears, the terrible gasping for breath. Sometimes Nora would wrap the young nun in blankets and wheel her out into the court-yard, not too far, a sheltered spot where the breeze was gentle. Some-times Nora caught herself holding her own breath. She would listen out for Frieda's wheezing as she tended her other patients: Sister Augusta, who had been dying for two decades, and Sister Clement, a grateful old soul who was run ragged by arthritis. Frieda, in the grip of her symp-toms, was terrified, although this went unsaid. Not much else did. To try and distract her, Nora would tell Frieda anecdotes about her past life and particularly, her girlhood. The life she had before her granny's wake. Small, harmless, humorous stories, quietly delivered; they were a silent order after all. When Frieda had the breath for words she would reply with her own tales of life in the orphanage. They were a generation apart and very different in temperament; Frieda was easygoing, Nora was often contradictory. But they laughed at the same things and were both drawn to the absurd. And so, the dark and difficult nights passed and the two became friends. It did not go unnoticed by Mother Superior, but knowing well her respective nuns she was perhaps wise enough to realize that they were good for one another even while she cautioned against such attachments.

Nora's first thought on hearing about Frieda's departure was panic. Should the young woman take ill, who would be there to care for her? Nora would try to reassure herself, as she tries to reassure herself now. Wasn't there a toughness, a perseverance to gentle Frieda that comes of long suffering? Frieda had been reared an orphan, she was alone in the world, yet she had a tenacity, a drive, and a will that propelled her out of the monastery gates. And into God only knows what.

CHAPTER 8

Nora finds herself alone for supper, facing down the tureen in a room that is especially gloomy at the dying of the day. The wallpaper is shabby, the cruets are sticky, the cutlery needs a good polish, there are ancient stains on the damask tablecloth. Nora thinks back to the scrubbed wooden tables in the refectory at High Dallow. The starched napkins and simple homely bowls and plates, one set for each sister. She takes a moment to acknowledge how strange it is to eat alone in this stale room. Having spent the last three decades eating in silence she is surprised how quickly she has become accustomed to chatter at the dining table.

Irene Rawlings clatters in with a tray of peripherals. Nora doesn't need to look in the serving bowl to know that cabbage is on the menu again. The housekeeper throws Nora a cold glance and stomps out again. It's the work of moments to gather a few small portions onto the tray, although Nora doubts it would tempt a grieving widow into eating. She herself can't stomach it tonight.

She climbs the stairs with the tray and knocks gently at the door of the second-floor front.

There's a Stella-size shape in silhouette against the window. There is light yet in the sky, but it is dim in the room she has lately shared with Teddy. Nora sets the tray down on the chest of drawers and goes to turn on the light.

"Leave it," Stella says. "I prefer the dark. Will you come and sit with me?"

Nora takes the other chair by the window. It's the same view as hers, the expanse of beach and the promenade.

"Me and Teddy would sit here for hours. He loved the sea."

Nora waits. Somewhere in the room a clock ticks. The sea can be heard through the closed window. The house is silent but for the usual shifting and creaking. The room is very cold but a little musty, like a sickroom. Stella hasn't left it since yesterday afternoon. Nora fights the urge to throw the window open. Instead, she watches as lights come on at the far end of the promenade, the twinkling town. To the right the dark bulk of the headland. Nora fancies there's a gaiety, an abandon, to the illuminations after all the years of wartime blackout. But really, what is she to know about that? High Dallow was remote and had no near neighbors other than the grouse on the moors and the odd stray sheep.

Dark falls, Nora waits. Until lately she has been very good at waiting: for the quiet voice inside, for the prayers that punctuated the course of the day, for the letter that never arrived. Not now. Now she feels a growing impatience.

"Is there anything you need, Stella?"

Stella becomes very still. "I need to find out what happened to Teddy."

Nora chooses her words carefully. "The coroner will prepare a report—"

"The coroner recorded death by misadventure. Inspector Rideout came by this afternoon to tell me."

Nora muses, an outcome that was perhaps to be expected.

"So that's it—case dismissed." Stella's voice is bitter. "They believe my husband murdered himself."

"Do you?"

"No. I don't." Stella meets Nora's eyes. "My husband had no reason to."

Nora frowns. She wonders if the young widow is simply feeling disbelief, grief, guilt—all common in those whose loved ones die by their own hand. Rideout certainly seemed predisposed to consider Teddy's death a suicide. Had Nora been through the horrors of active service perhaps she would think differently, perhaps she would understand why a young, healthy man would seek a way out.

"Oh, Teddy had the odd nightmare," said Stella, as if reading her mind. "The odd dark mood, it was in his nature."

"But the war—"

"We'd put that horrible business behind us," says Stella firmly. "Or at least tried. Teddy didn't drink or gamble. He didn't owe money. He adored me and loved his job."

"He worked at the amusement park?"

"Yes. His boss was happy with him. Everyone was."

Were you happy with him, Stella? Nora bites back the words. She frowns, reconsiders, tries to frame her question in a way that will not lead.

Stella's small hand comes searching for Nora's in the dark.

"Stella, you are freezing."

"Am I? It's odd, I've been so numb since yesterday. I can't seem to feel anything."

Nora diagnoses shock. "Have you any tea-making things?"

"Yes, but sit a while, please."

The view is peaceful, the velvety void of the sea and the illuminated crescent of the town in the distance.

"Teddy was frightened of the dark. We always had to sleep with a light on. I love it, though. It is so soothing, peaceful. Sometimes we went out walking when he couldn't sleep, only on a moonlit night he preferred to go out alone. He would be uneasy until dawn."

"Teddy always slept badly?"

"Sometimes he couldn't sleep at all. When he did there were the night terrors. Very bad dreams. He would rave and shout and sob and I could do nothing but watch him. He would wake covered in sweat and cry like a baby. Sometimes he didn't recognize me."

"Did he speak to anyone about this, get help?"

"Teddy? Of course not. He said it was par for the course. I've heard that so many of those who saw action suffer so." Stella's breath catches. "It was hard to know how to help him."

"I can imagine."

"Once I woke with him standing over me glaring, fists clenched, almost like I was the enemy."

"Did he strike you?"

"Of course not. Teddy would never have hurt me."

Nora considers. "How was his mood in daylight hours?"

"Variable. Sometimes—" Stella pauses. "I don't want to speak ill of him, especially not now."

Nora, drawing on her experience of sickroom revelations, sits and waits. But nothing more seems to be forthcoming.

Stella sniffs in the dark; a rustle as a handkerchief is found. "I'm sorry, I thought I had no more tears left."

Nora puts a smile into her voice. "I'm no expert but I think tears are generally regarded as better out than in."

"Don't you ever cry?"

"Not really."

"You must have had a very happy life?"

"More an uneventful life, I would say."

"I can't believe that, pitching up here all alone. We think you are quite the woman of mystery; Bill has you pegged for an heiress on the run."

Nora laughs.

"You already seem to know us so well, while we know so little about you."

"There's nothing much to know."

Stella snorts. "I don't believe that somehow. But I understand you are more interested in finding out about others than letting on about yourself."

"You make me sound very nosy."

Stella laughs a little.

"Was Teddy very changed by his experiences in the war, Stella?"

"I have no idea. I didn't know him before the war, I met him when he was on leave, but he told me from the start that he couldn't wait to return to civilian life and marry me when it was all over. He was true to his word."

"He never spoke about his part in the war?"

"No, never. But I know for a fact that he would not have poisoned himself." Stella takes a deep breath. "Because I'm expecting a baby."

"Oh, Stella."

Stella's tears come fast and almost angry, until finally with sobbing hiccups she seems to collect herself.

"Teddy was desperate to be a father. He was elated when I told him. We made so many plans. To leave this awful place and find our own little house. It seemed to improve his mood no end."

Nora frowns, remembering the stormy couple on the beach and Teddy surly at the dinner table. If that was Teddy in a good mood . . .

As if in answer Stella adds, "Teddy could be very sweet when we were alone. So, you see, he had everything to live for: our baby, our future."

"But if Teddy didn't take his own life—"

"It was Karel Ježek, he did it! He cleared out yesterday morning and he won't be back—isn't that bloody proof enough? I told the police to go after him, arrest him—"

"Stella—"

"Don't you see?" A weary edge creeps into Stella's voice. "They've let Teddy's murderer get away with it."

Nora's mind is full of questions, yet she waits in the dark for Stella's breathing to calm.

"You said that the ill feeling between them originated from your husband's belief that Karel Ježek was interested in you."

"Yes."

"Was Teddy not reassured by your happy news?"

"What are you saying? That Teddy didn't believe our baby was his?"

Nora hesitates—had this occurred to her? She glances at Stella but in the darkness cannot read her expression. If she could she'd no doubt see Stella's kind face offended, her clear eyes tearful. A dark thought rises in Nora's mind: what if there *was* something between Stella and Karel? Put paid to by the baby and then Teddy's death. Couldn't remorse turn to venom against a former lover?

"I wasn't insinuating that."

Stella replies solemnly, "I never betrayed my husband in that way—I swear to God."

Nora is struck by deep sincerity in the young woman's voice.

An intake of breath in the dark. "You have to understand: he was always around. Following us, watching. Sometimes late at night I sensed him standing there outside our door, I heard the creak of the floorboards as he passed. He was always out in the garden, skulking and smoking, looking up at our window. He would smirk across the table at mealtimes. Or stare if we passed him on the stairwell. Hateful man."

"What did Teddy make of this?"

"He told me to ignore him. Then he said he would talk to him. That's when they argued."

"You witnessed this?"

"No. But they both had faces like thunder for days."

Nora considers this. "Did Karel Ježek ever force his attentions on you?"

"No. And neither did I encourage them, if that's what you're getting at!"

Nora frowns in the dark. "Why would Karel Ježek kill your husband? I'm sorry, Stella, I just don't follow."

"He saw that we were happy and wanted to ruin everything."

Nora considers this. Remembering again the first time she saw the couple, emotions strained at the beach, their young faces exhausted at the dining table. And wasn't Karel Ježek stalking them then? Didn't his eyes follow Teddy as he walked out of the room? And what of his expression? Nora tries to remember. Was it hatred? Envy? She can't be sure now.

Stella's tone becomes quietly miserable. "If he couldn't have what he wanted he didn't want anyone else to."

Nora considers. People can be cruel, evil even, when their desire is thwarted.

In the back of her mind an unwelcome thread is pulled, with a corresponding lurch deep in her gut. A lifetime ago in a nighttime field, her own spinning head, drunk on wake whiskey and the smells of the late autumn. The harvest gone and the warm earth furrowed. A hint of peat smoke in the air from her granny's house beyond and the mineral cut of colder weather to come. Then a shape silhouetted against the sky, so solidly dark against the starry backdrop—

Nora forces her attention back to the room. "So, they fought, you believe?"

"He made Teddy very angry. My husband just wanted to keep me all for himself, protect me and keep me safe. Poor Teddy, he never quite believed that I loved him as much as I did. It was a whirlwind romance really, Teddy and I."

"How did you meet?"

Nora hears a smile in Stella's voice. "It was towards the end of the war. He spotted me in Piccadilly Circus. He said he fell in love with my hat first! It was a silly thing, all trimmed with silk flowers, but somehow it made me feel bright and happy even on a gray day. He followed me to work and waited outside all day long. He didn't move from the spot until I came out again."

Nora searches for a positive response. "That's dedication."

"Isn't it? I was working in a telephone exchange; of all the hundreds of girls in and out of that place he held out for me. We were inseparable, right from the start really. To be honest, I don't know what I will do without him."

Nora searches for a comforting response; finding none, she is silent.

"Have you ever been in love?" Stella is asking. "Did you ever have a special person, Nora?"

Nora smiles in the dark. "I liked the idea of love when I was young. My granny worried that I'd be flighty."

"I don't believe that!"

"Do you not? Am I so much the dour spinster?"

Stella laughs. "Don't put words in my mouth."

Nora laughs too.

"But really?"

"At the beginning there was one love. I suppose it put paid to all the rest."

"Did it end very sadly?"

"What makes you think it has ended? Perhaps we are just on a little break?"

"Is that so?"

"I don't know, Stella. I think there are many ways to love. I really do. Only sometimes we don't realize we have a choice."

"Maybe you'll find another love in Gore-on-Sea?"

Nora laughs. "Of all places."

"There are better places," says Stella. "I'm going to leave Gulls Nest. I can't stay, it's too painful, all these bad memories."

"Of course. Where will you go?"

"Back to London I expect."

"Will you have support there, when the time comes, with your baby?"

"I've friends there."

"You've friends here too, I'm sure, Stella. You are well liked."

"Could you imagine Mrs. Rawlings allowing me to boil up nappies in my room? Or Mrs. Wells with one of her heads and a baby crying at all hours?"

"No, probably not." Nora wishes she could be of greater service. She reminds herself that the young are resilient, but even so.

"I would have packed my suitcase already, only, if I leave, Teddy will never have justice. But then Karel Ježek has already got away with it."

Nora chooses her words carefully. "Stella, these are serious allegations you are making. Be frank with me, have you any proof?"

"No—but am I truly the only one who thinks it looks suspicious? On the very day Teddy dies under mysterious circumstances that man disappears. Where is he now?"

"It is a coincidence, I agree." Nora speaks calmly, quietly. "But leaving town doesn't make the man a murderer, Stella."

"It's a gut feeling, don't tell me you never have them, Nora? Call it a woman's intuition." Stella's voice is full of sad conviction. "I knew my Teddy and there is just no way he would have left me—left *us*."

CHAPTER 9

Nora Breen stands outside looking in. The sunshine is sharp when the cloud breaks, unflattering; she sees well her reflection in the window: quizzical face, shorn hair, secondhand dress. Hatless and baffled, like an escapee from an asylum. She really ought to throw a shape on herself at the start of a new week. Monday morning, bright but not terribly early. Is she getting slack? Fishing in her net shopper she extracts a beret, puts it on perfectly straight, and stands as upright as a mother superior; purposeful, haughty. Now she tilts it to a jaunty angle and gives herself a lascivious wink. Now she pushes the hat back from her head and pulls her lip up over her teeth in the way of a rabbit; she crosses her eyes, grins. Now she sweeps the beret off her head and peers again. Regarding her on the other side of the glass is the face of another. A man, heavily bearded, his expression one of amusement. The man, unbeknownst to Nora, had opened the curtains behind the window display. Now he beckons her in. Nora gives a prim nod of assent; she was planning on going inside anyway. She wonders if she ought to be embarrassed as she steps in through the door.

The foyer to the studio is old-fashioned. A wood-paneled counter, velvet chairs, parlor palms; it's like stepping back to Victorian times. The portraits on the wall, faded now, are full of stiff backs and watching eyes.

The proprietor steps forward, broad-shouldered and paunchy, shorter and older than Nora, with a hale heartiness and twinkly dark-eyed joviality to him. On closer inspection, his suit is a little threadbare and his beard a bit tangled, but his smile is warm and his handshake firm. He introduces himself as Mr. Hosmer, proprietor of Hosmer's Photographic Studio; Hosmer to his friends and his customers, who are quite simply friends in development. He has a pleasant accent that Nora cannot place and a caress to the voice that is not wheedling but rather can be found in those that take a genuine interest in their fellow humans. At least, these are Nora's first impressions. She reminds herself that first impressions are not always accurate.

"So, how can I be of assistance?"

Nora thinks quickly. However amiable the man might appear, she doubts if he will openly discuss the character of his employee with a complete stranger. "A portrait, Mr. Hosmer. I was hoping to have my likeness taken."

"Hosmer, please."

"I am not your friend."

"Even so." He seems to stifle a smile and gestures towards the window. "You were practicing? A woman of many faces. I rather liked the one with your beret." He mimes her rakish pose.

"We'll see." Nora turns to look at the albums fanned out across the countertop.

"Please, inspect," says Hosmer. "Our recent work."

Nora opens a heavy leather-bound album. Young couples with shy grins, immortalized against a diaphanous curtain and painted Tuscan landscapes. Stately matrons flanked by Greek columns and more parlor palms. Babies gurgling in nests of soft toys. Neat girls and boys in uniform with chubby knees, long socks, and pressed blouses and shirts. Venerable gentlemen in tweed looking like landowners and off-duty vicars.

Nora turns the pages; all these lives, all these faces, but she sees no one like her. Who is she? A washed-up nun. An inquirer into the deaths of strangers. An abandoned friend. Flotsam and jetsam. Perhaps Hosmer reads this realization on her face, for he gently takes the album from her hand and closes it. Then, from behind the counter he extracts a shabby cardboard-bound folder.

"For those who look beneath the surface," he says mysteriously.

Nora glances up at him to see he is smiling.

These are very different pictures. Starkly black and white. An old man's face fills the frame, skin pores, nasal hairs, and all. A middle-aged man glares into the camera. It is all oddly unsettling.

"We tried to capture their essence, a sense of who they are, not who they think they should be."

Nora turns another page and there is Frieda. Her hair is loose, shaken all around her face, her pupils deep, black, dilated. On her lips plays a smile that is in no way innocent. Nora is aghast. But this is definitely—unquestionably—Frieda. Only not the Frieda she knew. Nora looks at the title written in an artistic hand under the print. *Liberty.*

"When was this taken?"

Hosmer looks at the photograph. "Oh, a month ago or so. I can't claim credit, that was by one of my most talented young photographers."

"And the model?"

"Frieda Firecracker."

Nora frowns. "Why Firecracker?"

Hosmer taps the album. "Look at her! She lights up the frame! Beauty is one thing in a woman, passion another!"

Nora is feeling her own passion, a rising anger as she studies the photograph of the young woman. "I thought I knew her."

Hosmer is watching her. "She's your friend."

"Yes. But this isn't Frieda. I mean, the way she looks in this photograph isn't her character."

Hosmer nods. "And you show all your character at once? Eh? All the different sides to you."

"I've a front side and a back side, what else?" she replies furiously.

Hosmer bursts out laughing, warm and fruity. So that Nora can't help but laugh too.

She shakes her head. "I just feel as if I didn't know her, seeing this."

Hosmer pats her hand. "Frieda can be all different things. She can be your friend *and* this photographer's muse."

"Who was the photographer?"

"Karel Ježek."

Nora gasps.

"You know him?"

"Heartburn. All this talk about passion. Tell me more."

"He says he hails from Prague." Hosmer leans forward conspiratorially. "But I have my doubts."

"You don't think he's from Prague? Why?"

"Doesn't speak a word of the language. I have been to many places," he adds, by way of explanation.

"Yet you keep him on? Knowing he isn't who he says he is?"

"Is anyone who they say they are?"

Nora, frustrated, opens her mouth.

Hosmer puts up his hand. "I keep him on because he's a great photographer, obsessed with it."

"How long has he worked for you?"

"He arrived at the start of the year."

"Is he here now?"

"No." Hosmer hesitates. "We have an agreement. He is free to follow his own creative urges. Don't get me wrong, he worked hard enough during the high season. He did the work of three, four. Up and down that beach. I even threw him a couple of weddings. A real grafter."

"Do you know where he is?"

Hosmer looks closely at Nora. "Why do you ask?"

"I'd like him to photograph me," she lies.

On Hosmer's face a fleeting frown. "I don't know where Karel is." He turns away, goes behind the counter, lowers his voice. "And you are not the first to ask."

Nora realizes that Inspector Rideout has already been here; he had made inquiries at Karel's place of work—at least this is one lead he has followed.

Nora tries to talk nonchalantly. "The girl, Frieda, do you know where she is?"

Hosmer, distracted, is searching for something. "She's a friend of Karel's. She left town, I believe, he was quite upset about it."

"Were they together?"

"If they were, he wouldn't have told me. Karel keeps his cards close to his chest, as they say. She lived up at the same boardinghouse, out along the end of the promenade. An unhospitable place, he said, but convenient."

"He didn't say where she'd gone?"

"He didn't." Hosmer finds a box of mounted prints and puts them on the countertop. "What you must understand is that Gore-on-Sea is a place for roll-ins, roll-outs. Like the tide, yes? People come and people go."

Nora glances around, points to the photographs on the wall. "Some people stay, a very long time."

Hosmer laughs. "I took over this business five years ago, I have yet to breathe new life into it. I have many ideas."

"Sounds like you have settled?"

"In a way," he says. "Right, I think I have found inspiration for your portrait."

"There will be no lighting up the frame. Or passion. Or close-ups."

Hosmer smiles.

From the box he takes a series of photographs, wonderfully lit so that the subjects' eyes are bright and the skin flawless, women and men in elegant poses. "I worked for the theaters in London. Very classic, very timeless. Would you like to try something like this?"

Nora, suddenly taken by the idea, nods.

The backdrop is a simple white sheet. The puce coat, Hosmer deems ghastly; the gray dress unflattering. Instead, he holds out a length of gold brocade. He advises her to improvise, twine it about her, Roman style. He tells her the color will brighten her face, that he'll photograph only her head and shoulders.

Nora divests herself of clothes in the cubicle to the side of the studio and wraps the cloth around her body as best she can, pulling it in at her waist, throwing it over a shoulder. Swathed in this material she feels oddly relieved. Closer now to the decades when she sailed about in habit and veil. She looks in the mirror and sees a square jaw, a set of strong shoulders, shorn hair. Hosmer is right to choose this cloth; it lights and softens her face.

She feels only oddly excited as she pads barefoot back across the studio to stand on a little taped cross on the floor. The room is big and dark; Hosmer is doing complicated things with lights on stands.

"When you are ready," he says softly.

Nora is suddenly gripped with embarrassment. She shuffles into some kind of a pose, smiles.

"Only smile if you mean it."

Nora stops smiling.

"Wait." Hosmer goes over to the record player in the corner and switches it on; the disc turns and the initial crackling sound gives way to music. Jazz, Nora knows that much. Mellow sounds of saxophone and piano, a scattered arrangement, discordant sometimes but nice.

"Dance if you want, it might help to relax you."

Nora grips her makeshift tunic about her. "I am relaxed."

"Close your eyes and just drift. I'm still setting up."

Nora finds she does want to close her eyes; as for drifting, she'll give it a go. Soon she gets lost in the music and it seems entirely natural to be wrapped in an old curtain in a photographer's studio on the Kent coast.

Soon she can dance with her eyes open. She struts and glares, turns and pouts, laughs and grimaces. She scampers to the edge of the backdrop and strides back again. But then she notices that Hosmer is doing a corresponding dance with his camera and tripod, and she stops short. He grins, waves at her to continue. Oddly delighted by his grin, she does.

Nora picks her way back across the room, the music still in her head and her feet. It is at this moment that she thinks of Frieda and understands for the first time the pleasure the young woman might have felt in her newfound freedom. This is not just cavorting about in front of a camera lens; it is something more, something honest, maybe even courageous. For a moment Nora thinks of the starched veil and the wimple and how far they have both traveled from it. Was Nora dancing barefoot in a curtain before a complete stranger any less real or true than Sister Agnes? Was Frieda Firecracker any less real than the joyful novice Nora loved? Could Nora really blame Frieda for succumbing to the unruly joys of the world when here she was doing exactly the same?

Nora steps into the foyer, her face still a little flushed. She opens her bag and takes out her purse.

"Wait until you see the photographs first; if you are happy with them then by all means pay."

Nora nods a little sheepishly, well knowing that she can't afford them. "Thank you. I enjoyed that, unbelievably."

Hosmer laughs; he pauses, glances at her thoughtfully. "Frieda spoke of you. She said whenever anything interesting happened she would write about it in a letter to her good friend."

Nora's heart jolts.

"She described you." Hosmer's face is kindly. "Formidable but fun."

She nods, unable to trust herself to speak.

Hosmer goes back behind the counter. In a short while he returns with a large manila envelope. "Here are the photographs Karel took of Frieda. Would it help to have them?"

"Yes, I think it would, thank you." Nora takes the envelope. "Did Frieda speak to you about her life before coming to Gore-on-Sea?"

"Not to me. To Karel perhaps. And what about your life before, Miss Breen?"

Nora notes the change of subject. "It's a long auld story."

"One I would like to hear sometime." He looks at her thoughtfully. "You've left much behind, what made you do that?"

So, he knows about the Order, thinks Nora, surprised that she feels the need to justify herself to him. "I had to come to find her. You see, she just stopped writing. I feared something was wrong. But by the time I arrived she was gone."

Hosmer smiles. "That's not unusual. Like I said, in this town people come and go."

"Don't you see, it was out of character; she promised to write to me." As Nora says it, she realizes how trivial it sounds. A small promise, easily broken by a young woman out in the world. She reads this in Hosmer's face.

Hosmer's voice is kind, soft. "And her friendship was very important to you?"

"Yes." Nora collects herself. "If you hear anything of her, or if Karel makes contact—"

"Naturally. Where will I find you?"

"At Gulls Nest."

"I see. I shouldn't have spoken ill of the place."

"Not at all."

Hosmer opens his mouth to say something, then thinks better of it and closes it again. "Your photographs will be ready in two or three days. But come back anytime, to talk, to listen to music. You can dance if you want, the curtain isn't obligatory."

Nora laughs. "Thank you, Hosmer. I'd like that."

Nora leaves her beret on this time, the angle as rakish as she feels. She strolls through town, upright in her ugly coat, feeling not beautiful but alive, as if she inhabits her body. For so long her body was in the service of God, the best she could expect from it was to be sturdy, healthful, to serve her in her duties. Now it is as if her body is waking up. She passes a butcher's shop and catches the smell of blood and sawdust. She takes pleasure in the produce outside a greengrocer's: earthy root vegetables, sharp green cooking apples. The breeze up from the sea is a caress; the glances of strangers provoke a smile now and a smile is given to her in return. She even makes the most of the changeable weather. The sky is overcast, a light rain falls; she shelters in the window of a hat shop. She imagines what it is like to touch the felt and feather creations, admiring their colors and forms. The sun comes out and the pavement shines. Nora is swayed by the sudden optimism of a brightening day. Finding herself passing the opulent façade of the Marine Hotel, she steps inside.

The Garden Bar is quiet at this time of day, though it would be a peaceful spot at any hour. Marble tiles and lush green plants, tall iron-work windows with a conservatory feel to it. There is a polished wood bar. In the corner, a lady pianist plays soothingly to an audience of two. An older couple, who sit looking out at the sea, holding hands, their faces relaxed, contented. Nora feels a sudden pang of something. She wonders if it could be loneliness.

"Miss Breen, what a pleasant surprise."

It is Bill Carter, dapper as ever, now in his barman's livery of white waistcoat and bow tie.

"What can I treat you to?"

"What do you recommend, Bill?"

"Oh, a cocktail, almost certainly."

"It's barely lunchtime."

Bill smiles, suave. "An aperitif?"

Nora, buoyed as she is, nods her consent. Bill, with a flourish, pro-duces a dainty bowl of olives.

"We have all the classics—Gin Fizz, Old Fashioned, Margarita—or if you are inclined towards the experimental you could try our house cocktail."

"Which is?"

"The Marine Mermaid. Bubbly, with a tail-fin kick."

Nora laughs. "Your invention? Sounds just the ticket."

Bill offers a bow and returns to the bar.

Nora, knowing she can ill afford to order anything, feigns interest in the luncheon menu, watches him. His movements are so smooth he could be on casters. He deftly takes up a glass, then bottles, mixers, garnishes, measuring and mixing with a practiced eye. In moments he is back across the room, a cloth over his arm and a tray in his hand. On it is a bulbous glass of a startling green liquid.

There's a twinkle in Bill's eye as he sets a coaster down and the drink on top.

Nora throws him a look.

"Be brave," he says.

Nora takes a tentative taste, coughs, tries another sip. "It's frighteningly wonderful. I somehow feel it's realigning my organs."

"I'll take that as a compliment."

"Join me, Bill?"

Bill looks towards his only other customers, the older couple; they are engrossed with the view. The pianist is softly playing to herself.

"Just for a minute." He sits down.

Nora peers over the rim of her glass. "It's a classy joint."

"It was," says Bill. He lowers his voice. "Only the clientele these days—"

"Not *Quality?*"

Bill smiles. "No, not really. With the exclusion of your good self."

"Thank you, Bill."

He looks at her closely. "I must say, the sea air is doing some good; you look dreadfully well."

"Well, it isn't Irene's food."

They both grimace a little.

"You ever think of moving on from Gulls Nest?"

Bill shrugs. "There are advantages: an evening stroll down the promenade and the odd tipple with the professor."

Nora thinks of Poppy's gossip, Bill's unrequited love for Helena Wells.

Bill seems to read her mind. "That old rogue told you, didn't he, that I was infatuated with our landlady?"

"It's none of my business."

"You must think I'm a fool?"

"That's not a thought I'd think."

Bill nods, smiles sadly. "You are a generous soul, then."

"Bill, may I ask you a question?"

"Of course."

"What do you think happened to Teddy Atkins?"

"To be honest: I've no idea. He was more than a little tortured, up and down, so it's not impossible he took his own life."

"Stella will not contemplate the thought."

"They seemed very close, in the same boat so to speak, like some couples are."

"Do you think she's right?"

"Well, she knew him better than anyone. What's the alternative, Nora? That someone poisoned him? Is it likely a grown man would drink such a preparation?"

"Under duress? Accidentally?"

"I can't believe there's a murderer in our midst, Nora."

"Why would Teddy's murderer be in our midst? Could they not be a stranger?"

Bill frowns. "I suppose it's feasible. But poisoning? It's like something from a detective story, a film. Who in their right mind would poison a regular, ordinary fella like Teddy?"

"Regular, ordinary folk murder and get murdered, Bill. It's rare, of course, but it can happen in real life as well as fiction."

Bill doesn't look convinced.

"Did you see anything strange the morning of Teddy's death?"

"Nothing. It was a morning exactly like any other."

"Exactly?" Nora smiles, patiently. "The devil is in the detail, Bill. You of all people should know that."

Bill adjusts his cuff links with the slightest of nods.

"Tell me how your morning unfolded."

Bill hesitates.

"Please, humor me."

"I was up, dressed, and down to breakfast just before eight a.m."

"Stella was your only companion in the dining room?"

"Until you arrived, yes."

"No sign of any of the other residents?"

"None. Stella said Teddy must have gone out before she woke. She surmised he would be in the workshop; he was there most mornings, sometimes through the night." Bill hesitates. "She seemed in low spirits, tired. Not her usual bright self."

Nora notes this. "Anything else?"

"No. Only that Mrs. Rawlings had forgotten to platter the cold collation and Rose had a grumble about that. She did what she could. It was heavy on the Spam, I recall."

"And then you left us around—"

"Eight twenty. I had a meeting in town at half past."

"You walked straight to town?"

"I did."

"And attended your meeting?"

Bill glances around, lowers his voice. "Not quite, my contact didn't show."

"Can you elaborate?"

"It was a deal. A bit of commerce."

"What then?"

"I walked about the town a bit."

"Did you meet with anyone?"

Bill looks at her with a guarded expression. "Are you asking me if I have an alibi?"

Nora realizes that she is.

Bill holds up his hand. "Don't answer, Nora. I walked alone and I met no one I knew. I arrived about nine thirty. Check with the doorman, he'll tell you."

Bill was wandering about the town alone during the time that Teddy drank the poison.

She speaks, more to herself. "So, nothing odd? Nothing out of place?"

"As I said, only Stella in low spirits and an increase of Spam on the breakfast platter."

A woman and a man walk into the bar. Bill looks up; his gaze alights on the man and his expression changes, momentarily. Nora reads a pure kind of hatred before the barman's countenance becomes smooth, polite, bland again.

He quickly rises. "If you will excuse me, Nora."

Nora takes the opportunity to study the newcomers closely. The girl is very young, perhaps not much above sixteen. She wears a too-light summer frock with a fur coat. Around her neck is a pearl three-tier necklace that looks to be made for someone older and grander. Her lipstick is smudged and her eyes blank. There are dark circles under them, and her hair is more than a little windswept; it has not been introduced to a brush for a while. The man is older than the woman, perhaps in his early thirties; tall and thin and hungry-looking. Lascivious, thinks Nora.

The man's gaze sweeps around the room and briefly over Nora. Finding nothing of interest there, he turns to the bar.

Bill is right behind him when he clicks his fingers.

"Carter. Fizz, quick as you like."

"Champagne for you too, *miss*?"

The man glares at Bill. The barman's face gives nothing away.

The young woman shuffles slightly as if she's fit to drop.

"She'll have what I have."

The man steers her firmly by the elbow to a table at the opposite end of the room. In passing he bends and mutters something to the pianist. Her face reddens; she stops playing, shuts the lid of the piano, rises, and walks out of the room.

Nora gestures to Bill, who bobs back to her table.

"Who is that man, Bill? He looks as though he owns the place."

Bill's expression remains benign but his voice is bitter. "He does, in a way. Percy Ladd. His father, Harry, has Gore-on-Sea in his pocket, including this hotel."

"He owns the amusement park, Laddland, where Teddy worked?"

Bill nods. "Harry Ladd is bad enough, but Percy there, he's a piece of work."

"And the young woman?"

"He knocks about with a different girl every week. He's like the lion that hunts the plains; he picks off the weak and confused. If I'm not mistaken, that one's father is the local rag-and-bone man."

Percy, from his perch in the corner, looks round at Bill. He calls out in a braying voice, "Come on—fizz!"

"I'd better get on with His Lordship's order."

The champagne is brought.

Nora watches as Percy Ladd drinks. He offers a mocking toast to his companion, who barely touches her glass. Perhaps feeling himself watched, Percy looks over at Nora.

Nora holds his gaze, sees his irritation sparked, feels an odd rush of victory when he looks away first. She turns back to her cocktail, wondering if she should sink it like a sailor or sip it like a lady. She closes her eyes and opts for the former.

"Do I know you?"

Nora looks up. Percy Ladd is looking down at her, his face a-smirk.

She meets his eyes, unsmiling. Percy seems to recoil slightly, his grin falters.

"Not yet," says Nora.

"You were looking over. Staring, in fact, at my friend."

Nora glances to his companion, left behind at the table. The young woman is drinking champagne, holding the glass with two hands, still wearing her coat. She glances about herself, her eyes invariably falling on Percy. Nora wonders if she is frightened of him.

A feeling of rage grows inside her. Whether Percy has forced his attentions on this girl or not, it is clear she is disposable to him.

Nora returns her attention to Percy, her voice level, cold. "She looks a little young for you, bewildered even. But I expect you know that."

Percy laughs, there's a snort to it. "You're a nosy old—"

"And you're a rat. Tell you what, I'll down this cocktail and we'll take this outside, shall we? It would give me the greatest satisfaction to knock your fecking teeth out."

Percy reddens, then with a derisive bow returns to his table. Lifting the Champagne bottle from the cooler he tops up the girl's glass. From time to time, he glances over at Nora, his face sour. He pours the last of the champagne for himself and downs it. Then he upends the bottle in the cooler, grabs his date by the elbow, and ushers her out of the bar.

Nora finishes her cocktail; the taste of strong spirits gets stronger as she approaches the bottom. She's flittered now. Not even lunchtime and Nora Breen is three sheets to the wind. And now it hits her: a full recollection of the last time she drank. She looks at the empty glass and wishes that she hadn't downed the contents. It's too late, the memories are scrabbling and scratching out from the back room of her mind.

It was the night of her grandmother's wake. Nora purses her lips against the rim of her empty glass, feeling the heat of the drink move through her, unlocking mind and muscles. She had been young, not much above sixteen, as she had bent over the coffin and kissed Granny's cold auld face goodbye. The woman had been a horror, but the Mass was well attended and afterwards everyone came back to the house.

Her uncles had held the floor for they could sing, everyone agreed. Nora had watched her mother run about with sandwiches and a drop of something for the mourners. She wondered why her mother didn't have a song like her brothers. Nora's father was alive then. She loved to watch the two of them, her mother and father; the way they exchanged looks of kindness between them made her heart full and sore somehow. They were both quiet people and well suited for that. Nora felt a pang, even then, for what she somehow knew she would not have. It wasn't that she wanted the big love affair; she'd had notions for this boy or that and lost her mind entirely over them. She knew she had a vocation; as did the religious sisters at her school. It was an unwritten rule that there was a path that led straight from her parents' farm to the Carmelite Order. For however much she might feel for a boy, she craved something higher and everlasting. Still, Nora saw that there could be much comfort and contentment in the love between two people who understood one another. So, while her uncles sang of terrible heartbreak and wild joy, Nora thought about the little things, the quiet moments of contentment, that she would never experience with another person. The way her father dug over her mother's garden without complaint. The way her mother went out with a coat to him.

Bill passes her table and with a magician's sleight of hand swaps her empty glass with a fresh cocktail. She glances up and catches his fleeting wink. Then he is gone. Sliding down the length of the conservatory, smooth and obliging, to welcome new guests.

Nora considers the glass. The colors are more vivid than the last, maritime blues and startling oranges, sunset under the ocean. If she drinks enough of these maybe she'll grow a tail and swim away. She raises the glass and toasts the view. This drink is as good as the first.

But with the taste, the memories return.

Granny's wake. Nora's uncle back from America feeding her drink, and around midnight when the room was hot and the musicians in full flight and the mourners up and dancing, Nora slipped out. Down the field away from the cottage, glancing back to see the light shine from every window, the laughter and the music following her. She lay down trying to ignore the spinning of her head and the ringing of her ears as she looked up at the stars. Never minding the furrowed earth for it was a dry night and it would brush off. She wondered if God was up there looking down. Sometimes she was almost certain He was communicating with her. He was present in everything: sunlight on the water, dew on a spider's web, the swoop of a crow. Other times Nora felt empty and alone. The sisters told her to be calm and still and listen and then she would discover her vocation. This was hard for Nora. As she lay in the field flittered on porter and whiskey, sweet wine and goodness knows what else, under the enormity of the sky, she wondered what she was trading, what she was risking if she joined the order. A home, children perhaps, intimacy with another. The stars danced and the earth smelled sweet and the air cooled, for the summer was long over. And Nora gave herself a good talking-to. Better all the difficulties and doubts of a life of faith than shackling herself to some mortal fella who would be one moment marvelous and the next a gobshite. Then a rake of screaming kids. And for what? God was constant, she just had to keep listening and looking out for Him.

She shut her eyes. Perhaps she slept, she hardly knew, but when she opened them again a figure was standing over her. It was the sound rather than the sight of him that shocked her awake: a metallic ting, the rip of buttons; he was unfastening his breeches.

He did it quickly with his hand over her mouth, although she wouldn't have screamed out, shocked as she was. It hurt but not as much as when the child she carried for him was born eight months later. A tiny thing, a girl, that came too soon. Full mouth, long fingers, a freckle on the top lip. The sister at the home bent the rules and let her hold the little bundle, leaving Nora alone in the room for a few precious minutes. Nora wept over the baby and later regretted it; wasn't that her daughter's first sight of the world? After the baby was taken from her, her arms ached for the longest time.

Frieda couldn't have been that child—her child—she was born a decade too late, of course. Yet Nora's heart knew Frieda from the very first time she set eyes on her. Her full mouth and long fingers, the exact same freckle on the top lip. Frieda was an orphan, raised by the sisters. It was as if her own child had returned to her grown. And so, the sunny novice became a reminder of the darkest part of Nora's life. The sin and the shame—but also love for the child they let her keep for the briefest of moments. Nora had prayed to God. How should she navigate the waves of feeling that buffeted her? The pain and the rage, the grief and the yearning? Where was the safe harbor and peaceful water? But on this matter, she found Him curiously silent.

Nora puts down her glass, wipes her eyes, and takes a furtive look around. No one is paying her any mind, thank goodness. But then another thought comes. She would like to be asked what the matter is. To tell her own story, bear witness to her own crimes—such as they were—but the feeling swiftly passes.

Despite her precarious finances she tips Bill generously as she leaves. The memories it induced were bad, but they were good cocktails.

After a restorative walk along the seafront Nora heads to the police station. Here she spends the best part of the afternoon alternately dozing and glaring at the desk officer. When she is finally ushered into the interview room, she sees with satisfaction that someone has cleaned the table. Her suggestions, then, are taken on board, with a little persistence. Detective Inspector Rideout joins her directly. They sit facing each other, both rumpled. Nora feels her head lifting from her daytime drinking. Rideout offers her a peppermint strong enough to mask the smell of spirits.

Having unloaded the most recent content of her investigatory notebook, Nora waits. Rideout looks unimpressed by her gatherings.

He trots his words out slowly. "Mr. Ježek is not a suspect."

"If that is even his name, as Mr. Hosmer informed me—"

"No crime has been committed—"

"Now, that's where you are wrong, Inspector."

Rideout exhales. "The death of Mr. Atkins is not currently being treated as a murder investigation. There is every suggestion that the man took his own life." He holds up his hand. "Despite your hunch and Mrs. Atkins's belief."

"And what about Stella's pregnancy? Doesn't that put a different complexion on things? Her husband desperately wanted a family, so why would he leave them?"

"I wasn't aware of Mrs. Atkins's condition; but it makes no difference," Rideout says stiffly. "I can't investigate a murder without clear evidence pointing to foul play."

"What about launching a missing person case, or do you need clear evidence for that too?"

"You refer to your friend, Frieda Brogan? I said I would make inquiries, didn't I?"

"What inquiries, where?"

Inspector Rideout looks exasperated.

"Let's talk about the handkerchief in his pocket. Surely it links the two cases, Teddy's murder and Frieda's disappearance?"

"Will you stop referring to Mr. Atkins's death as murder!"

Nora looks at Rideout with interest. The policeman riled is rather handsome. A flashing intensity to his eyes.

"You heard what Mrs. Rawlings said, sometimes the boarders' laundry can get mixed up. That was verified by several residents."

Nora frowns. "What if it didn't?"

"He could have found it, someone could have given it to him, Frieda herself, even! Look, I can't possibly know—"

"That handkerchief is a clue; you should make it your business to know. If I were a detective—"

Rideout reddens. "This isn't a game, you know! Turning up here incognito, playing the amateur sleuth. Does anyone at that house know who you are and why you came here?"

"I'm not incognito, Inspector Rideout," says Nora coolly. "I go under my own name, unlike Karel Ježek."

Rideout groans.

"To enlighten my fellow residents at Gulls Nest would be contradictory to my purpose. I have been trying to gain their trust, to be taken into their confidence."

"To gain their trust you lied to them—isn't that a little contradictory, Miss Breen?"

"I did not lie to them. I merely neglected to give them the whole picture."

Rideout runs his fingers through his hair. "Has it not occurred to you that it might have helped your cause? Perhaps if they had known your personal investment in finding Frieda, they might have been more open."

Nora prickles to anger. "I had a hunch it was better not to tell."

Rideout's expression is scornful. "You and your hunches. What if they have cost you the most vital piece of information?"

"Such as?"

"Your young friend was merely fed up writing to some old busybody and wanted to bloody live a bit!"

Nora frowns down at the clean table. Her own strong, capable hands. Perhaps she made a mistake in not telling the whole story? Perhaps if she had she would have found Frieda by now.

"I'm sorry," Rideout says quietly.

Nora nods.

"I won't give your secret away, Sister Agnes."

"That is no longer my name and never will be again."

"You won't go back to your monastery, after you've solved my case?"

"I can't go back. I'd have to start from the beginning." She glances up at him. "If they'd even have me."

"Would you go back if you could?"

"No. I am in the world now."

On Rideout's face, the start of a smile. "Look out, world."

Nora notices that they are speaking quietly, the space between them closing, leaning in, elbows on table, palms down, their fingers almost touching. She sits back in her chair. "Rideout?"

"Yes?"

"With regards to the man pertaining to be Karel Ježek—"

"Not again."

"Would you not put the word out? If you won't arrest him, you could reel him in for questioning."

"If Mr. Ježek materializes, we will question him. As we questioned your fellow residents, and not because he's a murderer." Rideout slaps the table, rises out of the chair, a man of action. "Now, Miss Breen, if you don't mind, I have work to do."

"You do, of course; you are a busy man, are you not?"

Rideout looks gratified.

Nora picks up her bag, Rideout offers a smile. She returns it. But instead of standing she opens her bag and draws out her notebook and pen.

"But before I go, Rideout, tell me what you know about Percy Ladd."

Nora cannot help but relish Rideout's vexed state: the tension in his jaw, his glowering frown, the irritation in his eyes. She wonders if this makes her a bad person at all.

CHAPTER 10

It takes Nora a couple of days to be sure her timing is exactly right; after elevenses and before luncheon. This is when Helena Wells takes her daily constitutional. Today she intends to meet and interview Helena as she makes her circuit of the garden. With recent events, Irene has relaxed the rule that guests must vacate their rooms during the day. Professor Poppy has taken to his bed with bad health and Stella Atkins to hers with grief. Providing the guests are not demanding extra meals, nor burning coal to heat their rooms (coal that has not been purchased from her at inflated cost), Irene seems to accept the new order. This is a boon for Nora's investigation and particularly for finding a way to interview the elusive Helena Wells.

And investigation it is—Nora will not be disheartened by Inspector Rideout's laissez-faire attitude to events at Gulls Nest. With a freer rein of the house, Nora intends to learn more about the behavior of the residents and not waste valuable time holed up in the local library or meandering around town between the hours of nine and three. One such survey is exactly how the elusive Helena Wells spends her days.

The landlady, the housekeeper, and little Dinah occupy a confusing run of rooms that collectively jut out as an unsightly annex just along from the kitchen. Internally, this area lies behind a door to the left of the entrance hall marked STRICTLY PRIVATE. When visitors arrive, or outside of mealtimes, Irene Rawlings is generally seen to appear, grumbling, from this direction.

From the exterior these quarters are screened off from any guests enjoying the garden or the outside privy by a high wooden fence of recent construction. By diligently pressing out the wood knots in this fence Nora has furnished herself with a few spyholes from which she is able to work out the layout of the staff quarters. These seem to be constituted from an old washhouse and conservatory, linked together and expanded to offer a single-story carbuncle to the house's grand proportions. By changing her vantage point from one peephole to another, supplemented by positioning herself behind shrubbery and peering out of first-floor windows, Nora has been plotting Helena's habits.

The first sign of the landlady occurs just after nine o'clock in the morning with the rising of the blinds in the conservatory. Next, Helena throws open French windows and drifts onto the terrace. Her appearance at this time of the day offers a contrast to her usual elegant garb and demeanor. She appears neither polished nor measured. Instead of her natty widow's black she goes barefoot, clad in a voluminous white nightdress and shawl. Her unpinned hair, lustrous, thick, and tangled, falls about her shoulders. Nora wonders if poor lovestruck Bill Carter has ever seen the object of his affection thus. Perhaps it would be entirely too much for him? Perhaps, like Nora, he would be reminded of old tales of Victorian lunatic asylums. Helena stands on the terrace, blank-eyed, gulping the air, like a woman surfacing from underwater. After the gulping subsides, her mouth contorts, framing a silent scream. She pulls the roots of her hair, rocking on her feet. With these bizarre rituals over, she retreats inside. An hour or so later she reemerges, neat, trim, and altogether herself again, with a tiny coffee cup in hand.

Nora has made this careful note.

Helena Wells is a coffee drinker.

Helena then takes a few sips of her drink, puts down her cup, and buttoning her coat and pulling on her gloves and hat, sallies forth for her morning exercise. She treads the same loop of the garden and Dinah always follows. Helena pointedly ignores shaking foliage, or the scrabble of footsteps, as Dinah, clad in her usual outlandish way, creeps and scuttles after her mother. Nora wonders at their odd connection, Dinah's strange surveillance and Helena's tolerance of it. Perhaps it's just another game the two of them play?

They take in the old greenhouse and espaliered fruit trees, the forgotten pond, the toolshed and the mossy lawn and sundial, the spreading oak and its tree house, and Professor Poppy's stable workshop, where Helena stops for a reflective moment. Dinah too stops in turn, but she is never still, preferring to rip a leaf to shreds or hit the ground with a stick.

Nora records all of this, observing from an upstairs window, or behind a dense thicket of shrub. She concludes that every day in her landlady's life is more or less identical. At midday, without fail, a sour-faced Irene deposits a luncheon tray that is ignored. In the afternoon Helena swallows some kind of preparation brought by her housekeeper. Irene stands over her while she drinks it. Then Helena slumbers away the afternoon on a chaise longue. Nora ponders at this behavior; that a seemingly healthy woman in her prime does nothing, sees no one, and goes nowhere. It is the life of a prisoner or an invalid.

This morning Nora, spotting Helena putting down her coffee cup, takes a position in the rhododendron beyond the privy.

Helena approaches, her expression contemplative. As yet, there is no sign of Dinah following. Nora launches herself into her landlady's path.

Helena is startled but graciously brushes away Nora's apologies.

"I'll take a turn with you, Helena," she says firmly. "Isn't it a grand morning?"

It isn't. It's overcast and gloomy. The weather lends the garden a Gothic dreariness that Nora quite enjoys. She sees great fecundity here, even in the dying of the year.

"You are finding the house to your liking, Nora?"

"I am. Although perhaps like everyone at Gulls Nest, I'm troubled by recent events."

Helena looks puzzled.

"Teddy Atkins," Nora reminds her.

"Yes of course, ghastly."

"How is Dinah? Has she recovered from being shut away in the sideboard that day?"

"She will secrete herself away in odd places." Helena frowns. "I must say, poor Teddy's accident held quite a morbid fascination, but then again my daughter is apt to be macabre."

Nora glances at her landlady, her lovely wan face and dark coat. She catches that scent again, oddly familiar but one she cannot place. Nora draws a little nearer to Helena as the path allows. Then she realizes it is the smell of codeine syrup. Stella's fabulous gossip wasn't too outlandish; the landlady is likely addicted to a form of opiates.

"Do you think Teddy's death was an accident, Helena? The police seem to believe he died at his own hand."

Helena shudders. "Could we perhaps discuss something else?" She glances around and lowers her voice. "I fear the rhododendrons have ears."

They walk on in silence, behind them an occasional rustle in the bushes. Nora's sharp eyes catch a glimpse of Dinah hopping through the undergrowth. She accompanies them a little way, then perhaps finding something of better interest, bolts off in the opposite direction.

"She's a poppet, sometimes an absolute darling," says Helena blithely. "But I do find her ways unfathomable."

"You seem very tolerant of Dinah's ways."

"Too tolerant." Helena grimaces. "It is a matter of contention."

"Between you and Irene, you mean? Ought you care what your housekeeper thinks?"

Helena throws Nora a sharp glance. Was she too blunt?

"Perhaps not." Color rises in the landlady's cheeks. "It's not just Irene who believes Dinah should be taken in hand. I know what people say about me, that I'm indulgent, that I'm neglectful." She gives a little laugh. "How I manage to be both at the same time, I do not know."

Nora throws her a sympathetic look. "People can be judgmental."

"Not you, Nora?"

"I try to guard against it, keep an open mind."

They walk through the beautiful, moldering garden. Nora matches Helena's pace, which is unhurried, lingering.

"You are a nurse, Irene tells me?"

"Yes. For thirty years."

"What a blessing to be useful, to give of yourself in work. My health does not permit me to be useful to anyone."

"You suffer with headaches?"

"They are entirely debilitating."

"I am sorry to hear that. Has that always been the case?"

"In recent years; since coming to Gulls Nest, in fact. At first, I put it down to the upheaval of moving, the new environment, Dinah was a difficult infant, and I was on my own."

"Apart from Irene?"

Helena bites her lip. "Yes. Dinah's father is no longer with us."

Nora notes this somewhat oblique statement, but she reasons that many do not like to address death directly. A loved one may have *passed*, *moved on, left this life, met their maker*—all so much easier to say than that bleak word: *dead*.

"It must be a struggle, to be alone with a young child?"

Helena looks away. "Oh, Irene helps in her way and the house occupies Dinah. If only I felt stronger then I could steer her more, civilize her a bit, perhaps even get her into school and out from under everyone's feet."

"I'm surprised the truant officers aren't knocking on your door."

Helena glances at Nora with clear blue eyes. "Are you?" She frowns. "Dinah is not like other children. There was an *incident*."

"An incident?"

Helena nods, lowers her voice to no more than a whisper. "She tried to hurt another child. It was my fault entirely. I thought she ought to have friends her own age and not just an old Punchman."

"What happened?"

"Last year I encouraged her to be pals with the laundry woman's daughter. Unfortunately, one of their games went wrong." She casts a glance back at the pond, clotted with fallen leaves and slime, as they turn on to the mossy lawn.

"The child drowned?"

"All but." Helena looks away, her beautiful face harrowed.

Nora frowns. Could a child as young as Dinah maliciously hurt another child? Surely it wasn't intentional, premeditated, but rather an accident born out of some dare or other? As they walk on Nora glances back at the pond, this dank overgrown spot somehow seeming more sinister. Dinah's playground seeming dangerous indeed.

"Several doctors examined Dinah," Helena continues. "They said they found her lack of remorse disturbing."

Nora speaks gently. "Did you?"

"Yes, in a way. But then, Dinah was different from the start. She has never talked; the doctors said this was no doubt symptomatic of some awful shock or other, but I can think of nothing that fits the bill. In fact, Dinah has had a charmed existence."

"How so?"

Helena's smile is bitter. "She does exactly what she wants to do. She has the freedom of her beloved house and garden—she clings to Gulls Nest."

Helena is deep in her musings as they continue towards Poppy's workshop.

"But you'd go if you could?"

Helena doesn't answer.

"It takes a lot of strength to stay somewhere you're unhappy, Helena."

"It takes a lot of strength to leave too, Nora."

Nora, hearing some intimate tone in her voice, glances at Helena to see she is watching her with clear eyes.

"I know why you came, Nora. You knew Frieda from before, didn't you?" Helena speaks gently. "Please do not take offense but your hair, your manner, it speaks of a different kind of life."

"I hadn't thought, I suppose it does."

"Why didn't you say why you were here, Nora?"

"I had some kind of instinct it would be better to stay quiet about that. A hunch, if you like."

Helena nods. "I understand, I think."

"Is it very obvious that I've escaped from an order?"

"Perhaps." Helena laughs. "But people are generally not that perceptive, they are usually preoccupied with their own cares and worries. I know I am."

They approach Professor Poppy's workshop.

"So, you came to find Frieda and then another mystery presented itself to you?" Helena glances at Nora with some interest. "From your questions I take it that you think Teddy's death is a mystery."

"The police take the line that there is no mystery. That Teddy died by his own hand."

"You don't take that line?"

Nora is surprised by the intensity of Helena's expression, as if much rests on her answer.

"Possibly not."

Helena's brow wrinkles with this new anxiety. "I thought it was rather a cry for help; sometimes it is you know."

"He swallowed cyanide, Helena, he must have known there would be no way back."

"But it's too dreadful to think of an alternative—what, a killer in our midst?"

Nora finds herself asking a familiar question. "Why not a stranger? Why would the killer be among us?"

But Helena does not answer. She is cautiously pushing forward on the final leg of her usual circuit, round the back of Poppy's workshop through the nettles. Nora must work quickly.

"Did you notice anything odd, the morning of Teddy's death?"

"I didn't move from my bed. I woke with a very bad headache and didn't surface until midday, just after all the trouble."

"You didn't take your turn about the garden?"

Helena hesitates. "No. Not that morning."

They near the fence.

"Do you take anything, for your headaches?"

"Irene makes a preparation, a sort of syrup. It is preventative, really, I take it every day."

"But it doesn't work?"

Helena laughs. "Not entirely."

"Have you consulted a doctor?"

"Many." Helena pauses at the gate. "To no avail. I always get the sense that they think that it's all in my mind."

"But the pain is very real, isn't it?"

"Yes, it's rather sickening. I would do just about anything to be rid of it."

"One more question. You mentioned at our first meeting that you never drink tea—"

"I don't."

"You drink coffee."

"Yes, I do."

"Who prepares it?"

"Irene, of course."

"Poppy takes coffee too."

"Does he? I wouldn't know."

"Would your supply be kept in the pantry?"

"Probably. Irene will know where."

"Thank you, Helena."

Helena smiles.

"May I ask you one more thing?"

Helena's smile wavers: without it she looks tired. "Go ahead."

"You told me that I should not listen to gossip concerning the previous occupant of my room," continues Nora. "That Frieda Brogan simply left. What sort of gossip?"

Helena's pale cheeks color slightly. "Oh, that she was caught up with a married man or came to some kind of sticky end."

"What kind of sticky end?"

Helena turns away, opens the gate, wants to be gone.

"Please, Helena."

Helena takes a deep and even breath. Nora is reminded of her unrestrained morning gulps of air. With effort the other woman finds the words. "Girls fall all the time for the wrong man. Sometimes they take it into their own hands, one way or another."

With this Helena is gone. Leaving Nora behind with her scent. The sweet, cloying smell of an overblown flower.

CHAPTER 11

Nora turns the pages of her notebook, ignoring Dinah's scribbles as best she can. This notebook keeps score; it's a witness of sorts. Here Nora records her observations at length. She thinks about the sparse jottings she has seen Rideout make, deftly flipping open his pocket notebook. Perhaps she simply notices more than he does? Or perhaps she should be more selective? Only, how is she to know what's important yet? She feels a little thrill whenever she opens this book. Somewhere within its pages might lie the clue that will help her find Frieda. Identifying Teddy's killer would be a bonus, of course. Nora takes up her pen. Rideout can stick to his brief little notes. If she wants to write a tome she will, if it helps her to tease out these puzzles.

Nora records, in her firm, clear hand, the details of her meeting with Helena. Wondering as she does, whether she ought to have pressed her further. But what more could Helena tell her about Frieda? The landlady appeared to live in such languid isolation—what would she know about her residents? And what about Dinah? Could the actions of this strange little girl have a bearing on the cases of a missing woman and a poisoned man? Dinah could have taken Frieda's necklace—didn't Rose say the child thieved? Dinah tried to drown a playmate in a pond—could she poison a grown man? On the morning of Teddy's death, she was safely locked in a sideboard, by her own hand or by another's. Either way she appeared to be out of the picture.

On a fresh page, Nora writes:

Rose Briggs was in the kitchen or dining room all morning, only bobbing out around 8:45 a.m. to buy milk when she caught up with the milkman. Rose is known to dawdle and shirk. On her return she notices the coffeepot has been used by Teddy or his killer in the kitchen while she was gone. Rose had free access to coffeepot, etc., and is known to prepare coffee.

She reads it back to herself. Satisfied, she starts on a new line.

Irene Rawlings left Gulls Nest just after dawn. Not forthcoming regarding destination. Has she an alibi? Forgot to platter meat.

Nora leaves another line, then:

Stella Atkins breakfasted with Bill Carter until 8 when she takes tray up to Professor Poppy. Reads to him for a while then requests more milk around 8:45. Continues to read to Poppy until Rose's return and then goes straight out. During Rose's absence she hears someone FAMILIAR WITH OPERATING THE STICKY DOOR gain entrance to the house. Stella had not seen Teddy that morning. Alibi: Professor Poppy.

Bill Carter left the house at 8:20 to meet a contact in town on (dodgy) business. Contact did not appear. No alibi until he reaches work at 9:30.

Helena Wells is unwell in her room all morning. No alibi.

Karel Ježek possibly absconded the morning of Teddy's death or the night before. Has he an alibi? God alone would probably know.

Nora rereads the last line and then crosses it out. She'll not bring the Big Man Himself into this. His absence has been marked from the start.

Professor Poppy, late to rise after a night of poor sleep, is read to and brought a tray. Alibi: Stella.

Nora regards the entry next to Poppy's name. Somehow it is not enough. That Poppy was close to Teddy is evident, not just at the time of the event but as demonstrated by his behavior ever since. Hasn't the old man taken to his bed with declining health? After Stella, he perhaps knew the young man better than anyone in the house. And what's more, he was the one to find the body. A softhearted auld man, genteel and shabby, charming and seemingly harmless. Was it feasible that he planted the poison? After all, he supplied the coffee Teddy drank. Nora balks at the idea, then promptly reminds herself to keep a clear head, for isn't everyone in this house a potential suspect?

Nora knocks several times before she hears a low groan. Professor Poppy is propped up in his bed. It is evident from his bleary expression that he has been dozing. Toby Dog, however, looks fully awake. He greets Nora with a sprightly tail wag but holds his position at the foot of the counterpane, proud in his tatty collar, youthful, despite his graying muzzle. The room is no cleaner than the last time Nora looked in. The fug of the bedridden hangs heavy in the air, uncleared crockery is stacked on piles of books. There is a sharp stink of an unemptied chamber pot along with the tang of the unwashed, strongest as Nora approaches Poppy's bedside. The old man is joined under his covers by the entire cast of his puppet show. A motley crew lined up on either side of his pillow: Punch and Judy, the constable and the baby, the crocodile and the doctor. Joey the Clown, obviously a favorite, rests in the crook of Poppy's arm. The skeleton leers from the bedside locker.

"You are taking no chances, Poppy?"

"As I said, these puppets have long been dear to me, man and boy."

"No sign of Jack Ketch?"

"Not a scrap of fabric, not a whisper of wood." He sniffs the air. "Prop open the door, throw open the window, get a draft going would you, Madam Breen? My quarters are a little ripe for polite company."

"I'm a nurse, Poppy."

"Even so." The old man looks embarrassed.

Nora does what he asks.

"Please," says Poppy, gesturing to a chair in the corner. "Take a pew. That's Stella's chair. That's where she used to perch to read to me."

Nora notes the past tense. "Hasn't she been in to see you?"

Poppy waves this question away with a frail hand.

Nora takes the seat, moving the pile of books.

"The top book—that's the one we were enjoying together. We like a grisly crime. Or rather, Stella and I like *reading* about it." He snorts. "From memory, on the day of poor Teddy's death we had just embarked on chapter thirteen, unlucky for some."

Nora glances at the cover, the cheap kind of detective novel sold at train stations. A beautiful woman with pointy cleavage looks out of the window of a gothic house, a mysterious man in a trilby and raincoat skulks in the dark street below. The title: *The Boardinghouse on Blood Street.*

"Apt," she says.

"Isn't it? We rollick through 'em. I like a feisty private eye and Stella likes a bit of romance and the guilty brought to task. Neither of us likes a vamp."

Nora opens the book; a strip of ribbon marks a spot not so many pages on from the beginning of chapter thirteen.

"Take it. I wouldn't have the heart to read it now."

Nora closes the book carefully and puts it on her lap. She glances around her. Considers. From this seat she has a view out of the nearby window down to the kitchen door and the residents' exit beside it. Albeit if she cranes her neck and leans backwards. Stella hadn't troubled herself when she heard the door opening after Rose had left to fetch the milk. Nora agrees that there isn't a clear view, but neither is it totally obscured.

"Did Stella sit here to read to you on the morning of Teddy's death?"

"She did."

"This chair hadn't been moved at all?"

"No. As I said: that's her usual spot."

"Do you remember hearing someone returning to the kitchen, after Rose left to get the milk?"

In the bed, Mr. Punch stirs, the bell on his cap tinkles. Poppy glances at the puppet; a warning frown.

He answers Nora. "Of that I have no recollection. I was probably absorbed in our fictional bloodbath."

Another voice, a high mocking scream, answers: "*You wazzz azzz-leep!*"

Nora—startled—can't help but laugh.

The old man raises his eyebrows. "Mr. Punch. I'll kindly ask you not to interrupt! Miss Breen is interrogating me."

"Ah now!"

"Dear, we all want to solve the puzzle of Teddy's death." Beside him, the red-faced constable puppet gives a solemn nod. "Proceed if you please, madam."

"Is that true: did you doze off while Stella was reading to you?"

"No."

Mr. Punch nods. "*Yezz.*"

With effort Poppy smothers the struggling puppet under the covers. Mr. Punch disappears. "Now, where were we. To answer your question: I did not fall asleep—with a book that compelling, Blood Street Boardinghouse—are you kidding? I was hanging on every word. I was riveted. You know the housekeeper did it? Calamity; I've given it away!"

Nora smiles.

Poppy's face becomes serious. He takes up his Judy puppet and with gentle hands covers her ears. "If I'm right and Teddy's killer had me in their sights, if that concoction was for me, not him, they may be coming back to finish me off."

"So, you believe the killer prepared the coffee for you, then Teddy came across it and accidentally drank it? Wouldn't anyone who knew—or had studied the habits of the residents of this house—be aware that Teddy was to be found in the workshop early in the morning, whereas you rise later?"

"I can't explain it." The old man frowns. "But perhaps you are right."

"Do you have some reason to think that someone might target you, Poppy?"

"If you're asking do I have enemies, not such as would be motivated to bump me off. But then what could be the motivation for killing dear young Teddy?"

Nora pats his hand.

The old man looks anxious. "Should I die in mysterious circumstances, will you do something for me?"

Nora hesitates. As a nurse she's made many promises to the religious sick. They are usually prayers or the writing of letters. The old man fixes her with bright eyes. Toby Dog watches her with all the intensity of his terrier nature. Poppy's puppets regard her with their grotesque leers.

"That depends on what you are asking. And haven't we established that you've no real enemies, why would anyone want to kill you, Poppy?"

"But I've done harm to others, nonetheless. I'd like to make a confession." He puts Judy back down on the bed, straightening the lifeless puppet. "Please bear with me, the unburdening of one's darkest secrets is not easy. I am full of shame."

Nora sees, not without pity, how the old man becomes full of emotion. His hands shake as he pulls the cover over him, his eyes become furtive.

"Where to start?"

"Take your time, Poppy."

He glances at her gratefully. "I have led a profligate life."

Mr. Punch rises from under the covers with a joyful screaming cackle.

Nora rolls her eyes.

"Seriously though, you look like a woman of the world."

Nora snorts.

"Well, not quite of this world. What I'm saying is that I have collected enemies through no fault of my own." His smile falters. "In the eyes of the law, God too, perhaps, I am a bad man. In my youth I loved the wrong person."

"Poppy, do you really need to divulge this?"

"If it has a bearing on that young man's death, why ever not?"

"And this long-ago love affair could make you the target of a poisoner?"

The old man shrugs. "Either that, or it's a member of my own family seeking to do me in. Aside from being a profligate I'm very rich. Estates full of game birds and deer, gracious stone houses stuffed with paintings and priceless vases. I expect my greedy heirs want me out of the way. Perhaps they've finally found me, lying low in my seaside lair?"

The baby puppet gives a thin wail, its head revolves slowly.

"I don't know what to make of you, Poppy. Is any of this true?"

The old man taps the side of his nose.

"You are an auld rogue."

Poppy smiles and sinks back into his pillows. The puppets seem to sag against him. An easy peace descends on the room.

Nora surprises herself by asking, "Who did you love?"

Emotions pass across his face like a choppy weather front. She waits.

"My father's groom. He had a harder time of it than me, he lost his position. But the scandal had to be managed."

"I'm sorry."

"Are you?" Poppy takes a breath. "Don't be. It was the making of me. I ran away from home, from all those deadening responsibilities and expectations. And thus, I became a professor of the open road, king of the billowing canvas, lord of seaside misrule. I would rather be propped up here choking on Irene's cooking than fossilizing in some manor house. Some can toe the line, but others have no choice but to cross it, isn't that the case?"

"Perhaps you are right." Nora is thoughtful. "You were close to Teddy?"

The old man meets her eye. "We had much in common."

Nora tries to frame the words, but Poppy looks away. He rummages in his bedside table, draws out a piece of tatty foolscap paper. He puts it on the bed and taps it, businesslike.

"Should the worst occur, my funeral is paid up."

"Poppy—"

"Promise me just one thing: should I die in mysterious circumstances you'll be there for Dinah."

Poppy reaches out his hand to her. Nora crosses the room and sits by his side.

"Please, she has few friends." Poppy looks closely at Nora. "Have you heard tales about my little girl?"

"Helena mentioned something."

"The pond incident?"

"Yes."

Poppy looks at her slyly. "In your quiet way you have made it your business to know everything about us, haven't you? Your predecessor was the same; always asking questions."

"You are referring to Frieda Brogan?"

"The same."

"What kind of questions?"

Poppy frowns at Nora. "Aren't we talking about Dinah?"

Two of the puppets in the bed nod decisively.

"To continue: the pond incident was entirely Helena's fault. She inflicted the washerwoman's dreadful daughter on Dinah, a noisy hoyden of a child. No real harm was done."

"But Dinah did try to hurt her?"

"Dinah tried to silence her," says Poppy waspishly. "Another matter entirely. As you know, Dinah communicates differently."

"She writes beautifully. You taught her?"

Poppy looks pleased. "She's a sharp little thing." Mr. Punch surfaces from under the bedcover and peers around.

"Mr. Punch here is very fond of Dinah. It takes one to know one."

"One what?"

"Anarchist. Mr. Punch loves those who do not attempt to control him. Those who dance to their own tune."

Nora is careful with her words. "Do you think Dinah is capable of silencing anyone else?"

Mr. Punch puts his head in his hands. "Are you asking if Dinah, my odd little sunbeam, dosed dear Teddy?"

Nora hesitates.

Poppy holds up his hand. "In answer: I don't think so. Teddy wasn't exactly on her 'like' list but neither did she terribly dislike him." He turns to Nora. "She likes you; did you know that?"

"I didn't."

"Which is why I am asking for your help. Look out for her, be her friend; you have a skill with the wayward. Think of her as an unruly plant: you might not be able to train her, but you could encourage her to grow in the right direction."

"Poppy, what makes you think I'll be staying around to do that?"

Poppy looks at Nora closely. "Take no offense; this is a flotsam and jetsam sort of place. I think you like that, don't you? The strays and the waifs that wash up here with their dark mysteries. Isn't that what you're after, a dark mystery?"

With a little, happy whine Toby gets up, wagging a greeting. Stella is standing at the door, her face pale and tearstained, but she is wearing a smile of the small brave kind.

When Poppy sees her, his eyes fill with tears. Mr. Punch gives a sad and solemn bow.

"Silly Poppy," she says.

"My poor darling," he says.

Stella and Nora take a turn about the garden at Poppy's urging, for Stella has barely left her room since Teddy's death. They take the circuit that Nora recently walked with Helena. Stella is quiet. Misery and exhaustion are written all over her face. Nora could point out the glories of the neglected garden, the bright leaves in the pond, the misty cobwebs on the bushes but somehow Stella would not see them. She is lost in some kind of unhappy musing. Nora offers up a prayer, at least, she makes a start, only the words sound hollow, ashen in her mind.

"Don't pay any mind to Poppy. He was asking you to look out for me, wasn't he? I'm quite fine you know."

"Doubtless he is worried about you, Stella, but it was Dinah he was asking me to take under my wing."

"His protégée. They play with those puppets for hours. He has her laughing, soundlessly mind. With him she's as sweet as anything."

"You find her difficult?"

"Me, not really. She never gives me any problems." A thought appears to hit her. "Goodness, do you mean to say Poppy is leaving Gulls Nest?"

"Not exactly."

"What is it? It's about Teddy, isn't it? I can tell from your face!"

Nora hesitates.

"Please, Nora, no one tells me anything now—I shall go and ask Poppy—interrogate him!"

"He has a notion that the coffee was meant for him, that Teddy was poisoned by accident."

Stella's eyes widen; the expression on her face is strangely hopeful. Then she shakes her head. "I love Poppy really, I do, but he is full of the most ridiculous nonsense. Who would want to kill that soft old thing?"

Confronted with the sight of Poppy's workshop, Stella stops short. "But who would want to kill my Teddy?"

Her tears begin again. She seeks Nora's shoulder and sobs there for a while. Nora strokes her hair, wishing that she had said nothing rather than cause further pain.

As Stella's sobs quieten, Nora notices a movement in the nearby bushes. Dinah is watching them with interest. Her eyes meet Nora's for an instant and then she is gone.

CHAPTER 12

Nora sits in her room by the window. It is the awkward hour between tea and supper, although today Nora is partaking of no solid meals. She has had a dose of food poisoning.

The culprit: almost certainly Irene's potted shrimp which Nora suspected had been served for supper two days ago only to be resurrected at yesterday's breakfast.

In her darkest hour she had wondered if Teddy's poisoner had not returned and decided to pick off another houseguest. But if it were cyanide, she would not be sitting up at the table with a cup of weak tea at her elbow. Living and breathing, just about. She wears a bed blanket around her shoulders for she has the window open, to converse with Father Conway and for the fortifying breeze around her still-green gills. The seagull fixes her with a belligerent look, his feathers puffed up against the October cold. Like her, he is enjoying the dying rays of a bright, cold, sun-washed day of glistening sand and sparkling sea.

"I am not resting on my laurels, whatever you might think."

The seagull looks doubtful.

"What would you have me do, Father? Make rash accusations, jump to the wrong conclusions?"

The seagull looks unimpressed.

Nora finds that creeping feeling returning. The one that was all but absent through her years as a Carmelite nun. Kept at bay by the starched veil and the dawn prayer and listening out for a voice that wasn't her own. How could she ever atone? After more than three decades the horror of the lie she told still grips her. An innocent man accused; the perpetrator left to go free.

Nora shared with no one what had happened to her in the field the night of her granny's wake. She had gone home, washed herself between her legs, mended her clothes, and prayed. It took her mother days to get the story from her, for she knew that something had altered her daughter. Nora had begged her mother not to tell her father, for somehow him knowing would deepen her shame. But this was too big a secret for her mother to bear alone. Nora's father made no mention of it, only now he was a man broken, all the joy had gone from him. Worst of all, he couldn't meet Nora's eyes. He began to make discreet inquiries about the men who attended the wake, the villagers known to them, the outsiders, less so. He wrote down names in a notebook he hid behind the dresser and brooded over late at night. The priest advised Nora's parents to take the matter no further. He would personally write to Mother Superior; it wouldn't be a barrier to the girl's vocation. The whole affair was to be buried and forgotten about.

Only, Nora's body was changing and she knew enough about life to realize what this meant. She considered drowning herself in the river. She considered jumping from the hayloft. Adding a sin to a crime. She prayed for God's forgiveness.

Then came the day when Nora caught her mother looking at her belly. The expression on her face, before she turned away, was that of sorrow. That night Nora's father came into her room. In his hand he carried his notebook. He opened it and laid it on Nora's bed.

A terrible hot shame washed through her. How was she to tell her father that she couldn't name the man? Somehow it made things worse. Complicit in some terrible way she couldn't understand. She looked through the list as her father waited. When she glanced up at him, she saw the anger and pain in his eyes. Nora offered a quick prayer for guidance then picked out a name she did not recognize.

The man she identified was an itinerant thatcher. He was gone from the village the next day. Nora told herself that with divine inspiration perhaps she had picked right. When rumor had it that a second girl in the village had been attacked, she dropped this pretense and prayed harder for forgiveness.

Nora was sent away, before the child inside her was discerned by the other villagers, although the gossips had long been at work. She knew she would never be allowed to return. It was a relief in a way to leave that sad house. Her mother weeping in the kitchen. Her father outside raking over the same patch of soil.

"I will not make the same mistake again: if I accuse someone they will be guilty."

Father Conway regards her unblinkingly. She feels the weight of his judgment.

And now the heat is returning to her and with it the queasiness. She throws off the blanket from round her shoulders and stares down the gull.

"And there's the professional, Inspector Rideout, saying there's no evidence and no kind of case."

The gull shakes his wings in a desultory fashion then skulks off down the window ledge.

She sips her tea. She resolves to open the envelope first.

A can of worms, she thinks, then on account of her churning stomach, instantly regrets the thought.

At first it is hard to look at so many images of her missing friend. There are close-in head shots and full-length photographs. Glancing at the backs she sees they are dated in light pencil, the first photograph being only a week or so after Frieda's arrival in Gore-on-Sea. She begins to arrange them in order and gradually they tell a story of some kind. The earliest show Frieda as she knew her, clear-eyed and open-faced and smiling. But gradually other expressions are at play: Frieda ignoring the camera, playing with her hair, resting her chin on her hands with a look of sarcastic amusement. In the last portrait, just a few days before she disappeared, she looks dead at the camera: it's unflinching. A young woman, tired-looking but confident, resolute, entirely herself. A portrait that would attest to the closeness of photographer and sitter. Perhaps they were lovers; they were almost certainly friends. For a moment Nora feels a surge of envy; all these many faces of Frieda, some of them unknown to her.

She puts the photographs carefully away. They tell her little other than perhaps Frieda at Gore-on-Sea was more complicated than Frieda at High Dallow. Why wouldn't that be so. Out here there were all these other voices, influences, experiences.

With her musings she has not noticed the gull draw near. He lets rip with a startling keen.

"Merciful Jesus. Haven't I told you not to do that?"

The gull cackles and takes to the sky.

"Next time you'll be getting the potted shrimp, Conway."

Nora frowns and considers now Irene's face as she served the shrimp. Hadn't her instincts warned her against spreading it on that dry auld bit of toast? Hadn't Irene stood there and watched until she bit into it? As she left the room wasn't there the slightest of victorious smiles on Irene's face?

The housekeeper did it.

She thinks of Professor Poppy's book. *The Boardinghouse on Blood Street.* It has proved good company on her many trips to the privy. In the story the housekeeper is also sour. But this one is tall and hatchet-faced and a decent cook. The amateur detective is a beautiful young heiress, a woman with her own mystery, a tragic romance behind her. Jesus, who would want to read about a failed old nun with her stipend and secondhand shoes?

With no sign of Father Conway returning and every sign of dusk falling, Nora turns to her notebook.

Dating the entry, she realizes that tomorrow is Irene Rawlings's day off.

CHAPTER 13

Before the guests awake and Rose arrives to serve the breakfast, Irene Rawlings leaves Gulls Nest by the back door. Moments later so does Nora Breen. Irene heads down into town and up towards the station, stopping only to bob into a bakery. Perhaps not expecting to be followed, Irene is not acting furtive but then she has yet to reach the destination that she was so unprepared to disclose when questioned. Still, Nora takes every precaution not to be seen, ducking into doorways or skulking into alleyways, the early-morning darkness affording her some cover. And Nora has planned for this excursion. She has appropriated a buff raincoat and dreary headscarf from the boardinghouse's left and lost property box which allow her to blend in among the few commuters heading into the train station far better than the puce monstrosity would have. Irene buys a ticket and several moments later Nora does the same.

"I'm going where she's going."

The station officer raises his eyebrow, takes her money, and offers negligible change.

When the train arrives Nora boards the carriage behind Irene's. At each station, she looks out, until Irene disembarks halfway between Gore-on-Sea and London at a small station in a nondescript village. Nora scrabbles to follow, ignoring the glances of the commuters that have boarded her carriage at each stop.

Irene sets out from the station at a surprising clip, her round shape squeezed into a well-worn but clean suit and cape. Unlike most off-duty chars her hat is plain without trimmings. That she is musing over something is evident; she moves with her eyes on the road and her chin jutting forward. Her bag is hooked high on her arm. She looks entirely indomitable, as if she's on some kind of mission and heaven help anyone who would stop her. The privet hedges and wide driveways of nicely appointed houses give way to fields and the path, which is muddy in parts. Irene picks her way through what appears to be a familiar route to her. A few times, perhaps sensing she is being followed, she glances around her. When this happens, Nora aims herself through a hedge or over a wall. By the time they reach Irene's destination Nora is muddy of foot and skirt and has lost her hat and gained some leaves—but she has not blown her cover, as they say in the detective books. On this she congratulates herself, stealth being a premium skill for a good investigator.

At first Irene's big secret looks like a country estate. Nurses push patients in wheelchairs around flower beds. Other patients sit out along the veranda under blankets. Nora follows Irene through the gates.

Irene passes from the echoing foyer and into a maze of corridors. Nora keeps as close as she dares. When Irene glances behind her, Nora ducks into a staff changing room.

Here she furnishes herself, quite opportunistically, with a uniform she finds hanging on a peg. The disguise couldn't be better. As a visitor Nora would attract attention, as a nurse she can move about unhindered. Only, now she has lost Irene. Most of the wards are allocated for men, the majority of patients suffering from life-altering injuries sustained during the war. She finds a few female wards and scours them with a mad and hopeful notion in her head—what if Frieda is here? So engrossed is she with this thought that stepping along a corridor she almost misses sight of a nurse coming out of one of the private rooms, and in that room, sat by the window, Irene Rawlings and a young man who has suffered profound facial injuries.

It is only a glimpse, but in that moment, Irene looks up and meets Nora's eyes. If there is recognition there, Nora does not see it. What she does see is a very different expression than Irene usually wears. A tender sadness. A hopeless sympathy.

The door closes, and Nora moves on down the corridor.

Mrs. Rawlings's journey is twice as long as her allotted visiting time, bless her. Visitors usually only get an hour, whatever distance they travel. Nora learns this from an orderly in the sluice room. And she never misses a visit; she was of course here last week; she would be here next week. George's mother is a rock for him. The same could not be said for his wife; she visited once and sniffed behind a handkerchief, and, being the dramatic sort, left protesting a headache. And there was poor George with everything he had suffered. She would not even look the young man in his remaining eye. George is in good spirits, considering. He took his injuries from a land mine three days before VE Day. Poor bastard.

And now here is Matron. Will the new sister go and take George Rawlings's vital signs?

She will.

Nora watches Irene wind her way down the corridor. There's a different step to her than she arrived with. Uncertain, less than buoyant. As she turns the corner Nora can see the woman's face fall. Irene Rawlings is human and feels deeply. Nora goes quietly into George's room.

The young man's chair is by the window. He fixes her with one bright blue eye, a twist of a smile, a polite nod. George has submitted to many operations to repair his face and body; grafts and scars cover most of his head and neck.

"George, I'm here to do the usual checks. Is that all right with you?"

He nods slightly and makes a sound.

Nora sets about the work she's done a thousand times before; it calms her mind, the routine of it. She works gently. The room is warm and clean. Outside well-wrapped patients and tidy nurses drift across the lawn.

Her eye is taken by a framed photograph, amongst others, on George's bedside locker. It is Helena Wells.

When Nora looks back George is watching her.

"Is that your wife, George?"

George shrugs, his eye lit.

"She's very beautiful."

A low sound in George's throat affirms that she is. He nods towards the photograph; he wants it. Nora goes to the locker; next to the frame, under a little heart-shaped shell, is a drawing. One of Dinah's; she has signed it with a flourish.

"Dinah is an artist. Is this your daughter?"

George nods, the smile again.

Nora looks at the drawing: giant rabbits hop through a tangled garden. In the background, a house with eyes at every window.

"She's an imagination for herself, hasn't she?"

George gives a snorting laugh.

"Does Dinah come visiting too?"

George gives a slight shake of his head and looks away. Nora brings the framed photograph to him, setting it on the tray over his chair. George gazes at the picture for the longest moment, then with a look of frustration, reaches out a twisted hand and topples it.

* * *

Nora finds it harder to leave the convalescent home than to enter it, what with an emergency on one ward, a missing patient on another. She realizes how much she has missed feeling useful, efficient. She has a clear place here and a uniform, a purpose. She looks in again on George before she leaves. He is sleeping. Helena Wells is still facedown.

She hurries for the train and reaches the platform just as it pulls in. So intent is Nora on boarding that she does not see the figure behind her. Settling gratefully in her seat she looks up into the furious face of Irene Rawlings.

"So, now you think you know the story?"

Nora says nothing. She is waiting for the fury to abate, knowing behind it is a terrible, impotent sadness.

"What is wrong with you that you would follow a woman on her day off? That you would stick your bloody nose into her business?"

Nora nods. Perhaps it is time to level with Irene. And so, in a voice born of decades of appeasing community squabbles, she lays her case on the line.

Irene listens, then softens, but only slightly. "Why didn't you say you knew Frieda?"

"I had a hunch that it might be something I ought to keep to myself."

"So, you lied to us?"

This conversation feels dreadfully familiar. "No," says Nora firmly. "I just didn't disclose the whole picture. Would it have made a difference? Or would people just think I was mad, abandoning my vocation to find a young friend who'd drifted into town and could just as soon drift away again?"

Irene thinks about this a moment and seems to accept it. She opens her bag and rummages about. Extracting a roll of mints, she pops one contemplatively in her mouth and then offers the packet to Nora.

Nora nods her thanks, tries one, instantly regrets it; the mints are eye-wateringly powerful.

"Extra strong," says Irene.

"Bracing," Nora gasps.

"So," says Irene, "are you disappointed that I have a cast-iron alibi?"

"You were never my top suspect."

"You haven't read *The Boardinghouse on Blood Street*, then? I passed that one on to the old man."

"It seems you're not that kind of housekeeper after all."

Irene smiles, a real smile. It lights her face. Nora gets a sense of how Irene perhaps used to be, before the years, before George was injured.

"I'm sorry about your son. You must be heartbroken."

"Must I?" Irene's voice is sharp. "Are you a mother?"

Nora's breath catches. She can't answer.

"Don't presume to tell me how I feel." Irene's voice softens. "George is not dead and that is a blessing. As for what I feel, it's not important."

Nora looks out the window. The train is speeding out past the village. Houses, lanes, cars waiting at the crossing, all those lives lived. She suddenly feels envious of Irene. To know where her child is when she lies down to sleep at night. To be part of his story.

What of her own child? The baby who left Nora's empty arms aching. Where is she now? Had she survived? Had she lived through the war? Is she happy? Has she children of her own now? Does she know that she is loved? That her mother is in the world, sat on a train looking out at sky and fields, thinking about her?

"I didn't mean to be harsh with you, Nora."

Nora looks up.

Irene gestures to her face. "Have you a hankie?"

Nora, suddenly aware of her tears, fishes in her pocket, apologizes. Takes a moment to regain her composure.

"We have a way to go. And knowing you, there are bound to be a load of bleeding questions." Irene smiles to lighten the mood. "Fire away."

Nora laughs, sniffs, and considers. "You visit every week they said up at the home."

"George is my world. Always has been. A brighter, more loving lad you could not find."

Nora looks for words of comfort, until she sees the expression on Irene's face—pride keeping the tears at bay.

"Don't you tell me that God works in mysterious ways, or gives us only what we can bear, or any of that claptrap." Irene hesitates. "I'm sorry, I don't mean to be disrespectful."

"I'm the last person to hazard a guess at how God works; the Big Man Above and myself are not seeing eye to eye at the moment."

"That's your business."

They sit in silence for a while. Somewhere the conductor is checking tickets. Nora hears his raised voice.

"But I don't doubt it took guts to leave your order."

Nora nods.

"Well, I hope you find out what happened to the girl. She was nice—Frieda. She had a lovely way about her."

Nora is uneasy about the past tense.

Irene continues. "She didn't seem the kind to go off like that, but it happens. The young are inclined to be less steady, aren't they? Consequences can go out the window. A bit of freedom can go right to the head."

"Frieda wasn't giddy in the slightest." Nora's voice sounds more strident than she intended. She glances at Irene. "I knew her, that's all."

Irene nods. "I have the things she left behind, if it would help to see them. I kept them in case she came back. Would it help to see them, give you a clue?"

Nora nods.

"Well now, I know your secret and you know mine."

"Helena Wells is your daughter-in-law."

"She is not." Irene's face hardens again.

"They didn't marry," reasons Nora. "Why?"

Irene lowers her voice. "She already had a husband in London, an eminent doctor, no less."

Nora thinks of the drawing in George's room. "Dinah is your grand-daughter."

"So she says: I see nothing of George in her."

Irene looks out of the window again. The train has gained speed, the villages and towns, fields and outlying farms rush past.

"Her husband didn't want a scandal, you see," she continues. "He paid her off and I threw my bit of money in too and we bought Gulls Nest. It seemed the best thing to do at the time." Irene frowns. "I didn't know her as well as I do now and George adored her, of course."

"And then George was injured?"

Irene nods. "And I soon saw a different side to Madam. She would never visit; she blamed the headaches, brought on by the upset of seeing George injured. Helena thinks of herself first and foremost."

"And what of Dinah?"

"Another headache, although not for her mother; she has always let the girl run wild. To be honest, the child was born wrong."

Nora frowns. She will let this go for now. "Does Dinah know what relation she is to you and George?"

"She does."

"She doesn't visit him?"

Irene shakes her head. "The devil himself couldn't make Dinah leave Gulls Nest. And besides, that convalescent home is no place for a child.

As for the rest, the residents and the folk we know at Gore-on-Sea, we keep it to ourselves. It's nobody's business but our own. There are many widows since the war, it is easier to keep it like that."

"And Helena's husband?"

"On finding out that she'd been carrying on, he made an agreement with her. He was at an important stage in his career, he couldn't afford a scandal. She agreed to disappear quietly and stay away. *Like a toad under a rock* were his words, I believe." Irene bites her lip. "He hasn't changed his opinion since that time."

"How do you know?"

"A few weeks ago, I contacted him. It's George, you see, the home is increasing the fees. I want him to have the best, he deserves the best. Gulls Nest makes no money."

The reasons for Irene's mean-spirited housekeeping becomes clear to Nora.

"So, I went to ask her husband for more money."

"At Helena's urging?"

"She knew nothing about it." Irene's face reddens. "I told him that he must pay more for her silence, for her toeing the line with the story he had spun about her."

"Which was?"

"She had moved to Switzerland for the air. If the high society circles he moved in only knew she was a seaside landlady with a bastard child . . ." Irene takes a deep breath. "At that he became fierce angry. Oh, the language and from a professional man!"

"Well, you were trying to blackmail him, Irene."

Irene wrinkles her nose. "I might have saved myself the trouble."

"What did he say?"

"He told me that if Helena raised her head again, he'd knock it off."

The train jolts, the refreshment trolley rolls by. The two women stay silent, each with her own thoughts.

"Have you told Inspector Rideout about your visit to Helena's husband?"

Irene is defensive. "I have not. Why should he know anything about it?"

Nora frowns. "Professor Poppy has a theory; that Teddy drank poison that wasn't meant for him, that could have been prepared for another resident."

Irene gives a little bleak laugh. "A physician of note, a society man, travels to a seaside town to knock off his cheating wife?"

"He could have instructed someone else to do it?"

"For a religious sister you have a very dim view of people, don't you?" Irene turns to watch the landscape unfolding, her bag clenched on her knee.

And Nora watches Irene.

CHAPTER 14

Irene has an errand to run before heading up to Gulls Nest. Nora feels relief at the prospect of a solitary walk, the two of them a little awkward with one another, as acquaintances who have shared too much.

The days are shortening on winter's approach, but the sun is making a last effort as it sinks down to the horizon, torching the waves into ripples of light. The sea is a constant presence in this town, glimpsed at the ends of alleyways, or felt in the quality of air, more invigorating, more abrasive than inland. And then there are ever-present seagulls, turning and gliding, mewling and screaming.

Nora drifts down the lane towards Mr. Hosmer's photographic studio. On her approach she is accosted by an image.

Nora Firecracker. Dressed in no more than a gold curtain, striding off frame, leaning back to look right at the camera. Strong-jawed, challenging of gaze. An older woman and sensual for that, the bare shoulders round, the turn of the leg lovely. She hardly recognizes herself.

A car pulls up on the road behind her. She drags her eyes away from her portrait.

Inspector Rideout winds down his driver's side window. "I'm surprised you are not up at Gulls Nest, apparently there is quite a blowup. I'm on my way to referee."

Nora hopes he doesn't notice the portrait and then she hopes that he does. Either way she feels annoyed with herself.

"Karel Ježek has returned, which rather puts paid to your theory that he murdered Teddy Atkins."

"It wasn't my theory, it was Stella's."

Rideout leans over, opens the passenger door. "Give you a lift?"

Nora gets in.

Rideout is pristine today in tweed and smelling of some delicious woody soap, his mustache waxed neatly, his hair parted with accuracy. He glances up at Hosmer's shop window and throws Nora a grin. "What would Mother Superior say?"

Nora squashes any rising shame this question might provoke and settles him with a frosty glare. "I think she would have loved it. She was wonderfully open-minded."

Rideout pushes the car into gear, his grin widening.

They meet Stella on her way down to town, walking quickly with a vanity case in hand, her face set and dreadfully pale. When she looks up at them her expression is momentarily angry.

Rideout pulls over and jumps out of the car. Nora watches, as after a brief exchange, the inspector takes Stella's case and leads her round to the side of the car, opening the door for her. She hesitates before getting in.

Nora turns in her seat. "Stella?"

But Stella resolutely looks away. She has the air of a captured truant.

Gulls Nest is ominously still. The front door lies wide open, the hallway is empty. Rideout leaves the car on the gravel drive and springs out.

"Take Mrs. Atkins into the parlor."

"I told you: I will not go back into the house, not while *he* is in there," Stella hisses. "Would you have me share a house with a *murderer?*"

Rideout glances at Nora with exasperation.

Nora speaks softly. "Stella, I'll sit with you. We can close the door."

Stella glumly assents, allowing Nora to leave her case in the hallway. Stella settles in the easy chair while Nora lights a fire. The young woman is shivering but she refuses a blanket.

"I can't stay here any longer. Why won't the inspector let me leave? It's like I'm the criminal. Will you talk to him?"

Stella is at breaking point, Nora thinks. She kneels in front of her and takes her hand. "Leave the investigation to the detective inspector, Stella. He knows what he's doing."

"That's rich." Stella pulls her hand away. "If he's doing such a great job, why are you always snooping about asking questions?"

The sound of footsteps on the gravel drive and Stella is up and looking out.

"He's taking him away." Her voice is jubilant. "The inspector has arrested him."

Nora joins Stella at the window to see Rideout walking back to the car, only now he's accompanied by Karel Ježek. The small man looks even more diminished, his greatcoat swamping him, his brow furrowed. The two men reach the car, then Karel, buttoning up his coat, strides out along the drive, turning right, in the direction of the promenade.

Stella turns to Nora in pained confusion. "He's let him go."

Rideout is unapologetic. He has no grounds to arrest Karel Ježek. He merely asked him to put across his version of events on the morning of Teddy's death. Rideout glances towards the parlor window, where Stella stands watching.

"Has he an alibi?" Nora asks.

"Of sorts," says Rideout. "He was traveling. It's something we can check."

Nora nods. "Stella is adamant, she won't retract her accusation."

Rideout's voice takes on an ironic tone. "Even she must see it's unlikely that a murderer would return to the scene of the crime."

"Is it unlikely?" asks Nora. "I would have thought it fairly common; it is in detective novels."

Rideout throws her a look.

Nora returns it. "Why stop Stella from leaving? Why must she stay?"

"I've no grounds to keep her." He gets into his car. "Other than the prevention of a woman in her condition stampeding into town. You profess to be a practical woman; help her to see sense, Miss Breen."

Rideout has the car turned in the drive before the word leaves Nora's mouth.

"Gobshite."

Stella has gone from the parlor when Nora returns, her vanity case abandoned in the hall. Nora takes it up to find Stella has locked herself in her room. She can hear the abandoned sobbing. There's nothing for Nora to do, except say a prayer out of habit to whoever might be listening.

CHAPTER 15

Nora wakes in the night to a high harsh scream. It buzzes in her ears, familiar and shrill. She sits up in the bed, but the house is silent, only perhaps the light creak of feet on floorboards, which could be the night-time sound of the house settling. She finds herself drenched in sweat but this is no new thing.

A glance at the sky tells her nothing; the nights are long, and the mornings are slow to brighten. She checks the luminous dial of her alarm clock: a little after midnight. She listens and hears nothing but the wind and the sea. Lulled, Nora falls back to sleep.

It is as if only moments have passed when she hears a frantic knocking at her door: it is a gray morning and here is Stella, distraught and near speechless. She leads a barefoot Nora across the corridor.

Nora sees the dog first. Toby lies at the foot of the bed, his bright eyes dim now, his muzzle flecked with spittle, his tongue blue. His master's body is tangled in the sheets, on his face a terrified grimace.

Nora blesses herself without realizing. "What devil have you seen?" she whispers.

The remaining inhabitants of Gulls Nest collect in the parlor. Rose serves strong tea but only Bill Carter drinks it. Nora regards them; they are a grim-faced lot, herself included. She considers the last time they were collected like this. Only that time Professor Poppy sat in the chair that Stella is now occupying, her eyes downcast, a handkerchief in her fist. Nora is thankful that Karel Ježek is not present. Irene sits square and resentful nearest the door. The slight swaying of the curtain marks Dinah's presence. Now and again Bill glances in that direction but most of the time, as he sips his tea, his eyes fall on Helena. The lovely Mrs. Wells has taken a chair by the window, where she regards the ambulance and police car pulled up on her driveway.

Constable Griggs pops his head around the doorway and asks whether Miss Breen would kindly come to the dining room, where Nora finds Inspector Rideout standing by the fireplace, as dapper as a leading man. Only his face betrays an agitation Nora has not seen before: a deep-furrowed frown and a tightness to the jaw.

He does not greet her but merely waves his cigarette at the table. "Take a look."

Nora peers down at a small metal square lying on a clean cloth. "What is it?"

"It's called a swazzle," says Rideout. "Look closely and you'll see the reeds that make the sound."

Nora is mystified. "The sound of what?"

"Mr. Punch's voice. The doctor fished it out of his throat."

"He choked on it. And the dog?"

"Poisoned. The doctor puts the time of Poppy's death to somewhere between—"

"It was midnight," says Nora. "I heard him scream."

"But you didn't go and investigate?"

"I thought I was having a nightmare."

"Unfortunate." Rideout throws her a look. "Or perhaps fortunate for you. The time would fit."

"So, you don't think *he* died by his own hand?"

"Not unless he rammed that swazzle down his own neck."

"What about the dog? Someone must have killed it?"

"Must they have? Is it not impossible that the dog ate some of the tainted bait left down by Irene for the rabbits?"

Nora frowns. "It's too much of a coincidence."

"Yes, you're likely right. With the dog dead it would be easier for the killer to creep about the house."

Hearing Rideout talk of creeping killers sets Nora shivering. She has a thought. "Karel Ježek—"

"He's off the hook, for this one at least. Mr. Ježek spent last night at the Gore-on-Sea Royal Infirmary. He was dropped beaten and senseless on the doorstep just after pub closing time. I've to go on to talk to him after. Assuming he's regained consciousness by then."

"I'll come with you."

"You won't."

"You want me to keep my coulter out?"

Rideout swallows a smile. "If by *coulter* you mean *nose,* then yes."

"I can't promise anything." Nora gets up to leave. "Go easy on Stella, will you? She's not quite herself."

"Well, she doesn't have to worry about Mr. Ježek returning to Gulls Nest, for a while at least."

"His injuries are that bad?"

"I'm afraid so."

Nora heads to the door.

The inspector's voice follows her. "Not every sudden death is a murder, you know."

"I didn't say a thing, Rideout."

"You didn't have to, Breen."

CHAPTER 16

Karel Ježek is in a bad way. The nurse helpfully mistakes Nora for a concerned relative, leads the way to his bedside. It's a well-run ward, Nora notes as she passes a row of metal-framed beds on a polished floor. There are a small number of patients, all of them in an acute condition. The nurse quietly conducts her behind the green fabric screen and Nora rapidly makes her own assessment. The slight young man appears to have suffered a sustained assault with most of the damage to the left-hand side of the face. His nose is broken, and there is significant bruising and laceration visible among the bandages.

Nora has not seen injuries this bad since Sister Winifred was stampeded by a herd of dairy cows.

Sister Trigg adds a cranial injury, broken ribs, and a bruised spleen to the list. "He's very lucky to be here. He's a tough young man, isn't he? Despite his appearance."

"And the head injury?"

"Too early to tell, I'm afraid." Sister Trigg gives Nora a sympathetic smile. "Would you like to sit with him awhile? You can talk to him; he may hear everything we say, you know."

Nora looks at Karel's hands; his knuckles are unblemished. "He didn't fight back."

The nurse shakes her head. "He was likely set upon without warning. He took a blow to the top of his head."

"His assailant was taller than him."

"Quite possibly. And they went all out to do damage."

"Can you put a time on the attack?"

"Just before midnight we think. He was dropped here not long after; whoever brought him had a vehicle, the night porter heard it driving off."

"Did they leave a name, whoever found him?"

"They didn't. He was dropped outside the emergency door, I believe." Sister Trigg takes her leave. "Whoever they were, they saved your lad's life."

Nora sits for a while with Karel Ježek and ponders. The attack is so obviously an assault on an unwitting victim. There is an innocence to his face; with his delicate features and slim body he seems much younger than his years. He was a handsome lad, he will be again, although his injuries will alter him. Nora wonders at the hatred and suspicion the otherwise kindly Stella has for him. That the young man had an argument with her husband was clear but to peg Teddy's murder on Karel is another matter. But then sometimes frightened people look for a scapegoat when their questions go unanswered and their fears unassuaged. That dark thought rises in Nora's mind again and she wonders if there was something between Stella and Karel, that the young woman's anger might be misplaced guilt and shame.

The trundle of the medicine trolley signals a ward round. Nora has stayed way past the visiting hour.

She touches Karel's hand gently. "Hang in there, lad. I'll be back as soon as you are awake, then you can tell me your side of the story."

Nora calls by the nurses' station, stopping to thank Sister Trigg.

"About the young man's effects," says the nurse. "I don't think he'll be needing them for a while, would you take them?"

Nora would.

Moments later she finds herself in possession of a large paper bag and searching Gore-on-Sea infirmary for a quiet spot. She finds one in a little chapel just down the corridor from the X-ray department. The chapel is not much bigger than a broom cupboard but boasts wooden pews and a stained-glass window. Nora is impressed. She takes a pew towards the back and opens the bag.

At the top, folded neatly, is Karel's greatcoat. It smells strongly of stale beer and tobacco but also of the hedgerow and the sea. Nora realizes that this coat is quite simply an old-time traveling cloak. She feels certain that the young man has spent many a night sheltering in it, that it is a friend to him. Below the coat are his boots, equally worn and weather-stained. A battered box camera completes Karel Ježek's worldly goods. All have been blood-spattered, although care has been taken to sponge the worst of it off.

Nora glances up at the altar and mutters a precautionary prayer for forgiveness to no one in particular, then she begins to rifle through the pockets.

She finds a battered coin purse, all but empty. A small tin of pilchards, a smooth piece of green sea glass, and a photograph.

The photograph is battered, as is the little leather wallet frame that has kept it in one piece. Nora is only slightly disappointed that it is not of Frieda, although what would that really prove other than they were lovers perhaps. That they were close she can already tell from Karel's portraits. This photograph is of two boys, outside a single-story cottage. Nora very gently works the picture loose and turns it over—she is rewarded. She reads the faint ink on the back:

September 1939
Theo and John,
Cuddfan

The faces are just sharp enough to recognize: Teddy Atkins, around twelve, and Karel Ježek perhaps a little younger. Only Karel is smiling.

Teddy and Karel—*Theo and John*—were known to one another, long before they both came to be at Gulls Nest.

Nora tucks the boots and coat and other items back into the bag. She will put it in his room at Gulls Nest until he needs his things again. The photograph in the leather frame she will hold on to for now. She'll tell Rideout about it when he shows an inclination to listen.

At the desk Nora asks who was on shift when the man identified as Karel Ježek was deposited on the infirmary doorstep. She's in luck; the porter who found him is working today.

Frank is older, wiry, and with a dogged jut to his chin. He found the lad on the doorstep, a great deal of blood; he was certain he was a goner. As to the vehicle that brought him, well, Frank heard it more than saw it—something throaty, sporty. One thing Frank is sure about: whoever saved that lad didn't want any notoriety for it; they weren't hanging about.

On the way to the police station Nora mulls over the information on the back of Karel's obviously treasured photograph. Mr. Hosmer had intimated that Karel was not who he said he was and certainly not from Prague. So, he was using an alias but is John his real name?

She considers the word *Cuddfan*. A family name perhaps, or the name of a village, or the long low house in the background of the photograph? It is decidedly Welsh-sounding.

On her arrival at the police station, the waiting room is empty and the red-faced desk sergeant is nowhere to be seen. From the sound of swearing and roaring coming from the door to the cells, Nora deduces that any resident coppers are grappling someone into custody.

Nora takes the desk sergeant's place. A rifle through the daybook of the station's calls and visits tells her little she doesn't know: the serious assault on Mr. Ježek, the end of Mr. Poppy. The day of Teddy's death was a quiet morning at the station until the lad sent down from Gulls Nest arrived to get help. She turns back further, to the date of Frieda's disappearance. There is nothing remarkable to be read in the police notes, only that a complaint was made against Percy Ladd, who had been seen speeding through town at an ungodly hour. Driving too fast, the reporting officer noted drily, was a regular offense on Percy's part.

Nora copies the entry into her own notebook. This done, her mind returns to the puzzle of Karel's photograph. Who, if not the police, would stand a chance of identifying a long low house and two wartime boys somewhere, if the name was anything to go by, in Wales?

Her eye falls on the station telephone.

It is a common misconception, Nora knows, that a sister in an enclosed order has no interest in the external world. She has often found the opposite to be true: nuns may be insular, but they are not indifferent. The network of nuns up and down the country can spread news just as efficiently as the most diligent of local gossips, only the intent behind a carried story might be a little different. Through prayer requests and petitions, recreation time and letter writing, the world reaches into the furthest cloister and is heard and answered by the most obscure sister.

Knowing this, Nora lifts the receiver of the station telephone and asks the operator to connect her to the Carmelite monastery in Dolgellau. The phone rings for a long time. In her mind Nora sees the patter of sandaled feet down well-scrubbed stone corridors. The flutter of veil and skirts along cloisters, in and out of pockets of light and shade. The phone is answered by the lay sister Anwen.

The word *Cuddfan* is easy to decipher, says Anwen; it means *hide-away*. She would hazard a guess that it refers to the house. She listens carefully to Nora's description and asks questions about the appearance of the children and their surroundings such as Nora can make out. She'll ask around, she says.

Nora thanks her.

"Did you find Frieda Brogan?"

Nora is surprised not that this news has traveled but that it has been shared so quickly. "How did you know about Frieda?"

"Sister Ludivina of the Mystery of the Cross has not long joined our community. She has all the talk."

Nora smiles. "That she does."

"She said that you left your Order to look for Frieda."

"I left the Order. I'm looking for Frieda. Two separate issues."

"And God willing you'll find her." Another pause. "Then you'll go back?"

"No."

Silence on the other end, then, in a tone of quiet pity. "God bless you, Sister—"

"Nora, I'm just Nora now."

Anwen's voice is different now, efficient, impersonal, as if a connection between them has been broken. Nora is just a supplicant like any other, wanting prayers to cure gout or bankruptcy. "I will respond to the number you are presently calling from with my findings."

"Be sure to ask for a note sent up to me at Gulls Nest."

"The very place where Frieda Brogan disappeared?"

"Yes."

"The blessings of the Holy Family upon you; mind how you go, Nora."

As Nora walks back up the hill towards Gulls Nest, Anwen's words echo about her mind. *The very place where Frieda Brogan disappeared. Mind how you go.* It has never occurred to Nora to feel afraid at Gulls Nest but now it is different. What if whoever dealt with Frieda and the others deals with her? Frieda was inquisitive, Nora asks questions, what's the difference? In a house like Gulls Nest, curiosity might prove fatal.

Nora advises herself to tighten the screws. She must not give up hope. Frieda may yet be alive and out there somewhere. Besides, two residents of Gulls Nest remain unquestioned; they may yet have insights or clues crucial to her investigation. Although Nora predicts that neither will give up their story easily. Karel Ježek, she reassures herself, is going nowhere. Yet she must give him time to recover before returning to the infirmary to speak to him.

That leaves one resident—a dangerously curious individual—whose story Nora must somehow hear.

CHAPTER 17

Finding Dinah is easier said than done. Nora starts with all the obvious places: the dining room sideboard, the curtains. She calls from the top of the house to the bottom of the garden. The child is likely upset and grieving over the death of her friend Poppy, for the two were close. Nora takes this up with the others, but no one seems concerned. Rose hasn't seen Dinah for days, Irene says the same but there is no reason for alarm; the food they set out for her disappears and there are signs of life in the sticky handprints left here and there and the dirt walked in on the floor. It is common for Dinah to disappear, they say, especially if she thinks she is in trouble. Nora asks why would Dinah think she is in trouble? The others have no idea, there's no rhyme or reason to the girl. Nora decides to set some bait, as she would with any shy and wild creature.

Nora has obtained a brand-new notebook and a set of coloring pencils. She picks a clearing in the garden, the sundial on the mossy lawn, and she props up the book there. Attached to the book is a label bearing Dinah's name. Nora takes up her position, squeezed uncomfortably in a nearby bush, and waits. For a while nothing. Nora doesn't mind waiting; the day is lovely. The breeze stirs the leaves on the lawn into a waltz and a songbird gives a high clear song from a nearby tree and up through the branches the sky is a pure and brilliant blue without a cloud in it. Some leaves still cling to their branches, richly colored, trembling. A sudden rustle: Nora looks back to the sundial, but her bait has gone.

Nora follows in the direction of the rustle. Clearing a few bushes, she discerns a maze of passageways in the shrubs, too big for a rabbit or a fox. These are child-size. Ahead branches twang and wave as if they are calling her on. There is nothing for it. Nora drops to her hands and knees and begins to crawl.

The earth gives off the autumn smell of bonfires and dark days; the passages are made of beaten-down grass, sometimes slimy, sometimes muddy. All around branches and brambles have been shaped and sometimes tied. That Nora is in Dinah's wonderland she does not doubt; on turning corners or joining new passageways she finds treasures displayed: a row of strung beads, a broken jug, and a doll's head. Nora doggedly crawls as the undergrowth becomes thicker and more oppressive. Her clothes are wet, her hands and knees are filthy, she suspects she has twigs in her hair. She comes to a fork in the passageway and takes the side that looks to turn towards the light, having no real idea of where she is heading. There is a slight slope downward and then she sees a glimpse of lawn. Nora crawls towards it.

"Can I help you at all?"

The voice is gentle and utterly polite. Nora looks up at a man in curious attire. He wears a long apron of a butcher's kind, heavily pocketed. Most of the pockets contain sensible gardening objects: twine, hand forks, and suchlike. The topmost pocket, positioned over the man's heart, contains a small brown rabbit.

Nora straightens up, fully aware of her disheveled appearance.

Noting the high wall to the side of her and the man's clerical collar she makes quick deductions.

"I have come through the wall it seems; this is the vicarage?"

"Correct!" The man peers down at her. "Resident of Gulls Nest?"

"Yes. Nora Breen."

"Reverend Audley. Pleasure. You wouldn't be the first to visit by tunnel." The vicar and his rabbit both study Nora with inquisitive eyes. "Would you care to join us for afternoon tea?"

"I would, thank you."

Nora takes a seat at the table on the terrace. The housekeeper has left provisions; Reverend Audley tells her he will just be a jiffy; in the meantime, she must simply enjoy the vista.

It is a lovely vista.

The old stone wall creates a warm pocket of a garden, with well-tended flower beds. The garden of Gulls Nest looks overgrown and gloomy in comparison to the riot of color in the vicar's garden: late tumbling roses, exuberant dahlias, fiery chrysanthemums. The lawn is the color and velvety texture of a bowling green; there is no sign of wear or damage, despite the colony of rabbits that graze over it. There are rabbits everywhere. Elderly rabbits in old-fashioned wicker bath chairs. Rabbits sunbathing on flagstones. Young rabbits playing chase through a honeysuckle-heavy gazebo.

The vicar returns with a tray. He has changed his apron to reflect his new duty; it is a striped housekeeper's affair but there are still pockets and a rabbit still rides in one; the others boast an array of carrot tops and celery stalks. He busies himself with unloading dainty sandwiches and thin wedges of sponge cake, pouring tea, and helping Nora to milk. He sits down, lugging a nearby bunny up onto his lap.

"You have a beautiful garden, Reverend Audley."

"I have a host of excellent gardeners to help me." He waves his hand at the rabbits frolicking in a nearby border.

"You breed rabbits, I hear?"

The vicar's nose twitches in displeasure. "I am a fancier, Miss Breen. But really these rabbits are my family. Take Lady Davenport here, she has been with me for twenty-one years. Venerable old lady that she is. She is the matriarch of all my dwarf lops."

"I had no idea rabbits lived that long."

Reverend Audley looks gratified. He encourages Nora to take a sandwich. "Rabbits are greatly underestimated, you know. We have only just begun to find out what they are capable of." He frowns. "Mine are also capable of disappearing."

Nora thinks of Mrs. Rawlings's shed full of Cymag. "If they wander next door, they might get into difficulties."

"By *difficulties* you mean murder at the hands of that despicable woman." The vicar gently covers Lady Davenport's ears and lowers his voice to a hissing whisper. "She's a murderer. A poisoner of innocents."

Nora almost drops her teacup in surprise to hear the affable vicar talk this way.

"Still," says the vicar briskly. "We must not dwell on evil but trust that the Lord sees all and knows the contents of our hearts, rotten or pure. What is interesting is that there's a sort of natural selection taking place; the cleverer rabbits wouldn't dream of hopping through the wall. It's only the dim ones who go through."

"Or the explorers?"

The vicar considers. "Perhaps."

"You said I wouldn't be the first visitor here from Gulls Nest?"

"The little girl, she pops through the wall sometimes. I leave her a custard tart now and again. She seems to like them and is very sweet with the rabbits."

"You communicate with Dinah?"

Reverend Audley looks surprised. "Is she talking now?"

Nora shakes her head. "She writes everything down."

"Wise idea, then you can never be misquoted." The vicar pours Nora another cup of tea. "And what about you, Miss Breen, what brings you to Gore-on-Sea?"

Nora decides to be straight up. "I'm searching for my friend, Frieda Brogan. She was a resident of Gulls Nest. Did you know her?"

"Sorry, I only keep track of rabbit names really. I've very little interest in people. To be honest, I prefer my bunnies."

It takes all sorts, thinks Nora. "Why wouldn't you?" Her smile finds an answer on the vicar's face.

"So," he asks, "where did your friend go?"

"I don't know, she just seemed to disappear."

"Like my rabbits," the vicar muses, watching his bunnies. He stirs himself and offers Nora another sandwich. "So, you are here to solve a mystery?"

"Yes, but it seems that Gulls Nest is not prepared to offer me just one."

The vicar looks perplexed.

"The recent deaths," Nora explains.

Reverend Audley nods. "I was dreadfully sorry to hear about Professor Poppy and the poor young Teddy Atkins. I shared a sherry with the former on several occasions, the latter I did not know, I'm afraid." He lowers his voice. "You speak of mysteries . . . are you suggesting that there has been foul play?"

"My investigation is leading that way."

The vicar looks at her keenly. "So, you are a detective, Miss Breen?"

Nora considers. "Of the amateur variety, yes."

"Marvelous. The thrill of a good puzzle, eh? Only wouldn't it be better to stick to crosswords, what with a murderer on the loose?"

"I'm afraid I'm rather in the thick of it now. I can't leave off what I started."

"I understand. May I ask your professional opinion, you know, as a sleuth?"

"Go ahead."

The vicar gives Lady Davenport's head a gentle stroke. "Is there any chance Mrs. Rawlings might be next on the murderer's list?"

Nora stares at him in surprise.

The vicar laughs. "I'm sorry, I've shocked you, Miss Breen. Well, if you ever take a break from finding missing friends and solving suspicious deaths, you might help me with my rabbit problem. Take this morning; I let eighty rabbits out at dawn and now I only have seventy-seven."

"You've lost three rabbits today?"

"I'm afraid so. A Holland Lop, a Jersey Wooly, and a lovely little Lionhead. I could weep."

A rabbit the size of a dog catches Nora's eye.

The vicar notices. "That's Captain Lofthouse, he's a Flemish Giant. Mighty old brute, twice as big as your average Flemish and can eat a staggering quantity of carrot tops. Excuse me a moment while I refresh the teapot. You will take another cup?"

"I will, of course."

"Good show." Reverend Audley rises and returns with the teapot into the house.

Nora watches as Captain Lofthouse makes a zigzag passage through the garden, hopping heavily across the lawn, barreling through shrubs, charging back out of the border. At the far end of the garden, he plows into a large hydrangea in the corner by the old stone wall and is gone from sight.

Nora waits; Captain Lofthouse does not reemerge this time.

The other rabbits carry on about their business, gamboling about or lying on the terrace. Nora puts down her cup and goes to investigate.

Doubtless the bunny will be snorting around in the roots, or perhaps dozing in the shade. Captain Lofthouse is doing neither; he is wedged headfirst down a hole.

Extracting the big, frightened, struggling rabbit calls for another change of apron and some ropes. Hauled to safety by the joint strength of Nora and the vicar, Captain Lofthouse is none the worse for his experience. He accepts a carrot top and lopes ponderously away.

The two turn back to the hole, of fair size and opening into pitch black darkness. Nora pushes her arm in, up to her armpit, feeling air circulating around her outstretched hand, sensing the void beyond.

The vicar looks at her with excitement. "There is an old legend associated with this house. Long before it fell into the possession of the church it was owned by a local smuggler who carved underground caverns to hide away their booty."

Nora struggles upright. "Well, there is some kind of space down there. I believe that's where your rabbits have vanished, Reverend."

"Captain Lofthouse was too plump to fall through but the smaller chaps just slipped down?"

"Exactly." Nora peers down into the hole again. "We could widen it, find a torch?"

"I've an idea: I'll send for young Walter!"

Nora has her doubts about lowering a small boy tied about the waist with a rope into an unexplored smuggler's cave. Reverend Audley waves these away, as does Walter, the small boy with the monopoly on errands this side of the town, the same boy who came chasing down to Nora on the day of Teddy's death. Walter has been furnished with one bright coin for his troubles with the promise of another on completion of the task. Which is simply to keep his eyes peeled and shine the light around and report back.

"We'll split the loot," adds Reverend Audley. "If we find any."

Walter is ecstatic.

The circumference of the hole has been widened by the vicar's shovel and Walter's harness is securely fastened. Nora and the vicar take up the rope as Walter disappears by increments through the hole.

Walter may be a slight child, but even so, progress is slow. Nora clings to her end, her heart racing in her ears. The vicar, who mountaineered in his Oxford days, carefully lets out rope, bright-eyed with excitement.

It seems like an age before they hear Walter's voice, muffled and faint but victorious. They glance at one another; Reverend Audley grins.

"Jackpot!" He turns to the hole. "Walter, are any of my rabbits down there?"

There is silence.

The vicar's face falls. A frown. "Walter old chap, is everything all right?"

Now, faintly, Nora hears the boy begin to scream.

Walter sits pale-faced in the conservatory. He is wrapped in a blanket and holds a cup of sweet tea, Nora's best remedy for shock. A few rabbits hop up onto the couch next to him; he pets them absently. But by the time he has finished his drink, Walter appears revived. He shrugs off his blanket and potters off down the garden to get in the way of the police.

Nora can only hope that with the resilience of youth Walter will not be terribly marked by what he saw.

What did Walter see?

A woman, hair all over her face, head held funny.

Nora tries not to think the worst, but a sickness is rising in her, a terrible dread. She glances out of the conservatory window and across the lawn.

Reverend Audley stands grave-faced with Inspector Rideout by his side. Constable Griggs has drawn the short straw; another officer is knotting a rope round his waist. Readying the torch, he steps to the edge of the abyss.

As dusk falls, the police and the coast guard rescue volunteers shake hands, nod to one another, and begin to scatter across the lawn. An ambulance arrives and a stretcher is carried out through the vicarage's garden gate. On that stretcher is a small, well-wrapped form. Nora watches from the conservatory, having been relegated to this post several times by Rideout at his most strident.

Walter is long gone. He was driven home in a squad car despite living only three roads away. Nora understands why; let the boy's day of adventure end on a high note to wipe out the terror of his descent.

Reverend Audley has been nothing if not hospitable, providing tea and sponge cake and dainty sandwiches. None of which Nora has had the stomach to touch. Now the vicar is rounding up his rabbits. They are following him across the garden, big and small, lop- and straight-eared, brown and white, gray and black, and russet red. A little sea of furry bodies. It's a surreal sight. As he passes by the window he smiles at her sympathetically and her heart lurches. What does he know that she doesn't?

After a little time, here is Rideout himself. He wipes his boots as he steps into the conservatory, in his hands a small cardboard box, and in the box, a woman's shoe, of all things.

He addresses her with a strained formality. "Miss Breen, if we can verify that these items belonged to Frieda—"

"Items? Why would you not ask me to identify the body?"

Rideout looks pained. "It would not be possible to tell; the time elapsed and the injuries." He hesitates. "I want to spare you, Nora."

Nora feels a wave of nausea. She closes her eyes and takes a slow breath.

"We can do this another time," he is saying. "You can come down to the station when you are ready."

But then there would be the horror of not knowing, another hour, another day, another week of not knowing what had happened, not knowing where Frieda had gone to.

"No. Show me." Nora forces herself to open her eyes and look inside the box.

A woman's shoe, like any other, of smallish size, neat, black. The shoe is not familiar to Nora. Neither is the navy-blue headscarf folded next to it. Nora's eye falls on a little beadwork purse on a plaited cord, red and yellow, the beads glassy and green. A jolly thing, a little garish, almost something a child would have. It was a parting gift to the sunny young novice who couldn't stay. The nuns had made it collectively. Nora had plaited the strap herself. She looks at the little purse and her heart breaks.

"It's Frieda Brogan's."

"The deceased fits your description as far as we can make out." He lowers his voice, just above a whisper. "I'm so sorry, Nora."

Nora takes a slow breath. "How did she get there? Down that hole?"

"Chances are she fell. We first thought it was an old shaft of some kind but it's a labyrinth below the surface, the rock carved away. Tunnels and underground rooms that stretch out beyond the wall of the vicarage, it's quite some feat. Everywhere set with shells in intricate patterns."

"A smuggler's lair," Nora remembers.

"I don't know about that. Whether for storage or some other purpose, a few of the spaces are lit by roof lights, quite rudimentary, simple iron grates that have eroded over time. The land has crumbled in, widening them further. We found the body beneath one, a little bigger than the one you discovered in Reverend Audley's flower bed. It's rotten bad luck but she might simply have stepped onto it and that was enough for the grate to give way."

"And the fall could have killed her?"

"Certainly. The drop was over twenty feet."

"What I'm asking is," says Nora quietly, "were Frieda's injuries commensurate with a fall, or did someone hurt her first and then push her in?"

"I can't say."

Nora frowns. "You can."

Rideout hesitates. "It would be impossible to discern whether her death was accidental or deliberate, as we really cannot say whether the injuries were sustained before or during the fall. I'm sorry. None of this is what you wanted to hear."

Nora touches the little purse on the string. "I helped to make it. A leaving present from the sisters." She glances up at him. "I knew she would have kept writing to me. I told you that Frieda would never have broken her promise."

Rideout nods, walks away, folding in onto himself. Leaving her holding the little bag and a big grief.

Nora gives way. It is to be expected. First her legs and then her mind. Reverend Audley discreetly lowers the blinds and shuts the door. The rabbits give Nora a wide berth at first, the woman curled up so strangely on the conservatory floor. But by degrees they hop nearer, giving her side-eyes and twitching their noses gravely. One old veteran, seeking its own warmth, nudges alongside. Nora's fingers reach out and find the warm fur. She begins to sob. And with the tears come the memories. Bright snapshots, like a camera's flashes piercing the dark. Frieda waking after a long night, wan but smiling. Frieda, on a better day, moving through the light and shade of a cloistered walkway. Late for choir practice, if her light step and fluttering habit are anything to go by. Frieda in the vegetable garden, waxing lyrical about runner beans.

"I'm sorry, Frieda," Nora whispers. "I'm so sorry."

Frieda, spade in hand, backlit by autumn light, smiles.

When the vicar glances in again he sees that Nora is surrounded where she lies. Furry shapes of all sizes and colors envelop her in mute animal sympathy. In a while, he will bring her a cup of tea and a handkerchief and help her to her feet.

Reverend Audley has swapped his apron for a smoking jacket. An embroidered red affair, which seems a discordant choice. There are no discernible pockets in this garment, so he carries Lady Davenport in the crook of his arm, the old rabbit lying paws upward in a trusting slumber. Several more rabbits twitch and hop around his feet.

"I offer my condolences, for your loss." His words are spoken lightly but his face is grave.

Nora finds she can't speak. She holds a cup and saucer, but the tea goes untouched.

"Would it help to pray with me?"

His eyes are kindly, red-rimmed. Nora wonders if he ever twitches his nose like his charges.

"Perhaps you pray, Reverend, and I'll just be a bystander." Nora puts down her teacup and folds her hands on her lap.

He nods and bows his head. Nora watches him, listens not to the words but the quiet calm behind them. For a moment Nora envies the man his belief in a benevolent God, despite the indifferent cruelty of the world.

Reverend Audley sees her to the door. "Well, it seems as if your mystery just keeps getting deeper. Quite a rabbit hole you have popped through, isn't it?"

Nora nods, unable to speak.

"Well, I for one believe you are entirely equal to it. Good luck, Miss Breen."

Walking through the garden in the gloom of the dying day, Nora fights the urge to crawl back through the hole in the wall. Instead, she returns to Gulls Nest by the front gate, like any other respectable visitor. As she crosses the drive she looks up at the house and the house looks back at her blankly.

Nora finds herself shivering; Gulls Nest has never looked more foreboding.

This is a house that keeps her secrets well hidden. Her yew trees whisper together in their dour huddles and her windows reflect nothing more than the darkening sky. It is with effort and the deepest of breaths that Nora steps back over the threshold.

CHAPTER 18

Rideout had left her alone with Frieda's purse long enough for her to look inside. A few coins, a pot of rouge, and a book of matches printed with an illustration of the Marine Hotel. Nora had opened the book; three matches had been used. She had imagined Frieda striking them in the dark after she fell for the reassurance of light in her underground cavern, but Nora knows this wasn't so. Frieda died instantly from a broken neck.

Back in her room at Gulls Nest, Nora gathers her friend's letters and lays them out over the bed. Packed with information, yet they tell her nothing. The polite observations and anecdotes you'd share with an acquaintance: the look of the sea, a fortune told along the promenade, the excitement of a train journey. And then that last letter intimating so much more. What made Frieda write this? Was she somehow concerned? What was all this but passing the time of day, small talk, polite news? But how could Frieda tell of the complications and confusions of the world to a cloistered nun? How could the young woman write of sin or temptation or peril in a letter that Mother Superior would likely censor? How could poor dear dead Frieda share the dreams whipped up by the world with a friend who had long ago turned her face away from that same world?

What, after all, had they even talked about?

Nora tries to remember: observations about their days, memories of their lives before. Nothing more.

Nora touches each letter, trying to calm herself—hadn't she read between the lines? As perhaps Frieda knew she would. Nora left her vocation sensing danger in Frieda's little seaside intrigue and a broken promise to write.

Had she left sooner would Frieda still be alive?

Nora berates herself, but only gently. Today she feels her age, bone-weary with misery, her muscles sore with the strain of hauling a small screaming boy up from an underground tomb. She hopes that Walter is resilient enough to come through the experience unscathed. Even as she wishes it, she knows better.

Although it is not her day for bathing by rights, Nora decides to flout the rules. Taking her washbag along the corridor to the bathroom she passes by Poppy's room. Irene has been busy it seems. The door is propped open by boxes of books. More boxes are packed up inside. The bed has been stripped and the mattress sags sadly. If only the walls could speak, they might tell who came creeping in the night to finish off the poor old man. Rideout has interviewed the residents again of course but he isn't saying anything, at least not to Nora. It's not as if he has warned her to lock her door.

Who is left? Helena Wells and Irene Rawlings, locked together in mutual distrust, their history buried, a secret. Dinah running wild and left to her own devices. Poor, grieving Stella Atkins. Karel Ježek beaten half to death up at the infirmary. Bill Carter, chivalrous black-market trader and stalwart of the Marine Hotel.

The Marine Hotel. Nora will pay another visit tomorrow. Frieda must have visited to have the matches in her possession. Perhaps Bill could shed light on that?

Or could a past resident be responsible? Someone with a grudge against the house, its occupants? And as for the motive? The dead are all very different people, different personalities. Did they know their killer? What is it they had in common?

Nora reminds herself not to fall into Rideout's trap. She must keep an open mind. Frieda might have fallen by accident. Teddy may have drunk coffee meant for someone else.

But Poppy would not have poisoned his own dog and choked himself to death.

The bathroom at Gulls Nest is not inviting. It consists of a large rectangular tub, as deep and unwelcoming as a sarcophagus, and a wide and shallow handbasin. Both have questionable plumbing.

Despite the lateness of the hour, Nora braves the clanking boiler and fills the tub. Opening her washbag, she finds the sliver of soap she was supplied with on leaving High Dallow is all but gone. She does not regret that; the scent, faintly carbolic, takes her back to strip washes in cold water. There is still a great novelty in washing in hot water, let alone immersing herself in a bath full of it. Looking at the quantity of water already in the bath she knows the soap sliver won't cut it. Glancing in the cabinet built under the sink she finds a jar of bath salts of an abrasive kind and a bottle of ancient eau de cologne. She sniffs them; each are powerful in their own way. She opts for the salts but putting the perfume back into the cabinet she drops the bottle. It rolls, annoyingly, under the cabinet.

Nora kneels down. With some trepidation she slides her hand under, for Irene keeps the floor none too clean. Her fingers touch cold glass. She draws the object out, but it is not the perfume bottle she holds; it is a vial of smelling salts. She reaches in again; this time she is rewarded with a bottle of pills. Squinting at the label she recognizes the name of the drug, a sedative.

Smelling salts and sedatives. To wake someone up and to make them drowsy. But who would hide them under here?

She considers this as she lies in the bath. The condensation drips down the walls, the tiles an unwholesome green. It is a place of little comfort and yet Nora forces herself to stay. The water cools quickly in the unheated room. A scrap of a towel waits on the floor for her feet. The tap drips cold on her toes. She looks down at her limbs, distorted through the water. Aging, the skin puckered in places, a few age spots that can no longer pass as freckles. But she is strong yet, alive, less vital perhaps than she used to be, but fully capable. She wonders at the fairness of it all. Frieda with a whole life ahead of her, lost to a place of dank darkness.

She resolves to visit again the place of Frieda's fall. To make the descent and know for herself where her friend waited in the dark for someone to find her. She will speak to Rideout.

And with that thought of Frieda in the dark the tears finally come and Nora, half-submerged, gives in to her grief.

At first sight it seems a malicious act. Nora, wet-haired and in slippers and gown, returns to her room to see an act of terrible vandalism. Frieda's letters, which she had collected and cherished and then so carelessly left open on the bed, have been shredded, perforated, ruined. While she was in the bathtub someone has been busy. Nora is too stunned to cry. Too exhausted to shout out. She picks up the nearest scrap and then she sees it: letter after letter has been turned into a snowflake, each one different, each one unique. Confetti from a thousand snips litters the floor as Nora holds first one and then another up. Frieda's words, the familiar loop of her handwriting, is still readable in places, only her sentences are shot with holes.

Nora alights on the weapon of crime on the table: a pair of embroidery scissors. Taking out her sewing kit she sets to work with thread. In a short while she has Frieda's letters strung across the ceiling, where they flitter and turn in the drafts from the window. All her friend's words, somehow alive again.

CHAPTER 19

To Nora's surprise she is not breakfasting alone this morning. Seated at the table is Stella, thinner and graver each time Nora sees her. Bill sits opposite. Poppy's chair is vacant. Her fellow houseguests look up as she enters.

Bill immediately rises and pours Nora a cup of tea. Stella fusses with the milk.

"What is going on?"

Stella bites her lip and glances at Bill.

He pats down his tie and puts on a grave expression. "We are sorry for your loss, Nora."

"You were Frieda's friend, you left your order and came here to find her," Stella adds, her kind eyes pained. "Another tragedy for this hateful house."

"Who told you this?" asks Nora.

"It was a guess," replies Bill. "We put two and two together. From your questions."

"And we heard you crying," adds Stella. "I'm so sorry."

Nora nods, concentrates on her tea. It swims a little before her eyes.

Bill breaks the silence. "We've been summoned."

Nora looks up. He waves his hand to a note tacked up over the sideboard.

Mrs. Wells requests Gulls Nest residents to be assembled in the dining room.

Tonight, 7:00 p.m.

SHARP

"We think she might be closing down." Stella shrugs. "Who would come here with everything that has happened?"

Bill takes a sip of tea, pats his mustache with a napkin. "Oh, you'd be surprised, Stella. There are some ghouls who would be lining up ready to pay through the nose to sleep in a room that someone had died in."

Stella shudders. "I for one can't wait to leave. I think Inspector Rideout is utterly cruel to make us stay."

"The man has a job to do, a puzzle to solve. Think of it like a chessboard," says Bill patiently. "At least this way some of the pieces are still in place."

"But we are being toppled one by one!" exclaims Stella.

"We are not all of us still in place," says Nora quietly. "Karel Ježek is up at the infirmary."

Stella frowns. "Honestly, must you remind me of him? I am quite disturbed enough!"

Bill leans forward and pats her hand. "Lock your door at night, and any sign of funny business you come straight to me."

Stella nods, throws Bill a wry smile. "What would you do? Take them down with your blowpipe and poisonous darts?"

"Now, Stella, those are just trinkets from my travels." He glances at Nora. "And in no way poisonous."

"And what about Nora?" asks Stella. "Does she have your protection, Bill?"

Bill colors slightly. "I beg your pardon—"

Nora holds up her hand. "Thank you, Bill. But I'm fine."

"You have God at your side, I suppose?"

Nora glances over at Stella in surprise, hearing such uncharacteristic bitterness in her voice. But the young woman's face is open, benign.

"Poor Frieda didn't seem like a nun at all, neither do you really. Only you have a quiet way of moving about and talking. I expect that's why you are so calming. I can't imagine the two of you as friends. Frieda was so young, chatty and lively—"

Bill lays his hand on Stella's again. "Nora might not want to talk about this right now, Stella."

Nora glances at him gratefully.

Stella's cheeks flush slightly. "Goodness, I'm sorry, Nora." She clatters her plate and cup together, moving awkwardly. "I must gather myself; I return to work today. I have so much more time to dawdle without Poppy to read to."

Nora remembers Poppy's crime book, the ribbon marker, the progress made on the morning of Teddy's death. "How long would you have read to him for?"

"Oh, it varied. Sometimes only ten minutes, sometimes up to half an hour, longer."

"Did he ever fall asleep when you read to him?" asks Nora. "Poppy was given to dozing, wasn't he?"

Only perhaps someone like Nora, used to watching for small, almost intangible signs, would notice the barely perceptible pause as Stella stacked her crockery on the sideboard. A pause accompanied by the very slightest intake of breath.

"No. Poppy never fell asleep when I read to him, the stories were far too riveting."

Bill watches Stella out of the room and then turns to Nora. "The poor girl suffers so. She's alone in the world." He smooths down the tablecloth. "I suppose we all are."

Nora decides not to take up this comment. She changes tack. "Can I ask you something, Bill?"

"Fire away."

"Frieda was carrying a matchbook from the Marine Hotel when she died."

"Is that right?"

"So, Frieda visited the hotel?"

"Likely." Bill straightens his cuff links.

"Bill, tell me."

Bill takes a deep breath. "She drank there with Percy Ladd a couple of times."

Nora thinks of the young, empty-eyed woman she saw at the bar with Percy Ladd. Percy, a known predator of young, bewildered girls.

"Why didn't you say?"

Bill looks awkward. "It was after-hours. Percy paid me not to bleat."

"He met with Frieda there alone?"

Bill nods. "I would set their drinks out and make myself scarce."

Nora thinks of the local gossips. They would have had a field day knowing Frieda was being corrupted by Percy Ladd.

"It was Percy and not someone else's husband she was stepping out with." Nora feels no relief at this, on the contrary.

Bill holds up his hand. "I wouldn't jump to conclusions there, Nora. They could have been just friends."

"Come on, Bill. You know what kind of man Percy Ladd is."

"Think about what kind of girl Frieda was. Would she have got herself wrapped up with him? Now, I didn't know her as well as you did but I would credit her with more sense. Perhaps she had another reason to meet him?"

"At night, in an empty bar, with champagne? I was a nun but even I know what that means."

Bill looks sheepish.

Nora nods. "All right, Bill. I suppose you told Inspector Rideout about Frieda's clandestine meetings?"

Bill shakes his head.

"Bill!"

"I will now, of course. Don't blast me, Nora! You don't understand— if Percy Ladd wants to make life difficult for you, he will. If you cross him, you might as well be dead in this town."

Bill looks at Nora, realizing just what he's said.

"I think I need to go and have a few words with Percy Ladd."

Bill's face is strained with worry. "Leave it to the police, Nora, please."

"I will not."

"You really don't want to provoke him."

"Perhaps I do."

Bill seems to wrestle with some internal demon. "If you won't give it up, Nora—"

"I won't."

"Then I'll come with you. Backup, solidarity, that sort of thing."

"You would risk your job, Bill?"

"It's the decent thing to do. Stand ground, look the enemy right in the eye."

"We don't know Percy is the enemy yet," volunteers Nora.

Bill hardly seems to listen. "Frieda, Teddy, Poppy—all decent people; they didn't deserve what happened to them."

"No," says Nora gently. "They didn't."

Bill lights a cigarette. She sees the tremble in his hand; Bill is scared.

He inhales sharply, exhales slowly. Gives her a nervous smile. "I'll help you get to the bottom of it, Nora. I'll do my bit."

* * *

Laddland is found at the opposite end of Gore-on-Sea to Gulls Nest. It follows a sprawling crescent that starts on the flats of the sandy beach and curves all the way back towards the station. Out of season it is a singularly joyless affair. The perimeter is fenced to an unwelcoming height, which is not quite disguised by the brightly painted billboards promising a world of fun for the family. The painted grins on swimsuit-clad young men and women, happy parents and delighted children are not matched by the few punters who take a chalet here even at this time of year. These are a grim and shivering lot on this gray and windswept day.

The chalets have an air of the penitentiary about them, bunker-like and identical. The rides and attractions, including a lake with paddleboats, a petting zoo, crazy golf, the hall of mirrors and a miniature model village are at the center of the park. A scenic railway winds all around ferrying punters. The train stops running at the end of the summer. As do the headliner rides: the roller coaster, the pirate boat, the dodgems, and the Ferris wheels, big and small. But then the holidaymakers get a discount so they can't complain.

Bill hails a wiry-looking old man in work boots who is sweeping up around the chalets.

"Is the gaffer around?"

The old man eyes them charily. "Ladd senior or junior?"

"Junior."

The old man snorts. "At this time of day? Not a chance. Come back this afternoon. You might be lucky."

"You worked with Teddy Atkins at all?"

The old man turns to Nora, frowns. "Who is asking?"

"My name is Nora. I currently reside at Gulls Nest. You could say I'm a friend of his widow."

His face softens slightly, his voice becomes less gruff. "Where are my manners? I'm Stan." Stan takes a deep breath. "For Mrs. Atkins's loss I am sorry."

"You knew Teddy well?"

"He was a good worker, not a lot of chat from him, which to my mind makes an even better worker."

"What did he do?"

"Gardening, carpentry, he was even starting to have a go at big ride maintenance. Mr. Ladd liked him, knew a grafter when he saw one. He had Teddy earmarked for great things."

"You mean Percy Ladd?"

"No, his father, Harry Ladd, the big boss himself. I daresay that put Percy's nose out of joint."

"How come?"

"There's no love lost between father and son. Harry is a businessman and Percy is a wastrel. Harry is not about to hand over the reins anytime soon. He built this up from scratch."

"And Percy wants to take charge of things?"

"He has *ideas*," says Stan ironically. "Pie in the sky if you ask me." He glances at Bill. "This here chap will tell you: Percy Ladd is good for chasing young girls and driving fast, nothing else."

Nora considers. "What is all this about driving fast?"

Stan smiles. "For the thrill. Haven't you tried it?"

Nora smiles too. "I can't say I have."

"Well mind you don't get caught if you do. Of course, Percy Ladd is above the law."

"What makes you say that, Stan?"

Stan glances at Bill, who nods very slightly. Stan addresses Nora, his voice low. "Harry Ladd has this town in his pockets, some say coppers included. Percy can misbehave all he wants and it's covered up, bribes and the rest. Only don't let on I told you this."

"I understand."

Stan picks up his shovel. "All we can hope for is that one day Percy Ladd gets his comeuppance."

Nora walks through the park with Bill at her side.

"Penny for 'em?"

"It was reported to the police that Percy Ladd was speeding through town on the night that Frieda disappeared. I sneaked a look at the desk sergeant's report book when he was away from his desk."

"Nora! You're a woman of God!"

"Not anymore," replies Nora grimly.

"So, what do you make of it?"

"Could Percy's speeding offer a sign of guilt—away from or to the scene of the crime?"

"Like Stan said, Percy Ladd speeding is a regular occurrence."

Nora frowns. "Would you say there are many sporty cars in this town?"

"Since the war, not many. Who can afford to run one?"

Nora nods. "That's as I thought." She glances at Bill. "The person that dropped Karel Ježek at the infirmary didn't leave their name, but they were driving a sports car. The porter heard the engine."

Bill stops, frowns. "I can't keep up with you, Nora. Are we investigating Frieda's death or Karel's assault now? Is Percy Ladd a baddy or a goody?"

"That's just what I'm here to ascertain, Bill."

They continue a few steps.

"I don't see it myself, Percy helping anyone but himself."

"Perhaps the two men fought over something and it went too far? Then Percy, fearing for his own skin, dumped Karel outside the infirmary?"

"You think Percy would risk getting blood on his upholstery?"

"Good point, and one that might be settled by a look inside Percy's car."

Rounding a corner, they walk through another clutch of holiday chalets, bigger and more ornate in design than the ones they passed earlier. Nora reads a sign: WOODED GLADE, PREMIUM HOLIDAY VILLAGE. There are no woods and no glade, just a row of regimented chrysanthemums. But there is a beautiful blue car parked in its own gravel swerve.

Nora smiles. "That can't be?"

Bill grins. "That is."

Nora draws closer to inspect it. The vehicle is dazzling, kingfisher in color with accents of gleaming chrome that look almost molten. The interior is dressed in a fawn leather.

"It's French. He had it imported—he's not shy about sharing that fact."

"Is that right." Nora glances around; her eyes fall on a nearby chalet with the curtains closed tight.

Bill follows her gaze. "Chances are he's knocking off some young one in there." He blanches. "Goodness, I'm sorry."

"No need," she says grimly. "Say it as it is, Bill."

Nora opens the car door and gets in behind the steering wheel. The keys on a fob are still in the ignition.

Nora smiles. "Slapdash, Percy, very slapdash."

She peers at the dials and opens the glove box. She turns her attention to the passenger footwell, scrutinizing marks on the upholstery. A few telltale rusty smudges on the leather of the seat.

"Bill, this looks like blood."

The sound of a front door slamming and a roar.

"What the blazes do you think you are doing? Get away from my bloody car!"

Percy is stampeding through the flowers and onto the gravel. Behind him standing at the doorway is a blank-faced girl. Nora wonders what it is he drugs them with.

"Me again, Percy."

Percy looks at her with disgust. He turns to Bill. "Keep away from her, she's a mad old bitch."

Bill frowns. "That's no way to speak to—"

"I offered to knock his teeth out for him." Nora walks around the car, running her fingers over the paintwork. "Pristine."

Percy's face is red with fury. "Don't you touch my car!" He turns to Bill. "Tell her!"

Bill shrugs. "Nora Breen won't be told."

The younger man turns to Nora. "What exactly is your problem?"

Nora glances up at the young woman watching from the doorway of the chalet.

Percy follows her glance and smirks. "Oh, yes, you're the guardian of morals. Probably because you're not getting any yourself."

Nora rounds the front of the car, opens the door, and hops into the driver's seat.

Percy lets out a howl, wrenches the door open, and reaches inside to drag Nora from the car.

Bill Carter intervenes, grabbing hold of Percy's Italian sports jacket. Percy turns on him, spitting. To his credit, Bill keeps a tight grip.

"Calm down, Mr. Ladd. You don't want to be assaulting a lady."

"She's in my bloody car! That's trespassing!"

"Language, Mr. Ladd!"

"It's all right, Bill. You can unhand him."

Bill follows Nora's order.

Percy straightens his clothes, musters his swagger, shoots a hard glance at Bill. "Consider yourself sacked, Carter."

"That's not down to you. Is it, Percy?" says Nora smoothly. "Daddy

Ladd has all the clout around here. By the sounds of it you're just an embarrassment."

Percy's eyes narrow. "You old—"

"Change the record." Nora taps the passenger seat. "Why don't you hop in a minute, Percy? There's something I need your help with."

"Now if you think . . ."

Nora pulls the driver's door out from under his hand, slams, and locks it. Then she slips on the seat belt.

"You'd be doing me a favor really. I haven't driven since 1923 and that was a tractor." In one quick action Nora turns the key in the ignition and cocks her head to listen to the first throb of the engine.

Percy looks horrified. Bill, emboldened by Nora's actions, can't help but laugh. A smile appears on the face of the young woman watching from the chalet.

Nora jerks the car forward, brutal on the clutch.

"Dear God." Percy is running around to the passenger side.

Nora jerks the car backwards, stamping on the brakes. "Whoopsie."

Percy, panicking, opens the door and gets into the passenger seat.

"Now, I know your reputation, Percy, keep your hands where I can see them. Any false move on your part is liable to have me crashing into a wall. It would be a tragedy to scratch your paintwork."

"I'll call the police."

Nora glances at him coldly. "Course you will." With a screech and a roar, she sets off around the park.

The car might purr with another driver, but Nora drives it heavily, smashing through the gears, taking the corners haphazardly so that the car sounds more like a rally banger than a beautifully engineered machine. Percy's face is a picture of horror. Nora's first circuit takes in the major rides, the petting zoo, and the bank of the lake. Percy winces as she plows the car over curbs and up verges. By the third lap holidaymakers and staff alike have gathered to watch. A few people even begin cheering them on, several more stand laughing. Percy is red with rage, but he gives the thumbs-up on passing, else he would certainly lose face.

"Right, so, Percy," shouts Nora as she decimates a sea-themed parterre. "Here's the deal: I drive you around and around until either your gas runs out or you answer the questions I ask truthfully."

"You're mad."

Nora takes a corner wide. "Don't make me madder."

"All right!"

"Did you go afterhours to the bar at the Marine Hotel with Frieda Brogan?"

Percy looks at Nora in bewilderment. His brain seems to catch up. "Never heard of her."

Nora slams on the brakes and Percy's nose hits the dashboard. She reverses into a rubbish bin. Percy screams, blood pouring from his face.

"I'll give you a moment to get a hankie. There's one in the glove box."

Percy, whimpering, holds it up against himself.

"Let's try that again shall we. Marine Hotel, after-hours, Frieda Brogan?"

"Once!" screams Percy.

"Liar," says Nora and she clips the driver's wing mirror on the side of a ticket booth.

Percy howls. "Just stop the car."

Nora does, halfway along the paddleboat pier. She stops the engine, it ticks over, behind them dust settles.

Percy dabs at his face miserably with the handkerchief.

"Well?"

"Nothing happened with Frieda."

"Would you like me to drive off this pier and into the water?"

Percy shakes his head. In a gloopy voice with his nose still bleeding, "Nothing happened, that's the God's honest truth."

"Don't you bring God into this— Swear on this car, that's more believable."

"I swear. We just talked."

"What I can't fathom is why Frieda would agree to meet an article like you." Nora switches on the ignition.

"To mediate!" Percy looks, for the first time, shamefaced.

"Mediate?"

"Between me and Teddy Atkins."

Nora frowns. "I don't understand."

"It was Teddy's wife, that little brunette—what's her name . . ."

Nora scrutinizes Percy, knocking the car into gear. "Liar—you know her name—"

"Stella! Stella put Frieda up to it. Said I was worsening her husband's nerves or whatever. I ask you: what man needs a woman to do his dirty work?"

"His nerves?"

"I had it in for him. Bullied him. I ask you, like kids in a playground."

She tightens her grip on the gearstick. "And did you have it in for him?"

Percy reddens. "There was something about him I didn't like."

"Your father liked him well enough, is that it?"

Percy swears under his breath.

"So, it galled? That he was your father's favorite?"

"Who told you that? Bill Carter? He's an utter—"

Nora softens her voice. "Did it gall?"

Percy quietens. "Yes."

She considers. "This doesn't make sense. Why would Stella send Frieda, why didn't she talk to you herself?"

Percy frowns and looks away.

Nora puts the car into gear.

"We had form."

She studies him closely. "Something happened between you and Stella?"

Percy glances at her. "I wanted it to but she was loyal to him. God knows why. Little stunner like her, he barely touched her."

"And you know this *how*?"

Percy puffs himself up. "I know girls. All they want is a bit of fun."

"You don't know your arse from your elbow." Nora speaks coldly. "Gobshite."

Percy throws her a look of concentrated hatred.

"Did Teddy know that his wife had sent Frieda to mediate?"

Percy sneers. "I made sure to tell him. He wasn't best amused."

"Where were you the night Frieda disappeared?"

"Honestly? I've no idea. Probably out whoring."

"A complaint was made against you to the police; your car was seen speeding through town at a late hour."

Percy laughs thickly. "What's new?"

"You took Karel Ježek to the infirmary after he was assaulted. Why was that?"

"What and *what*?"

"The porter heard the throb of a sports car's engine as you drove away. You have bloodstains on the passenger seat." Nora points to a rusty patch on the leather. "Not a very thorough cleanup operation, Percy."

"This is nonsense—"

Nora puts the car into reverse gear. "Maybe I should drive you to the police station? Perhaps Inspector Rideout can confirm my findings—"

"Wait."

"Did you assault Karel Ježek?"

"Of course not! I spotted him slumped on the road, thought he'd been brawling, saw it was serious." Percy's expression is injured. "For God's sake, can't a man do a good turn?"

"Percy, don't talk shite. You are not known for your good turns."

Percy grabs hold of a thought, his expression turns triumphant. "Which is exactly why I didn't leave my name at the infirmary. Why would I ruin my reputation?"

Nora turns a cold eye on him. Percy visibly blanches. "If I find out that you are lying to me . . ."

Percy, with an attempt at bravado, smirks. "What can you do to me?"

"It wouldn't be yourself I would worry about." Nora switches off the engine. She strokes the steering wheel. "This really is a beautiful car, isn't it? One of a kind. French, is it? You must worry about it parked up here and there. Someone might scratch it for instance. Big long gashes running all down the length of it. Or empty a bucket of fish heads into this lovely interior. Imagine the smell, you'd never get rid of it!"

"I'm not lying," says Percy.

"And stay away from young girls."

Percy laughs.

Nora's voice is low and dangerous. "I mean it. One day your predatory behavior will bite you on the arse. That's a guarantee."

Percy stops laughing. "You're mad."

"Evidently." Nora takes the keys out of the ignition, unbuckles her seat belt, and gets out of the car.

"Can I have my keys back now?" asks Percy.

Nora gives him a withering glare. "And are you going to promise to drive sensibly?"

"What, like you did?" says Percy with derision.

Nora feels carefully the weight of the key fob in her palm as she steps out of the car and onto the pier. She takes aim. The trajectory of Percy's keys as they fall into the dead center of the lake describes a perfect arc.

CHAPTER 20

Nora has a bad feeling about this. The dining room has been cleared of sickly plants and cruets and the sideboard. Even Irene's signs have been taken down. The heavy tablecloth has been rolled away, revealing polished wood. The chairs are six in number and three candlesticks have been set along the sideboard.

Only one of the chairs is currently occupied. Bill greets Nora with a winning smile and pulls out the chair next to him. His round of spontaneous applause on seeing Nora stalk away from Percy stranded in his car was joined by a few of the braver staff members and a few bewildered holidaymakers, who thought it was part of the entertainment.

No one so far had lost their job. Bill Carter had given himself the night shift off. After all, they had been summoned by the lovely Mrs. Wells, and he would not miss a chance to hobnob with her, whatever the subject of the meeting.

Nora nods to Bill and takes the chair.

They are presently joined by Stella, who seems a little revived by curiosity, and only moments after this, Helena Wells and Irene Rawlings. Helena is luminous in a black fitted gown, her glossy hair drawn into a chignon. Bill orbits around her. Irene, dragged away from scouring pots, is aproned and sour.

Helena chooses Poppy's seat, the unofficial head of even a round table. She sits down and takes a deep breath.

"I expect you are wondering why I've gathered you here?"

Bill smiles encouragingly.

"We have tragically lost a few of our number." Her sad gaze falls on Stella, then moves to Bill, and finally Nora. "To accident and misadventure," she lowers her voice, "or worse. But we are still a family of sorts."

Irene grunts.

Helena continues. "Our thoughts are with Mr. Ježek. We must hope and pray for his speedy recovery."

Stella, eyes cast down, fidgets with her wedding ring.

Helena takes a moment. "What I'm proposing, what I've arranged for this evening, may not seem regular or commonplace, but then neither are the events that have recently befallen us."

"Quite right," says Bill.

Irene rolls her eyes.

"I have questions," says Helena. "I know many of you do too. Our hardworking constabulary haven't given us many answers yet, have they?"

A few mutinous murmurs of assent are heard.

"Right," she continues, "so, it's time to ask questions a different way. Some of you may be skeptics, of course, but we must all cooperate to make this work. Something to do with psychic energy, you see."

Nora frowns. The bad feeling grows.

"I implore you all to do two things for me: stay until the end of the sitting and keep an open mind."

"Of course, Mrs. Wells," whispers Bill.

Stella, her interest caught, spark returning, nods her consent.

Irene gives a grumbling affirmation.

Helena smiles warmly, gratified.

"What exactly," pipes up Nora, "are we promising to sit through?"

"A reading," replies Helena. "I'm sure you will have all heard of the illustrious Miss Elspeth Dence."

Nora glances around the room. Her fellow boarders look none the wiser.

Helena goes to the door and calls out, her voice high and nervous. "Miss Dence, would you be so kind as to join us?"

Miss Dence is a neatly presented, formidable-looking woman of around Nora's age. By appearance she could be a headmistress or a parish secretary. There is a tweedy formality to her, a resolute, no-nonsense air. She wears wire-rimmed spectacles and is not given to smiling unnecessarily. Miss Dence takes the vacant seat, Karel Ježek's, with an abrupt nod to her hostess.

"I shall outline the rules," she says firmly.

Even Irene Rawlings looks impressed.

"No breaking of the circle, no asking questions outside the duration that I indicate, no crying out, sobbing, or fainting. Is that clear?" She glances around the table with the look of a schoolmistress daring an errant class to misbehave.

Everyone nods.

"Then we will begin."

Miss Dence turns to Irene. "Light the candles and make the final checks, if you please, Mrs. Rawlings."

Irene stands. She opens the sideboard doors and checks for stowaways, then closes and locks the dining room door. Next, she lights the three candles on the sideboard one after the other and switches off the electric light.

Miss Dence carefully removes her spectacles and puts them in the breast pocket of her suit.

"In a house as beset by misfortune as this one"—her voice is still firm, only quieter now, as if in concession to the intimate candlelit dim—"where deaths both sudden and violent have occurred, and mysteries abound, the spirits of our friends and loved ones might linger. Does that make sense?" The medium quickly moves on. "I am here, at the behest of Mrs. Wells, for a twofold purpose. Firstly, to find answers to your questions as to the manner in which these people met their end. Secondly, to encourage our dearly deceased to find rest." Miss Dence looks around the table. "I must warn you that this is an imprecise science. The dead are like cats; they don't come when they are called. And anyone who has tried to put a cat out on a rainy night will have a sense of how persistently a haunting might cling to a place." She glances around the table.

"Has anyone here had a creeping sense of being watched? Or found that objects have moved of their own accord? Or heard footsteps and tapping or some such noise when they perceive themselves to be alone?"

Irene snorts. "We all have but that's just Dinah."

"Dinah is in spirit?"

"Oh no, Dinah is alive, very much so. She is my daughter," Helena volunteers, blushing.

Miss Dence throws her a cold glance. "To continue: today's séance may improve a psychical blockage or worsen it."

Nora, unable to help herself, laughs.

"Madam, there is nothing at all funny about this business. People's lives and deaths may be at stake here."

Nora sniffs, straightens her face.

"I am what's called a forensic medium. You may not have heard that term before, this is because I invented it. I work with the living and dead in cases where the passing of an individual is unresolved or unsatisfactory. I am here to give you comfort, if I can, that in passing through the veil your friends and loved ones are in a better place. But more importantly, to uncover, if I can, how they passed—"

A little sob from Stella. Miss Dence glances in her direction.

"Come now," she says, her voice stern but not unsympathetic. "You must be brave. Mrs. Atkins, isn't it? Don't you want answers? Can't you be brave?"

Stella sniffs.

"Jolly good. Right. Let's all join hands and make an inviolable circle."

Nora puts her hand in Bill's, who offers her a quick nod before turning to Helena, whose heavenly hand he is holding. He offers Helena a reassuring smile, which she returns.

Bill looks ecstatic.

Nora reaches out her other hand to Stella.

"The veil between our worlds is thin but difficult to negotiate," says Miss Dence, with the air of someone reciting. "If the conditions are right a spirit might make contact. You can't corral them, nor can you summon them. We must simply be open to them, receptive." With a stern gaze she makes one last sweep of the room before she closes her eyes. "I shall now enter a trance so that the spirits, such as wish to contact us tonight, can speak through me. Do not be alarmed, should my demeanor or appearance change; this is because I have become, temporarily, a mouthpiece for the other world."

Miss Dence closes her eyes and takes three deep breaths.

Nora squeezes Stella's hand. She looks wide-eyed and horrified in the dark.

The candlelight flickers, the grandmother clock in the hallway gives a muffled tick. The room suddenly feels close, airless. As if the walls are closing in on Nora. The space is shrinking and now it is full of the smell of Bill's hair oil and Irene's soap suds, Helena's perfume and the starch on Stella's collar. All this mingled with the smell of the supper they will be eating late tonight: scrag-end stew and dumplings. And another smell beyond this, just a waft, that comes and goes. Nora can't catch it—something dank, something briny.

Nora follows Miss Dence's voice. She closes her eyes. She focuses

on the inviolable circle. Never minding the darkness. She stays receptive
to those spirits who might drift about the corners, just out of eyeshot,
muttering, whispering, watching.

Miss Dence calls out to the void. "Is anyone there?"

There is no answer, only the odd smell grows stronger, dank sea
caves and moldering shells, underground passages, a draft of sudden
icy air.

Nora opens her eyes and looks around. Everyone else has their eyes
firmly shut and their hands linked around the table. The muffled clock
ticks, somewhere in the house a floorboard creaks, Miss Dence calls out
to the dead in a voice soft and plaintive so that it hardly sounds like her
own anymore.

The candles on the sideboard flicker gently. Nora focuses on one
of them; the flame burns quite steady in the still room, only now and
again wavering, a slow dance. Starting to feel drowsy in the close dark,
with the drone of Miss Dence's voice, she closes her eyes. A flame burns
on in her mind's eye. Nora's memory returns to her the flames she has
seen and known in the past. As a child at Mass, as a novice carrying her
candle in procession. The flame she held during the profession of her
vows. In the flickering candlelight she had felt the cold kiss of wood as
she lay facedown on the floor and died to the world. Never for one moment did she think she would ever return. The dank sea breeze comes
again, blowing sharp; the flame goes out.

And now comes the voice. *Whose* voice?

Wait for your eyes to adjust. You are in a tunnel, no, a pit. The walls
are patterned, smooth raised bumps, waves and whorls. There's light,
cool-toned, so, it must be moonlight. Moonlight through an opening to
the sky above. You are alone but for a slumped figure. Need you ask: a
woman. If she were alive her hands would be cold. She would hate the
chill of this place. The dank walls glisten. She would mind that dripping

sound. That scuffle of rats, near and nearer. If she were alive, she would look up to the light. She would shout out. Only her eyes are unseeing, a veil has passed over them.

Nora comes to. A crowd of faces peer down.

"Give her room," orders Miss Dence.

Nora's eyes fall on Stella, who stands apart from the rest. Nora sees, for only the briefest of moments, hard eyes in a blank face before the young woman's expression softens to one of concern.

Shivering violently and with her legs still feeling beyond her control, Nora is helped into the parlor by Bill and Irene. Miss Dence follows. The medium requests that strong tea and something sweet, marzipan ideally, is brought directly. Irene raises an eyebrow.

Ensconced in an easy chair with a blanket, Nora feels her shivering begin to lessen. A tray arrives with tea and a heel of stale madeira cake. Miss Dence takes the tray and requests that the others regain their seats at the table. She will be back in a jiffy. She closes the door and sets the tray down. Then, drawing up a footstool, she pours tea and hands Nora cake.

Nora tries to find words.

"Don't talk," she says. "Eat, drink."

Nora does what she's asked. To her surprise, she starts to feel better.

Miss Dence takes her spectacles from her breast pocket, puts them on, and peers closely at Nora. "Where did you find yourself, during the séance?"

"I heard a voice; it took me down to the place where Frieda fell. I thought it was you speaking."

"Not me, I was getting to grips with the Victorian consumptive who haunts the coal bunker. And did you sense Miss Brogan?"

"Yes. She was holding something out to me."

"Bingo." Miss Dence looks elated. "What was it?"

"I don't know; it was too dark and then I woke up."

Miss Dence looks a little disappointed. "No matter." She pats Nora's hand and gets up. "You have the gift, you ought to pay more attention."

"What gift?"

"For the spiritual, the otherworldly. Didn't you know?"

"I had an inclination."

"Don't rule out what you can't see. Don't discount what you struggle to understand. Keep an open mind, Miss Breen. You will, won't you?"

"Wide open."

CHAPTER 21

The morning after the séance, Nora sleeps in. She ignores the gray dawn and the sound of a beak tapping on the window. The day can wait and so can Father Conway. She ignores the sounds of the house waking, the doors opening and closing, the tread on stair and landing, the breakfast being served and cleared again. The milkman can go whistling down the road. The dim bunnies can keep on hopping through the wall. Life can go on without her. She turns her face to the wall.

But the memories come unbidden. So many mornings at the monastery. The velvet darkness in the winter. The cloudless sky in the summer. Moments of pure peace as well as moments where biting cold, or lack of sleep, or the uncertainties of faith made life something to be tolerated rather than enjoyed.

Nora remembers these times as the house quietens again.

She sits up with a start.

Stella is perched at the end of the bed. Her eyes have the same unblinking focus that Nora noticed last night. Like a sheep dog eyeing a flock.

"I didn't mean to startle, Nora!" she says. "I brought you a cup of something. I was worried about you after last night."

Nora follows Stella's gaze to a cup on the nightstand. Beside it a sugar bowl.

Nora realizes two things: that nothing in the world would incite her to drink the contents of that cup and that she herself feels, suddenly, heart-poundingly alert. Nora wonders at this strange overreaction on her part. The events of the past few days are no doubt to blame for her irrational response. Even so, Nora decides to trust her instincts.

"Don't let it get cold. It's cocoa." Stella measures a teaspoonful of sugar into the cup and daintily stirs it in.

Nora's mind clatters with the speed of a Laddland roller coaster. "What a kindness, Stella," she says. "Could I trouble you for more hot milk?"

Stella hesitates, the ghost of a frown. "I'll go and ask Rose."

With Stella gone, Nora springs into action; she decants the cocoa and pours a few grains of sugar into two separate twists of paper. Hiding both in the pocket of her robe, she jolts the nightstand with a quick firm shove. The sugar bowl goes over, the cup falls on the floor.

Stella comes in with the milk in a jug.

"Apologies, Stella. I am still a little dizzy it seems. What a terrible waste!"

Stella is gracious but Nora fancies her smile looks fixed. The young woman fetches a cloth and mops the puddle of cocoa. She retrieves the cup and sweeps the stray grains of sugar into the bowl.

"Thank you," says Nora. "Will we have some fresh air? Come, sit by the window with me."

They look out at a drear gray sky and a flat gray sea and a wet gray beach.

"I'm keeping you from your work, Stella."

Stella shrugs. "I'll go directly." She keeps her eyes on the horizon line. "I hated last night; that meddling medium."

"Did you, Stella? Were you frightened?"

"Of course not! But I don't blame you for fainting. It was perfectly awful. The dark, stuffy room and that awful bossy woman banging on about the dead."

"You think it wrong, meddling, as you call it, with the dead?"

"Oh, I don't believe in all that. I just feel it was a little insensitive to those of us who have lost people."

They sit in silence for a while.

Stella exhales. "You know, sometimes I think it might be best just to let the whole thing go. To stop asking questions and just move on with life."

"Do you really feel that, Stella? Don't you want to find out what happened to Teddy?"

Stella rubs her eyes, attempts a smile, but it's bitter. "No one seems to really care about that but me."

"I went to visit Percy Ladd to ask him some questions. Frieda had been seen with him at the Marine Hotel. He said that you had sent Frieda to talk to him about Teddy."

Stella meets Nora's eyes with her own clear gaze. "That's not fully true. Frieda rather took it upon herself. She had seen how miserable Teddy was becoming and how that affected me too."

"Why didn't you tell me about this?"

Stella looks awkward. "Because that first meeting led to other meetings between them. I felt responsible in a way, for putting Frieda in the way of harm. Percy doesn't have a good reputation."

Nora watches Stella closely. "I asked Percy why he thought you didn't go yourself."

Stella flushes. Her eyes flash. "What did he tell you? That he's been after me for months?"

Nora doesn't answer.

"When it comes to Percy, I've done nothing wrong. He chases all the girls. The more you resist him the more he wants you. The chase is more exciting than the kill."

Nora studies the young woman. It occurs to her that despite her innocent demeanor, Stella has a shrewdness about the world and most particularly men.

"I needn't have bothered," Stella continues. "Percy told Teddy of course and it caused such problems between him and me. He was angry at Frieda too. I suppose he felt as if we were conspiring behind his back but Frieda practically volunteered to stick her oar in!"

Nora changes tack. "Can you describe how Percy Ladd treated Teddy?"

Stella seems to calm a little. "Oh, he would set him impossible tasks or have Teddy do all the lowliest work. He would deride him before the others. Teddy was dreadfully sensitive, but he would never complain, at least not to him."

"Do you know why Percy acted like this?"

"Jealousy, I suppose. Teddy was popular with old father Ladd, I think. Everyone thought well of him."

Nora considers the photograph in Karel Ježek's possession, the two men as boys. "Teddy had many friends, then. Anyone in particular?"

Stella speaks firmly. "Teddy was well liked but he wasn't interested. He just wanted to stay quietly at home with me."

Nora chooses her words carefully. "Was he pals with Karel Ježek? Before they fell out?"

"No, they barely spoke to one another."

"He didn't know him from before?"

Stella looks confused. "Of course not, why would he? That man was a perfect stranger. He moved into the house the same week as us."

"And you are certain he was a stranger to you both?"

"Of course. Really, Nora, you ask the oddest questions."

She sees Nora watching her and smiles, her expression frank, guileless. Something like the old Stella returns and Nora wonders if she could have been very wrong. What is it about this place that even the innocent might appear malevolent?

"Where do you think Frieda was going on the night she disappeared?"

"I really don't know."

"Do you think that she went to meet Percy?"

Stella shrugs. "Does it matter now? How would we ever fathom what happened?"

"By searching for clues, compiling evidence—"

Stella laughs but not unkindly. "You're talking about the world of stories. Life isn't like that. It's twisted and messy and nasty things happen to nice people quite randomly. Bad luck is just that, it doesn't need an explanation."

CHAPTER 22

The desk sergeant barely looks up when Nora comes into the police station.

"Sergeant," she says. "If you could apply yourself to the pressing and unsolved cases in the town with the same diligence as you attack your little pad there, you would surely get a nice shiny medal."

No answer.

"Sergeant, if I could just have your attention."

No answer.

"Sergeant?"

This time the thrown shoe lands just short of the police officer with a satisfying clatter. Startled, he looks up.

"There now, that wasn't hard at all, was it?"

Yes, a message has been left for Miss Breen. No, Miss Breen cannot use the station's telephone. On this the desk officer is adamant. The findings of lay sister Anwen will just have to wait. As will the opportunity to speak with Inspector Rideout, it appears.

Hasn't she heard? The inspector suffered an injury in the line of duty. He's at home, just been discharged from the infirmary. No, the desk sergeant is not prepared to divulge the details of how said injury came about. Neither is he willing to divulge Inspector Rideout's home address.

Nora wonders if she might create a diversion to give her time to snoop through the daybook, make a quick telephone call, find out where to locate Rideout.

She could report a fire, a nuisance, a brawl, a murder.

Looking at the copper's fat head hunkered down, she knows he wouldn't buy it.

Nora walks through the town. She wonders when it became so difficult to find answers. Or has the truth always come hard-won? People rarely say what they mean, relationships are fraught with misunderstandings, who can really be objective? How can she even hope to pinpoint motives and actions, drives and desires when they are all so muddled and slippery, even in the best of us? Who among us really knows our own heart, let alone someone else's?

She passes by Mr. Hosmer's photographic studio. Her picture has gone from the window. She feels a pang of relief but also disappointment. Her image has been replaced by one of a smug couple, nattily dressed, their hats at corresponding tilts. They could be about to catch a plane, or a train, or a boat. They have glossy hair and bright eyes and are poised and ready for adventure.

Nora feels suddenly jaded, knowing, deeply, that she hasn't the hat, the hair, the time for adventure. For a moment, she yearns for her old life. For a moment, she wishes she had never agreed to Frieda writing to her. That she had asked her friend to keep her experiences out in the world to herself. Nora would be at High Dallow right now if she had. At this time of day, she would be working in the kitchen gardens, mulching, pruning, and tying. Not sticking her coulter into other people's business.

Her mind would be a still, calm pool, or at least, barely rippled. Gone now are the certainties of knowing her place in the greater scheme of things. Gone now is her purpose and peace. In her old life every waking moment was prescribed, ordered. That order will never return. Panic washes over her. Nora takes a breath or two. When the feeling subsides, she reminds herself to be honest, knowing, as she does, that sometimes we lie to ourselves most of all. Was the split with her community, her vows, her God, really caused by Frieda disappearing? Or was that just the catalyst? Hadn't there been certain moments, turning points, incidents— She stops herself. Now is not the time to open that particular can of snakes.

Either way, she must accept that now she is flotsam and jetsam.

So, she drifts.

She goes into the cheap café and orders what she can't afford. She eats three iced buns and barely tastes them. She sees her face in the metal teapot. Peering. Baffled. A fluff of peppery hair growing back. A well-used face. She walks. She sees herself moving past shop windows. Wandering. Aimless. She watches other people, weaving down pavements, stopping to gossip, rummaging in bags, wondering at the weather. Turning a corner, she finds herself outside a gentleman's tailor's shop of an expensive-looking kind. In the window, a single jacket is displayed. A sharply cut garment in rich mossy tweed. The jacket is pinned open so that passersby can catch a glimpse of its marvelous silk lining. The colors bright, the design birds of paradise, if Nora is not mistaken.

Half an hour later and she is entirely delighted with herself. Her coin purse is terminally depleted. Now she will struggle to find the price of a clutch of mackerel heads for Father Conway. Because she holds, wrapped in tissue paper, a paisley silk cravat in a fetching deep Bordeaux. And, from the customer order book on the counter, a memorized address.

Without the tram fare Nora has a fair walk. She roams inland, away from the sprawl of the seaside town, where the lanes narrow and become quieter. The afternoon brightens, the hedgerows are painted with autumn color, and the clouds scud away. She gets into a good stride and her body thanks her for it and her earlier despondency falls away.

She asks directions on reaching a picturesque village, with gnarled trees, a pub, and a duck pond, turning up a gentle slope to a handsome redbrick house.

The garden, she notes, is neglected and the curtains drawn against the day, but it is a lovely spot. She rings on the doorbell. Finding no answer, she negotiates with trepidation the overgrown path around the side of the house.

Inspector Rideout is on the terrace. He wears a Panama hat tilted forward over his face. Rounding the terrace, she sees his arm is in a sling.

"Inspector Rideout."

The man is up from his chair, swearing. He frowns as if trying to place her. His face, already scarred, has sustained further injuries, seemingly to the region of his ear, which is covered with a bulky, clumsily applied bandage.

"You were not at the station, they said you were injured in the line of duty."

Rideout gapes, sways, seems to recover, frowns. "You came out to my house."

"I did." Nora's glance takes in the empty bottles and overflowing ashtray surrounding his chair. "Will I put the kettle on?"

Rideout sits at the kitchen table. He is surprisingly tractable. Nora puts this down to the fact that he's still inebriated. Checking through the pantry she finds many more empty bottles but also fresh milk and a few provisions.

She makes strong coffee for them both and sets it down.

Nora sips hers as she watches him negotiate the coffeepot and sugar bowl one-handedly, his bandaged hand still in the sling. He is unshaven, the scars to his jaw and neck are described by the patches where stubble does not grow.

To his credit he comes to himself more quickly than she anticipates. While he does, she looks around the room. An old-fashioned house, with a heavy wood dresser in the country style and wallpaper that has seen better days. It is not filthy but neither is it well maintained. Given the moldering provisions in the pantry, Nora suspects the inspector has only an occasional char.

She glances back to find him watching her.

"It was my mother's house. She died last year."

"I'm sorry for your loss."

"Thank you." He gestures towards the French windows. "Garden, it was her joy."

Nora glances out at a tumble of overblown roses, gone-over spears of hollyhocks, and leggy lavenders. A swath has been cut through the lawn to a toolshed, otherwise the whole has been ignored.

Rideout fixes her with his light brown eyes. "How on earth did you find me?"

Nora slides the tissue-paper-wrapped package across the table.

"What is this?"

"From your tailor. They also gave me your address."

"They wouldn't."

"Inadvertently."

"Detective Breen." He picks up the package with his good hand and goes at the ribbon with his teeth.

"It's a cravat."

"You barge into my house and give me a cravat—"

"I hardly barged, you opened the door and stepped aside."

Rideout raises his eyebrows.

Nora changes the subject. "What happened to you? They wouldn't say at the station, or at least not the specifics."

"Got shot at. Armed robbery."

"Goodness, any damage?"

"Top of my ear and a finger. Nothing vital." Rideout laughs. "I managed to get through the war with the best part of my face intact and a gang of louts from London nearly did for me. They took aim, I dodged."

"Were they louts?"

"Actually, they were quite organized, considering. They'd come to the seaside on an away day and saw an opportunity. The Marine Hotel was counting up the money after a big convention."

"The Ladd family won't like that."

"No, I don't expect they will. But every officer in Kent will be on the case."

"Isn't it a world of difference where the rich and the powerful are involved? I suppose this means your other cases are let to slide?"

Rideout eyes Nora closely. "By other cases, you mean the Gulls Nest deaths?"

"I do."

"One suicide and two accidents."

"It's doubtful that Teddy drank poison to kill himself, questionable that Frieda just fell—but to consider Poppy's death an accident—that's ridiculous. Who says?"

"The coroner."

Nora frowns. "How do you know that?"

"Tip-off."

"You don't believe that, surely? The deaths of Teddy Atkins and Professor Poppy only days apart. And there were Frieda's suspicions."

"Only she never wrote them down, did she?"

Nora frowns. "There was one more letter; Bill saw it in the letter tray the night she disappeared. What if someone took it?"

"More likely it got lost in the post."

"Do you know how reliable the postal service is?"

Rideout looks weary. "Why are you here? Is it just to berate me?"

Nora fishes in her bag and brings out her sample pots. She puts them on the table. "Stella made me cocoa."

"And?"

"I want your laboratory to test these."

Rideout laughs again. "My laboratory? Of course, it's at your disposal."

Nora feels her cheeks begin to warm. Her armpits will follow suit. She tries to think cool thoughts.

"Test for what exactly?"

"It doesn't smell like bitter almonds." She frowns. "She was acting suspiciously."

"Come on, sunny little Mrs. Atkins? I thought she was your friend?"

Nora frowns. "It's hard to tell with everything that's gone on."

Rideout's voice becomes kinder, almost gentle. "Perhaps you ought to leave that house? Start afresh in digs more calming to your imagination?"

"You told us to stay!"

"So I did."

"You must have thought there was foul play?"

"Miss Breen, we've been through this; our resources are very stretched—"

"Not for the likes of the Ladds."

"Look, Gore-on-Sea is only a backwater; a prudent person would visit, have their fun, leave again. It's a place no one really cares about full of people that just drift through."

"Is that why they've chosen you to police it?"

A shadow flickers in his eyes, the twinge of some forgotten pain.

"I'm sorry," says Nora.

Rideout gets up from the table and goes over to the sink. He finds a glass among the empties and fills it with water. He drinks, looking out of the window.

"Apologies, force of habit, living alone—do you want some?"

Nora shakes her head. She thinks a moment. "I know as well as you do that Gore-on-Sea is not a backwater. Think of all the money that flows into it, the Ladds, their empire."

Rideout exhales. "Once Gore-on-Sea was considered quaint, now it is ugly and sprawling. I never wanted to come back here, after the war."

"Why did you?"

"Oh, Mother and her garden." He salutes at the window with his glass, as if they are both bearing witness to him.

"You never married?"

"What?" Rideout smiles. "No, almost, but no. And you? Apologies, I forget sometimes, you are so worldly now."

Nora laughs. Rideout looks back into the garden.

"Were you a police officer before you served?"

"Good God no. I was an engineer."

"Why did you change?"

Rideout gives her one of his twisted smiles. "I wanted to make a difference. And there were openings. It meant I could be around for the final years. It was only me and her, you see."

Nora nods.

"What about you? I expect you were earmarked young for the religious life?"

"What makes you say that?"

"Oh, I don't know. You seem so strong-minded, uncompromising."

Nora thinks about this. "Traits that may not make a religious life easy. I was a nurse as well as a nun."

"So you were, I forget."

"And as a nurse I'd ask who dressed your ear. Surely they didn't send you out of the infirmary with that?"

"I'm afraid they did. Are you shocked?"

"Greatly."

"Can you rectify it?"

"I'd be glad to."

Rideout directs her to the first aid box. It is kept in a little adjoining washhouse. The bandages and gauzes are old and yellowed but serviceable. At her request he takes off his jacket and loosens the top button of his shirt. Nora removes the dressing with a gentle hand. The bullet has sliced through, claiming almost a third of his ear.

"Is it ghastly? Are my good looks ruined?"

Nora smiles. "You'll live. It's clean and healing well, despite the dressing."

"Then the infirmary did something right."

When she is done Nora lays a comforting hand on his shoulder, absentmindedly, as she would with any of her patients.

The smallest exhalation from Rideout brings her to her senses. She looks down and there's her hand and his shoulder beneath it. His head is bent forward slightly, his nape oddly vulnerable and his hair thick and curling and in need of a cut. She feels the warmth of his skin through his shirt, the scent of smoke and woody soap from him.

His voice comes to her quietly. "Am I done?"

"You are." Nora takes her hand away.

She is all bustle. Packing up the dressings, returning the first aid box, patting dry her forehead with a tea towel. His eyes trail her about the kitchen, lit with some kind of amusement, a half smile on his lips.

"What about my hand?" He flaps the wing of his arm in the sling.

Nora pauses, glances. "Now that's well bandaged."

"The ward sister did it."

"I can tell."

"I looked in on Karel Ježek before I left the infirmary. He's awake now."

"And what did he tell you about the assault?"

"He's refusing to talk."

"To you?"

"To anyone."

Nora considers this. "So, we don't know who left him for dead. But we do know Percy Ladd took him to the infirmary. He admitted as much when I interviewed him."

"For pity's sake, Nora." Rideout looks at her in exasperation. "I really wish you wouldn't! Playing detectives, at your age!"

"What about my age? By my reckoning I'm not above five years your senior."

"I'm not yet forty-five."

"Give or take."

Rideout's vexation is tempered by a smile.

Nora takes a seat opposite, glances at him coolly. "Do you want to hear my findings, such as they are?"

Rideout rubs his forehead with his good hand. "Do I have a choice?"

Nora, in brief and with no extraneous details or deviations, outlines her experiences of the past few days. Rideout listens, only raising his eyebrows when she describes her joyride with Percy. Nora chooses her words carefully when she describes her collapse at the séance.

"You found her in the dark with her hand outstretched, as if in supplication?"

Nora recounts the positioning of Frieda's body, watching Rideout's expression change from skepticism to wonder.

"Yes. We found her exactly as you describe."

* * *

Nora walks out along the terrace. She needs some air. A few moments. She'll be as right as rain. The day darkens so early now, she can see in through the French window, Rideout is switching on lamps. She folds her arms around herself; her dress is thick, she is not chill. She just wants a breeze on her face but inland the weather is less bracing; she is sheltered by a dead mother's garden that smells of lavender and leaf loam. She wonders about her own mother. Nodding by a fire in a neat cottage in Mayo. Growing her few greens. Fussing after her chickens. Tuning in her radio. Living for the bit of news. Nora's own father up at the graveyard, his last years spent grinding his jaw against the misery of seizing joints. She wonders if she'll visit them now that she's at liberty in the world.

And now here is Rideout coming out to her, with her coat in his hands.

He lights a fire in the sitting room grate. It's a smoky affair but she thanks him, although she's not cold and didn't catch a chill at all.

They share a meat pie and a slippery clutch of pickled onions and he tells her anecdotes about the RAF, the hilarious ones, not the one that saw him shot down, fuselage flak-punctured, spiraling through the sky into enemy territory. She tells him anecdotes about the sisters she nursed, the charming ones, not the one about the sister who died roaring without faith and with her life sacrificed for nothing.

Laughing still at her stories, he disappears into the pantry and returns jubilant, with a bottle of wine. Nora knows it's time to go and says as much.

He falters, nods, offers to run her back to Gulls Nest.

Following him into the hallway Nora has a thought. "Do you have a telephone?"

*   *   *

It is late, but lay sister Anwen has been up packaging communion wafers. The sisters have been having great success with mechanization in the manufacture of hosts. This is the machine age after all. They are trading farther and farther afield. Supply and demand. Anwen says she experiences nothing short of joy in packing all those little round disks. Just the thought of them all going out into the world to be blessed by the hands of unknown priests and placed on all those innocent tongues.

Nora has no answer for that. She lets Anwen rattle on while she watches Rideout.

He waits for her in the front porch, she can see him through the glass door. He is smoking, hatless. He has his collar turned up, the bandage on his ear won't allow for a hat. For all this he still looks the part: a leading man, albeit of the rumpled and tortured kind. Nora sits in the hallway, telephone receiver cradled in her hand, Anwen blathering. She leans forward, takes in the view up the stairs. A lovely oak staircase, the carpet good but dusty. On the wall there are paintings, mostly landscapes, among them a half-length portrait of a mild-eyed young woman just at the turn of the landing. Rideout's mother perhaps, with the man himself never marrying. Nora frowns at an unseemly feeling of relief at this thought and applies herself to her telephone call.

"As you might know," continues Anwen, "*Cuddfan* is not a very unusual name for a house, so I had scant hope in finding the location of the photograph for you, let alone the identity of the children in it."

"I do understand," replies Nora, disappointed that a network of nuns could fail to uncover this information. "Thank you for trying."

"However, that did not stop me asking around, extensively, tirelessly, on your behalf, Nora."

"Much appreciated, Anwen. I'm sorry to take up your time on a wild-goose chase."

"That's just it." Anwen's voice bubbles with excitement. "I've found that house and the boys."

"Fair play!"

Rideout glances in, Nora widens her eyes. He looks away again.

"It just so happens that one of our sisters, originally from the area of Carmarthenshire, knew of a farm with the same name. A sad story, like so many sad stories from the war."

A pause for reflection at the other end of the line. Nora waits.

"The tale goes that the farmer, who had one young son, called John, took on an evacuee from London. His boy was by all accounts an insular little chap preferring his own company and that of the animals and birds. Nevertheless, he took to the evacuee, whose name was Theodore, and the two became inseparable. They went everywhere together, two handsome boys: bright-haired, smiling Theo and dark, scowling John."

Nora feels a shiver run through her, hearing the foreshadowing in Anwen's tale.

"Until, for reasons only known to him, in 1943 Theo enlisted."

"He wasn't old enough, surely?"

"Barely sixteen."

"Theo lied about his age to enlist?"

"Like so many, Nora."

A silence falls between the two. Anwen is no doubt praying for the souls of fallen underage soldiers; for their sins, such as they had time to commit. Nora would have done the same once. Now all she thinks about is the waste of young lives.

Anwen continues. "John, who was furious with his friend for going away, promptly joined up to be with Theo. He was half a year younger."

"Could their families do nothing to get them back?"

"What could they do? Two willful lads lost overseas and the whole world at war."

"Not quite the whole world, Anwen."

"Granted. But here's the tragedy of it: only one of the boys came back."

"Which one?"

"Theo. John Morgan was killed in combat. Which was perhaps even more of a tragedy as the young man had acted with remarkable bravery and was awarded medals posthumously."

"He was killed?"

"He was."

"Not missing?"

"No. Definitely killed. Theodore returned to the farm he had been evacuated to all those years before. It is said that he grieved terribly. The farmer, who appeared to hold no grudges for the loss of his son, asked Theo to stay and work on the farm."

"And did he?"

"For a time, yes. But it seems that Theo could not settle. I suppose the place reminded him of his lost friend. Some friendships run very deep, don't they? Sometimes to the detriment . . ."

Nora detects a note of accusation in Anwen's voice.

She ignores it. "Where did Theo go?"

"Nobody knew. There was talk locally that he'd gone to London and fallen in with a bad crowd, got himself into trouble. If the old farmer knew he wasn't saying anything."

"Thank you, Anwen."

"As, in my view, so often happens to impressionable young people out in the world who are not guided by Christ's light—"

"Anwen, *thank you.*"

"You are welcome, Nora."

Inspector Rideout pulls up, at Nora's request, at the bottom of the road. He kills the engine. Outside it has begun to rain, a pleasant sound on the roof.

Nora has enjoyed the ride: the dark country lanes, the empty pavements, and now the lights along the promenade. They merge and bleed as she looks through the raindrops on the window. She traces the descent of one drop as it winds down the glass and wonders why so few things take a direct route.

The dark made it easier to tell John and Theo's story. Nora told it plainly and Rideout listened in silence, making no comment.

A motion; Rideout has turned to her in the dark. "Good work, Breen."

Nora says nothing. She traces another falling raindrop.

"I'll pay another visit to Karel Ježek tomorrow," Rideout says.

"Don't you mean John Morgan?"

"Let's wait for the whole story before we refer to him by that name. I'd like you to come with me."

"What for?"

"He'll talk to you."

"And not to you?"

"There might be things he doesn't feel comfortable disclosing, you know." Rideout hesitates. "To another chap."

Nora finds another raindrop, one moving in a different trajectory to the others, erratic, diagonal. Perhaps blown by the wind. Perhaps charting its own course, if a raindrop can do such a thing. Nora traces it, absorbed.

Rideout's voice breaks in. "You have the photograph?"

"Up in my room, shall I fetch it?"

"Bring it with you. I'll pick you up after breakfast."

Nora considers. "You think I can take the lead on this interview?"

"I wouldn't expect anything less, Breen."

CHAPTER 23

Rideout is true to his word. He is waiting in his car as she steps down the promenade. She gets into the passenger seat, glad to see him spruced and alert, the mustache reinstated, his hair brushed, bandages still in place.

"You look like a leading man again."

Rideout laughs and puts the car into gear with his good hand, steering with his knees. "It's safer than it looks," he adds.

"I'm saying nothing," says Nora.

It's a bright October morning and Gore-on-Sea is already busy with day-trippers. A full coach passes them and heads down the road towards Laddland; a passenger salutes Nora with a paper cup.

"The fun starts early."

"A work's outing," says Rideout. "Some of them get raucous."

"They never stop coming, do they?"

"The season extends every year. Wait until summer arrives."

"I won't be here in the summer."

Rideout glances at her. "Is that right? Where will you be?"

"I expect I shall travel."

"Good for you."

Rideout swings the car into the grounds of Gore-on-Sea Royal Infirmary. The existing Victorian façade has been extended to give new wards and an accident and emergency department as befitting a popular seaside resort. Karel Ježek has been moved to a general ward since Nora last looked in, which means he is improving, she tells Rideout.

A young red-haired ward sister at the nurses' station welcomes Rideout back with—to Nora's mind—a predatory variety of smile.

"Back so soon, Inspector?"

Nora glances at Rideout. He's returning her smile, all teeth and eyes.

"Not that you aren't welcome anytime." Nurse Smiler turns to Nora. "Can I help you, dear? Is she lost?"

Nora scowls at the nurse.

Rideout intervenes. "This is Breen. She's with me."

The nurse looks doubtful. "Sergeant Breen?"

"Inspector Breen," says Nora. "We've come to question one of your patients. Mr. Ježek?"

The nurse nods. "Of course. If you'll come this way, Inspectors, his bed is at the end of the ward."

Nora and Rideout follow her.

"It's rather that you are with me," hisses Nora. "Since it's my lead we're following up on."

"Magnanimous of you."

The nurse glances behind and throws Rideout another smile.

"That one bandaged your ear, didn't she?"

"She did."

"She wants to concentrate less on smiling and more on dressings." She meets Rideout's amused glance. "What?"

And here is Mr. Ježek's bed.

The young man's injuries may have healed since Nora last saw him but he has got so much thinner, a ghost of himself. He is lying on his side facing the window, his eyes closed, seemingly asleep. Bundled under his head is the army greatcoat.

The nurse speaks low to Nora. "We don't quite know what to do with him. Physically he is almost well enough to leave but he won't speak and will barely eat. The doctors are looking to find him a place at Park Mount if he doesn't perk up."

"An asylum not far from here," explains Rideout.

Nora glances at the young man in the bed. "Will you both give me a moment?"

Rideout looks surprised but steps back as Nora draws the fabric screen around Karel's bed. She sits down on the visitor's chair and taking the leather-framed photograph from her bag, gently slips it under the young man's hand.

She watches closely and waits. For all the world it looks as though Karel Ježek sleeps on, but Nora can discern a shift, a change in breathing perhaps, a flicker of his eyelashes.

She gets up slowly and exits through the curtains.

Inspector Rideout stands a few beds away. He looks round as Nora approaches.

She turns to the nurse. "Keep the curtains closed for a bit. I'll visit again soon."

Nora strikes out towards the entrance hall.

Rideout catches up. "You were quick, what did you get?"

"Nothing today."

Rideout frowns. "But you interviewed him?"

"I did not."

"So, when you actually have permission to stick your nose in, you don't? You are perverse, Breen, has anyone ever told you that?"

"The thing is, people don't all communicate in the same way. Sometimes you have to draw a story out gradually. Like hooking a fish."

"Is that right? So, how long have we got to solve this case? All the time in the world?"

Nora glances at Rideout, who immediately looks away, making a big point of rummaging in his pocket for cigarettes.

She stifles a grin. "How long have *we* got? As long as it takes, Rideout."

Rideout lights two cigarettes, passes her one with a curt nod to let her know this is expediency not romance.

Nora accepts it and inhales without thinking. She catches Rideout looking at her, narrowing an eye against the smoke, like a gun slinger. She wonders if he knows he's cinematic.

"So, what's next, Nora Breen?"

"I have other fish to catch. A very big fish and a very little one."

Nora heads to Laddland, following the trail of the work's outing coach, now parked at the entrance of the amusement park, its driver already dozing at the wheel. Its occupants have spilled out among the attractions. They still clutch their paper cups; added to this are hats and sashes bearing the name of their employer. They come from a jam factory it seems, which explains why some have dressed up as soft fruit. A group of tipsy raspberries have boarded paddleboats and are making raucous turns about the lake. A middle-aged plum is trying his hand in the shooting gallery. A gaggle of strawberries bicker on the crazy golf course.

There is no sign of Percy Ladd or his marvelous French sports car, but then, Nora hasn't come to see Percy. A gardener directs her to a vast four-tiered yellow stuccoed building. It has the look of a sandcastle a giant's child might build. Each of the four turrets boasts a flag emblazoned with the Laddland logo, with colors garish in the harsh October sun. The foyer is full height, the walls painted with waves, sea creatures the size of buses hanging on wires: a crab, a leaping fish, a mermaid. A map tells her that the sandcastle houses the Coral Ballroom, Penny Arcade, Gaiety Theatre, Wild West Bar, and the offices of Harry Ladd. Harry Ladd, who mixes with the great and the good even as he is rumored to know every sordid undercurrent that washes through this town. The challenge will be to extract any information out of him at all; he is said to be a man who gives nothing freely. But he may, even inadvertently, shed light that will help Nora make sense of the puzzles at Gulls Nest. At the very least he might give clarity to Percy's actions of late.

At this time of day only the arcade is open. Lights flash and flicker on the coin machines, the Lucky Dip, the Cupid's Secret. A few grisly old fellas hang about a bank of peep shows. Younger men doggedly play pinball, cigarettes hanging from their mouths. A group of young women queue for an automaton palm reader. The place smells of stale smoke and popcorn, candy floss and spilt beer. With its windowless rooms and high ceilings, the space has a cavernous feel. The noise of the machines at play and the roars of the players, the metallic music piped through loudspeakers, all find echoes as the sound clatters around. Nora takes a wrong turn in her confusion and finds herself in the hall of mirrors. There is Nora, her face distorted, her mouth wide, her head a pin, her legs like trunks, her neck four feet long. She closes her eyes and gropes her way out.

More by luck than by design she stumbles across a staircase. The walls are red velvet, the carpet is red too and thick on every tread, the banister is gold. But at least the heavy door that swings closed behind her muffles the noise. The staircase winds around a central column housing a gated elevator, a smart affair in gold and black. Nora tries the gate but finds it locked. High above there is a domed skylight. She decides to climb. A few turns up the staircase and she passes long narrow

windows, mock arrow slits. She has found her way into one of the turrets. As Nora climbs the views open up and the grounds of the amusement park spread out below her, the sun glancing off the lake and the
tiny paddleboats, the Big Dipper and the Ferris wheels and all the little
stalls and flower beds that punctuate the rides. A ringing sound and a
clank and the elevator starts to rise as if magically summoned, passing
Nora effortlessly by as she labors up. Breathless, Nora reaches the point
where the stairs and the lift terminate in the middle of a dazzling room.
The floor is white marble veined with black, windows are set in all the
walls so that the space has the feeling of a lighthouse. On one side long,
low couches are ranged, tomato color and of shiny leather. They sur-
round a huge oval table of smoky glass. Nora keeps walking round. Here
are glass display cases with tiny scale models of the park and ahead a
desk, a dark slab of wood, a brutal shape. Sat behind the desk on a chair
made from chrome and leather, there's a man, watching her.

He is late middle-aged and dressed like an old-time banker, curiously at odds against the stark setting. His suit is black, his waistcoat
too. Over his large belly a gold watch chain is strung. His nose blooms
red and his face is gimlet-eyed and flabby. His wide mouth is down-
turned like that of a toad, in fact there is something very toad-like about
the man. The broad back and the thin limbs, the pockets of loose flesh.
If his son could represent Lust, this man could represent Greed. His
eyes, like Percy's, have a lascivious gleam to them that years of excess
have done little to dull. He waves his plump hand.

"Take a pew. What can I do you for, love?"

Perhaps he catches the grimace that Nora tries to hide, for his smile
widens. Nora sees all at once she has wasted her time coming here. This
man would give nothing away, not even if it were free.

"You made short work of the stairs; I'll give you that. Wait now, get
your breath back."

"Mr. Ladd—"

"Guilty! Call me Harry."

"I've come to talk about Teddy Atkins."

The smile falters. "And who are you when you're at home?"

"A fellow boarder at Gulls Nest."

Harry points a fat finger towards the window to the left of him. "Right there. That's where the trouble started. I've staff lodgings here, him and his natty little wife would have been right comfortable. Wouldn't hear of it. Staying in that hole, that's what did him in."

"Teddy had worked for you since the start of the year?"

A flash of what appears to be genuine emotion, regret, sympathy crosses Harry's face. "Teddy was like a son to me. A better worker you could not get. Turn his hand to anything, ever so polite. But then he had a wicked sense of humor too, he had me in stitches. Not an ounce of badness in that lad."

"His wife believed Teddy was mistreated during the course of working for you, that it was the cause of considerable upset for him."

The mouth turns down. "She's suing me? The little bitch!"

Nora frowns. "No, she wants to get to the bottom of his death."

"Poor girl, she would of course. Topped himself. That's the bottom of it."

"That might not be the case. I believe the death of Teddy Atkins is somehow linked to two further deaths of Gulls Nest residents."

He hoots. "Two more, is it? Beggars belief why you're still living there! I've a nice chalet I can let to you on the cheap, if you like?"

"I won't be leaving."

"Balls of steel."

"The other deaths—"

Harry holds up a plump hand. "Stop you there. I read the local rag. Besides, I don't do death before luncheon." His eyes fall on her. "Join me?"

"I'm not hungry."

"Cockles? And chips, if you're lucky."

"Let's get back to Teddy Atkins. Your son allegedly bullied him."

"*Allegedly* is the word there."

"Are you disputing it?"

"No." Harry's jowls soften, as does his voice. "Percy had it in for the boy, that much I know. To be honest, I think he was after Teddy's wife."

"Stella?"

"Stella, is it? She's a flossy, by reputation."

"I don't know what that is."

"A girl who is married but still tempts other fellas."

"That's what they say about Stella?"

"Teddy's missus, yes." Harry smiles. "I think Percy went after her and she turned him down. Jealousy. Percy had much to be jealous about. There was Teddy, everyone liked him, everyone wanted to pat him on the back, shake hands with him. Honest, good-looking, quiet lad. Then there's Percy and—apologies to the memory of his dead mother— he's a twisted shit who no one likes."

"There are elements in Teddy's death that point to foul play."

"And you think that Percy killed him? My son's an unctuous bastard but he's not a murderer."

"Frieda Brogan."

"Dead girl in the hole?"

"She was my friend."

"Condolences."

"She'd met Percy at least twice at the Marine Hotel."

"Her and a hundred others, they're not dead."

"She wrote me a letter to say that she was uncovering secrets. It was in her nature to be curious."

"You know what they say about curiosity." Harry joins his hands together, puts his doughy chin on them. "She was uncovering no secrets of mine, dear, I didn't know her. My son is a nasty bastard, granted, but

I doubt if he finished her off. Push her down a well? He wouldn't have had the mettle."

"It wasn't a well; it was an underground shell grotto."

"Does it have an owner? Sounds ripe for a public attraction. And the third death? What did Percy have to do with that one?"

"You read the gazette, figure it out."

Harry smiles. "Percy never liked Punch as a child. No real sense of humor. Poppy was an old character in a town of old characters, knew him well. So, he choked on his swazzle? He was a showman—who's to say it wasn't the way he wanted to go?"

Nora pounces. "Poppy's cause of death wasn't reported in the newspapers."

"Wasn't it?"

"No."

The smile widens, like the toad that caught all the flies. "Look out that window, love. I built that, every ride, every slot machine, every twinkling dream. I was born at the bottom of the heap and I've worked my way up to these dizzy heights. King of the seaside. Top of the world. How did I do that? By looking around myself, knowing what's what, keeping my eyes and my ears open. A seagull can't fart in this town without me knowing about it, Nora Breen."

Nora is taken aback but hides it. "I'll get to the bottom of it."

"I expect you will. In the meantime, mind how you go."

"And if Percy—"

"If Percy turns out to be responsible, I'll be the first to turn him in; he's neither use nor ornament to me. His mother spoiled him, you see, rest her soul. Coddled him. Takes after her side, I see nothing of myself in him."

"Maybe you underestimate your son?"

"I don't think so."

"What about Percy's recent act of compassion?"

Harry laughs. "Come off it."

"Didn't he drive Karel Ježek, also a Gulls Nest resident, to the infirmary the other night? Percy's actions certainly saved his life; Karel had
been beaten and left for dead. You didn't know? Perhaps you don't catch
every gull's fart?"

The flicker of anger on Harry's face is almost too fast for Nora to
see, only that his gimlet eyes narrow, his wide mouth sags. But then the
toad, slippery to the last, smiles wider.

"Isn't it sometimes the way," observes Nora, "that the person we
think we know best is the one we know least?"

CHAPTER 24

A change has occurred this past week at Gulls Nest. Nora wonders how it has slipped her by. But then, the change, if not gradual, has been subtle. The removal of Irene's more strident signs from the walls. The appearance of fresh-cut flowers on the supper table. In the parlor, the china dogs have moved gradually nearer to each other, and there seem to be a few more coals on the fire.

Nora wonders if the management are trying to offset the disadvantage of living in a boardinghouse with the highest death rate in Kent.

And now, as she passes by the kitchen door to the dining room, the sound of wireless music and giggling. She stops, opens the door a crack, listens hard, and recognizes Bill Carter's voice.

He is flirting.

Surely not with Irene?

Nora feels compelled to learn more, she walks through the door marked PRIVATE.

She finds Bill at the kitchen sink with his shirtsleeves rolled up. Helena is perched on the edge of the table watching him. She wears a kimono and her hair is long and loose. The kitchen smells deliciously of baking. The two are singing along with some nonsense on the radio.

They turn their radiant faces to Nora, who waves the empty jug.

Helena, coffee in hand, saunters out along the corridor. Bill promises her he will bring her warm madeleines shortly. Before she closes the door, she blows a kiss and Bill catches it.

He grins at Nora's look of bafflement. "Today, I'm in charge of breakfast," he says.

They sit at the kitchen table. Nora accepts a custard tart and admits it is quite wonderful. Bill recounts with sparkling eyes how, following the séance, the two of them had become closer. The magic happened, he thinks, the very moment they held hands. A spark ignited between them. Now it will be garden walks in the moonlight and beach walks at dawn and him creating all manner of patisserie delights for his beloved. Life is becoming as sweet as his landlady's tooth.

"Where is Irene?"

Bill shrugs. "She's been acting funny since Helena and me got together. She has threatened to leave." He lowers his voice. "To be honest that would be no bad thing. Imagine, we could run this place together, myself and Helena. Top-notch rooms and restaurant. A change of name perhaps, *Doves Nest*. Isn't that romantic? Less heckling. I could cook and Helena could grace the house with her luminous presence."

Nora raises her eyebrows.

Bill crashes back to earth. "But my darling won't hear of it, she seems so scared of offending Irene. It's like that old baggage has something over her, as if the poor darling is frightened of her. But I can guarantee you that Irene won't be an obstacle to our marriage."

Now Nora is amazed. "You are getting married?"

Bill smiles and holds his finger up to his lips in a gesture of secrecy. He rummages in his apron pocket and takes out a neat little ring box.

With a flourish he opens it: a lovely aquamarine flanked by two sizable diamonds.

"Isn't this all a bit sudden, Bill?"

Bill looks unconcerned. "Strike while the iron's hot! I'll propose tomorrow night. I'm planning on cooking a top-notch, fancy meal to celebrate. You are, of course, invited. All the residents are."

"What about Dinah?"

Bill lowers his voice. "I plan to pack her off to school. Residential. It will civilize her."

Nora frowns. "And Helena has agreed to that?"

"I'm sure she'll see sense," says Bill. "As I've said before, the child needs reining in."

There's a clatter outside and the back door handle turns. The door sticks as it always does, a small foot boots it, the door opens. Dinah comes in backwards, dragging a toy pram up the step after her.

"Talk of the devil," mutters Bill. "And up pop the horns."

Dinah, if it is possible, is even more bedraggled and dirty than the last time Nora saw her. Her face is smeared with jam and her hair is tangled with feathers. She is still dressed like an old lady going to the opera, only her hem is torn and her slippers muddy. She parks the pram by the pantry and hops over to the table, ignoring Nora and eyeing Bill warily.

She puts out her hand for a slice of tart.

"No," says Bill. "Wash your hands first, Dinah. We've been over this."

Dinah rolls her eyes. Bill beckons her to the sink, where he upturns a bucket. She clambers on and looks away as he runs the tap. Then she holds out her hands with an aggrieved expression as Bill dries them with a tea towel.

"You have a pram, Dinah?"

Dinah regards Nora coolly with her large blue eyes.

Bill nods. "A present from Uncle Bill. Show Nora your pram, Dinah."

Dinah turns her frosty gaze on Bill, who withers slightly under it, but she pigeon-steps across the kitchen floor and drags the pram, one-handed, rocking over to the table.

"Careful." Bill smiles. "What about your baby?"

But there is no baby. Nora sees, under the pink frilly canopy, that Dinah has filled the pram with rocks.

Bill sees it too. "Look at the mud! The pretty quilt all spoilt! Why would you do that, Dinah?"

Dinah ignores him. She takes the whole tart from the table, carrying the plate carefully with her two hands. Then she drops it into her pram, pulls up the hood, snap. With a derisive glance at Bill, she shoves the pram across the kitchen floor and down the step and slams the door behind her.

Bill opens his mouth to speak but the buzzer goes off on the oven. He puts the tea towel over his arm and turns to rescue the madeleines.

Nora goes out into the garden. She looks for signs of Dinah: a small footprint, or the trail of her pram's wheels, or a bead, or a feather. Passing under the oak tree Nora has the sense that she is being watched and looks up. Dinah is hanging blithely, high up in the tree, with one foot twisted in the rope ladder of the tree-house platform.

"Merciful Jesus!"

Dinah's upside-down mouth laughs soundlessly.

Nora shows her what she has: two freshly baked madeleines. She hopes that the smell will travel up. Perhaps it does, for in a while Dinah slowly comes down, rung by rung, on each rung revolving with her head thrown back like a circus performer.

Nora draws on three decades of patience.

Dinah insists on bringing her pram with them. Only now it seems lighter, bouncing over the path. The muddy quilt is pulled up over something smaller, a little humped shape.

"You've lost the rocks?"

Dinah shrugs and veers through weeds with her teeth gritted.

They go to the pond, which surprises Nora. She thinks of the crime Dinah was accused of; the attempted drowning of the laundry woman's daughter. Dinah sits down on the paved edge and peers briefly over the side, wrinkling her nose. Then she holds out her hand for her cake.

"I'm surprised you can manage this. You cleared most of Bill's tart."

Dinah mimes being sick then she points. Nora sees that the tart is splattered on the wall behind.

"You're a horror."

Dinah takes this as a compliment and smiles graciously.

They eat their treats in silence. Dinah pecking bits and then nibbling with her front teeth, Nora in the usual fashion.

"You found the notebook I left? And the coloring pencils?"

Dinah nods.

"And have you written in it, drawn pictures?"

Dinah gulps the last of her cake. Holds up her finger and stands. She steps over to the pram and lifting the mattress slides out the notebook.

"I'm glad you could make use of it. I thought it would stop you writing in mine." She throws Dinah a glance. "You haven't cut the paper to shreds then?"

Dinah frowns.

"You found my letters, didn't you? At first, I was sad because they were from my friend. But I suppose it doesn't matter, they are snowflakes now. I strung them up across the ceiling in my room. They dance in the breeze."

Dinah nods happily.

"You've seen them?"

Dinah nods sheepishly.

She has of course, thinks Nora, doesn't she let herself into every room when we are out? The sticky fingers, the peering face.

"There was one more letter I would very much like to see. One that I haven't read yet, so I'd be even sadder to see it cut up. It was from Miss Brogan, maybe the last letter she ever wrote. Do you remember her?"

Dinah shrugs.

"Would you have seen such a letter? It was in the post tray, but then, like Frieda, it disappeared."

Dinah glances at Nora slyly, then shakes her head.

"All right, so. Will we look at your notebook?"

Dinah, hugging the notebook to her chest, hops back and sits down. She hands it to Nora and gestures to her to turn the first page. The drawing, colored carefully, is unmistakably of Irene: the wide red face, the curranty eyes, the housekeeper's way of standing in her slatternly clogs.

"Mrs. Rawlings?"

Dinah nods, Nora turns the next page. Now Mrs. Rawlings's head is lopped from her body; it floats in a giant tureen. From the stump of her neck gushes a fountain of red. Nora is reminded of the bad dream she had not long after she arrived. She wonders that the tureen would feature so in the imagination, then she thinks of the frights that come out of it.

"Goodness. I'm not sure Mrs. Rawlings deserves that, does she?"

"She's drawn worse."

Nora looks up. The subject of the portrait is standing before them.

"No doubt she's drawn a horrible picture of you too, Miss Breen," says Irene. "She's like that."

Dinah grabs her notebook from Nora, pushes it back into the pram, and she's off, clattering over the mossy grass.

"She'll go back up into her tree house and sulk." Irene crosses her hands high on her chest. Her voice softens. "I'd rather she didn't. It's too high. I've told her mother that it's dangerous but as with most things she won't listen."

Nora is surprised. This is the first time that Irene has volunteered any consideration of Dinah's welfare. Perhaps despite her harsh pronouncements against her granddaughter, there is a kernel of love.

"Ah, she's grand," says Nora. "It takes great bravery to be your own person. Imagine who she'll grow into."

"I dread to think."

"Well, who remembers the tractable people in life?"

Irene smiles, a small smile, but it's like a glimmer of sunshine on a wet bank holiday. "Shall we take a turn?"

"We will."

They walk down to Poppy's workshop, the long low building all shuttered and closed. The place looks forlorn somehow, missing its owner.

"What will happen to all Poppy's things?"

"His nephew is coming for them." She glances at Nora. "He's a viscount."

"Well, I never. The auld rogue did speak the truth."

"On occasion." Irene points to the workshop. "There are spirits in there."

"You're not coming over all Miss Dence, are you?" Nora replies.

Irene laughs. "I meant brandy, gin, rum—Poppy kept the lot. What about a snifter? Wouldn't do us any harm."

"May even do us good?"

The two go inside. Nora fetches another chair and Irene lights the little burner. They find more than the spirits. A pouch of good pipe tobacco and something to convey it. Nora pours brandy into two clean jam jars with a generous hand; Irene stokes the pipe. Filling and cleaning, lighting and puffing expertly.

"You've done that before, Irene?"

"My granddad was a great pipe man, worked for the Port of London; he taught me everything I know."

"Well, you smoke like a docker."

"I thank you."

The two raise their jam jars.

"*Sláinte*," says Nora.

"Your health," says Irene.

They drink.

"Powerful stuff, Irene."

"Hairs on your chest, Nora."

Nora looks around herself, the place already gathering dust. The workbench where the cup and saucer and spoon were all laid out in a line. The place on the floor where Teddy's body was found.

"Another toast," says Irene. "Absent friends."

"Absent friends."

"I miss that old bastard," says Irene. "Poppy was a gentleman when all is said and done."

"Perhaps he did right not to stay in his castle then, to take to the road?"

"Perhaps," says Irene. "Although it would take something to leave all that behind."

"Maybe it was a millstone. He left for love you know?"

"He did?"

"Wanted someone he couldn't have. He gave up everything for them."

"It's an old story."

"People fall in love. It's not a question of wrong or right. I'd say if it happens, grab hold of it with both hands."

"Is that what you'd say, Nora?"

Nora pours another drink for them both. "I would."

"Were you ever in love?"

"Not properly. You?"

Irene smiles. "I was. I went into service in a house in Pimlico. He was the groom. Fine pair of legs, to see him in his uniform, the tights, the jacket."

"He was a looker?"

"He was. I loved the bones of him and for a short while, he loved me."

She passes the pipe to Nora, who takes small puffs. Irene nods. "You're not so shoddy yourself."

"I could get used to this. A short time, Irene?"

"The other staff warned me; he was flash, they said. I didn't listen. I had to leave my position, no reference, I couldn't even go home. He left me with nothing, you see, only my George."

"You were on your own in the world?"

"I had George."

"As Helena has Dinah."

Irene frowns. "It's not the same. She had a husband; she should have stayed with him."

"She didn't listen to the warnings either."

Irene looks disgruntled. "I cared for my child."

"Maybe she does too, in her own way?"

"You think so? Well, now she's hooking up with another fella." Irene takes back the offered pipe and enjoys a few reflective puffs. "It's time for me to leave, Nora, if he gets his feet under the kitchen table. You know what they say: too many cooks."

"Where would you go?"

"Oh, I'd open a little establishment of my own. Any corner closer to George. A fresh start, put behind everything that's happened here. Bill Carter is welcome to that kitchen. He'll have to run things on his own with Rose having left."

"This is new, when did she go?"

"A few days ago. She got a job in the café, waitressing. She said she won't miss my sharp tongue. She's a good girl, skittish though. I knew all about her sloping off to have a read of her romance books and a smoke."

Nora laughs.

Irene's face is serious again. "I hope you get to the bottom of things, really, I do. I daresay you will, Nora, a damn sight faster than the police."

To this end, Nora, after splashing her face with water and sucking a menthol lozenge, returns to the infirmary. Nurse Smiler is on duty. She looks up from her desk.

"Inspector, you've just missed the other inspector. He was here all evening and again this morning. He's gone for some fresh air." She fights against her natural proclivity and pulls a downcast face. "I'm afraid it's not going very well."

"The patient is still not talking?"

"Or drinking, or eating. We have him on a drip, the doctors are considering administering a feeding tube. He is going to be transferred to Park Mount this afternoon, perhaps they'll have more luck."

"Can I see him? I know the way."

"Of course. Anything you need, Inspector—"

"I'll let you know."

The lad in the bed looks like he hasn't moved. Turned to the wall, the greatcoat under his head, eyes closed. Slight before, there is nothing of him now.

Nora closes the curtains and pulls up a chair. She watches for signs in his body that tell her that he knows she is there. The slightest change in his breath, a muscle twitch. Nothing.

"John Morgan," says Nora, her voice just above a whisper. "I once did what you are doing now; I turned to the wall and tried to die. It didn't work for me, as you can see; I'm still here, in all my glory. There were times when I wished I had succeeded and times when I was happy that I didn't. In the hope that you might tell me your story I'll tell you mine and you'll be the first I've told it to."

Silence from the bed.

"You're a good listener, I'll tell you that. It came about after a starry night. It was my granny's own wake and I had taken drink." Nora stops and considers her breath; she hopes he's getting menthol not whiskey fumes. "I'm not averse to a dropeen, just so you know, but I don't make a habit of it. Anyway. There I was alone under the night sky, thinking about God and death and marriage, all the big questions of my little life. What should I do? What was before me? When it happened." Nora allows herself a slow breath. "I remember thinking, after he had finished, that's the worst of it over, then. But it wasn't. I was with child and before long the whole parish knew. The question was, could I identify my attacker? I couldn't but I did. The man was run out of town. A thing in itself unusual in those days when the theft of a goat was worth more than the destruction of a girl. I went away to have the baby. After she was born—tiny little thing that she was—and taken away, I also found a wall to turn my face to. From the outside I must have seemed as dormant as a stone. From the outside nothing seemed to be happening. That couldn't have been further from the truth. Inside my mind everything was racing, a thousand fears and thoughts, a whirlwind of pain. After a time, I learnt to quieten it, pick out one strand and then another. A course of action presented itself to me. Some, who don't know the finer points of religious life, might say it was a course of inaction." Nora closes her eyes. "There was a time when I believed purpose was enough, even without peace."

She opens her eyes to find John Morgan looking at her.

He won't eat but with Nora's help he sits up and takes a drink. Slowly, slowly. In a voice no louder than her own he asks for a cigarette. Nora finds a wheelchair and helps him into it. He is pitifully thin, all elbows and knees. When she pushes him back along the ward Nurse Smiler stares at them as if a true miracle has taken place.

"We'll be back in a jiffy," says Nora.

They pass Rideout in the corridor. John Morgan turns his face away and Nora takes his cue and pushes faster. Glancing over her shoulder she sees the inspector, hands in pockets, continuing.

They find a corner of the memorial garden, bright with bedding plants and in view of the ambulances. His cigarettes are in the greatcoat, which John carries bundled on his lap. Nora helps him fish them out, and he gestures to her to take one. He cannot manage the matches, so she lights them both.

"So now," says Nora, "you have my story, John. Will you tell me yours?"

"It's strange to hear that name again. He would never say it, even when we were alone."

"You mean Theo?"

John nods. "It was his idea to come here. An anonymous place for drifters. All we needed to do was be careful, live like strangers. Only, somehow it was worse to be near him every day like that, to have to pretend. To have to hide what we meant to each other."

They sit in silence. John looks out over the car park.

"You met as boys, didn't you?" asks Nora gently.

"Theo was evacuated to my father's farm."

"And you became friends?"

John nods. "Theo was like no one else, you can't imagine. Carefree and funny, adventurous. He was never surly; he grew into that living with her."

"Stella?"

"He wanted to be like everyone else, not stick his head over the parapet. He was always far more frightened than me of what we had. What we did. Ashamed even."

"Is that why he enlisted?"

John glances down, sees his cigarette has run to ash. He taps it, takes a cautious inhalation. "He thought he would do the right thing for a change. Stupid bastard."

"And then you followed him?"

"What else would I have done?" John smiles, the shadows that haunt his face disappear. "And I found him. We had three days' leave together. Beautiful days. At the end of them he told me that he intended to marry Stella."

"That was when you decided to walk away from your old life."

John looks at Nora. "How perceptive. To be honest, I felt dead anyway. As John Morgan I was dead. The things I'd seen during the war, then losing Theo. I wanted to be free of the past, start anew. A different identity, a different life."

"Your identity?"

"I took it from a soldier." John looks away. "Who didn't need it anymore."

"You took from a dead man?"

"Yes. His papers, uniform, tags, and then I gave him mine." He hesitates. "God forgive me, I stoved in his face, in case someone who knew me came across him."

Nora reaches out and touches John's hand. He takes her hand in his own, pats it, and then returns it.

"The war was ending and in the chaos of people trying to get home it was easy enough to slip by unnoticed. I roamed Europe, I never intended to come back to England." John launches his cigarette into the flower bed. "But I suppose I wanted to know he'd come through the war and that he was all right. I told myself I would take one last look. From a distance, you understand?"

Nora sees that John is shivering now. She arranges the greatcoat over him, pulling it up over his shoulders; he nods his thanks.

"I'd already tracked him down once. I did it again. They had settled in Slough, of all places. It suited them; quiet, dull, pleasant enough. I became fascinated by their life together. I watched them both, oh, for days."

"That must have been painful."

"Yes, like reopening a wound. One day Theo spotted me, I suppose I wanted him to. It was in a pub, the two of them huddled together in the snug, him with his half pint of bitter, her with her sherry, the old married couple." John laughs. "When he saw me at the bar his face paled. I felt like the ghost of bloody Banquo."

"What happened?"

"I sank my drink and left. I felt I'd done enough."

"And he followed?"

John's smile is bittersweet. "Yes, he followed."

An ambulance clangs up to the entrance of the emergency room. A porter and a doctor come out. John watches disinterestedly, some other human drama unfolding.

"Did Stella know about your relationship?"

John turns back to Nora. "Theo thought not."

"What do you think?"

He shrugs. "We were careful. But Stella disliked me from the off, I had a sense of that. Maybe she had her suspicions that we were more than strangers. Sometimes I would catch her watching me."

"On the morning of Teddy's death—"

"To my eternal regret I left Gulls Nest the night before. I traveled to London and stayed in a hotel there. Inspector Rideout has been furnished with an alibi. I didn't intend to come back; I'd told Theo as much. I had asked him to come away with me, leave his wife."

"What did he say?"

"We argued. He wouldn't give me an answer, so I left. I told him I was going to Paris. I'd wait a few days for him, no more." John closes his eyes. "It seems rather cruel in retrospect to give such an ultimatum."

"No crueler than living in the same house as strangers."

"Perhaps not."

Nora chooses her words carefully. "Do you think Teddy died at his own hand?"

John looks at her, a world of pain in his eyes. "Honestly? I don't know."

They sit in silence for a while.

"Can I ask you another question, John?"

"Go ahead."

"You knew Frieda Brogan?"

"Yes, for a time."

"She was my friend."

"I know. Hosmer said. I'm very sorry."

Nora nods.

"He gave you my photographs of her, didn't he? I'm glad." John smiles. "He came to visit and talked jazz at me for hours. Didn't get anything out of me. I suspect Inspector Rideout put him up to it."

"I don't think so. Hosmer holds you in high regard."

"I work hard." John gives a lopsided smile. "I gather he likes you too, he was singing your praises."

Nora meets his smile with her own wry one. "I danced around his studio wrapped only in a curtain."

"Of course you did. The audacious Miss Breen. So, you left your monastery to search for Frieda."

Nora hesitates. "Yes, I suppose you could say that. I was concerned when she didn't write. Did you not think it odd her just disappearing?"

"As awful as it sounds, I thought it was my fault. The evening before she went, we took wine up onto the headland. We told each other our dreams. My wish for a life with Theo, her ambition to act."

"She wanted to act?"

"Couldn't you tell from my photographs? She was uninhibited, brave. I told her she should run off to London and get right up on the stage." John glances at Nora. "She had such passion for life."

"Did you walk back alone?"

"No, together. I said good night in the garden at Gulls Nest. But she didn't show the next morning at breakfast. Then there was the whole furore about her leaving her room and all her things."

"What did you think?"

John's face looks pained. "Honestly? Initially, I was worried, but I was so damned wrapped up in my own woes that I did nothing. I told myself that Frieda had caught the early train, that she'd struck out and not looked back. I wanted very badly to do the same of course." He meets Nora's eye. "I am so sorry."

"You weren't to know," she says. "Can we return to your last walk with Frieda?"

"Yes, of course."

"What time did you return from the headland?"

"Around ten."

"And she had no plans to go out again that night?"

"Not that I knew of."

Nora looks at him thoughtfully. "You know who put you in the infirmary?"

"I do."

"Was it Percy Ladd?"

John tries to smile and winces. "He wouldn't be up to it, despite his bluster. He paid a couple of hired thugs to rough me up, teach me a lesson. He admitted as much before he dumped me outside the emergency room. He didn't know I was listening."

"Why would Percy do that?"

"Someone put him up to it. It went too far and I expect he lost his bottle. If I died, he knew he would be to blame, in part."

"Who put him up to it?"

John glances at Nora. "Who do you think? Head of my fan club. Stella."

"Stella, really? Percy told you this?"

John shrugs. "It's common knowledge he'd do anything for a woman who refuses him. Stella has led him a merry dance." He rests his head against the back of the wheelchair.

"You're exhausted," says Nora. "I'll take you back."

Glancing up, she sees Inspector Rideout step out of the main entrance of the infirmary. He is crossing the grounds, heading for the memorial garden.

"I'll pay the price for what I did in the war," says John. "I often wondered about his family, the other soldier, waiting for him to come home, never knowing."

"You distinguished yourself, that must count for something, doesn't it? What you did wasn't for reasons of cowardice, John."

"Perhaps it was cowardice in a way, to turn my back on the life that fate had dealt me?"

"Do you believe in fate?"

John thinks a moment. "Probably not. No more than in God. And you?"

"I'm reserving judgment."

They share a smile as Rideout approaches.

John Morgan salutes him. "She'll fill you in." He nods to Nora. "Thank you. It's been a breath of fresh air."

They walk down towards the promenade, Nora and Rideout. Nora keeping to her own thoughts and ignoring Rideout's glances.

"We can put out a request, on the wireless, in the local papers, ask for any witnesses to step forward. Someone might have seen her that night."

Nora nods. "In a way I don't know what's worse: knowing a terrible thing has happened to someone, or never finding out. Either way, how can you settle their spirit?" She looks up at him. "And I don't mean that in a Miss Dence way."

"A missing person offers another type of ghost story."

"I suppose it does. People will fill in the gaps." Nora takes a deep breath. "Tell me, the pathologist's findings on Frieda, your own deductions."

They head down onto the beach. Nora slips on the first swath of pebbles that gives way to flat sand at the shoreline. Rideout steps forward, has her arm. She smiles him her thanks. They walk a few steps together before he lets go.

"I anticipated it would be inconclusive as to whether she sustained her facial and head injuries prior to the fall or as a result. Her hands showed no defensive injuries, broken nails, fingers, and so forth, and there were no marks to her body to suggest a violation."

Nora closes her eyes, nods. "So, she might have been pushed but it's also plausible that she simply fell?"

"Yes. On examining the area around the skylight shaft to the caves below, we found that the grate was weak, metal fatigue. The vegetation surrounding the skylight was overgrown. It was a sprung trap; it was just unfortunate that Frieda walked into it. At night she wouldn't have seen where she was walking."

"Is it possible that the grate could have been tampered with? The trap sprung, if you like?"

"Not impossible I suppose, but the metal showed no recent tool marks or signs of force."

"And the coroner will rule that it was an accident?"

"Without further evidence, that is likely."

"If there is further evidence I will find it."

They walk over hard, flat sand. Nora has taken off her shoes; she holds them by the heels. Rideout turns against the breeze and lights a cigarette in the shelter of his jacket. She gestures and he hands it to her. She takes a few puffs and hands it back, their fingers touching quite naturally.

"You know, it's in human nature, to want to parcel things up neatly," says Rideout. "The war hasn't helped. It has blown us apart in so many ways; the old rituals, the old beliefs no longer hold. We want death, like life, to have a reason. Every action pegged, every motive understood, every coincidence unpicked. Otherwise, what is there but chaos?"

"What are you saying?"

"Sometimes we have to accept that when it comes to matters of life and death, we can't know everything and never will. And let it go."

Nora looks up at the gulls, flashes of white in a darkening sky. A bank of dark clouds looms over the headland but looking out to the far horizon there is bright sky yet.

CHAPTER 25

Nora dresses for dinner. She makes the effort, changing into a new secondhand dress of navy velvet, brushing the hair that's growing back
strong, the brown strands and the gray. The curls frame her face and
soften its severity a little, the strong jaw and the wide mouth. The dress
hangs well, flattering her tall boyish frame. Her granny always told her
to smile at herself in the mirror, to greet politely the person she saw
there as she would anyone else. Nora gives it a go. She would be the first
to admit the effect is not unpleasant. Her reconfigured wrinkles have
a cheekiness about them, the gap in her front teeth is winsome; both
point to a woman who smiles and laughs often. But you would need to
know her to see that the smile does not reach her clear gray eyes tonight.

She glances up at the paper snowflakes that adorn her room, they
flitter on. They are never still, for there are always drafts in the room,
even with the windows closed. It's almost as if Frieda communicates
with her still, her words on paper are somehow still alive. Nora watches
them and feels the same flittering inside her. Nerves, or excitement, she
cannot tell.

Now that the hour of Bill's dinner has arrived Nora can't help but wonder what such a gathering might unleash. All day long she has sensed a storm brewing. The morning began with a stream of deliveries: the butchers, the florist, the grocer's boy. Setting Bill jogging in and out of the kitchen in his chef's apron and shirtsleeves. The weather, which was unexpectedly glorious, saw Helena take to her terrace on a lounge chair. Pushed out of her kitchen Irene forfeited a suggested day off to sit smoking an old pipe of Poppy's on the back doorstep. She spent the best part of the day there, scowling at the kitchen's new incumbent and making disparaging comments and acrid smoke clouds. But visiting Bill just a few hours ago, Nora was impressed; the kitchen was spotless and the bright pans on the hob bubbled in chorus. The smells were tantalizing, of fresh baking and sharp herbs and rich sauces. The dishes already prepared were ranged on the sideboard, carefully covered over. Bill was in control. As dapper as ever, apart from the bead of sweat on his forehead. Nora's offers of help were waved aside. Stepping past the dining room Nora saw that Bill was truly as he said: in advance of himself. The table had been set with linen and fine silver, candlesticks and flowers. The crockery in evidence on the sideboard was not the usual chipped stoneware affair that Irene's meals were served on but rather immaculate blue-white bone china. Bill was indeed a wonder to gather these things to the house.

Nora gives herself a final smile. She will do.

The guests assemble in the parlor, according to directions on the invitations they have been given, Nora's having been slipped under her door sometime in the afternoon. *You are cordially invited*, said the printed cream card, *to the Gulls Nest Banquet. Cocktails 6:30 p.m. sharp.* Stella is already there waiting, wearing a scarlet bolero jacket and neat-waisted dress, her hair put up in a style that somehow ages her. She pats the seat next to her and Nora takes it.

"What do you make of this?" whispers Stella. "A little fancy, isn't it?"

Before Nora has time to answer, Irene grumbles into the room. She wears her habitually sour expression, but she too has dressed for the occasion in a mauve dress and ice-blue cardigan. Helena and Dinah follow, hand in hand. Helena is as elegant as ever in black silk with pearl earrings. But the greatest transformation has taken place in Dinah.

Nora notices Irene's eyes light up with pride as she watches her granddaughter enter the room. Dinah wears a moss-green dress with a sash, her red hair has been brushed into plaits, and her face is clean. She doesn't hop or creep but rather walks sensibly and nods at the others. To Nora she offers a small smile.

And now here is the man of the moment—Bill enters the room, impeccable in a dress shirt and evening suit and balancing a tray of glasses. He deftly takes command of the evening. Nothing is too much trouble! Don't the ladies all look wonderful! His eyes alight on Helena, of course.

The cocktail he is serving is of his own invention, created just for tonight! Something peach and fizzy and not unlike a Bellini, only with a twist. Perhaps Nora is not the only diner who thinks of cyanide. She glances at Stella, who holds her glass awkwardly by the stem, hesitating to drink, looking round at the others. Seeing Irene still upright after knocking back half a glass, Stella takes a cautious sip only to exclaim how divine it is.

In no time it seems they are called into the dining room, lit entirely by candlelight. But this is of a very different kind to the somber murk of Miss Dence's séance. Long tapered candles in silver candelabra decorate sideboard and table, their soft light reflected in the cut-glass vases and crystal goblets ranged about. Swags of roses, Helena's favorite flowers, crimson and white, spill across the table. Bill has thought of everything. Handwritten place cards and menus are to be found propped up next to fan-shaped napkins. Stella counts the courses and makes ten—a few named in French! Even Irene looks impressed by the notion of beef bourguignon and chicken consommé, fish terrine and quince tart.

And so, the meal begins.

Bill serves the first course. The chicken consommé is flavorsome and accompanied by dainty rolls. Bill explains that every course will be complemented by its own specially selected fine wine. The diners soften and the candlelight flatters and the conversation is convivial. Bill's anecdotes are charming, and Helena laughs at them prettily. Dinah's plait may trail in the soup, but she makes an effort to sit nicely on the chair.

Bill brings out the terrine, piped around the base with mayonnaise flowers, set in the perfect shape of a leaping salmon.

Stella claps, Helena laughs, and Dinah grins. Perhaps Nora is the only one to notice that it isn't a nice grin. Neither does anyone else seem to notice how, with an odd and quiet diligence, Dinah has lined up her side plate, fork, knife, glass, and napkin, all in a line. Just like the mice, Nora thinks.

Just like . . .

Nora frowns. This organizing habit of Dinah's reminds her of something that she's currently too flittered to remember.

Bill, with a napkin over his arm, tops up their glasses. It's too soon for a toast, he says, but he can't help but propose one. It's nobody's surprise when he toasts his beautiful landlady. Helena basks in the attention.

Now, with a fork and a silver slice, Bill announces that he will portion up the terrine.

Stella makes some kind of comment about the wonders of aspic.

Irene's expression is one of begrudging respect.

Helena smiles vaguely.

Bill makes a confident first incision. As he does, he recounts the first time he created this dish, for an admiral in the navy, at sea, of course. Perhaps distracted from the task at hand he does not notice what several of the diners have. The first portion of perfectly layered and seasoned fish in jelly comes with a foreign body. The tail of which, pinched between fish slice and fork, allows the body to swing a moment before the serving reaches the plate. In this way, Bill Carter serves up a dead mouse, fur slick, eyes dull, to his intended fiancée.

Helena shrieks, Irene curses, and Stella looks on in horror. Dinah erupts into soundless laughing. She meets Nora's eye, her face flushed and jubilant.

Bill points the fish slice at Dinah with a shaking hand. "Get out! Get out! You twisted little bastard!"

Dinah jumps down from the chair and runs, her grin wide and joyful.

Helena raises a napkin to her face and lets out a sob.

Bill turns to her, mortified. "Dearest—"

Helena shakes her head, gets to her feet, and sweeps out of the room.

There is silence but for the clatter of a spoon. Irene helps herself to a large portion of the terrine. She returns the stares of the other diners. "What? There's no mouse in this bit."

"Even so, Irene!" Stella's expression is a picture of disgust.

"Waste not, want not," Irene says truculently.

Other than Irene, no one has the stomach for further courses. Bill waves away offers of help to clear away and disappears into the kitchen with the bottle of vintage port that was to take pride of place with his Offering of Cheeses.

Nora turns down Stella's offer of a cup of cocoa. The young woman looks tired and besides, after an evening like this one Nora would prefer a drop of the hard stuff and the company of the moonlit sea view through her window. They exchange good nights and Stella continues up to the next floor.

Nora has no sooner closed her door and kicked off her shoes than she hears screaming above. She's out the door taking the stairs two at a time and runs into Stella on the landing. Stella is beside herself.

Nora quietens her as best she can as Bill rushes up the stairs with a rolling pin. Irene is soon to follow, already wearing a hairnet and dressing gown.

"It's there," sobs Stella. "In the room."

Nora opens the door. In the bed, dressed all in black, wearing a black mask and a leering grin, is Professor Poppy's missing puppet: the hangman, Jack Ketch.

Stella won't entertain sleeping in her own room, so Nora takes her into hers. She dispatches the others; it will not do to discuss this tonight, with Stella already so fearful and distressed. She settles Stella in the chair by the window, where she alternately shivers and cries.

"It's just horrible," she whispers. "Who would do such a thing? Who would creep into my room and put that loathsome puppet in there?"

Nora considers. Every one of them was accounted for. No one left the dining room until the meal broke up. Dinah rushed out first, of course, then Helena, but would there have been time for either of them to climb the two flights of stairs to Stella's room to tuck the puppet into her bed?

Stella turns to Nora with a look of horror. "What if it means they are coming for me next?"

Nora tries to comfort the young woman but must admit that her own sense of foreboding is growing. Why would this unknown figure continue to attack the Gulls Nest residents? Why would anyone attack Stella, especially in her condition? But then, likely no one else apart from her and Rideout knows Stella is expecting.

"Stella, you're exhausted. Lie down and rest on my bed for a while."

Stella protests but she does what she's told like a tractable child. Her hands are frozen, and her face pinched with crying. Nora adds another blanket to the bed and puts the kettle on the burner for a hot water bottle.

Stella holds out her hand. "Don't leave me. My mind is full. The shock of seeing that terrible puppet. Its face smirking at me."

Nora pulls the chair over beside the bed.

"Read to me, Nora. It always soothes."

Nora, weary herself now that Stella is calming down, picks up a book and begins to read, automatically. Stella closes her eyes.

By the turn of two pages Nora realizes she has picked up the book Stella was reading to Poppy on the morning of Teddy's death. How tactless, what on earth made her do that? She stops.

"Oh no keep on," says Stella. "What is this story?"

Nora checks. She has just read aloud the part immediately before the ribbon bookmark, the last pages Stella read. The girl must be tired not to recognize this. Nora considers the pages that comprise that final reading. Starting at chapter thirteen, as Poppy had remarked, and ending at the ribbon bookmark. Very few pages indeed. Stella must have read at a very slow pace, or perhaps she broke off to chat with the old man?

Nora glances up but Stella is asleep now. Any further questions must wait until the morning. Nora switches off the bedside lamp and takes the chair to the window.

The house quietens. Nora hears just the rush and the pull of the sea outside. The occasional whistle of the wind. And the creaks of the house, as if it is all at sea too, only sailing through calmer waters now. If she listens, she can hear Stella's soft breathing as she sleeps. Nora moves as soundlessly as she can, which given her decades of living without noise is more silently than most. She closes the door behind her and on second thoughts, locks it.

She climbs the stairs cautiously to the second-floor front, refraining from switching a light on, feeling her way. She opens Stella's door and senses the dark room. There is no sound or movement within, nothing to suggest a killer lurking, ready to pounce. The curtains are open; despite the moonless and starless night the window lets in a little light. Nora feels about for the switch.

Jack Ketch is still in the bed. Mocking and sinister. She is not surprised that Stella startled so on seeing him. Nora had told the others to leave the room exactly as Stella had found it. She casts her eye around and is saddened.

Nothing has changed in the room since the first time she saw it. Teddy's slippers and toothbrush still share the space with Stella's. The toy car and the nightie case are still poignant reminders of the couple's childhoods. The wedding photograph, seen now through eyes that are more knowing, has a tragic quality. The couple seem impossibly young, Stella lovely in white, Teddy scowling up at the sun.

There are no signs of any disturbance in the room, nor are there signs that an assailant passed through here. Whoever tucked up Jack Ketch in Stella's bed left no trace; the rug has not been rumpled, the bed's coverlet is smooth, the drawers show no signs of ransacking. But as Nora turns to go, she catches sight of something. A covered bucket by the fireplace, perhaps for ash, or rubbish. Following the same instinct that caused her to hesitate, Nora crosses the room and opens the lid.

Inside, steeping in water, are several bloodstained rags. Nora frowns, looks around for the fireside poker, and dips it into the water, extracting a sodden wad of cotton. The realization comes to her: Stella is on her courses. Either she has lost her baby, or she was never pregnant in the first place. As Nora returns the poker and replaces the lid of the bucket, she ponders both thoughts. If Stella had suffered a miscarriage, wouldn't she have sought Nora's help, knowing that a nurse was close at hand? Had Stella sought medical treatment or seen a doctor? The second idea—that Stella lied about her pregnancy—seems less plausible. Why would Stella make up such a thing?

But now Nora begins to look at the room with different eyes, paying closer attention.

She turns to the kitchenette and sees two cups laid out, the pot of cocoa standing by and the little bowl of sugar. Stella screamed almost immediately on entering her room. That meant that she would have set the cups ready at the beginning of the evening with the intention of inviting someone up for a drink. Or perhaps, like having Teddy's slippers and toothbrush still, poor Stella had not come to terms with her life alone and could not bear to set a single cup?

Finding nothing else of note, Nora gathers up grinning Jack Ketch and leaves the room, closing the door softly behind her.

CHAPTER 26

Nora spent an uncomfortable night and is relieved to be up, not with the lark but with the gulls, which are less poetic entirely. Not wanting to disturb Stella by returning to her own room, she had curled up in a chair in the parlor. Awake but bleary-eyed she will go and make breakfast and take a cup of tea up to Stella. Nora's thoughts return to her discovery of the lidded bucket and its contents. In what way will she bring up a matter so personal? She decides to think further on the subject. She glances at Jack Ketch; the puppet is propped on the chair beside her, his power to terrify somewhat lessened in daylight. The paint on his face is flaking and his hangman's mask is fraying. He looks well loved and well traveled, a macabre but comic figure. Not at all the harbinger of doom he appeared to be last night.

"You look how I feel," she says to him.

She takes Jack Ketch to the bookcase and slips him in a drawer, where she hopes he can stay out of trouble.

Nora goes into the kitchen. It is empty and, to Bill's credit, spotless. The porcelain dishes are packed up in a tea chest and the flowers from the table are piled at the back door, already wilting and no doubt on their way to the compost heap. There is no sign of breakfast; Irene may be on strike of course and Bill, after last night's failed dinner, may not be inclined to take possession of the kitchen again in a hurry. Hearing whistling and the clattering of bottles Nora exits the back door and rounds the house to see the milkman setting today's delivery down, covering the top of every bottle with the flat stones evidently put aside on the window ledge for this purpose.

He glances up as Nora approaches and gives her a nod and a grin.

"The birdies like the cream," he explains. "I never forget, else Mrs. Rawlings will have my guts for garters." He hands her a pint bottle.

Nora wishes him good morning and carries the milk back into the kitchen. In no time she has the range lit and the kettle boiled. Bill has put the covered remains of the dishes untainted by Dinah in the pantry. Nora finds butter and a roll and makes tea.

When Nora returns to her room, Stella is gently waking. If she has heard Nora unlock the door, she makes no remark. She sits up in the bed and stretches.

"I slept better in your room than I have for ages. I suppose half of me lies awake wondering when Teddy will return."

They have their breakfast at the table by the window.

Stella seems sunny, chatting. She hops from subject to subject. Last night's fiasco. The horror that Dinah is and how someone really ought to teach the child some manners. Whether poor Bill's love affair with Helena can survive Dinah's attempts to dismantle it.

"I came across Dinah in the garden yesterday," remarks Stella. "All secretive with that new pram of hers. She had something, a book, I think. She hid it under the mattress and practically ran away. Something stolen, no doubt."

Nora finds herself bothered by this unfair accusation. "It was probably a notebook. I gave it to her; she didn't steal it."

Stella smiles. "Is that right? Whatever for?"

"She likes to draw, to write. It's her way of communicating."

"Well and good, but who knows what sort of disturbing things you'd find in it! Perhaps her devious plans to sabotage Bill's meal?" A thought appears to strike Stella. "You don't think Dinah was responsible for putting that dreadful puppet in my bed? She isn't afraid of upsetting people if that mouse is anything to go by."

Nora considers. It would not be impossible; it certainly appears to be the sort of trick Dinah is fond of. But then how and where did Dinah come across the puppet? Did she take it from the workshop herself? Or find it discarded by Teddy's killer? Could it be possible that Dinah visited the workshop at some point after Teddy's death and before Nora noticed the puppet was gone? If so, this would mean that despite appearances, Dinah did not remain locked in the sideboard until Rideout discovered her.

These were questions she could try to put to Dinah.

Nora looks up to see that Stella is watching her closely. Some instinct leads her to answer lightly, "I wouldn't have thought so. Even Dinah has her limits and she's fond of you, isn't she?"

Stella nods. "Oh, yes."

Somehow Stella's enthusiasm seems empty.

Nora pours them both another tea. Stella refuses a bread roll.

"I don't have the stomach for it," she says, her hand on her belly, comforting, maternal. "The mornings are the worst. But I'm all right, really."

Nora sees that Stella is not all right. Not in the least. There is a glassiness to her eyes, dark circles beneath, as if her good night's sleep has barely refreshed her.

Nora must ask but will go gently, "Stella, you don't seem well, is there anything—"

Stella stridently interrupts. "What am I thinking of? I must go." And now she is up and leaving.

"Stella?"

"I can't be late for work again, really I can't." Stella's smile is forced. "Jack Ketch might be coming for me but there is still rent to be paid."

Nora goes for a walk to clear her head. She turns away from the headland and walks down towards the promenade. After an inauspicious start the sun has come out and the sky is a pure blue and the clouds scud across the sky like a clean wet wash and the seagulls turn and mew. The light on the wet sand is enticing but Nora turns from the wide and lovely space of the beach and heads into town. She passes Hosmer's photographic studio. The portrait of the globe-trotting young couple has been replaced by a plump and happy baby who gurgles out at the viewer from a nest of soft toys, clutching a rattle in its fist. Nora would like to call into Hosmer's for a drink, a bit of jazz, a dance even, but something is forming in her mind. She won't say it's an idea, or even a notion, just the faintest waft of a niggle. Like following a loose strand in a knot she's been trying to unpick. What she needs, she decides, is a strong and decent cup of tea. The kind a spoon could stand in.

Nora steps into the cheap café, where the tables are clean and the décor nicely austere. She takes a corner table so that she has the glance of the room. The waitress has yet to notice her arrival, engrossed as she is with something just under the counter. Nora would bet that it's a romance novel. When the waitress finally looks up and squints over, she gives a smile of recognition.

She brings a pad; the pencil is already tucked behind her ear. "What will you have, Miss Breen?"

"A pot of tea and a moment of your time, Rose."

Rose says she has more than a moment, it's been a slack morning for one thing and another. She brings the tea and a bun, on the house.

Nora smiles her thanks. "How are you finding your new position, Rose?"

"I won't lie," she says. "My nerves have improved no end now that I'm away from Gulls Nest."

Nora smiles. "You don't strike me as someone with a nervous disposition, Rose."

"That place would make anyone a wreck! I was glad to leave." Rose hesitates. "But I still can't help thinking back to that morning, what happened to Mr. Atkins, and wondering . . ."

"What do you wonder?"

"Well, if I hadn't gone out to fetch the milk that morning then things might have been very different."

"How so, Rose?"

"Well, we would know who made that coffee for a start." Rose shivers. "But then perhaps I wouldn't be here now? They might have done me in too."

Nora feels the knot that she's teasing give way a little. She pulls ever so gently on a strand of thought.

"Can we go back to the milk, Rose? You said the birds had squabbled over it and upset the bottles that morning?"

"That's right."

"Do you remember anything else different about the milk? How you found the bottles?"

"Knocked over, pecked, milk spilt, what else?" Rose frowns. "I'm not sure what you're asking."

"How did the birds get to the lids?"

Rose's face brightens, like a child who has worked out a tricky sum. "There were no stones. The milkman hadn't set them over the bottle tops—wait—there were no stones to be seen. Someone had taken them away."

"Good girl yourself." Nora pats her hand, gets to her feet, and grabs her coat. "I'll have that cup of tea later."

Perhaps by some innate sense of self-preservation the red-faced desk sergeant doesn't argue back with Nora Breen this time. He merely eyes her warily, closes his book, and disappears to fetch the inspector. But then, Nora, for expediency's sake, does have the two shoes held ready in her hands and this time she's not planning to miss.

As they drive away from the station, Breen tells Rideout to step on it. He may glance at her wryly, but he doesn't have to be told twice.

CHAPTER 27

Rideout takes the house, Nora takes the garden. She has a hunch that this is where she will find her. Opening the kitchen door as quietly as she can, she steps outside. Late autumn sunlight dapples through tree and hedge but the corners are dim and there are many places to hide. Nora checks the privy, lodged behind a bank of rhododendrons; the gazebo, stuffed with old furniture; and the small toolshed. Her search takes in the mossy sloping lawn and its sundial, the Victorian greenhouse with delicate ironwork, and moldering panes, the pond with fallen yellow leaves, bright against dark water. The overgrown path takes her closer to the old high boundary wall, adorned with the skeletons of espaliered fruit trees. Tucked away behind a bank of dank bushes is a wooden hut. A recent path has been trampled through the weeds. The door is still well secured with two padlocks but around the side of the hut the twiggy saplings show broken branches. Nora rounds the hut, thorns snagging, nettles stinging. She is unsurprised to see that the boarded window has been breached. She swings herself up and into the hut. In the dim she looks to the top shelf and sees the row of red and white poison tins. Nora's heart turns sideways as, looking closer, she sees that the row has been disturbed: one tin is missing. She hurriedly climbs back out and keeps searching.

Nora comes to the lovely sprawling oak. At the foot of the trunk a child's toy pram is parked. Nora looks up; high in the tree's branches is the tree house. No more than a platform with a rope ladder. Too high for a young child, certainly not for someone without a head for heights. Like Nora. Rabbits are massing around the tree, perhaps drawn to the bundle of lettuce heads left on the parcel tray of the pram. As Nora nears, she sees the pram's mattress has been turned over. If Dinah's notebook was hidden there once, it is not there now. A muffled sound from above draws her attention. The rope ladder is down so she begins to climb.

Nora cautions herself against looking down. The ladder swings and turns horribly and before a few rungs Nora's hands are slick with sweat and her legs trembling. Halfway up a strong breeze finds its way in off the sea, buffeting her. Her foot slips on the rung, Nora looks down. Far below now lie the pram and the bunnies and the ground. Should she fall—

The muffled noise again. Nora closes her eyes and takes a deep breath and keeps climbing. In her mind she does not pray but she does give thanks to the long hours spent in the monastery gardens or mopping endless corridors or moving and settling her patients. Nora has strength for this yet. Her arms tell her differently. It is with gritted teeth that she hauls herself up on the platform.

Dinah is still in her moss-green party dress, her face tearstained and her blue eyes large. Stella sits next to her with her arm around the little girl's shoulders. Dinah appears to shrink from her touch. Before them lies a gingham tablecloth, spread over the boards of the platform. The cloth is set with a teapot and cups. There is a milk jug and a sugar bowl. In a basket nearby lies a thermos flask, a stoppered bottle of milk, and a little white and red tin. Nora doesn't need to guess the contents of the sugar bowl. Beside the basket lies Dinah's notebook, pages splayed open and facedown.

Nora sees that two cups have been poured; one has been set before Dinah, the other is in Stella's hand.

Stella smiles at Nora. "Why don't you join us, Nora. Will you take tea?"

Nora meets Dinah's eye. The child is terrified.

Nora moves forward. "Come, sit by me, Dinah."

"Stay where you are, Nora," says Stella coolly. "No nearer."

Nora complies.

Stella rewards Nora with a smile. "You will have a cup, otherwise you will be the odd one out. Here, let me serve you." She takes another cup and saucer from the basket, lifts the teapot, adds a splash of milk, and then diligently measures three heaped sugars.

Nora takes the cup.

"It's too late in the morning for coffee," says Stella. "And I prefer tea, don't you? Now we have all got a cup. Drink up, don't let it go cold."

Nora watches Stella. Had she not known what was in the sugar bowl she would never have suspected. Stella is acting her usual amiable self.

"Did you mix it like this for Teddy?" Nora asks.

Stella shakes her head. "No, I watched while he added his own sugar."

"You slipped down to prepare the drink and took it to the workshop while Rose went out to buy milk?"

"Of course."

"After drugging Poppy so he fell asleep?"

"It hardly took much, poor old thing."

"Then reviving him with smelling salts so that he would think you had been sat with him all along?"

"He would never admit to dozing off."

Nora glances at Dinah, gesturing very slightly with her head, willing her to move away, very slowly to the side. Dinah understands and begins to shuffle away on her bottom.

Stella turns to Dinah. "Where do you think you are going?"

Nora's heart goes out to the little girl, who freezes on the spot, crying silent tears.

"Teddy wrote me a letter and carried it for days in his overcoat. Do you know what it said? That he loved someone else and was going to leave me. Which in itself was neither here nor there."

"You didn't care if he left you?" Nora frowns. "So why take his life?"

Stella looks at Nora, her expression scornful. "I had been through so much with him, sacrificed so much, tolerated so much. Moving from London to this pit. Putting up with his terrible moods. Days on end silent and moping. Screaming nightmares when he did sleep. An empty bed when he didn't. He looked through me. Has anyone ever done that to you? I began to feel as if I didn't exist." Stella takes a breath. "I was out walking when I heard that odious man talking to Frieda."

"You mean Karel Ježek?"

"They were discussing his secret love. How they had previously known one another, how they had conspired to arrive in this same seaside town and live together under the same roof pretending to be strangers."

"You eavesdropped this conversation?"

"It concerned me. They were debating whether Teddy should leave me or not. I really saw red. I wanted to run at them there and then."

"Did you?"

"Of course not. Revenge is a dish best served cold, isn't it?" Stella picks up Dinah's teacup and holds it out to her. "Drink up."

"How did you take revenge?"

"I haven't finished with the why yet. I would ask you: did I really deserve that? The lies, the deceit, the scheming, their unnatural love?

And little innocent Frieda practically acting as their go-between, egging them on."

"So, you planned to punish them all?"

"Yes. Only Frieda fell by accident."

"I don't believe you."

"Why would I lie?" says Stella blithely. "I've already told you I killed Teddy. I would happily have pushed her down that hole. Only I didn't need to. I simply had to steer her over that grate and she tumbled in all by herself. Easy. I listened there at the hole for a while. You know, I don't think she died straightaway; I swear I heard some little mewling noise." Stella feigns surprise, as if a thought has just struck her. "Perhaps I might have saved her? Instead, I enjoyed a nice, slow stroll back to Gulls Nest. It was a wonderfully clear night for stars."

Stella regards Nora closely, her eyes glittering with amusement. Nora cautions herself not to take the bait. She must not show her anger else the situation will escalate, which in Stella's mind may give her cause to act. But beyond all this Nora is surprised to find she wishes to extract every ounce of Stella's confession.

"And Frieda's last letter?"

"Sorry, burnt it. She outlined their sordid romance; none of the particulars, but it would have been incriminating."

"And Poppy?" she asks, evenly. "I thought he was your friend, Stella?"

"He was, sadly."

"He realized that you had slipped out of the room when he was drugged asleep and fed your husband poison."

"You are rather ruining the tone, Nora. I thought we were having a tea party?" Stella turns to Dinah. "And didn't I tell you to drink up?"

Dinah picks up the cup, pours the contents onto the floor, and puts the cup carefully down again with the merest glance at Stella.

Stella stares openmouthed, then in a heartbeat, slaps Dinah hard across the cheek. Holding the child around the shoulders, Stella grabs a handful of the substance from the sugar bowl. Dinah turns her head away, closing her mouth, her lips a compressed line, making choked little sobbing noises.

Nora is horrified. "Stella, she's a child!"

Stella pauses. It's enough time for Dinah to scream. Stella—shocked by the sudden sound from the silent child—lets go. Dinah scuttles over the other side of the platform to Nora. Stella scrabbles to her feet and makes a lunge for Dinah.

Stella trips. Time slows suddenly like a dream. Stella falls backwards, stretching out her arms to Nora, who shrinks back, pushing the child behind her. Then the sound of Stella hitting branches, ripping leaves, and then a dull thud.

All is silent but for the sound of breeze though the tree canopy scattering the last of the leaves. In the distance the sea can be heard, as constant as a heartbeat.

Dinah wriggles out of Nora's hold, patters to the side of the platform, and peers over. She points. Nora looks.

Stella lies facedown but Nora can tell she has gone. It's there in the awkwardness of her limbs, the angle of her head. The rabbits, unfazed, hop by.

CHAPTER 28

They sit at Rideout's kitchen table, a pot of tea brewing nicely between them. Rideout turns the pages of the notebook. It's all there, the whole story, illustrations drawn in color pencil and imbued with Dinah's strange, skewed view of the world. The faces may be grotesque, but they are recognizable, portraits with an element of the Punch and Judy show. Here are two young women walking arm in arm down the path, Frieda and Stella. Here is Stella serving a cup of death, the skull and crossbones drawn in the steam that rises. Here is Stella looming over the bed of a diminished Professor Poppy. At the foot of the bed lies poor dead Toby Dog, paws upwards, a twisted blue tongue hanging out. And here, finally, are Teddy and John, happy together wrapped in John's greatcoat, out on the headland, the sea below and the gulls dancing overhead.

"Dinah saw it all?"

"She did. What she didn't see from her tree house she witnessed with Professor Poppy's borrowed binoculars as she crept around the house. Stella knew well that she had to get Dinah out of the way the morning of Teddy's murder, for the child had a habit of spying. What she didn't know was that Dinah had already witnessed a great deal. It

was easy enough for Stella to lock her in the sideboard just after breakfast. She knew Dinah's habits. But Stella didn't realize that Dinah could
work the lock on the inside."

"So, Dinah witnessed Teddy's murder?"

"Not the act, but she saw Stella carry the coffee into the workshop
and walk out again minutes later. Dinah was the first to find Teddy dead
on the floor. The coffee cup was in disarray, so Dinah tidied it. She likes
to line things up," Nora explains.

"And she took the Jack Ketch puppet?"

"She did. In her own way she wanted to communicate what had
happened. Later she would put the puppet in Stella's room."

"Why didn't Dinah say anything? Tell an adult?"

Nora frowns. "That's something I haven't been able to fathom. I believe Dinah was still attached in some way to Stella. The young woman
had been kind to her in the past."

"Perhaps it worked both ways? After all, Stella killed other witnesses, why not Dinah?"

"Maybe so."

"If Dinah had only come forward."

Nora nods. "I believe she was scared. Remember that she was im-
plicated in the attempted drowning of the laundry woman's daughter?"

"I remember."

"Well, maybe she thought she might somehow be blamed?"

Rideout nods. "Or a mixture of all those things? How is Dinah now?"

"Surprisingly well, considering."

"One moment," says Rideout.

The inspector gets up and goes into the study. Nora looks out of the
French window at his dead mother's garden. She resists the temptation
to go outside and tidy it up. She reminds herself that sometimes a little
chaos is beneficial in life. She thinks back to the overgrown margin in
the gardens at High Dallow, alive with butterflies and bees.

Rideout returns with a book and hands it to her. A nicely bound notebook, the pages a little yellowed with age but quite serviceable.

"For Dinah. Perhaps it might help her to fill another? You look out for the child, don't you?"

"Well, I promised Professor Poppy." Nora smiles. "We go out to tea, Dinah and me."

"I thought Dinah wouldn't leave Gulls Nest?"

"I bribe her with cream teas at Rose's café."

Rideout laughs. "Whatever next!"

"School, hopefully." Nora looks at the notebook. "This was yours?"

He smiles. "I bought it before the war. I was going to write my experiences down. Get it on the page and out of my head. I never did, too busy staying alive."

"Then write them down now?"

"One day. In the meantime, let Dinah express herself in whatever way she can." He glances at her with the hint of a smile. "So now, you're all packed?"

"I am. I've the train at five."

"Have you time for a walk on the beach?"

"I have."

Inspector Rideout takes Nora Breen back to town. There is no emergency to attend, no killer at large to chase down. Even so, he drives fast and they both enjoy it. But then, all too soon they reach their destination. He parks up along the end of the promenade, not far from the spot where Nora first saw Stella and Teddy walking. She glances up at Gulls Nest, to her empty window there. Soon someone else will be looking out of it, another Miss Brogan or Miss Breen, or a Mrs. Atkins or a Professor Poppy. Some new character washed up along the shore of Gore-on-Sea with a suitcase and a story to unpack. She wonders at the sight

she and Rideout would make to someone looking casually out. Would
they look like a couple? Of course not; when they walk there's a polite
distance between them. Not the distance of strangers, perhaps, but of
friendly acquaintances. Perhaps this onlooker might wonder as to how
their relationship will develop? They might notice that the man's glance,
which falls often on the woman's face, is warm, perhaps a little more
than amiable. And that should the woman stumble, the man would no
doubt offer his arm in a chivalrous way. As for the woman, her shoes are
in her hand and her eyes are on the horizon. She has the look of someone with a headful of thoughts. The two move towards the water's edge,
where they stand together looking out at the sea.

"Of course, you could stay."

Nora glances at Rideout in surprise. "I've given my notice; they'll
have rented my room by now."

He laughs. "Even with Bill's grand plans for the boardinghouse it
would take a certain type of person to live at Gulls Nest."

"*Doves* Nest," Nora corrects. "Waifs and strays, of those there are
plenty in Gore-on-Sea. They'll find another lodger. Besides, what have
I got to stay for?"

Their eyes meet, he grins.

Nora laughs, hardly knows why. "*What?*"

"It just so happens that I have this case. Damnably difficult. Would
you hear the bones of it, Breen?"

Nora must admit it is decidedly rakish, that eyebrow of his. She has
always liked the rakish ones.

"I might, Rideout."

They head up off the beach, the woman and the man, with a favorable wind behind them. Favorable only in that it's going in the same
direction, otherwise bitter, with a rough lick of salt, coming in, as it does,
off the wide cold gray sea. They make their way along a long snake of
a promenade.

ACKNOWLEDGMENTS

Huge thanks go to my brilliant agents Sue Armstrong, C&W, and Amelia Atlas, CAA, whose advice and encouragement means the world to me. Thanks also to Catriona Paget and the C&W family. I am immensely grateful to the team at Atria who are always a delight to work with. My thanks to Loan Le, Elizabeth Hitti, Natalie Argentina, and to Susan M. S. Brown, Lisa Nicholas, and Barbara Greenberg. To my friends Mark LaFlaur and Janet Cameron, in deep appreciation for your kind encouragement over the years.

To Eva, Elise, Sharon and Annie, heartfelt thanks for your love and support. To my mother, who always spins a great story, much love. In gratitude to Sister Margaret Healy for her insights on a spiritual life. With thanks to Damaris Armstrong and Dave Jelley, wonderful readers and lovely friends. This book would not have been possible (or at least would have been a lot less fun to write) without the encyclopedic knowledge of my pal Edmund White, chemist, pathology expert, inventor and all-round brilliant partner in crime. Any oversights and omissions will be mine and certainly not Professor White's. With love to Andrea Enston for always cheering me on. Big thanks to Melanie Tucker who is my lifelong ally. Finally, with much gratitude to Claire Martin for our Sunday night conferences and being the best of friends.

ABOUT THE AUTHOR

Jess Kidd is the award-winning author of *The Night Ship*, *Things in Jars*, *Mr. Flood's Last Resort*, and *Himself*. Learn more at JessKidd.com.